The Warring States

Also by Aidan Harte

The Wave Trilogy
Irenicon

The Warring States

BOOK II OF THE WAVE TRILOGY

AIDAN HARTE

Jo Fletcher

New York • London

Jo Fletcher Books
An imprint of Quercus
New York • London

ISBN 978-1-62365-417-7

Library of Congress Control Number: 2015931870

Distributed in the United States and Canada by
Hachette Book Group
1290 Avenue of the Americas
New York, NY 10104

Manufactured in the United States

10 9 8 7 6 5 4 3 2 1

www.quercus.com

To Des

THE PRINCIPAL RIVERS AND CITIES OF
ETRURIA

EUROPA

the Venetian Gulf

CONCORD

1

the Concordian Gulf

RASENNA 20

19

ARIMINUM

2

ANCONA

CORSA

18

3

VOLSINII

VEII 16

17 15

PESCARA

The Adriatic

4

5

6

Dragon's Island

14

CAIETA

13

12 7

BARI

BRUNDISIUM

SALERNO 11

9

TARANTO

8

Gulf of Taranto

THE
BLACK
HAND

10

SYBARIS

MESSINA

Messina Strait

THE
THREE
SICILIES

SIRACUSA

The Ionican

The Tyrrhenian

THE
CAGLIGARIAN
ISLES

1 The Irenicon
2 The Ariminus
3 The Potenza
4 The Pescara
5 The Sangro
6 The Trigno
7 The Ofanto
8 The Bradano
9 The Basento
10 The Crathis

11 The Silarus
12 The Volturno
13 The Garigliano
14 The Liri
15 The Allia
16 The Albula
17 The Cremera
18 The Marta
19 The Tora
20 The Ombrone

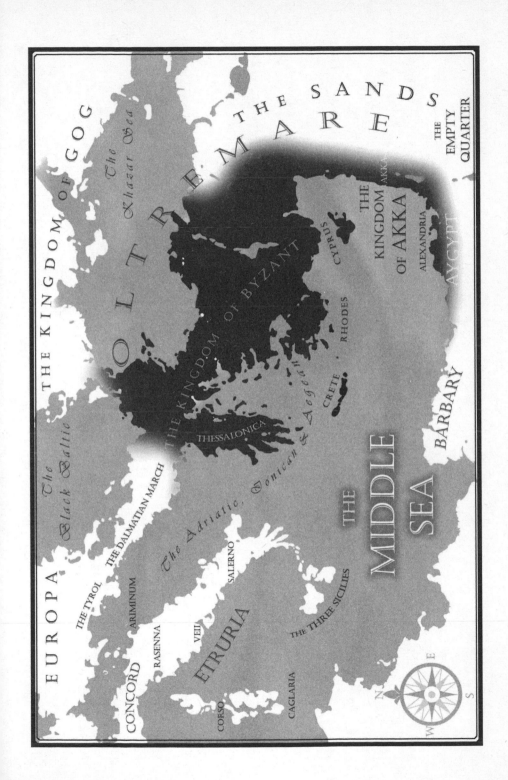

PART I:
STATE OF INNOCENCE

And she brought forth a man child, who was to rule all nations with a rod of iron.

Revelation *12:5*

Chapter 1

Two years before the Siege of Rasenna, the Year of our Lady, 1367

"You're pretty slow for an engineer if you can't see he's lying."

"Signora, *you* can see there are others waiting. Step aside."

"I want something!"

"'Course you do. But even if your son wasn't too young—how old are you?"

"Eight," the boy said.

"Even if he were old enough, the Guild only pays for children smart enough to be engineers, and if he were even half as clever as you say, the examiners would have spotted him years ago—and he'd have got further in the al-Buni test today. I'm sorry, but I need you to step aside."

"But I told you what a great *liar* he is. Torbidda, do it properly, or I swear—"

"I want to go home."

The examiner shared the boy's sentiment. He had been sitting in a fine mist of drizzle all morning. His clothes and papers were soaked and his nose dripping, and the dark clouds circling the Molè presaged a squall. He'd seen it a hundred times: destitute parents trying to pawn off mouths they couldn't feed, never mind that their children were every bit as dull as they were. The Apprentices ought to trust the examiners and stop the annual open testing; they were nothing more than an invitation for fraud. The boy was obviously no Bernoulli—he had a stubborn, ox-like brow and a grim, set jaw. The examiner didn't blame him for being angry—his mother *was* trying to sell him, after all.

"Test him again!" She struck the boy, an open-handed slap. He didn't cry, but the examiner could see a scene developing. She turned back, smiling sweetly. "This time he'll do it right."

"Signora, look—"

"Problem here?" A tall man stopped beside the inspection desk. He was in his late forties, but still fit and strong. He wore a stream-lined toga that fell open across his barrel chest as if to advertise his strength. The youthful body was belied by white dartings in his neat beard and the faded ink of the Etruscan numerals beneath the stubble of his shaved head. His bitter mouth pulled down his sharp features.

"No problem, Grand Selector Flaccus; just a slight delay."

The woman, recognizing in the examiner's voice that Flaccus had the authority to give her what she wanted, turned to him. "I insist that my son be tested again. He's only *acting* dumb." On the sheet she held up there were a dozen grids, each with five squares filled in, the rest blank. The pattern had to be recognized, replicated and, in later stages, elaborated. "He makes things like this out of his head. Tell him, Torbidda."

Flaccus snapped the test from the woman's hand and studied it for a moment. "You obviously understood the sequence up to the second line, so why did you put a five here?"

The boy looked down at the grids in bewilderment. "Was that wrong?"

Flaccus abruptly dropped into a crouch and grabbed the boy's chin. As the Grand Selector looked at him—*into him*—Torbidda noticed his missing finger. It was an old wound, the stump worn rough.

"You'll have to do better to fool me, boy. I deal with liars every day, the best Concord has. Take the test again, and do it right, or your mother will end her days in the belly of the Beast. Don't doubt my word."

The woman began to cry and Torbidda shook his head as if deeply confused, as if there had been some terrible mistake. He looked at the man again, searching for sympathy. Finding none, he acknowledged defeat with a stoic sigh and leaned down on the examiner's desk. He filled in the grid without pausing and handed it to Flaccus.

The Grand Selector scanned it and said quietly, "Give me the last sheet."

Hiding his skepticism—no child ever got that far—the examiner fumbled for the form.

Flaccus pointed in the final box on the final row. "What goes here?"

Torbidda scanned the first row and paused a moment. Then he said, "Don't you know, Grand Selector?"

"I am asking the question," he growled ominously.

"Sixty," Torbidda said.

"Pay the woman," said Flaccus as he pulled Torbidda away. The boy turned to call to his mother, but her attention was rapt on the money the examiner was counting out, her grief and her son, the object sold, already forgotten.

Flaccus steered him uphill, his grip firm on Torbidda's shoulder. For want of anything pleasant to consider, Torbidda pondered the Grand Selector's absent finger. Amputation was a severe punishment, marking engineers with the stamp of civilian incompetence. The first lesson of Concord's assembly line was that its blades were *always* thirsty; his generation needed only to examine their parents to see the savage surgery the engines could inflict.

They were soon in the highest part of Old Town, where the little wooden houses of civilians were replaced by tall stone buildings with taller stacks belching smoke and steam, all surrounding the base of Monte Nero, the rock upon which Bernoulli had planted his great triple-domed cathedral.

Flaccus stopped and looked down at the boy. "What's your game?" he asked, sounding genuinely puzzled. "Most Old Towners would kill to join the Guild. There's third-year Cadets who couldn't get to page four of the al-Buni, but I believe you found it easy. You *really* don't want to be an engineer?"

"I'd prefer to be free."

Flaccus chuckled heartily at this and relaxed. "Not even the Apprentices are free, boy. Only the dead. But let me make this clear: if you give less than your best from here on, then I'll make sure you get what you wish for."

He left Torbidda in a pen with a dozen other children—despite what Flaccus had said, none of them looked happier than Torbidda about being selected.

As Torbidda took his place in the line, the tall boy in front turned around to examine him. "Hello," he said cheerily. "How did you do in your al-Buni? Damn hard, wasn't it?" His simple, well-cut clothes spoke of wealth as eloquently as his New City accent. His dark complexion was not uncommon among the aristocracy; most likely one of his ancestors had been in Oltremare long enough to take a native wife—many Crusaders had returned with their bloodline spiced with some of that Ebionite warrior prowess.

When Torbidda kept silent, his eyes fixed on the ground, the boy shrugged and turned back.

Torbidda looked up slowly and studied the back of the boy's head. Then he examined the tall girl holding a clipboard at the head of the line. A weeping blond boy entered the pen and she directed him to wait behind Torbidda. She was older than the other children, perhaps ten or eleven, and had the composure of an adult. She wore a Cadet's white gown, with its distinctive wide neck and shapeless cut. Her hair was dark like his mother's, but very short, almost patchy. She dealt with the inductees with a brusque confidence he found impressive.

After some time Flaccus reappeared and pushed another boy, heavyset and scruffy, into the pen, then walked swiftly back toward the examination desks. This new boy stared furiously after the Grand Selector, as if debating whether to hurl an insult or a stone, before finally looking around at the girl, who pointed to the end of the line. He walked with the lumbering shuffle of a pit-dog, and Torbidda realized he was a real city boy, the type who made the New City stairwells so dangerous; he probably ran along the partition walls and dropped down on unsuspecting ferrymen. He was probably an orphan who'd volunteered himself.

The city boy looked disdainfully at the sniffling blond child and barked, "Move!" When the blond boy stood aside, he pushed ahead of Torbidda, growling, "You too."

The Cadet calmly set down her clipboard and walked over to them. The city boy tensed, but she sounded quite relaxed as she spoke. "This will take all day unless everyone waits their turn."

"I don't take orders—" he started defiantly, but she stepped forward, planted one leg behind his and pushed his shoulders, hard. The boy went onto his back.

Before he could rise, her foot was on his neck. "You have all year to prove how hard you are—all you have to do today is wait in line. Do yourself a kindness."

Without waiting for assent she released him and returned to her station. The city boy silently took his place at the end of the line.

"Best give second-years a wide berth," said the tall boy in front, as if Torbidda had asked his advice. His expression was sympathetic. "Sad about leaving your family?"

Torbidda saw he wasn't going to give up. "Not really."

The tall boy looked surprised, then said, "Yes, quite right, we'll see them in a year. What's there to be scared about? Plenty of children have been through it all before."

Torbidda eyed his inquisitor with suspicion. "So what happens next?"

"We'll get our numbers soon. We're supposed to forget names—mine's Leto, by the way." He lowered his voice. "Leto Spinther," he said in an undertone, as if he didn't want to sound boastful.

Torbidda had heard of the Spinthers, of course. He didn't offer his own name, but Leto dispelled any awkwardness by ignoring it and carrying on with his cheerful patter. "They'll tell you engineers don't have names—don't you believe it. A third of the students here are from good families, even though most probably didn't get to the second page of the test. The First Apprentice is an Argenti. *That* hardly slowed his climb up the mountain."

"I'm not from a good family."

Leto had the tact not to laugh. "Don't worry, there's still perfect equality in the Guild. 'No number greater than another,' as they say."

Torbidda was bemused by such an innumerate statement from a prospective engineer; he didn't get Leto's courtly sarcasm. But he listened carefully, picking up the rhythms in Leto's speech, cataloging his words, sifting meaningless gossip from information that might prove *useful*, just as every other child in the pen was doing: working out the *rules*. Caution dictated that becoming friendly with *any* Cadet this early on would be premature—better to wait and size things up properly before committing; a bad alliance was worse than none—but this boy's friendly, relaxed manner was obviously unfeigned, and with his family background . . .

"I'm Torbidda," he said with a shy smile.

Leto beamed and shook his hand. "I got to the fourth page—mind you, this wasn't my first attempt. My parents paid for tuition."

The older girl made no small-talk as she processed the Cadets. "Take nothing that will slow you down," she instructed, and they obeyed, leaving behind bags and purses, even emptying their pockets. As Torbidda drew closer, he could see that a set of keys hung around her long neck instead of a Herod's Sword. She had shadowed Grecian hair and olive skin that was more common further south of Concord; her robust features suggested she might even have some Rasenneisi blood.

After taking their details she pointed to the narrow stairway clinging to the side of the mountain and the children proceeded under a rusted arch that read *Labor Vincit Omnia*.

A few steps up and out of her sight, the city boy pushed in front of Torbidda, pausing only to give him a murderous look. Clearly he needed someone to blame for his humiliation and the girl was obviously not an option. Torbidda made a fist, but Leto said, "Not here. You're liable to get yourself killed too."

Torbidda ignored him and yanked on the city boy's hood. The boy turned with it and pushed him, making Torbidda fall back, jolting down several slippery steps until he caught himself. Leto stood aside as the city boy climbed back down to where Torbidda was looking around in vain for a weapon, a loose rock, anything.

The city boy was about to pounce when he abruptly froze. "Catch you later," he said, then pushed by Leto.

Torbidda looked around for the reason for the boy's retreat. The second-year girl was coming up the steps toward them. He held his arm out, but she walked over him. A few steps up she looked back and called, "Get up, Cadet! You're on your own—haven't you figured that out yet?"

Leto waited until she'd gone before helping Torbidda up. "I *did* warn you."

"You don't believe in fighting?"

"Not at the wrong moment. It's an especially bad idea on terrain this bad, when the other fellow has the high ground and more experience in combat—well, street brawls anyhow."

"What should you do?"

"Maneuver—make him surrender those advantages. Then attack."

They climbed through rain that fell like whips, clinging to the slippery stone. Far below, Torbidda could see the factories of Old Town, wreathed in a perennial yellowed fog. The sheer number of factories wasn't appreciable from below, but they worked night and day, engines churning out war engines just as the Guild Halls manufactured engineers.

The Guild might be brutally logical, but the buildings it inhabited were a monument of improvisation, hastily supplemented whenever needed. Though Monte Nero's slope afforded little level ground to build upon, there were extensions, and extra towers and outhouses perched wherever space could be found upon the great rock. The towers that originally housed the Molè's builders were connected by iron bridges and narrow passages cut through the mountain itself. They were never meant to be permanent—they formed a strangely chaotic venue for training ordered minds—but proximity to the Molè trumped all other considerations. Now, the higher the building, the greater its importance.

A third of the way up, a particularly stout tower sat isolated on a little summit: the Selectors' Tower, a hub to the surrounding minarets. As well as bridges and stairways, Torbidda could see a tangle of wires connecting each tower, like a web. He couldn't begin to guess their purpose.

At the end of their climb the children dragged themselves, panting and perspiring despite the cold, under a second arch that read *Homo Homini Lupus,* where a long rectangular building dominated the space: the Cadets' quarters. The baths were in a bunker below the building.

Following orders, the children hurriedly stripped and ran the gauntlet of pressured water jets that struck their skin like hail. Torbidda emerged from the dousing to discover his clothes gone. In their place was a ticket. Leto quickly whispered what was coming, and Torbidda tried to compose himself.

Baaa baaa—

Baaa baaa—

He listened to the gleeful jeering as he waited in line; it made him shiver more than the bitter wind on his wet, naked skin. As he entered the refectory he felt his face redden and his eyes water. Leto had a distant, small smile on his face, but he kept his head bowed. The city boy, still angry after his humiliation at the hands of a girl, was like a trapped animal, constantly looking around for a means of escape. Torbidda thought he was just making it worse for himself—this need only be endured. To distract himself, he studied the lectern at the top of the hall, a great silver eagle. Leto said edifying Bernoullian maxims were read out from here as Cadets took their meals, but today the new second-years were to be edified with a different spectacle.

Baaa baaa—

Baaa baaa—

The refectory echoed with the mocking calls. Torbidda caught the eye of the dark-haired girl for a moment. Although she wasn't joining in with the taunting, she was watching proceedings with interest as she ate.

Three at a time, the new inmates were summoned to the top of the hall, where an ancient trio of bored-looking legionary barbers waited, grizzled antiques who probably fought at Montaperti.

"Ticket. Sit." A mechanical exchange and a rough shearing. The message was clear: *A bad job is good enough for you.* Torbidda had always been able to distinguish between what adults *said* and what they *meant*; the two were generally at odds. This here—this methodically orchestrated spectacle with all the nakedness, the jeering, the renaming—it was an induction into a new family. If they were lambs, they were lambs without a shepherd, for this was an abattoir where children were efficiently ground up and recomposed as engineers.

When his hair was scattered on the ground, the wheezing old drunkard pressed a waxy piece of paper against his skull and braced his head with that hand as he took the hot knife in the other. Torbidda didn't flinch, but he couldn't stop the tears rolling down his cheek. Unfair, he thought, to pry out this evidence of weakness.

Pulling off the stencil, his shearer told him flatly, "Your name is"—*rippp!*—"Sixty." He poured a foul-smelling orange oil onto Torbidda's head, which burned as he rubbed it in. Cold drips streaked Torbidda's neck and back. "Let the scabs heal by themselves. Stand and dress yourself, Cadet."

He was finished just before the other two. The side of Leto's head read LVIII and the stupefied city boy's read LIX. Torbidda was walking away when he turned and glanced back as three new naked children took their place. Already he felt different. They were *civilians*. He was a Cadet, Cadet Number LX. His name was Sixty.

Chapter 2

His mother screamed curses at the Grand Selector as they dragged him away. "My baby! Don't take him from me, please!"

It was too unbelievable not to be a dream. Torbidda opened his eyes and listened instead to the storm outside the dormitory, and children weeping in the dark, weak islands adrift in a predatory archipelago. Other voices catcalled and teased, but no one ventured out of their cubicles. That first night was a period of watchful waiting, of study. Like an al-Buni grid, they had to learn the rules before advancing.

RATATATATATA TATTARATA TA TARA RAT AT AT AT T T T

The bell was the lambs' first lesson: that belligerent mechanical rapping would henceforth marshal Cadets' hours, dictating when to study, eat and bathe; when to sleep and when to rise—

"Let's go, maggots! An engineer's got to outpace the sun!"

The second-year who'd processed them yesterday was a monitor today, and her first duty was to familiarize the lambs with early rising. "Anyone still sleeping when the bell rings tomorrow gets a visit to Flaccus' tower. Next week, it's automatic expulsion. That's right: back to the mills. Back to mines. Back to the streets. You don't want that, and I don't care. Let's go! Let's go!" Torbidda was learning already to distinguish between the babble of new accents; her broad singsong came from the Concordian contato.

The dormitory was a long, wide hall with a curved roof. Light beams from high circular windows crisscrossed the dusty space, making Torbidda think of the belly of an overturned ship. There were four rows of cubicles, with a corridor running alongside either wall and in the middle; the two doors were in opposite corners. Each cubicle had a single bed and a wardrobe, and a modicum of privacy was provided by thin blue curtains hanging from a steel bar. The back-to-back wardrobes formed a narrow walkway for adventurous midnight prowlings.

"Keep Flaccus waiting down at the shooting course and he's liable to use you for a target!" the monitor shouted as the last of the lambs ran out. Somehow, Torbidda didn't think she was making that one up.

Bernoulli, the Guild's founder, had wanted his Cadets as deadly as possible, as quickly as possible. They would first be taught to use projectiles, including hand-cannons and bows, and then knives. Only those who survived the initial cull to become Candidates would learn the more sophisticated martial arts, which were more deadly than any weapon.

The lesson took place on the shooting course. The mountain face above the course was upwind from the factories, and pockmarked with craters. Though yesterday's gales had ebbed somewhat, a misting rain obscured their targets—but Grand Selector Flaccus made no allowance for these difficulties. "Think the Forty-Seveners had your advantages?" he drawled. "Conditions in battle aren't always favorable, Cadets."

By the day's end, their brains would be exhausted from calculating arcs and rates of descent, their eyes and throats raw from the gunpowder and their fingertips bleeding from plucking bowstrings—but everyone's aim would have improved. Flaccus was an impatient, harassing tutor, and the Cadets were soon grumbling, and taking revenge by making up increasingly fanciful reasons for his missing finger, from condottieri proof-of-life to the Guild's punishment for incompetence. Leto said Flaccus was a field commander who had lost his first command, and the Guild had had to pay his ransom; teaching Cadets was his demotion.

"For which he's determined to make us pay," Torbidda said grimly.

Although Leto couldn't match Torbidda's speed at calculating distances and slopes—none of them could—he proved to be an adept archer. Leto had grown up on the Europan frontier, in the legionary camps commanded by his famous father, Manius Spinther. Most of the aristocracy lucky enough to survive the Reformation held onto their empty titles until their purses were empty too, but the Spinthers were different; they adapted to the changing times. While Bernoulli's star was rising, various prominent Spinthers renounced their titles and sent their sons off to learn the mechanical arts, and when the storm came, they escaped the worst ravages of the mob—by being part of that mob. "Engineers have no family," Leto liked to say, "but a Spinther is always a Spinther." His cousins had all been through the Guild Halls and now it was his turn. Torbidda, perceiving that Leto's first loyalty was to family, stored that away and counted himself lucky to have found such an ally.

He was clumsily nocking an arrow when Leto whispered, "Torbidda, look! That's Filippo Argenti!"

Flaccus was whispering deferentially to the newcomer, a stolid, middle-aged man with the blank, weather-beaten face of a mason. The vivid red of the First Apprentice's gown looked unreal against the scarred landscape of the firing range. Others began to notice his presence and soon every Cadet was hitting wide of the mark—all except Leto, who continued to hit bulls'-eyes with perfect nonchalance. After watching for a few minutes, the First Apprentice clapped his hands and walked onto the firing range. The Cadets immediately lowered their weapons.

"I need a volunteer. Someone willing to shoot me. Anyone?" He paused, then sighed with theatrical relief when none stepped forward. "Well, that's gratifying."

Laughter dispelled the tension still remaining from yesterday's induction.

Argenti looked around, and then started, "Brothers and sisters, welcome. I once stood where you stand. You're asking, will I make it?" He looked from face to face, nodding as if to say this was quite natural. "I won't lie, some of you won't. First year *will* be tough, but just remember that you're not alone. If the Guild seems cruel, remember: it is not senselessly cruel. We winnow with reason. We need the best."

He looked up at the brutalized crags behind the range. "The Guild is a mountain with many peaks—Old Town, New City, the Guild Halls—but really, they are one. Our strength is our unity. What is our strength?"

"Unity," came the eager response.

"Just so. Unity depends on team spirit. No tower can stand with each brick vying to be higher than the others."

He stopped in front of Torbidda. "Each must be content in its place. The mortar that binds them must be—"

"Trust?" said Torbidda in a dry whisper. He felt Leto's unease.

"Trust! Exactly. I am First Apprentice not because I learned how to climb, but because I learned how to trust. It's all very well to say so; you need to see it." Like a cheap magician he produced a small red apple from his sleeve and looked around brightly. "I need a volunteer. Whom can I tempt?"

Leto subtly shook his head, but the warning was unnecessary; Torbidda had already spotted Flaccus' ill-concealed eagerness. The boy who'd been crying in the line yesterday put his hand up.

The First Apprentice smiled kindly. "What's your name, son?"

The blond boy had to think for a moment. ". . . Forty-Two, First Apprentice."

"Not your *number*. Don't you have a real name?"

"Oh! Yes, First Apprentice. Calpurnius Glabrio."

"Well, Calpurnius, I am a decent shot, and I need a volunteer."

"What must I do?"

"That's the spirit. Step up to the target. Place this on your head."
There was an intake of breath and the Apprentice said in a loud
voice, "Go back if you're afraid. There's no shame in it."

Calpurnius solemnly took the apple and walked up to the target.
"I trust you, First Apprentice."

The Apprentice took careful aim and released. The arrow took the
apple with a wet *thunk-kuh-kuh*. Calpurnius joined in the applause.
Quickly, the Apprentice nocked another and shot again. The force
drove Calpurnius back and pinned him against the target.

As the boy screamed, the Apprentice turned around. "Why have
you stopped applauding, children?"

He looked back at Calpurnius, took another arrow, drew back
and released. The screaming stopped. "What are you thinking now,
Cadets?" he snarled. "That this was *unfair*? I tell you: it is *necessary*.
The Guild is an army, and an army is only as strong as its weakest
member. You're here because you're clever, so I won't patronize you.
We take you young, when it is still possible to change you—to *mold*
you. You have begun to climb the mountain, and now the only way
out is *up*. Your peers will not help you. They will do everything to
make you stumble. Each summit is further up, and the higher you
go, the purer the competition—and the further to fall. There's no
safety down here, either. Believe me, the laggard will quickly find
himself without allies." This time his smile was sour and weary. "As
you climb higher, you'll appreciate that we Apprentices are not to
be envied. Having reached that final peak, we can only watch as
our competition surrounds us. But that"—he looked around with
hostility—"is as it should be."

He turned once more to Torbidda. "You, boy: what is your name?"

"*Sixty*, sir."

He smiled kindly. "I mean your *real* name."

"Sixty, sir."

The smile disappeared. "Fetch me that apple, Sixty."

"No, sir."

"That's the correct answer." The Apprentice turned and walked over to the target. "You will hear talk of factions: engineers against nobles, Empiricists against Naturalists. Ignore these chimeras. All alliances are temporary. Your competition is all around you. Make alliances, by all means, but know this: *all friends must eventually become rivals.*" He pulled out the arrow and removed the apple. "Calpurnius wanted to be loved. You must rise above that temptation."

"This"—he threw the apple to Torbidda—"is for saying no to me."

As Torbidda caught the apple, the First Apprentice's fist moved.

After a moment's numbness, sharp pain spread throughout Torbidda's chest. He sat up and coughed blood. He was several braccia from where he had been standing. Every Cadet was staring openmouthed. The man in red looked down at him. "And *that* is for not shooting me when you had me in your sights. I wait for you, all of you. Come and cut my throat someday."

Torbidda watched the First Apprentice walk slowly back to the Guild Halls, wondering how, if that day ever came, he would find the courage to do it.

First Apprentice Argenti's demonstration had left Grand Selector Flaccus almost giddy. "*That's* what it's all about, Cadets," he huffed with admiration. "Man domesticated himself along with the dog. We must be wolves again."

One of the Cadets threw up, and Flaccus snatched Torbidda's apple and threw it at him viciously. "What did you expect? The Guild is not the Curia. The Guild Hall is not a seminary. Don't start feeling sorry for yourself. You're receiving an unrivaled education at great cost to the State. Some say war's a cheaper and better school for engineers; some say it's wasteful to educate so many when so few of you will survive . . ." Flaccus obviously shared this view. ". . . but the Colors say waste's inevitable when mining. They want the best, and the best are those who survive. All right, break's over. Back in line."

As they reassembled, Torbidda caught the eye of the boy who'd vomited. The boy blushed in anger as he wiped his mouth. He stood shoulder to shoulder with the others and nocked an arrow. Torbidda looked away and did likewise.

"Take aim—" Flaccus roared.

Chapter 3

Argenti's demonstration had strange results on the children. While some became cautious, others took it as license to indulge all their passions unrestrainedly. That night the city boy, Fifty-Nine, cornered Torbidda in his cubicle. Three other city boys joined in, while a fourth stood at the curtain, watching proceedings. The onlooker was the boy who had caught Torbidda staring. When he said, "Enough!" they stopped. He was handsome, and had a New City accent like Leto's.

Curtains had to be drawn in the morning to display tidy cubicle, locked wardrobe and neatly made bed. Torbidda was just pulling his open when the monitor walked by. She must have seen his black eye, but all she remarked on was his tardiness: "Do better, Sixty. It gets faster."

And she was right. Those who made it would be landed on the front line, so the Cadets had to become accustomed to the pressure

from the start. As days turned to weeks new subjects kept coming, as
if there was no time to waste. Flaccus taught the "hard" arts, including Mechanics and Geometry; those subjects requiring anything
resembling intuition and imagination he left, contemptuously, to
Selector Varro.

The Anatomy Hall had no viewing gallery. "Dissection's not an art
learned from afar. We must get our hands wet!" Varro said gleefully.
    It was situated in the large cavern where the main canal entered
and exited the mountain. The floor was solid rock, interrupted by a
metal grid under which dark channels of water flowed from deeper
caverns within Monte Nero. High circular windows allowed smoke-
stained swallows and exhausted daylight to enter the cavern, though
the shafts of light were bisected by the gauntlet of thin stalactites
and dripping chains that hung from the roof and soon dissipated
into the larger gloom within. At the back of the cave was a wall of
metal, which turned constantly, producing a dull animal groan that
vied with the water's roar. On some of the dozens of workstations
suspended from long chains were the drying remains of previous
dissections. They were bloated with formaldehyde, which added to
the stench hanging in the frigid atmosphere. As well as the weight-
bearing chains, there were others, great swathes of links that shivered with the same icy luminescence illuminating the orbs of New
City. The blue crackling current gave the cave a shifting twilight
quality that made even those occupants with peeled skin and gaping
chest cavities seem nervously animated.
    The Cadets were still searching for tools and fighting for worksta-
tions when the selector shuffled to the podium. Varro was short, com-
pact and profoundly hairy. His large, ape-like hands and long dexterous
fingers were, like every other part of him except his skull, covered in
wiry reddish-brown and gray hair. His heavy red beard, braided in the
Ebionite fashion, was a startling contrast to his pale skull.
    Ignoring the chaos around him, he launched into his first lecture.
    "You weren't thinking of taking my workstation, were you?" The
boy's drawl sounded bored, almost a yawn.

"I don't see any names," said Torbidda, defiantly.

"They shouldn't let slow learners be Cadets."

The boy's followers laughed on cue. They were straining with anticipation, like a dog pack, but the boy moved leisurely as a peacock, raising his fists up to Torbidda's face as though inviting inspection. "No names here either. Or didn't you get enough last night?"

His number was Four. His striking face was perfect, except for the fleshy lips that were set in a perpetual sneer. He had been one of the first inducted on Examination Day, and he acted as if he had been privy to deep secrets his whole life. Four's swagger drew the rowdier first-years into his orbit; there were a few nobles, including the Fuscus twins, but most were poor city boys, including Fifty-Nine, of course. Like Leto, Four was from the New City, but unlike the Spinthers, his family had only just taken the leap; he was the first son to be sent to the Guild, and he was loud in denigrating both the Curia and aristocracy as yesterday's men. The nervous boys admired his bluster, and anointed him their seer, to lead them through this strange land and chase away its shadows.

"Well?" said Four.

Torbidda recognized there was no way of winning the contest; Four had the high ground. He abandoned his claim to the workstation and found another.

"*Madonna,* don't take it personally, Torbidda. You're a means to an end, that's all. Four is consolidating his position—"

"—by creating opportunities for his crew to prove their loyalty. I know that."

"You did the right thing backing down. Don't let yourself become an object-lesson."

Leto was right, of course, but Torbidda looked up with dissatisfaction from his colorless lunch and scanned the other tables in the refectory. The Apprenticeship Candidates sat at the high table at the far end of the room. To reach the third year was no small achievement, but still only a handful—a maximum of twelve, usually fewer—were deemed worthy to apply for Apprenticeship; the rest were posted abroad, scattered across the empire. The Candidates' solemn intensity was a fascinating spectacle, but one might as well look for example to the saints. The second-years at the opposite table, however: they were still mortals.

Usually Leto's evaluation of military problems was sound, but though Torbidda had backed down to Four, just as the first-years deferred to the second-years, he *knew* servility wasn't a long-term stratagem. He looked across at the monitor, who was discussing something while the Cadets around her listened courteously. Compared with the first-years' rowdy fighting and posturing, the second-years were serenity itself. How was it that peace reigned on that side of the room? How had they learned to cooperate?

Leto saw the direction of his glance and said softly, "Forget it, Torbidda. Second-years won't help—they'll kill you faster than Four will. At least he needs an excuse."

But Torbidda was looking for answers, not allies. It would have been easy for the Guild to segregate the lambs from these veterans, so this example had been placed before them for a reason. His life depended on discovering why.

"Come on," said Leto. "Flaccus will kill us both if we're late for Mechanics again."

The water cut through the stone like paper. Torbidda held the gem to the light, examining it with the intensity of a poacher stalking prey. Gem-cutting had something of Geometry's precision: the light was perfect or flawed, just as an equation was correct or incorrect. Others complained, but Torbidda understood why they were expected to master practical arts as well as theory. The Guild needed more than rote-trained mules; each Cadet was expected to travel the same road Bernoulli had.

As the Cadets proudly admired their own work and showed their gems off to the others, Torbidda wondered at their pleasure—and envied them, a little. Their work was pedestrian compared to his, but when he studied his jewel's icy new clarity he felt only confusion at the nausea it inspired in him. It was like fire scorching his insides. He had worked hard, finding the planes then grinding and polishing to reveal the flawless gem within, but now the urge to ruin that perfection was taking hold of him.

He carefully placed it down and moved on to his next task. With Gem-cutting, progress was tangible; some subjects were more about learning to stumble through the darkness.

Alchemistry was taught in a cave cut even deeper into the mountain than the Anatomy Hall—but it was far warmer, thanks to the great furnace at its heart that fed on coal and dripping animal fats. Its roar and the feverish scent of scorched cinnabar filled the cave. The furnace sat on a raised platform beneath a bramble of tubes that stretched to the ceiling and tangled into ever-darker, more intricate knots. The far wall was lost in the gloom; it was only when they got closer, and their eyes had adjusted to the crepuscular light, that they could see it was moving, albeit with glacial slowness.

Varro collected a lubricating yellow syrup from taps that punctured the wall's metal surface. He was more human than Flaccus; he treated the Cadets like fellow explorers, and took for granted that they shared his curiosity. As he tended to ramble, his classes were an oasis of calm in their crowded schedule, not to mention a chance for some of the Cadets to indulge in games of correspondence chess.

Varro was working the bellows when he suddenly pointed and shouted, "You! What's your name?"

"Sixty, Sir."

"And were you named for your father? The Grand Selector may prefer numbers to people, but he's not the one asking. Come, lad, your *real* name."

". . . Torbidda, Sir." He felt exposed before his fellow students; there was safety in anonymity.

"Torbidda, is it? And how many elements are there?"

"Ninety-two occur naturally. We'll make more eventually."

"Ninety-two? Flaccus told you that, I suppose. Does *that* sound like the name of God? *We'll make more*, you say, as if it's a simple thing— it's easier by far to create a new letter in the alphabet! What would we do if we found it? It would remake all texts. What babble was wrought leaping from Four to Ninety, and you blithely propose to go on? To rebuild the Tower until God throws it down again and sends a more lasting Flood so that we remember the lesson this time—"

This mystical tangent set eyes rolling.

"Didn't God die in Forty-Seven, sir?" said Leto.

Varro erupted with laughter that filled the cave. "Oh, very good. What's your name? And don't give me a damned number."

"Spinther, sir," said Leto loudly.

"Ah! I knew your father. Well, yes, a certain priestly deity *was* a casualty of the Reformation. But I'm not referring to the idol of those paper-shuffling clerics. Our prey's an older beast, and killing Him would be a great deed, great indeed. Perhaps one of you will manage it." He looked fondly into the furnace. "Where was I?"

"The elements, sir?"

"Ah, yes!" Varro threw the bellows aside and picked up a beaker of water that reflected the dangling lights like falling stars frozen. "When speaking of primordial matters, best not multiply explanations. Simplify. This glass is the world. This glass is each of you. You are not numbers! You are water! You are air!"

He cast the water on the pipes and it hissed and bubbled and steam wafted up. "Look, children: the ghost flees! Catch it, and we'll have power to move mountains. Air and water are God's initials, the Aleph and Beth of a world at war. Fools like Flaccus will count the stars and list the elements and remain blind to the larger pattern. The Wave, children! It is majestic and merciless, and it is *everywhere*, even in the elements. Consider the valence of ordered atoms. It flows up—one, two, three, four, and down, three, two, one—and up again. As below, so above. As above, so below."

There was a long, embarrassed silence during which Varro collected himself. "So," he said, "that's what we're about today: extracting oxygen from water. You'll see the bitch holds on as fiercely as a mother does her child. Find a station. Take a beaker."

The Cadets went through the experiment noisily, everyone competing to impersonate the old man's eccentric manner. Torbidda tried to play along, but it wasn't easy.

This was just a basic alchemical exercise, yet his hand trembled and his heart pounded. Frustrated at the sluggish pace of Flaccus' teaching, he'd begun to study independently, and his grasp of Wave Theory was now sufficiently advanced to recognize that Varro's hints of some grand hidden tapestry were at the very heart of the Bernoullian art. But though Torbidda might be suddenly conscious of the gravity of their search, he was in the minority. Cadets with a family background in engineering had more conservative ideas about the limits of Natural Philosophy, and Four spoke for these: "No wonder they keep this relic buried down here," he said loudly.

"He's the last Naturalist in any position of influence."

"But they say Bonnacio is one of his protégés," Torbidda said mildly. They were back in the refectory, and Torbidda was keeping his eyes on the second-years, even as he tried to find out what Leto thought of Selector Varro.

"So much the worse for the Second Apprentice," Leto said. "The other two are Empiricists. Look, Torbidda: it's easy to be taken in, but that kind of talk isn't politic. The old man gets away with it because he fought the good fight in Forty-Seven but if *you* want to get a decent posting in third year, be an Empiricist. Or at least pretend to be."

"Sure."

Torbidda understood this was a warning. Cadets were always under scrutiny, and not just by the selectors. Although he affected a carelessness, Leto was as manipulative as any of the Cadets; he was just more subtle than most. He'd known exactly how well Torbidda had done in the al-Buni when he had befriended him—indeed, all of Leto's friends had turned out to be top students—but Torbidda didn't resent him for his calculation. He took it as a compliment. Now he decided to heed Leto's warning. Aside from the tyrannical bell, they were given no guidance outside the classroom; no behavior was proscribed or recommended. They were on their own, and conspicuously following the wrong crowd could be fatal.

His first real fight, however, had nothing to do with political calculation. It was over a girl.

Chapter 4

Torbidda sprinted to reach the dormitory door before the bell sounded, but he was too late. It opened in front of him.

RATATATATATA TATTARATA TATA RAAT AT AT T T T T T

"Still too slow, Sixty," said the monitor walking by.

She marched down the row, glancing at the neat beds in the cubicles to her left, and stopped at a closed curtain. "You had *better* be dead, Fifty-Nine."

She pulled back the curtain and the boy in the bed shifted with a tired groan and pulled the sheet tighter. Furious, she stepped in and pulled back the bedclothes.

"Morning!" said Fifty-Nine with a happy yawn.

A hand shot out from beneath the bed and grabbed her ankle; and two silent boys appeared behind her. One slipped an arm around her neck and pulled her head back as the second closed the curtain and stood watch outside.

At the far end of the dormitory, Torbidda stood in the doorway looking back. He paused for a second before continuing out and closing the door firmly behind him. Whatever was about to happen was none of his concern.

A third boy emerged from the wardrobe with a whoop.

"Please—" she whimpered, and stopped struggling. When he came closer, she kicked his crotch with her free leg. As he keeled over, Fifty-Nine hopped out of bed and punched her exposed belly. The same moment another hand grabbed her other ankle and she lost her footing. Fifty-Nine and the other boy unceremoniously picked her up and threw her against the wall above the bed. She fell onto the mattress with a grunt.

"You're so smart, how'd you get in this mess, huh?" Fifty-Nine bared his teeth in a grin. "Well? Answer me!" He hammered his fist into her nose.

"Cover her face!" he ordered the freckled boy emerging from beneath the bed. The city boy was shrill and somewhat panicked by the sight of blood, and at how abruptly the girl had stopped flailing. But as well as revenge for his earlier humiliation at the monitor's hands, he intended to show his peers that he could organize fun and games as well as Four. Tackling a second-year was dangerous—she had a year's combat training on them—but they'd come in strength. They piled pillows and sheets on top, and two large hands held her wrists while other hands pulled at her robes.

Torbidda knew he shouldn't be here—he'd seen the boy standing watch and guessed what was going to happen. Now he was trying to walk crouched and quietly along the narrow walkway formed by the top of the wardrobes. The old wood creaked, but the boys were too excited to notice. He could hear them whooping with excitement. He should let them go about their business before they noticed him. She—*she herself*—said it: every Cadet was on their own, and the same rules applied to her.

Yet here he was.

Fifty-Nine was squirming on top, trying to get her legs open and his robe up at the same time. The boy holding her under the bedclothes was concentrating on his job, while the other was staring with something like reverence. The boy behind the curtain glanced in for a moment, then reluctantly returned to sentry duty.

Four would have enforced better discipline, Torbidda thought. Still telling himself this was none of his business, he dropped onto the nearest boy. He landed feet-first, clumsily, but his weight was enough to knock the boy into the one standing watch, and he pulled the curtain down with him. The boy holding the pillow didn't wait for orders but abandoned his post to rush Torbidda, and as the girl felt the pressure ease, without even trying to remove the blankets, her fingers shot up, searching and finding Fifty-Nine's eyes. The pillow boy had pulled Torbidda down and the three of them were kicking and punching him until he curled into a ball. Fifty-Nine's scream made them turn just in time to see the girl pull her thumbs out of their leader's face with an audible *pop*. She stood onto the bed and pulled herself up onto the wardrobe.

The boys forgot about Torbidda—he was stupid with the beating anyway—and leapt up on the bed to follow her. She'd get them individually if they let her escape. The three leapt for the walkway together, figuring to rush her. She kicked one in the face and knocked him back onto the floor, and as the other two got to their feet, she backed away carefully. She took the set of keys from around her neck and threw them at Torbidda's fetal body. "Hey, Sixty!"

The jangle as it landed made him open his eyes.

"Lock the north door behind you," she ordered.

Torbidda grabbed the keys and as he started crawling to the door she turned and limped toward the other, then stopped abruptly and turned to face her pursuers.

"You're trapped," one of the boys shouted, and laughed. "We blocked that door."

"I guessed you would," she said calmly, and raced toward them. She knocked the first boy aside with an elbow as she threw herself bodily at the other. They tumbled off together, but she twisted as she fell so that he took the impact. She smashed his head on the floor, just to be sure, then went to examine the other three. The one she'd kicked in the face, the first to fall, had broken his neck.

As he limped back from the door, Torbidda saw her kneel beside the one she'd elbowed off the walkway. He was clutching his ribs and moaning. She tenderly lifted his head into her lap, then twisted it sharply left. The moaning stopped.

Fifty-Nine was writhing on the bed, streaming blood from the holes in his face. As she carefully rechained the curtain, she looked at Torbidda and said flatly, "You're late for class, Cadet. Leave my keys in the door."

She didn't need to say she owed him. It was obvious. Torbidda limped to the door, unlocked it and shut out Fifty-Nine's smothered screams behind him.

Chapter 5

"Flaccus believes in a mechanistic universe that can be mastered with levers and winches. Be warned. Nature is a far more subtle monster, and one that you must first understand if you are to tame her."

The class stood in the Alchemistry Hall at the edge of a massive circular sheet, shivering in the frigid air. Five long chains were connected to the sheet. Varro ushered them closer. "Get comfy—not that close, Signore Vitale! Step back, Signorina Inzerillo. All right, let's see . . ." He looked at the levers in front of him, feigning confusion.

Torbidda stole a glance at Four and his acolytes and looked away quickly; Four was watching him. Fifty-Nine's suicidal attempt to establish his independence had allowed Four to consolidate control of the city boys, making life trying for everyone else in general and Torbidda in particular: the girl was too big a target, so by default he had become the focus of Four's campaign of vengeance.

Leto observed that avenging fallen comrades was an excellent cause to unite a group—but Torbidda was less interested in history, than practical suggestions as to *how* he could survive.

Varro pulled one of the dangling chains, the sheet lifted and the children stepped back. The water started only two braccia down, but it looked at least five braccia deep. The pool's surface was *alive* with writhing limbs, spastic hands and gnashing animal jaws as shapes turned and shifted unstably and cubes and spheres broke the surface and dissolved.

"Look, children, at the monster our wisdom captured. Beautiful bride, isn't she? The pseudonaiades are pure water, and water only. We compromised creatures are at once less and more than these elementals."

"All right, Torbidda?" Leto whispered.

"Fine," he said, fighting rising panic as Varro went on.

"We're going to get in. Don't worry, it's safe. To study pseudonaiades we must come to know it *intimately*. But let's not get carried away with romance: the water of life is death to Man. First, I shall render it neutral."

He began to work the crank beside the levers and blue sparks hopped from the turning spokes. Varro watched the dial as he worked. "Spinther, be a good fellow and pull that switch—that one, there."

As Leto did so, the slowly moving wheel changed direction suddenly and started spinning fast. The water's surface was flooded with the cranking energy and an acrid metallic smell filled the room. The surface shot up in several agonized arcs and then, just as suddenly, was still.

Varro moved to another wheel and strained against it. There was a clunking noise, followed by sustained sucking, and the level of the water started to sink quickly. When it got past four braccia, the top of a tall rectangular box became visible, a layer of rust covering it like moss. As the water sank a little lower, they saw it was actually two connected boxes. Each had a door of thick greenish glass. The door on the left was open, and they could see an empty seat inside. The water level within the other container had not sunk.

Varro was climbing down even as the last of the water drained. "Come on, it's safe. The monster's sleeping." He jumped down into the quarter-braccia that remained and waded over to the box. "Wakey, wakey," he sang, tapping the other compartment. He turned to the class. "Well, come on! Don't be scared."

The children climbed down one by one, and by the time they were all in the hole, Varro was sitting inside the compartment on the right, strapping two domes over his ears. He inclined his head to the partition and the Cadets watched a column of water form, moving tentatively at first, as if testing the bonds of its prison, then it began to flow over the glass walls, searching for cracks. Torbidda took a step backward, glancing at the ladder.

"Look," said Four, "Sixty's scared of water. It's so true what they say about Old Towners and washing."

His crew snickered, even though the majority of them were from the Depths.

"Can you hear it?" Varro's voice was distorted, each word echoing and overlapping, and there was a shifting vibrato to each syllable. *"The peak of our Natural Philosophy is the Wave, but it would have been impossible without this device. The Helens had the Delphic Oracle. The Etruscans had the Cumaean Sibyl. We have this! Bernoulli called it the Confession Box. Remember, frame your queries in numerical terms, or you'll get answers that only a theologian could decipher. Who's got a question?"*

Four made a suggestion.

"Bit morbid," Varro remarked, but he pushed the dial, cleared his throat and asked, *"Water, how many of these children shall survive the year?"*

The water column merely continued its swaying. Varro pumped the dial for a few moments then pulled hard on it. The floor of the glass compartment crackled with blue bolts. They vaulted up the walls passing through the pseudonaiad and bending in transit.

"How many?" Varro repeated firmly, his voice authoritative.

The sound that came out was like a staccato wail, *Aaaam-neeevvvaaa*. Varro fiddled with dials and the dulcimer sound was heard again, distorted and marred by moments of blank silence.

"laaaamneeed vaaaav—"

"Anyone know what that means?"

Doubtfully, Torbidda spoke up. "It's the Ebionite High Language, Sir."

"Madonna!" Varro exclaimed. "We have a linguist! Very good, what does it mean?"

Torbidda swallowed and said, "Thirty-six."

"That's all?" said Four. "But how do we know that's correct? Ask it how many will die today."

Varro was preparing to relay the message when an answer came unprompted.

"Khaaaaaaheeeeee—"

"It means eighteen," said Torbidda doubtfully.

"Eighteen? What, in one day?" Four exclaimed. "This is bunk!"

Suddenly animated, the pseudonaiad reformed as a square pillar, reared back and butted its "corner" on the glass. The Confession Box shook, but Varro only laughed. The pseudonaiad lost cohesion for a few moments after the blow, then sluggishly reformed. Ripples undulated over its surface. Suddenly it struck again, hitting the same place.

"*Settle down now,*" said Varro, once more pumping on the switch.

A crack appeared in the glass, jerkily spreading out, fast and slow, but always getting wider.

"*. . . perhaps we should return to this another time.*"

Four was first up the ladder, Leto fast behind him.

Varro called, "Spinther, wind up that wheel, would you, that's a good boy. The rest of you, take your time, nice and orderly."

The pseudonaiad struck the glass again, and the climbers' pace speeded up.

CraAAAck

"Let me up! Let me up!" Varro pushed by Torbidda and pulled a girl off the ladder. Torbidda helped her up, all the while keeping his eye on the box.

The pseudonaiad again flowed over the glass, studying the crack, judging what it needed. A few drips fell from the crack and wriggled on the floor like worms. It reeled back again.

KRAAK

The glass shattered and the children screamed as the water came rushing through the fracture and hit the ground. It reformed quickly, orientated itself on its human quarries and threw itself at the ladder, narrowly missing a boy who pulled his foot away with a yelp. Torbidda and the girl were stranded in the pit with this monster. Above, Varro checked the control board and shouted "Keep turning, Spinther! Needs a little more."

Varro ran to the side of the pit. The class was watching the pair stranded below with interest. No one offered to help.

"Shock it!" cried Torbidda.

"It's not charged yet. You!" Varro pulled Four out the circle. "Help Spinther turn it." He pushed him toward Leto. He looked back down and shouted, "Keep moving, Cadets! Don't let it corner you."

"What are you doing?" said Leto as Four pulled against him on the wheel, making it impossible to turn.

"Sixty's going to get a bath after all!"

The male Fuscus twin was circling. Leto didn't have time to argue—and anyway, it would be pointless. He let the Fuscus boy get behind him, then let go of the wheel, which yanked Four off his feet as it spun wildly in the direction Four had been pulling. Leto elbowed the Fuscus boy in the nose, then reached out with one hand to brace the wheel before turning back to Four, who was still sprawled flat. He stomped hard on Four's stomach then he returned to the wheel and started winding desperately.

The girl, terrified, clung to Torbidda as the pseudonaiad reared up. If he did nothing, they would drown together. He needed more time.

He elbowed her in the face and dived aside as the water stampeded, enveloping the stunned girl as Torbidda ran to the other side of the Confession Box. He slammed the door behind him, but there was no lock—why would there be? As he clung onto the handle, the girl dropped lifelessly out of the pillar of water, which collapsed into a wave and crashed against the glass.

Torbidda felt it pulling against the other side. He couldn't hold it much longer. He screamed into the head set, *"Help!"*

The door was wrestled open, Torbidda screamed and the water filled the compartment.

Then there was pain, and blue light—

When he awoke, the last of the lifeless water was going down the drain, once more subject to gravity. Varro was looking down at him with an expression of wonder, and Leto with one of concern.

Torbidda noticed his bloody lip. "You fought for me, Spinther? *Idiota.*"

"Don't take it to heart," said Leto. "I didn't have time to think it through."

"Oh, what a mess," said Varro, regarding the girl's body. She was dead, with no wound but the bloody nose Torbidda had given her. "I don't suppose anyone knows her name?"

"I know her number," Torbidda said. "It was Eighteen."

Chapter 6

Every workstation had a fresh subject, hyperventilating and struggling against their bonds, ready for dissection.

"Sixty! Big day! Excited?"

Torbidda responded dutifully, "Very, sir." Varro's attentiveness, stemming from guilt, no doubt, had rapidly become annoying. Torbidda was worried that it would mark him as a Naturalist partisan.

Varro shuffled to the top of cave. "Now, pace yourself. You have just one subject each. You need to keep it fresh until noon, which is, let's see"—he glanced at a water-clock—"three hours. You'll be surprised how much punishment a subject can bear if you avoid the major organs."

They'd had weeks of lectures and cadaver butchery, and this was their first *real* dissection. Varro, shaken by the Confession Box accident, had brought in those second-years specializing in Anatomy to assist. The monitor tutted as she walked past Torbidda's station.

"Call that secure? You won't learn much wrestling the subject for the scalpel."

She refastened the straps and then looked at him, appraising his fresh black eye. "Why don't you fight back?"

Torbidda carefully laid out his tools. "He's not that much trouble."

"You should make eye-contact when you lie. Makes it more convincing."

As the students got under way, the screaming started.

Torbidda smiled in embarrassment. "He'll get bored and move on."

She looked at him intensely. "Listen, you have to start thinking long-term. If you take it from Four, others will follow. You don't know what's coming in the next few months. I didn't." She looked around again and then pulled up her tunic. An ugly pink scar bisected her flank in the shape of an N. "I didn't realize how fast it could escalate. This saved my life. It told me what I had to do to survive."

Torbidda watched as she circled the room, helping other students. She wasn't telling him anything he hadn't already worked out—so why was he waiting? He wasn't scared, exactly. He had just expected an adult to step in at some point—that was how childhood worked. Those were the *rules*.

When she returned, he asked, "What should I do?"

"Give him a target."

Her name was Agrippina. Her father was a farmer, one of the few still trying to make a living raising chickens and harvesting dust in the Concordian contato. At the end of another drought year he'd realized the worth of his unusually canny daughter. He made the trek to the city bringing her in the trailer with the other livestock. Although she was determined not to let anyone ever own her again, she wasn't bitter. Her father had done them both a favor.

"I love it here," she said simply.

Every second-year had this reverence. Torbidda was beginning to understand where it came from. The Guild was a machine: it never gave back more than you put in, but it never promised anything, and it never lied either.

"Madonna, what a din!" exclaimed Varro. "I *told* you: cut the vocal cords first!"

Initially, the complete absence of rules gave rise to clumsy sexual experimentation late at night. That carnal holiday didn't last. Eventually there was no one foolish enough to drop their guard. Nights were one long tense silence now.

Torbidda could hear the approaching whispers. He knew what was imminent; Agrippina *had* warned him. He had brought this on himself by his servility. It was dark and he was outnumbered here; there was nothing for it but to endure. They came in strength, rushing in to overturn his mattress, and piled on, whooping and hollering. Blows rained down on him in quick succession, on his legs, torso and face. It was not a serious attack—there was nothing sharp involved. He covered his head and waited for the end. Four probably thought he was making an example, but you don't make examples when nobody can see.

You wait for daylight.

Torbidda rose before the bell and limped to the sinks to wash the matted blood from his body. He entered the refectory and sat alone, eating breakfast through scabbed lips, hood down to show his bruises to the world. Naturally everyone ignored him; talking to a sinking Cadet was impolitic. As Four and his followers filed by Torbidda, each greeted him with a smack on the back on his head.

"Morning."

"Morning."

"Morning."

"Morning."

Torbidda's swollen face usefully masked his anger—though the anger wasn't directed at Four but at himself. He had survived the night, but what incompetence, to have let it come to this.

He felt a hand on his shoulder. "You all right?"

Leto's imprudence was touching. He had troubles of his own with the Fuscus twins. The New City brats were minor nobility; their family had a long-running feud with the Spinthers. Leto's indifference to the incestuous quarrels of the old nobility infuriated them nearly as much as his indifference to his status, which was far grander than theirs.

"Go away."

"What? I'm not going to—Look, I wasn't one of them last night—"

"I know that! Please, go, but first hit me."

Leto's eyes narrowed. "What are you planning?"

"Please."

"Fine!" he shouted and struck Torbidda hard on the back of the head. There was general laughter as he walked away.

"Even Spinther's got sick of the smell," Four drawled.

Torbidda limped through the day, dutifully dissected, solved problems and calculated and drew and read, and all the while dispassionately examined his plan from different angles, holding it up to the light to see its flaws.

He arrived early for Mechanics to select a workstation that would put his back to the classroom. He powered up his water-saw and cut a small wedge of wood. He took his half-carved table leg from the lathe and practiced swinging it, getting the feel of its weight and balance. After class began he informed Flaccus that there was an impatient consul waiting for him in his tower. Flaccus left in a hurry, telling the class to continue work. Torbidda followed him to the door, wedge in hand, but there was no need for it. Flaccus had left his keys behind.

Torbidda turned the lock and pocketed the keys. Then he returned to his own isolated workstation, taking care to shuffle past Four's desk. The absence of adult supervision would be irresistible—he knew Four still thought of the selectors as surrogate parents. He busied himself splitting wood with water. With the din from the saws it would be impossible to hear Four's approach, so he just had to be ready.

When it came, time seemed to slow. An arm came around his neck; the other braced his forehead. Four meant to tip him toward the blade—he probably just planned to scare him. Instead of resisting, Torbidda pulled, leaning to the left as he went forward, and Four's arm went into the water's path. There was a whipping sound and the stream ran red for a moment. Four's scream was louder than the saw.

Now Torbidda pushed against his weight and Four fell backward, trying to keep his balance even as the blood spewed from his severed forearm. Torbidda snatched up the table leg as he turned and put his whole body behind it. It caught Four under the jaw and lifted his feet from the ground.

He landed on his back and lay there, coughing blood, not understanding what had happened—or what was happening now. His eyes darted from his pumping wound to the onlooking classroom.

"*Please*," he gargled, "get help!"

One of his crew ran to the door, only to discover it was locked.

"I've got the key," Torbidda said clearly.

Four's crew dared each other to rush him, but a minute passed and still no one made a move. He stood guard over Four until the blood slowed to a languid ebb. At the end of it, Torbidda had the high ground. They had watched their leader die, and everyone else had watched them watching.

When Torbidda unlocked the door, Flaccus was waiting. Torbidda got a slap for locking him out of his own classroom and a mop for the mess. The selector didn't mention Four. No one did. He was forgotten before his blood was mopped up.

Chapter 7

Heads turned in the refectory as Torbidda sat at the second-years' table.

Agrippina smiled. "I didn't invite you to join me. There are rules, you know."

"But just one counts."

Agrippina laughed. "I heard about your woodwork."

"Already?"

"I see you've been practicing eye-contact—but don't pretend to be surprised. Everyone's talking about it."

Torbidda felt no elation about the killing, nor any remorse. He wondered if he had always been so heartless, or whether it was a logical response to a heartless environment. He knew now why congress was civil among the second-years: they all knew the consequences. They still quarreled, but their quarrels were swift, unflinching things and the loser was not left bruised or lame but out in the cold, another example to his peers.

Agrippina studied him coolly. "You did what you had to. I know you're too smart to waste your time with guilt, but don't start reveling in killing either. Some Cadets start thinking it's *that* type of competition, and they don't last."

"I understand. It's a means to an end. I don't understand why you care."

"You helped me."

"True but you didn't *have* to reciprocate. I'm only a first-year."

"Exactly. You're talented and you won't ever be competition. I'll need competent allies when I become Third Apprentice."

"Don't you mean *if*?"

"I mean when."

He offered his hand. "My name's Torbidda."

First-bloods were students to watch. He'd set a record in so quickly learning the Guild's key lesson—that notoriety was safer than anonymity—but it would take more than one killing to impress the selectors; they had seen the passage of numerous prodigies. A few, including the current Third Apprentice, fulfilled their promise. Most, like Giovanni Bernoulli, grandson of the *Stupor Mundi*, did not.

A fearsome season followed as Torbidda's peers raced to catch up, but still there was more to learn than fear; there was delight, discovery and inspiration as Cadets began to discover their particular affinities for individual subjects.

". . . Architecture begins and ends with Man. Literally. The Etruscans compared man's footprint with his height and replicated the ratio in their temples. See, the capita of this column, one sixth. There are no accidents. What made this idea important, anyone? You, Spinther."

Leto yawned. Aside from the practicalities of bridges and siege-engines, architecture bored him. "It was new?"

"Even bad ideas are young once," Varro said impatiently. "Anyone?"

"A pleasing ratio," Torbidda said, "applied consistently makes a pleasing building."

The Drawing Hall was a huge space embellished with a brighter touch than Bernoulli's. It had once been a scriptorium, and the dappled light that filled it hummed of noble dreams and honeyed memories. A line drawn here had clarity as nowhere else. Before the Guild overthrew the Curia, before her engineers became soldiers, their study was innocent; you could see it in the spiraling plant motifs tumbling joyfully from the columns that interlaced like bending trees. The scribes had willingly shared their desks with the Guild's draftsmen, and both celebrated the Word of God: the scribes paid homage by embellishing it, the engineers by uncovering the gears of his great work, Nature.

The light was dispersed further by several three-braccia-wide parabolic mirrors. The artifacts, dating from the Guild's early days, leaned against the walls like the discarded shields of some Homeric band. Inspired by fanciful legends of Archimedes, the Curia had attempted to create a weapon using giant mirrors to focus and target light. These optical experiments were discontinued after Bernoulli demonstrated water's vastly greater potential.

But the Maestro was gone, and the few draftsmen required now worked under the harsh mechanical lights of the factories. An age of synthesis required different men, Flaccus said; he called it Progress. Like the old scribes, these new draftsmen were copyists who looked upon original creation as vanity. If a war-machine was needed, no one sat down to draw it. Instead, one filed a request to the Collegio dei Consoli, who forwarded it to a clerk, who consulted the index and rooted out the appropriate design. But it was obvious that the age of discovery had never ended for Varro. He especially enjoyed the paradoxical aspects of architecture, the illusions employed to flood the hearts of men with joy or awe or dread. "See how a pillar will appear straight only if it bulges at the center. If it *was* straight it would not *appear* straight."

"*Entasis*," said Torbidda, struggling with the Greek.

"Don't be embarrassed," Varro laughed. "It's good to know words you can't pronounce; a true student must outstrip his teacher's pace! *Entasis*. What perversion that lovely word implies—that perfection displeases Man. And experience bears this out, does it not? A perfectly tuned instrument sounds *wrong*; there must be twelve uneven semitones in an octave to please our imperfect ears. Yes children, we prefer the lie."

While Varro carelessly imparted his eccentric doctrines, Flaccus trod a more cautious path. Any interpretation of Bernoulli's legacy necessarily favored one of the factions at war for the Guild. The Empiricists championed the *antediluvian* Bernoulli, the youthful iconoclast, the first among a generation of engineers of equal wisdom, with all his energy, his anticlericalism, his military triumphs. The Naturalists' idol was the *postdiluvian* philosopher passing from mere knowledge into wisdom, soberly weighing his famous deeds and finding them petty, electing instead to remake the world after he had washed it clean. He was David *and* Goliath, joyful giant-killer and tyrant executioner. All of the Collegio and two of the Apprentices were Empiricists, so naturally Flaccus concentrated on the younger Bernoulli, skating over those later years with no stronger admonition than "Regrettable."

Expedience was the real lesson, and the Guild took only fast learners.

Torbidda wasn't surprised to see how quickly his example was emulated; the lesson required no further explanation. As the boy who killed first (anatomical subjects didn't count), he enjoyed brief notoriety, but others soon joined the club and the more time passed, the more gruesome proofs of the principle, the more attentive every student became in Anatomy and Military History class. Cliques formed and sundered as the lambs scrambled to find security, but the truth was plain: there was no safety in numbers, nor any place to stand aloof from the race. If the Guild was a family, it was a family of wolves, all against all. To the average citizen, this brood of killers, merciless, inventive and quick, were devils, but even Hell has its reasons, and even in its depths there were all the games and laughter that make up childhood. After a fashion.

And there were friendships.

* * *

The storm was vicious enough for Ballistics to be canceled. Cadets used free time to work on their own projects—it was good practice; in their second year they would be expected to be autonomous. While Torbidda lost himself in Wave Theory, Leto's interests were more practical: he was designing a trebuchet that used the recoil of the throw to load its next. Torbidda had been sitting in a nook parsing a particularly thorny theorem when he had spotted the Fuscus twins surreptitiously edging toward the Drawing Room, where Leto was working alone.

Five minutes had passed. Instead of rushing to his friend's aid, Torbidda was walking the Halls, struggling to justify his inaction. Leto had breezed through first year so far, aside from occasional confrontations with the Fuscus siblings. His winning manner, his connections and his father's reputation had seen to that. The only thing that fazed him was Anatomy. He could dissect cadavers perfectly well, but whether from tender feeling or sheer queasiness, he hated to work wet. Torbidda had long worried that Leto could not leap this most important hurdle. He knew he was being logical— helping someone who wouldn't help themselves was pointless—but that didn't make him feel any better.

The Drawing Hall was empty. Dust motes hung expectantly in light shafts, waiting to baptize new creations with their soft veil. "Leto?"

He's not here. Just go.

Cursing his sentimental weakness, Torbidda walked through the empty rows of desks. Automatically he glanced at his own desk. Strange: his pair of compasses was gone. Something else too was *off*—what? He scanned the light-filled space, marveling, in passing, at the thick iron windowpanes, wrought into the semblance of ivy. That was it—The light. The uppermost window was open.

He prayed that the ivy was strong enough to bear him; though it groaned when he began climbing, it held fast.

Don't get involved.

* * *

The roof was a rounded vault of beaten metal held fast with studs and tar that gleamed in the rain as if new. It was cold, but that wasn't what worried him. One false step on the slippery roof would send him plummeting.

On the top of the roof Leto sat hugging his legs, thoroughly soaked, staring sullenly at the Molè. It was a temple designed to humble. Its interlocking forms and its awful height entangled the eye until one forgot all truths and whichever weak god one was pledged to. Its stone demanded terrified worship.

Beside Leto lay the body of the Fuscus girl. The rain had washed the wound clean, and now it looked as if Leto had inserted the points into her neck without pain or protest. His stained robes gave the lie to that. Torbidda looked down and saw the smashed body of the other twin on the rocks below.

"And Varro says you don't know one end of a pair of compasses from the other."

When Leto kept his eyes on the Molè, Torbidda said, "I'm sorry I didn't come to help earlier."

At last Leto turned. "Madonna! You don't have to explain! I know the rules—I've always known them. It's folly to protect a weakling in a world where weakness kills. You figured that out for yourself, but I've heard stories about this place since I was young. I told myself that I could do things differently."

"You did good."

"I did what I had to. It's not the same thing. It was easy, too. I did it the way you did Four: gave them a target, chose the day, chose the terrain. Easy."

"You're being melodramatic. How many did you kill before you became a Cadet?"

". . . none."

"What do you think they've been training us for? If you get a chance to cull the competition you take it. Being guilty for being rational is foolish. You're here; you have to fight, same as the rest of us. Of course you planned it. That's what we do."

Leto shakily got to his feet. "And there's no escape."

"Of course there is: get through it," said Torbidda with a grin. "By the way, I'll need my compasses back."

As Torbidda scuttled back to the window, Leto yanked the instrument out. It came free easier than he'd expected, and he lost his footing, fell and began sliding down the vault roof, crying, *"Ahhhahh!"*

There was nothing to hold but curved wetness.

At the last second, Leto managed to grab the railing. He looked up and found Torbidda standing over him. His smile poorly disguised his fear. "That stuff about getting rid of competition—there're *some* exceptions?"

Torbidda grasped his hand. "If you were competition, I'd have killed you long ago."

Chapter 8

Grand Selector Flaccus hammered the notice onto the refectory door and strode away officiously. Lambs no more, the first-years gathered around to read it. Torbidda's eyes dropped to the final condition: *Designs to be submitted anonymously*. Influence could get you into the Guild Halls, but the annual competition was to ensure that all Apprentice Candidates were engineers of genuine ability.

"How come the second-years aren't interested? They're the only ones eligible."

"They read it last year," said Leto. "The challenge is always the same."

That made sense; the commission that had brought Bernoulli to fame was the audacious one-span bridge that remained the city's main entry point. There was nowhere to hide on a bridge. Designing one was the purest test of an engineer.

Torbidda and Leto were still discussing it when Agrippina sat down beside them. She tilted her head to the notice. "They say you're an excellent draftsman."

"Not bad," said Torbidda. "What do you have in mind?"

"I'm a better anatomist than an architect." She smiled in embarrassment. "Something lofty and grand, I suppose."

"That won't get you noticed," said Leto. "That's what you want, right?"

"Who are you again?" Agrippina said archly. "Oh yes, the Spinther boy. A mediocre engineer trading on his family name. Mind your own business." In the Halls' hothouse rivalry, everyone kept abreast of their fellows' talent.

"Down, girl," said Torbidda. "Don't be offended by her country manners, Leto."

"Oh, I'm not. I know my limitations. As do you, Signorina, otherwise you wouldn't have asked Torbidda's help."

"*Torbidda's* help," she replied, then softened. "Oh all right, I'll bite. How do I get noticed?"

"Say you design a great bridge. What good is it? The last thing this city needs is another bridge."

"So?"

"So I grew up in a legion camp, and a better bridge is exactly what the *legions* need. Momentum's the key thing in any campaign, but if you think Etruria is bad, look at a map of Europa: rivers, rivers and more rivers. You know what's involved in building a pontoon bridge? Tying boats together, making it level so carts can cross, keeping it stable so the animals don't take fright—all that fuss, and Madonna help you if a storm hits. And then you have to dismantle the damn thing. Design a bridge with practical military application and they won't just make you Candidate, they'll throw you a Triumph."

After a pause, Agrippina smiled. "Not a bad idea, Spinther. I'll keep you close when I wear the red."

Leto gave a courtly bow. "I should be honored."

Torbidda said, "Well then, for starters it'll need to be quick to assemble and disassemble . . ."

* * *

For the next few days they met in Drawing Hall to discuss ideas; working closely for the first time with Agrippina, Torbidda at last understood what was meant by the old saw, "Sober as an Anatomist." She was practical as sinew and bone, and got quickly to the nub of engineering problems. Working beside first-years lacking his grasp of Wave Theory, Torbidda was used to stopping to explain himself. Collaborating with someone with an understanding equal to his was novel and fun. Both had initially thought of a portable, prefabricated truss bridge, but they rejected it because of the lifting equipment needed—and because both felt that something more ingenious was required.

Agrippina finished outlining her new idea and said, "Got anything better?"

Torbidda shyly showed his sketches. The idea had struck him during Ballistics: the arches of a bridge could be drawn by the arced path of a disk skimming across water, the supporting pillars forming wherever the disk hits the water. A stable surface, say tightly bound logs, could be rapidly unrolled and fastened to the arches before the army marched over.

Agrippina studied the sketches for a long time. She looked up at last, and said flatly, "A bridge that makes itself."

"Exactly!" Torbidda said excitedly, "and it can be swiftly dismantled when the last solider crosses. One could bridge any distance of water, simply by shooting the disk further and—"

"Torbidda, Torbidda, even if that were possible," she cut him off, "we don't have the ability to make something like this."

"We don't.have to *build* it. You're just trying to get noticed."

Agrippina made a face. "The Apprentices won't be impressed with a clever design if the theory's unsound."

"It's sound. Remember the first week I was here you sent me to Flaccus' office?"

"You sure can hold a grudge."

"You've seen that egg on his desk? It was designed by Bernoulli's grandson. They say he showed potential."

Agrippina's lip curled. "That burn-out—. Yes, I've seen the egg. It transmits a phased current that repels pseudonaiades—nothing special."

"No, but think about how it works: by inducing density in water. Take that a step further and you could create a temporary structure, like foundations. Why not? Everyday ice is just one type of water polymorph. There's no reason that we couldn't create a more stable crystal structure."

Agrippina shook her head. "Ice is weak, but that's precisely why it forms. Ice, rivers, bones; nature always finds the quickest way. At low temperatures, controlled conditions, your polymorph would hold for a few seconds, *maybe*, but in the real world, in running water with applied pressure, forget it. Military engineering isn't the rarefied theory of the Guild Halls. It's more like politics: the art of the possible."

"But—"

"And, as for bridge itself," she continued, "well, it's very elegant, but the ballistics idea is pure fantasy; no cannon's that accurate, that consistent. So you're left with a bridge that has the same limitation as all 'self-supporting' structures—it can't support itself until it's complete. A marching army doesn't have time to build elaborate formwork. Aside from practicalities, considerations of speed rule it out."

Torbidda disagreed, but he could tell Agrippina was getting frustrated so he turned back to her plan of a parabolic swing-bridge. It had two fulcrums—that was what made it original; once it swung to the other side of a river and the army had crossed, it could be detached from its first base and swung across, disassembled and packed up again. It required a rope-and-pulley system and it had a limited span, but it would obviously work and it could be quickly transported.

"Well," Torbidda sighed, "it's practical."

Those with families to visit took advantage of the brief end-of-year break. Torbidda spent the time in the Drawing Hall. Agrippina had remained intent on her swing-bridge and he had drawn it up handsomely, but his original idea kept going around in his head. It was foolish to devote more time to it, but Agrippina's lack of imagination irked and he wanted to prove her wrong. An idea with merit had merit; it was an intellectual problem, nothing more. Her dismissal of the ballistics aspect stemmed from poor understanding; much error could be eliminated with more precise cannons.

But her criticism of the foundations was sound. He decided they would work better if they grew up instead of down: the moment that the disk connected with the water surface, it would send a powerful signal down to the bedrock, which would form a seed crystal of super-cooled ice, which would prompt a phase-transition to a crystal lattice in the water around it. The problem was to prevent that nucleation from dissipating randomly. Agrippina's words came back to him: *Nature always finds the quickest way.* The water through which the initial signal-burst traveled would be affected by its passage, if only temporarily, so all that was required was to make this dissipate slowly. That done, the column of super-cooled water above the seed would be the path of least resistance. The whole process would happen quickly, making rows of ice-trees appear in the wake of the disk skipping over the water.

He got up to stretch his legs and looked at the strange warped reflections in the great mirrors. The evening sun made the wrought-iron leaves of the windows look autumnal and fragile. He thought of the year, the struggles, violence and cruelty and the lessons learned, and he admitted to himself something that he could no longer deny: his mother had not betrayed him. *He* had betrayed *himself*—and that betrayal had begun before he could walk, from the time his hands could manipulate tools: fixing broken things, improving and making queer machines, the babble of numbers that grew louder every year; the comical patterns in the footsteps of a lame neighbor, the guilty rhythm of the midnight doorknocker, the somber ratio of colored leaves falling among the dead ones. He was as far beyond the other Cadets as they were beyond other children. Problems that stumped them, he solved effortlessly; his destruction of Four had merely been the first example.

"Knew I'd find you here."

"Spinther! What news?"

They embraced in the warm reflection of the mirrors. After Leto filled him in on city gossip, the Bocca della Verità's latest slanders, and developments on the Europan front, they discussed their electives. Torbidda had decided on Architecture, believing the mother of all arts would bring him closest to Bernoulli. Leto chose Military Applications for the same reason. The dark star they revolved around had mastered all arts.

They looked at their reflections, which curved around the edges as if they repelled each other, seeing the distance traveled in a year. Torbidda was taller now, and though Leto's uniform was newer they might have been doubles.

Leto ran his finger around the mirror's rim, producing an ethereal wavering note. "Perfect."

Torbidda looked closer, and his reflection became distended, a vision of himself as a man. "No, there's a flaw in it—see? There. Likely the alloy cooled unevenly. It's subtle, but it distorts the light. It wouldn't have been apparent before it was polished."

"I still think it's beautiful."

Torbidda silently smiled. Leto could never be a Candidate. The mirror was a weapon; its function was not to be beautiful, its function was to kill.

"Come on, or we'll be late for the shearing."

When he saw the new first-years assembled, naked and shivering, Torbidda could hardly believe that he had once been such a lamb. It was more than another life; it was another person. In truth, *he* had not survived; the excess had been ground and cut away, leaving a brute, uncuttable stone. The coming year must polish it.

Chapter 9

The backstreet surgeons who flourished during the reign of the Curia disappeared under the engineers. What forced them out of the market was neither prosecution nor social opprobrium, but competition from the State. Submitting to the engineers' deft knifes was safer and, initially at least, more lucrative. The financial incentive was discontinued in 1359 to cut the waiting-lists: too many were giving birth before their embryos could be harvested.

from The Bernoullian Reforms *by Count Titus Tremellius Pomptinus*

"It's three months old. Most malformations have occurred at this point. *Cazzo*, my subject's all right. Anyone? Yes, Sixteen? Oh indeed, that spine is an absolute mess! Everyone be sure to have a look at Sixteen's before you finish; we learn from Nature's mistakes no less than from our own. Now, as you can smell, it's started to urinate into the amniotic fluid . . ."

Second-years had no monitor, so Torbidda had to wait till Anatomy to see Agrippina; Varro said he still required her help—but, as Leto observed, Varro always surrounded himself with the brighter students. It made Torbidda sad to think she'd soon be gone. Most third-years were sent to the front.

"Well, your posting must agree with you. You're looking happy."

"Should do!" said Agrippina, grinning, and proffered the thin yellow ribbon tied to her left arm.

"Is that what I think it is?" said Leto.

"I'm a Candidate!" she whooped.

"Congratulations!" they shouted simultaneously.

"Cadets!" Varro shouted over the din. "Pay attention. This *will* be on the test. Notice that the eyes have now moved laterally to the anterior and the eyelids are shut. They won't open until the sixth month, but we don't have to wait. Work carefully, keep the eye intact. You can see the pigment has already colored the retina. Ah, this one has nice brown eyes. Tear ducts have already formed, and—look! They're functioning!"

Torbidda expected Agrippina to thank him, but instead she turned to Leto. "Spinther, I'm about to find out what competition really means. You always know who's out, who's in. What would you counsel?"

Leto checked to see that Varro was busy. He advised Agrippina as he had once advised Torbidda: "For starters, distance yourself from him." He looked at the selector. For most Cadets, Guild politics was wasted mental effort, but those in line for Apprenticeship had to take an interest in the murky topic. The summit of any hierarchy attracts awe and envy in equal measure from those below and here was no different: first-years studied second-years; second-years studied third-years, and all studied the Candidates. Even though the Candidates were the best, the majority would rise no further—only the death of one of the three Apprentices would create an opening. As consolation, every Candidate became a member of the Collegio dei Consoli; they were all eligible for election to its governing board. Relations between the Collegio and the Apprentices were fractious, with envy on one side, contempt on the other.

Leto told them both that the Collegio's advisory role had expanded under Filippo Argenti. "His appointment as First Apprentice is telling of the Collegio's growing influence. Argenti's generation of engineers is the first trained in the Guild Halls out of the Curia's shadow. He's got no reverence for the myths of Forty-Seven. The Girolamo Bernoulli he knew was an old man past his prime who was reverting to medieval thinking."

"The dogs on the street know that," Agrippina said. "How does he stand with the army?"

"Well, that's the question, isn't it?" Leto was less neutral when it came to the army, his criticism less guarded. "In comparison to Bernoulli's lightning campaigns, Argenti's wars are pedestrian. He inherited the best army Etruria has ever seen—and how does he use it? The legions are scattered in a great continental-wide pushing match, with Concordian machine grinding on barbarian brawn. The tribes make obeisance, then as soon as the pressure lifts, rebel again. It makes us look weak."

"He can't break the deadlock?" asked Torbidda.

"He can't concentrate on it. The repeated need for expensive rearguard actions in Etruria drains all momentum from the Europan campaign. This feckless policy more than anything else is behind the wistful revival of Naturalism led by the Second Apprentice."

"Does Argenti see Bonnacio as a threat?" Agrippina asked.

"Bonnacio's an apolitical dreamer, content to haunt the Molè's domes, tend the lantern flame and watch the stars while Argenti and his clique direct policy. He's probably more concerned about Pulcher."

"I heard the Third Apprentice said Argenti was no fitter to wear black than he is to wear the red."

"That remark was widely disseminated—younger sons don't enjoy seeing their elders fritter away their fortune. By leaning so heavily on the Collegio—Consul Corvis and that lot—Argenti's making the red pale. If Argenti's watching anyone, it should be Pulcher."

* * *

The first-year whose turn it was to read valiantly struggled to make himself heard until he finally gave up. Leto's prediction had been borne out sooner than expected: Filippo Argenti was dead and the Candidates' table was empty. Both sides of the refectory were alive with gossip about how Pulcher had actually done the deed. Leto, of course, was intimate with the various versions, but Torbidda wasn't interested in gossip. "That's that," he said glumly.

"What do you mean?"

"Think about it!" he snapped. "Argenti was getting on, but Bonnacio is in his early twenties, Pulcher's still a teenager and the next Third Apprentice will be a third-year. That means we'll never—"

"—wear the red?" Leto finished and laughed. "Madonna, I never thought I had a chance. Did you?"

Torbidda was looking balefully at the high table where the Candidates usually sat.

Leto followed his glance, "Well, it's not all bad. Agrippina's got as good a chance as any Candidate. We could have friends in high places next year."

Chapter 10

ON THE ORIGINS OF CONCORDIAN GOTHIC

To avoid taxing the gentle Reader's patience, the Author will follow convention in referring to Concord's cathedral as St. Eco's[1]
until 1347, and thereafter as the Molè Bernoulliana. Whatever
name the cathedral goes by, its foundations are inseparable
from the Reformation's.

Some ambitious young historians have argued that we will not
find those foundations in Concord, nor even Etruria; they tell us
we must venture to that water-scarred land of dark savage for-
ests: Europa. We are accustomed to thinking of the Reformation
as uniquely Concordian, but they suggest that many of the larger

---

1. Saint Eco, a follower of Saint Francis, traveled from Gubbio to Concord to
    minister to those unlucky Crusaders who returned from Oltremare with the
    venereal affliction known as *Roland's Horn*. The miracles ascribed to Eco are
    too numerous and repetitious to relate, but his popularity was such that the
    Curia named their cherished cathedral for him.

Europan cities also had the necessary conditions at the turn of the century.

This is not the place to dissect that argument;[2] while it may be true that every city important enough to have a cathedral[3] had a similarly unstable dynamic of tight-knit engineering firms working for unimaginative clerics, only Concord had Girolamo Bernoulli.

2. The Author demolishes this jejune theory in Volume II, showing how the Curia's inertia could not have been overcome without a force as dynamic as Bernoulli.

3. Today the giant skeletons of these cathedrals litter the continent. To many engineers the real tragedy of the Europan wars is they will never be rebuilt; walls expected to be bombarded cannot soar.

Chapter 11

The winds were brutal and the steps tall. Slime riverlets streaked them treacherous. It was a strain to breathe. This was higher than he had ever been on Monte Nero, even higher than the Drawing Hall roof, which caught the white sunlight below him—yet still the summit was an impossible distance. The sky was cold and empty and scarred by a web of crisscrossed wire that intersected at the Selectors' Tower as though tethering it to the isolated rocky peak. Torbidda knew the reason he'd been summoned. He'd broken the rules. He'd been discovered. Expulsion would surely follow.

The summit was even clearer in the office, but Torbidda tried to ignore it and listen to Flaccus. For want of anything else to focus on, he stared at the egg-shaped device on the desk and heard words spilling from his mouth: "Grand Selector, I made a mistake, but you can just—"

"You're being moved up a year," Flaccus interrupted, then added angrily, "Don't look at me, it's not my idea. That's not all." He held up the ribbon as if it were a loathsome yellow worm. "Our new First Apprentice, in his wisdom, found your design, speculative and impractical as it was, remarkable—so remarkable that as of now"—he flung the ribbon at Torbidda—"you're a Candidate."

"But—but I'm not ready."

"I told him that. I told him that you should be punished for breaking the rules, too. He disagreed—*he* thinks you're *gifted.*" Flaccus picked up the egg and regarded it philosophically. "I think he's mistaken. The only other Cadet to be made Candidate this young was Bernoulli's grandson, and *that* was a disaster . . ."

On he went, but Torbidda had stopped listening. He was thinking about the little yellow ribbon that meant he and Agrippina were competitors now.

". . .course, *Varro* put in a word for you, and that carries a lot of weight with the First Apprentice, starry-eyed mystic that he is. If you ask me, *that's* why he nominated you. Naturalists know their own."

Flaccus waited for him to deny the charge or confirm it, and Torbidda realized with surprise that Flaccus was as uncertain as the most guileless inductee. As above, so below. "Grand Selector, I do want to be an Apprentice someday, but—"

"Don't get ahead of yourself. Being a Candidate doesn't mean you'll ever make Apprentice."

"I mean, there are more worthy Candidates."

"Certainly: Cadet Seventy-Nine, for example." Flaccus laughed. That was Agrippina's number. "Just do as you're told. They can make you a Candidate, but they can't make you what you're not."

Torbidda descended from the Selectors' Tower feeling less apprehensive than he expected. He was committed now, and he must accept the price commitment demanded. The only alternative was to pursue advancement in the legions, where it would not always be Concordians under his knife. But inevitably the day would come when he'd be up against Leto. Competition was universal, unavoidable. And merely thinking of retreat—that was impossible. The summit was calling. He must answer.

He took a bowl from the stack, handed it over and watched it being filled with morbid fascination. He had become used to the colorless gruel, but he had never learned to like it.

A sudden push knocked him into the stack. The bowls tumbled and smashed.

"Agrippina—" he began.

"Keep away from me, you sneaky little bastard!"

The lectern reader paused. Torbidda felt every eye on him, just like the first days again, and he turned to stare them down. By the time he looked back, she was gone. He sat alone thinking of the fight ahead of him, playing out scenarios.

"So it's true." It was Leto, looking at the ribbon on Torbidda's arm. "Can I sit?"

"You don't need to ask. Agrippina—"

"I know. Be glad she didn't kill you."

"Where is she, Leto?"

"She doesn't want to see you again."

"Where?"

"I should have guessed," Torbidda said when Leto finally led him to the Drawing Hall. He followed him up the ivy frame and out of the window. Agrippina was sitting there beside the spire, hugging her legs. She'd been crying. Her back was to the Molè and she was looking out into the Wastes as if waiting for a rider to come to her rescue.

"What do *you* want?"

"Give him a chance to explain," Leto said.

"Agrippina, I didn't ask for this."

"Do you think I'm a *child*? You submitted your design."

"I'm an *engineer*. I thought I had the better answer."

"You're just a disinterested natural philosopher, is that it?"

"So I'm ambitious! I want to be Apprentice one day, yes, of *course* I do—but Third when you're Second, Second when you're First. I don't want to compete with you. I *won't*."

She started to reply, then turned back to the Wastes. Torbidda turned to see what she was looking at. He saw only clouds of loose dust burling over the barren soil. When she spoke again all anger was gone. "I wanted to be the first female Apprentice. I thought—it's stupid—I wanted to prove to my father I was worth a damn."

Torbidda realized she was looking beyond the barrenness to a faraway farmstead that probably didn't exist anymore.

After a moment, Leto said, "Didn't he sell you?"

Agrippina laughed, and she wiped her face. "I wanted to prove it to myself, then."

"You will," said Torbidda. "Listen, even if I could, I wouldn't take the Apprenticeship from you. I'm young enough to wait. The other Apprentices don't have to die of natural causes. We'll train together, so no other Candidate has a chance against you."

"What about me?" said Leto with mock outrage. "When you're Third and she's Second, where will I be?"

"In Europa, winning Triumphs."

"Getting scalped by some gruesome Frank, you mean. If one of you does make it, I expect a soft posting: some backwater where nothing happens anymore, like Rasenna." He did a Flaccus-like growl: "Cadets, are we clear?"

Torbidda and Agrippina saluted. "Yes, Sir!"

Below them sunlight made New City shine like polished ivory. It even penetrated the smoke plumes drifting lazily from the gloom of Old Town. While the Molè's shadow fell on the far side of Concord, a child could believe that Fortune dealt fair.

Chapter 12

Flaccus marched proudly along the top of the aqueduct, one of the many that fed the canals. The day was windy and getting dark, but hardly enough to merit the flickering torch he carried. The twelve children followed the Grand Selector like a trail of mourners, their robes and yellow ribbons fluttering. The aqueduct was the oldest structure above ground in Concord—only the sewers rivaled its antiquity—but Torbidda knew enough about Etruscan architecture to trust its stability.

He had less faith in his new classmates. He felt conspicuously vulnerable beside the third-years, a songbird in an eagle's aerie. A competitive tension had already settled over the small group, but for him they reserved special hostility. They had put in their time, won their position by merit; he heard them arguing about what species of cheat he was, whether it was patronage or skulduggery that had enabled him to join their table.

Only Agrippina spoke directly to him. "You don't like heights?"

"Heights I don't mind. It's the water. It doesn't care for me."

Agrippina took this as a joke. "I'm the same with dogs, got bit once. You fell in?"

"Not technically. My mother, before she had me, she got . . . sick."

"How so?"

"Her mind was ill. She claimed that a pseudonaiad visited her to warn her that the child she carried was 'dry.' The best thing, it advised, was to kill herself. She jumped into the canal. They pulled her out half-drowned and raving. I protected her from my father, and when I was older from herself, but no matter what I did she said I was an abomination. She got rid of me as soon as she could."

Flaccus had stopped by a set of narrow steps that wound around one of the aqueduct's massive supporting pillars. "If you're quite finished, Sixty?" He looked around the class and brandished his torch in an apelike manner. "Fire is a club. Water is a scalpel. Engineers can increase that power by funneling it into narrow canals, by letting it fall from heights. Our task is to harness that pressure by older means. Some of you are too skeptical, some insufficiently so. Water Style is about force, precision and—yes, belief. As we descend we will probe the very edges of Natural Philosophy. Keep your wits about you."

The twelve followed Flaccus down the steps. Torbidda was last, trailing slowly, looking at the intersecting net of aqueducts.

"What is it?" Agrippina said.

"All that water. Why did Concord never became a sea power?"

"Is it all that surprising? To Bernoulli, water was something to be controlled. To sail is to put oneself in the sea's hands. Besides a fleet's not much use without a harbor."

"We've turned rivers on our enemies. Why not send one to join the sea? We're slaves to geography until we do."

"I'll be sure to remedy that when I wear yellow. Let's get through today before conquering the world, shall we?"

They raced each other until they caught up with the rest. Halfway down, the stairs stopped winding around the pillar and plunged into it through an arch. The steep descent continued within and the darkness became so total that Flaccus' torch became the single point of light. They emerged into a chamber somewhere far below the pillar's base and continued through several more until they came to one much larger.

"Welcome to History's graveyard," said Flaccus.

"He's enjoying this a bit too much," Agrippina whispered to Torbidda.

As Flaccus lit the cressets they saw it was a deep, high-ceilinged place, too damp to be dusty. Tall pillars divided the space and between them stood spectral totems, statues shrouded in pale, half-rotted sheets.

Flaccus stopped at one and waited for the class to assemble around him. "This was one of the Guild's first factories, long before Forty-Seven, back when Natural Philosophers were the Curia's loyal servants, when Concord's finest minds were enslaved by idiots. There is no better place to learn humility." And saying that, he pulled away the sheet.

The statue depicted Saint Barabbas, identifiable by his conventional symbol of a dagger half-concealed in his cloak. "These statues were meant to 'decorate' the Molè, like lice infesting some noble beast's skin. Those who carved them gladly tumbled them during the Reformation—heady times. This cemetery of saints are the ones who got away."

Flaccus breathed out and suddenly struck the sculpture's torso with a flat palm. The impact echoed around the vaulted roof and when it dissipated, there was a growing sound of fracture. The sculpture cracked into thirds and the head, torso and fist-gripping-dagger smashed as they hit the floor separately.

"A rock's destiny is the same as ours: to be dust. I merely helped it achieve that potential."

The impression the demonstration had made on the Candidates swiftly dispelled; the Grand Selector was too obviously pleased with himself.

"How?" said Agrippina.

"It's hard to explain." He pursed his lips. "See, Time has a direction: after night comes morning. The Etruscans, clever buggers they were, created a martial art that harnessed that flow. It's what made them so strong."

"Yet their empire fell," said Torbidda, looking at the broken statue.

There was a flicker of displeasure before Flaccus composed himself and returned to his Sage-like pose. "Well, night follows morning, doesn't it? When the darkness fell, the Curia managed to hold onto a mangled version of Water Style, but it was as degraded as their Hebrew. Eventually it too was forgotten. Then, from the ashes, two powers rose up. Our war with the Rasenneisi ebbed and flowed for a generation, until *he* was born."

"Bernoulli," said one of the Candidates reverently.

Agrippina rolled her eyes.

"Bernoulli," repeated Flaccus in a stage-whisper. "He rescued Concord from darkness and Water Style from the mystics."

"How?" Agrippina asked again.

Flaccus cleared his throat. "By returning to first principles, I suppose. He interrogated the element itself until it confessed its secrets."

Torbidda looked around uneasily, but none of them had been in Varro's class the day of the incident. Flaccus led them deeper into the chamber and stopped in a space surrounded by five water-worn columns. In the center was a puddle fed by a steady barrage of drips from the ceiling and leaks pouring down the columns. He turned before their footsteps had finished echoing.

"Anyone know where we are now?"

Torbidda said, "Under the main canal?"

"That's right," Flaccus said, again slightly annoyed. "You can't hear it, but it's there, like a great wind." He pointed to the roof. "When you've learned more you'll *feel* it in your bones. Now, do as I do. Do *not* disturb the water."

He entered the circle and where he stepped, ripples did not spread out. "If you fight against it, your energy dissipates in thousand directions. Go with it—"

He slammed his foot down suddenly and the puddle *exploded* into a thousand floating drops. A Candidate with a toe in the puddle went flying back into a pillar; the rest were buffeted by a momentary gale-force wind. Just as suddenly, the drops rained down around Flaccus.

Do as I do.

A simple, effective method. The only drawback to the repetitious exercises that ate through the morning was that the Candidates never got to explore alternatives, or make mistakes. Flaccus corrected faults so intolerantly that it became difficult to do the most elementary things. But despite their teacher's limitations, these children knew how to learn. By the first day's end, the canal's water was barely audible; within a week, it roared.

Each day they practiced, each session extending as their stamina improved. The enervated Candidates at the high table in the refectory were a diverting spectacle for first- and second-years. The regular absence of two of the Candidates was remarked upon.

They worked until Agrippina gave in to exhaustion, then Torbidda continued alone. He had most to learn, so he practiced longest, rising early, working till late. Agrippina confessed that she could hardly relate to old friends anymore, and Torbidda sympathized. He saw Leto rarely, and when they met it was as if years had passed in the interval. Leto was excelling in Military Applications, but Torbidda could muster little enthusiasm for his tales of siege and stratagem.

The more he practiced, the louder the current became. It drowned out the din of ordinary life. A shadow had slipped between his eyes and the world; it made everything that had once seemed important fade to gray. Torbidda knew that Candidacy entailed sacrifice, and he had resigned himself to seeing his other studies suffer, but instead he excelled as never before. Impossible problems were effortlessly solved, new connections made, the paradoxes of Bernoullian Wave Theory no longer benumbed him. He *understood* with new depth. How was unclear, and Flaccus had no answers: to him, Water Style was sets and drills; he certainly didn't believe they were harnessing the power behind the Wave. He blithely exposed the Candidates to dangers he could not see, and it changed them in ways that they didn't understand. The loud fell silent, the subtle became frankly violent.

One morning Agrippina and Torbidda discovered they had had the same dream, of sinking into cold water and darkness. They realized they could easily lose themselves, and swore to pull each other back if the other was going too deep.

For lack of such a partner, the other Candidates suffered. As weeks turned to months, casualties mounted: two were murdered, two died in a suicide pact and two more were expelled (one had become incapacitated, the other insane).

"They broke because they were weak," was Flaccus' pat, unvarying explanation. Although he didn't know what, he knew that there was *something* in the depths. His solution was to avoid it. "You can't draw on what's down there. Once It feels your presence, it'll draw you in and consume you. So learn to float and concentrate on controlling the water's flow. Ignore the rest." Constant pressure was his answer: "If you wish to master any wild animal, you break it."

"You don't think it's possible that Water has more than animal instinct?" Torbidda asked. "That it has some sort of higher intelligence?"

"No. Intelligence is revealed by election, discrimination. Water is a slave to its nature."

"Men are no less bound by causality"—Torbidda pursued his question—"and perhaps more so. We can't choose to make effects precede cause, but the pseudonaiades exist in a state where Time is liquid—"

"Bah! The anthropomorphic theory didn't sound any less preposterous when it came drooling from Bernoulli on his deathbed. If the pseudonaiades could act on the past, they wouldn't still be our prisoner. And if they could see the future, they wouldn't have let us capture them."

"Not necessarily," said Torbidda. "They could be *obliged* to act a certain way, though aware it will be disastrous."

"Obliged by what?"

"I don't know," Torbidda admitted, "some force stronger than Time's arrow—"

"Stop embarrassing yourself. I told the Apprentices you had a child's understanding of Wave Theory. *Nothing's* stronger!"

The last Candidates were too exhausted to sneer at Torbidda, but only Agrippina took his side. "Then perhaps they know their bondage has a grander purpose."

Flaccus rounded on her. "'Purpose'? I thought better of you. Soon you'll be talking about God's plan for us." Flaccus was extra-hard on Agrippina; he saw her solidarity with Torbidda as rank insubordination. He wanted the Candidates at each other's necks, not cozying up together. "Water Style's not the secret of the ages. It's a way to fight. It won't get you to Heaven but it *might* keep you alive through Conclave."

Chapter 13

Footsteps among the columns. "Agrippina?"

Flaccus stepped out from behind a statue. "Candidates don't help other Candidates."

Torbidda didn't bother to respond. He went back to his steps. The ripple only occurred when he willed it. Flaccus watched for a while, waiting for some slip. He said at last, "I didn't teach you that combination."

"I worked it out with Agrippina. It's obvious really," Torbidda said coldly.

Flaccus stepped into the puddle, upsetting its placid surface. "Yet it took the wonder child to discover it. I see brats like you every year. You learn a little and hear stories of Bernoulli and start to think that you're like him. You're nothing like him."

Torbidda continued his set. "If you think you can goad me—"

Flaccus suddenly brought a knee into his stomach and stood aside so Torbidda tumbled face-first into the water. There was a moment of darkness before his eyes opened. Half his face was submerged. He felt Flaccus' foot between his shoulders, keeping him down. "You're scheming to let Cadet Seventy-Nine win, aren't you? The moment I saw you I knew you for a liar."

"That's what you taught us!" Torbidda shouted, gagging as water entered his mouth.

"Oh no, no one had to teach you. You're a natural. I needn't have worried—you'll fight her because you want the yellow more than anyone." He leaned down and pressed Torbidda's face until his nose and mouth went under.

Torbidda tried to lift himself up, but it was impossible under Flaccus' much greater weight. He was drowning. He twisted his lower half and spread his legs wide and brought them together against Flaccus' supporting leg. The Grand Selector fell, and Torbidda rolled over, gasping for air.

Flaccus picked himself up triumphantly. "See?" He walked away laughing, "When the moment comes, you'll fight. There's a wolf in you and I can't wait to see its teeth."

The embarrassed streak of yellow was the nearest thing to color in an otherwise gray sky. They sat on the roof and looked down the barren earth laid out hopeless as a corpse. Winter had withdrawn its stranglehold and the sun resumed its faithful passage, but it was a pointless trudge, with no warmth to wake the slumbering roots.

Talk was exhausted.

No one else understood the transformation they were undergoing but their rivals. They huddled together like lotus-eaters, yearning for the next dose and terrified of it. Their senses had attained a new pitch of sensitivity, resulting not in clarity but cacophony. Everything was too loud, too sharp, too bright, too cold. The canal below them pulsed with energy. The Molè behind them was a malevolent hunger, and they were always aware of it, just as magnetized needles always know the poles. It was a relief to watch the pathetic sun and know they were not the only ones struggling.

Before the cold broke their feeble bones, Agrippina suggested they walk the city walls. She was on edge. Earlier that evening, Torbidda had discovered her unconscious in the crypts. "I went deep," was all she said when she awoke. The sentinels saluted as they passed. Strange feeling, to be recognized—in the Guild Halls everyone was a number, anonymous, divisible, easily substituted.

She took him to the southern wall and pointed to the Wastes. The flat horizon shifted as gray winds passed over. The emptiness was perfect, but for a few sun-blackened husks that had once been trees and a long straight road covered in parts by the creeping dust.

"Beyond that," she said, "a few leagues before the Rasenneisi contato begins, near Montaperti, that's where my father's farm is. It gets green eventually—well, greener, I should say. Nothing prospers. The Molè leached all the good out of the land," she added without looking over her shoulder, "like a big greedy tree spreading death with its shadow. The higher the Molè rose, the worse the land got, my father used to say. I told him it was a consequence of diverting the rivers, and that when the trees died, erosion made the land barren." She turned to him with a vehemence he'd never seen before. "I was *wrong*, Torbidda! There's *something* else, deep in the roots of the city, and it's hungry. You've sensed it too, haven't you?"

Torbidda demurred, and sought to change the subject. Half a mile out, a dust-trail rose from a procession, slowly circling the city, crossed the road to the city as if wasn't there, making their own path across the dry thorns and sharp stones.

"Who are they?"

"Fraticelli," said Agrippina with distaste.

Torbidda had seen mendicants before; some wandered into the city every few years. Many were haruspices of sorts. Lacking schooling, they invented rituals and preached eccentric sermons to the Small People who were seeking entertainment more than enlightenment. The Guild ignored new preachers until they began to preach sedition—all of them did eventually—and then they hanged them.

"My father called the Fraticelli chickens coming home to roost. Lots of lost souls end up in the Wastes, people ruined by our legions or condottieri, but the refugees from Gubbio are unique. They think they *deserved* punishment. They believe that the Wave that made them homeless was God's opening salvo in a new war on Man. They wander Etruria like Noahs warning of deluge, recruiting as they go. I've seen whole farms emptied in a day, families throwing away everything to join the pilgrimage."

"Where are they going?"

"Jerusalem—at least, that's what the Fraticelli tell them. But they all end up here, circling. It's the Molè that does it: it draws and repels them at once."

"One desert's as good as another, I suppose."

"No. This is the worst." She turned back to the city. Tears rolled down her face as she whispered, "Torbidda, what will become of us?"

"We stick to the plan." He spoke with an assurance he didn't feel. "You'll win the Conclave and become Third, ally with the new Second, kill the First and both move up a step. Then you can make the argument that I'm still eligible since I moved up a year. Who's going to argue with the Second Apprentice?"

"Won't the orange grow pale in turn? And when I'm First and you're Second, and some other young villain is Third, what then? Aren't we just putting off the inevitable? The day one of us must—"

Torbidda grabbed her by the shoulder and spun her around to look at him. "That day will *never* come! We're powerless now, but when we're Apprentices, we can change the world."

She smiled sadly. "You're right. We can change it. Anything's possible."

"Come on," he said. He wondered if she really believed it. "I want to show you something."

They walked down through the keep to the city gates, then took an old stairway to the Old Town. Agrippina had never been before, and he wanted to show her the boarded-up corner house he'd grown up in.

They paused in Piazzetta Bocca della Verità to read the latest Truth. The small landing halfway between worlds was named after its antique fountain. Water had never flowed from the leering Mouth of Truth; instead, a stream of innuendo, gossip and satire poured from the satyr's lolling tongue. Those too lazy for conspiracy could exercise their spleen with epigrams and rhyming couplets. It didn't matter whether one's complaint was trivial or weighty or if the target was Guild bureaucracy, imperial wars or a particularly inept general; what did matter was the elegance of the attack. Especially good Truths would be swiftly replicated around the city. Like the Curia before them, the Collegio took a tolerant attitude: let the Small People vent—it was harmless and a useful gauge of the public mood.

As Torbidda read, he fancied the satyr was laughing at him:

Who killed the First? I have a notion:
It was someone seeking fast promotion.
An impatient and ambitious fellow,
You'll find him wearing orange or yellow,
But when he seeks to wear the red,
Who wears the red must needs be dead.

Torbidda was surprised that the circumstances of Argenti's murder were known outside the Guild Halls. Cadets always imagined themselves privy to great mysteries, but the poem made it clear their imagined secrets were common knowledge, even as it satirized their pious protestations of fidelity to each other.

Agrippina seemed to share his thoughts. "Let's get drunk."

Theology students were a thing of the past and Cadets were generally too conservative to drink, but old Concord's taverns were still busy. The nobility had nothing else to do. Cadets were not supposed to leave the Guild Halls, but Torbidda and Agrippina felt no fear. Though the streets were unsafe for ordinary Old Towners this late, engineers roamed where they pleased, no matter what the hour—everyone understood the dire consequences of offending engineers. They found a suitably derelict tavern in the Depths and an hour later were toasting each other loudly. The Rule and Compass, formerly

The Cardinal's Hat, was one of the older drinking holes in the so-called officers' quarter. Though its population possessed that blood formerly considered noble, this part of old Concord was as filthy as any other slum in the Depths. What would be the point of improvements when the residents were just passing through, or so they insisted as decade followed decade.

Torbidda tilted his mug at the corner. "Damn nerve. That soldier's been staring at us all night."

Agrippina tossed her head back. "Let him stare." She toasted the man. "Salute, Signore!"

Clearly inebriated, and clearly surprised to be noticed, the man lurched to his feet and stumbled toward them. The barman, following every unsteady step, mumbled warningly, "Geta . . ."

But the soldier ignored him and stopped in front of the Cadets. "Why don't you lovebirds keep it down?" he growled.

As Torbidda stood, he took his hood down to show his number. "How dare you—?" he started, but Agrippina pulled him back down.

"Forget it," she said. "He's just a drunken fool."

The drunk spun around. "I *beg* your damn pardon, Signorina, but I'm a hero of a dozen sieges! While you damn engineers sat around and plotted, I'm the one who scaled the damn walls. I opened the damn gates. And who gets the bloody credit? Damn engineers, that's who. But you baldies look like Cadets to me." He turned to look at the rest of the tavern's clientele. "Baby lice," he announced, "know how get 'em? Pinch the head, that's how—" and he reached for Agrippina.

She allowed him to get close, which gave her time to grab the bottle. A streak of green smashed over his head and wet emeralds rained down. She kicked forcefully into the soldier's knee and he fell forward and smashed his chin against the table.

She pushed his unconscious body off the table into the fragments of the broken bottle.

The barman insisted that their drinks were free, and offered to call a night guard. "I needs my license," he said, his voice low.

Agrippina just wanted to leave. "No harm done."

"You *do* have some Rasenneisi in you," said Torbidda, smiling to hide his disquiet. It was not the drunk noble—nothing strange there—but the speed with which Agrippina had put him down. Perhaps it *was* an accident that she had gone so deep this morning, but he was now certain that she *had* been holding back in practice—just as he was.

"*Cin cin*," he said, and clinked her glass.

She smiled back.

In their hearts, each knew the competition was real.

Chapter 14

ON THE ORIGINS OF CONCORDIAN GOTHIC

Even before the first stone of St. Eco's was laid, the Cathedral's singular aspect atop Monte Nero made it unique. Most of Etruria's great cathedrals were built in urban settings, which placed restrictions on construction. Free of these considerations, the Opera del Duomo of St. Eco's decided to forgo scaffolding in lieu of the large ramps used by the Ancients. This is just one of the ways that the Curia's plans reflect the rebirth of interest in the Etruscans. They were inspired by newly translated texts that revealed that the sun-bleached temples still standing in the remote pastures of our contato[4] had once been full of color. Consequently, it was decided that St. Eco's façade should blend colored marble with playful ornament.

---

4.   In the cities, their marble had been long cannibalized.

Given the contemporary pace of discovery and innovation, St. Eco's architects assumed that the ambitious dome they sketched would be possible by the time the walls to support it were built.[5] The Curia intended St. Eco to proclaim Concordian superiority to all Etruria. They were to be disappointed. As successive capomaestri grew to manhood and sank to senility, the cathedral's walls grew ever more elaborate, but not a braccia taller. St. Eco, the domeless cathedral, became instead a byword for Concordian hubris.

5. Since the fall of the Etruscan Empire, the dome had presented an insurmountable logistical challenge.

Chapter 15

Her body leaned back in elegant surprise; the smooth undulations that composed Her face invited reverence. He leaned forward with parted lips.

"She's the real enemy, you know."

Torbidda dropped the veil quickly and looked around. No one. Just the frozen ethereal silhouettes of shrouded statues. He cursed his stupidity in isolating himself with no escape route and prepared for ambush.

"You'll catch your death standing in a puddle all day," said Varro, emerging from behind a column. "I'd thought you'd have enough of it after that accident with the Confession Box."

Torbidda stepped away from the statue as the old selector shuffled toward him. "How did you get in?"

"Flaccus thinks he's the only one who knows about this place. Ha! I know *every* secret. I roam these vaults with the ghosts and listen to the echo of the great days." Torbidda watched with mild nausea as Varro stripped the shroud from the statue and ran his hand, hungry as a blind man's, over the form of the shy maiden.

"The Madonna. Oh, I'm sure that you were thinking of someone else—a sister, a mother, a sweetheart—but the sculpture represents your enemy. The snake at Her feet? That's us. That's why She hates us. We would dispel the darkness of ignorance. Curiosity is the only sure path to wisdom."

"I'm not a lamb anymore," Torbidda said. "The Madonna's a myth."

"Oh, she's real."

"She lived—but two thousand years ago. She's dust now, like the Curia and its fancies. Engineers build with stone and iron." Although Torbidda did not respect Flaccus, by now he had little for Varro either.

"Engineers require imaginary numbers to solve certain equations, do they not?" Varro said equably. "Without them, certain truths would remain inaccessible."

"That's different," Torbidda said impatiently. "They're . . . useful fictions."

"We know that *now*, but someone somewhere once took a chance. Different problems require different tools, and faith can be useful as logic."

"Logic's a tool for preserving truth. Its first law is that nothing true can be derived from false principles."

"Yet every law has exceptions. I've extracted nobility from base metals. Torture can compel truth from liars. Kings have been born in mangers."

"Selector, these are false analogies."

Torbidda's polite response was wasted effort. Varro wasn't listening; he was lovingly caressing the statue's curves. Torbidda cleared his throat and the old man leered at him knowingly. "I was a mason, you know, before the Reformation. I might even have carved her. I don't remember. Our work was uniform. These days every craftsman's striving to be original and the result is cacophony. We strove then to forget ourselves, to let ourselves be God's hands. All Bernoulli had to do was insert himself in God's place to acquire an army of devoted slaves."

Although quick to criticize Flaccus and his coterie, Varro usually limited himself to bland generalities when discussing Bernoulli. Curiosity compelled Torbidda to ask, "What was he like, really? Tell me, no one's listening."

Varro smiled conspiratorially. "He had an eye for talent. I came to his notice on the building site of St. Eco's, as we called it then. I was always good at uncovering secrets, and bad at hiding them. When I realized he wasn't building an ordinary cathedral he could have killed me. Instead, he told me his *real* secret and sent me out into the world to learn more. I wandered on his behalf and met other wanderers, older and more powerful, and when I returned, he showed me the Confession Box. He no longer had to search for secrets; they came to him and whispered the history of tomorrow. He told me one would come to destroy his work, and afterward, *another* would come to complete it. I waited for so long that in my eagerness I mistook the signs! I thought his grandson, Giovanni, was that man." His fingers tightened around the statue's throat. "How wrong I was."

Torbidda said nothing.

"You're studying deep things down here in the dark. Flaccus lacks the wisdom to enlighten you."

"Can you?"

Varro walked across the puddle. Torbidda noticed that he did not disturb the surface. "Follow me."

The Alchemistry Hall echoed with the sound of crashing waves. The pool was already drained. Below, a pseudonaiad stalked up and down, flowing over the curved walls, crashing against them and then reforming. When Torbidda approached the edge, the restless movement ceased.

"See: it remembers you."

Though it was eyeless and faceless, Torbidda felt it *looking* at him. "I can't get in there. It'll kill me."

Varro pulled the ladder up. "If you don't face your fears, I promise that you'll die in Conclave. You know that Flaccus has been secretly training Agrippina. Do you think she'll hesitate?"

"Is *that* why you want to help me? To spite Flaccus? Perhaps Agrippina is willing to lower herself to simony, but if I win the yellow I won't be a pawn."

"Precisely why it must be you," Varro said high-mindedly. "Girolamo Bernoulli wanted the best to climb the mountain. In this faithless time I remain his last faithful servant."

Torbidda didn't give much credence to that, but he was out of options; *that* was undeniable. With a silent prayer, he leapt down. As soon as his feet touched the ground the water rushed for him. His reflexes were considerably better now, and he dodged it—but only just. He backed away, but there was no escape in the cylindrical prison. The elemental hurled itself at him again, and again he rolled out of the way at the last moment.

"Varro!" This was foolish. "In the name of sanity, lower the ladder!"

"No," Varro said simply.

Torbidda's Water Style was sophisticated enough now that he could sense the water's will, and he could anticipate its attacks. But no entirely defensive strategy could win here: the water never lagged, it never got tired or gave him space; it just kept coming. Eventually he'd make a slip, and then—

Soon he was up against the wall again.

Varro yelled, "You need to attack!"

Torbidda knew he was right, and in desperation, he threw a punch. His fist sank into the column, where liquid entrails gripped his fingers, pulled his hand in and swallowed his wrist, his arm— Torbidda leapt, kicked both feet against the wall and pushed himself *into* the pseudonaiad. He landed on the other side, thoroughly soaked, but free.

He gulped for air. "Damn you, Varro! How can I hurt what I can't hit?"

"Think, boy! It's water—only water. You're that and more."

Torbidda's mind worked desperately: *water, air*—could he harness air the way he harnessed water? Surely that was impossible. Water was in him, in his blood, saturating his matter. Air was outside. How could he control that? But with nothing to lose, he threw another punch, this time stopping scant inches before the column's surface. The focused blast of air burst through the elemental and it reeled back, looking like a tattered flag, then reformed.

"That's it, attack! *Attack!* Don't let it rest."

Torbidda didn't need to be told now. Another blow, and another: he had it now. The elemental fell back from the pneumatic onslaught shedding water from liquid wounds. He herded it back against the wall and, eyes shut, fists together, struck mercilessly, pushing air into it like a hammer, inflating it . . .

The explosion drenched him. He opened his eyes to find himself standing in a cloud of mist. Around his feet small, trembling puddles were desperately combining. It wasn't dead—it couldn't die—but he had bested it.

Varro dropped the ladder and held out his hand. Torbidda climbed up and stood beside the selector, watching the pseudonaiad reforming. It moves sluggishly, punch-drunk.

"Now you are ready."

"Varro," Torbidda gasped, "I'm grateful for what you did, but, please, tell me the truth. I know there's more."

Varro smiled proudly. "I can't fool you. When the water recognized you, I knew you would be the perfect vessel. That's all the Apprentices are—red, orange, yellow, they're all just potential vessels. Like a thief in the night, the master will return—at what hour, no one can say, but it is *imminent*. One Apprentice must sacrifice himself so that Bernoulli can live again, and it must be the most worthy vessel. My dear boy, I think that honor is yours! You have all the requisite qualities."

"What if I don't want this honor?"

Varro's shoulders began to shake with mirth.

"What if I refuse?"

"Oh, poor boy, your *wishes* are irrelevant." Varro's face creased in hysterical laughter. "You think your will could withstand Bernoulli's? Your fate was sealed the day you entered the Guild Halls—AAHHhh!"

Crrackk

The selector landed badly. He had not expected the push. The distinctive egg-white color of fresh bone glistened from his shin. The water sensed him.

"Take your reward," said Torbidda, covering the pool with its shroud, "O good and faithful servant."

Chapter 16

The Molè's construction continued apace after the Reformation, to the chagrin of many. Nobles found on the Curia's register of donors were still expected to pay. A graduated income tax supplied the rest; the engineers' efficiency extended to money-gathering. Even the prostitutes were levied.

from The Bernoullian Reforms *by Count Titus Tremellius Pomptinus*

Torbidda crept from the Halls down to Old Town wrapped in a long cloak. It was an indirect route, but one that would not be noticed. He requisitioned a horse from the heralds' livery and rode across the Ponte Bernoulliana. The guards at the gate stood under the empty gibbets and studied him. Torbidda gave them a brusque salute, which allowed them to see his yellow armband. "Guild business," he muttered. One advantage of being a Candidate was the fear it inspired. The dark green gates rippled open and, for the first time in his life, Torbidda left the city of Concord.

To what end he knew not.

For all his doubts, as soon as he was outside the walls he felt invisible chains drop away: he had escaped a malign will that had directed every step of his life. He rode a mile or two before a gruesome spectacle slowed him to a walk. The procession of mendicants he had observed the other day had become a trail of bodies, tended by buzzing flies and crows. He rode on warily until he came to a neatly stacked mound. One Fraticelli was living still, and he was piling bodies by the light of a small fire.

He turned with the contented smile of a farmer completing his harvest and Torbidda flinched when he looked into the pits where the Fraticelli's eyes should be. Agrippina had told him the Fraticelli rejoiced in poverty; they never washed, and wore their habits until the cloth fell, rotting, from their bodies. If this was true, then here surely was their king. His shapeless, filthy rags were the gray of a donkey's pelt, and looked as if they had been made from matted tail hairs.

"Where goes't thou, Brother?" The blind man's voice was like a sharp quill scratching rough parchment.

"No idea," Torbidda said, carefully keeping the revulsion from his voice. He had worked on emaciated specimens in the Anatomy Halls, but he had never before seen such desiccation in living flesh. The blind man was all knee and knuckle: his limbs were bones covered with an uneven layer of thin, bruised skin, burned the same angry pink as the bodies on his pile. The bone of his skull showed clear through his bald pate. His mouth was large, and crowded with yellow teeth, perhaps four or six too many, and his smiling lips were chapped and broken.

"If you don't know where you're going, no one is waiting for you, so what hurry? Rest a while."

Torbidda couldn't fault his logic, but he looked back at Concord anxiously.

The Fraticelli laughed. "Ah, you're running! These poor pilgrims, they thought to run too. They believed they'd be safe if they reached the world's center."

"They didn't get far," Torbidda remarked.

"They got as far as they were meant to. Each star is given a path and may not choose another. Men are no different. The day Men are free to choose their own path, that day History ends. But these fools understood nothing of Astronomy. They fell into the thrall of yonder city. Some said it was punishment; some said they were not worthy to see Jerusalem. Others, mad with the sun, said Concord *was* the new Jerusalem!"

"I don't know what Concord is," Torbidda said, and dismounted, "but it's not that. Had they no guide?"

The Fraticelli's head tilted like a bird. "Perhaps they thought I was their guide." He scratched his chin-stubble and giggled. "Perhaps I was."

"Why did they perish?"

"There's little else to do in the desert. Three paltry revolutions and they started dropping. A blind man makes a poor guide," he confessed, "but I'll try to be a better host." He took a fiery brand from his campfire and threw it onto the pile of bodies. The dry clothes caught quickly and soon the crackle of skin peeling, fat sizzling and bones snapping filled the air.

"That's better. So, how shall we pass the time? A story! Have you one to tell? I see you're shy. I'll start. There once was a town besieged by condottieri. The thing went on till every larder in town was empty. The magnates got together and decided that there were simply too many mouths to feed, so they evicted the Small People. Well, you can imagine that when the condottieri saw this army of beggars coming toward them, they didn't like the look of all those hungry mouths either. So they persuaded the beggars not to advance further—arrows, pikes and swords made their case—and the beggars fled back to the town. But the gates remained closed. 'We know ye not,' the magnates said, and cast down stones and darts on their heads."

"Was the siege successful?"

"The show of unity against the Small People proved to each side they had much in common. A deal was struck, money changed hands and the keep marched out, flags up, honor intact, between the skeletons of the beggars and beggars' wives and beggars' children, and if that was not success, I don't know what is."

Torbidda felt the story's moral was somehow dubious, but lately he'd found such distinctions impossibly difficult. "Are you a pilgrim too?"

"I was, but now I wait in this wilderness to make ready for the king."

"Ours just died," Torbidda said wryly.

"Permit me to contradict you, Child. The First Apprentice is merely a steward. He keeps the lamp burning and awaits his king's return. See—?" He pointed to the city.

"I see nothing," Torbidda began, but just then the lantern atop the Molè lit up, its glow taking its place among the stars.

"Behold! A star in the east. It burns for you."

Torbidda watched it for a long time. "If I go back, I'll have to do a wicked thing."

"You have no experience in this area?"

"Nothing like this. I fear my penance for it will be to become a sacrificial lamb."

"Who told you so? We all have parts to play: handmaid, king, wise man, fool—but you're no lamb. I see better than most—you're a wolf! And a wolf must wolf. These pilgrims chose to run; you see how Fortune rewarded their cowardice. Choose life and fight, or stay here and fuel my fire."

The fat-fueled fire burned frantically, the Fraticelli's voice was a drone like a sated fly and Torbidda felt sleep creeping up on him. "And how do you know my part?"

The blind man looked heavenward. "I read it," he said, then laughed as if he saw Torbidda's look of skepticism. "Oh, not there! The stars are one book, but I prefer another." He moved to the side. A little away from both fires lay an old man's body, abdomen open, entrails exposed. Torbidda gagged, even though he was an

experienced dissectionist—this looked like the work of a raven-
ing beast. The blind man reached over and held up some trailing
guts. "Here's the honest part of a man. That fellow was the pilgrims'
guide. He led them to me, and he *told* me"—he shook the entrails
like prayer beads—"to wait here for my king." The seared air between
them warped and twisted tiresomely. Before his eyes shut, Torbidda
heard him say, "Turn, Majesty! Turn and be a wolf."

Torbidda awoke with his horse nuzzling him. He sat up and turned
into a swollen, unblinking Cyclopean sun. It blinded him momentarily and robbed heat from his vision so that he saw the world in
tones of blue. He did not recognize it. There was no sign of the Fraticelli, nor the charnel mound, only a few scattered bones the sun had
obviously been parching for years. The wind doused him with foul
dust. He wrapped a scarf around his face and rode back to the city,
to take whatever Fortune had in store for Cadet Number LX.

Chapter 17

ON THE ORIGINS OF CONCORDIAN GOTHIC

The Opera del Duomo wasted lifetimes in procrastination, wasted them as waves beating on the rocks are wasted, before it was dismissed in disgrace. In the Twenties, when a young Girolamo Bernoulli was making his name, the embarrassment of Concord's unfinished cathedral was compounded by the triumphant completion of Rasenna's. The subsequent appointment of an unconventional and relatively untested young man as capomaestro (St. Eco's youngest-ever) was either an inspired choice or a sign of how desperate the Curia had become.

Far from letting this task overawe him, Bernoulli caused a minor scandal by scathingly dismissing the Curia's unrealized designs.[6] He described St. Eco's walls as "squat, sober and thrifty, like a merchant's wife, and just as ugly." The dome that had defeated

---

6. The centuries-old plans had been elevated to holy relics at this stage.

generations of brilliant architects he pronounced "unambitious."[7] Before he would place a single brick atop another, he insisted on knocking down the walls that had stood for decades. That he was allowed to do so is revealing of the Curia's desperation.[8]

7. In our era of rampant egoism, it seems natural, predictable even, for an architect to disparage his predecessors. Students should be wary of projecting contemporary values onto an age when slavish ancestor-worship was the norm. It was then a given that those who wished to succeed had to adorn the dead with laurels and spew bile on innovators; this complacent ethos sat well with an institution like the Curia.

8. Revealing also the influence of Bernoulli's ill-fated patron, Senator Postumus Tremellius Felix.

Chapter 18

He had climbed for hours, and each hour the wind grew more outraged and assailed him more wildly. It screamed abuse as it whipped between the ragged peaks, so intent on hurtling him down that he had to hug the steps until his fingertips fused with the cold rock. He did not feel his skin coming away as he ripped them off the freezing stone.

He was numb: best to be numb when there is nothing left to feel but pain. He had not even bothered to justify the morning's events to himself. His conscience must be numb too—perhaps it had atrophied. It was certainly superfluous at this altitude. *Take nothing that will slow you down.* Agrippina told him that before the ascent began. He remembered seeing emptiness rush into her eyes as the hate disappeared. He remembered the perfunctory applause as he limped out of the Conclave. He remembered Grand Selector Flaccus' confusion as he shook his bloody hand and dazedly pointed to the steps.

Take nothing.

When he reached the summit of Monte Nero he found himself standing between two rows: men and women in long black gowns on the right, soldiers on the left, consuls and praetorians. The plain was utterly flat, as if some giant sword had cut the stone with a clean swipe. The cathedral occupied most of it but there would have been space enough for a legion to assemble if such a thing were legal: the only soldiers allowed up here were senior officers and praetorians. At the end of the path was the Molè. Steep steps led to the great Doors of History, and there, flanked by Castrucco, the Prefect of the Praetorian Guard, stood a figure whose orange robes whipped around him like the last leaves of winter.

Torbidda paused to catch his breath. The consul on his right, a short, genial-looking fellow with a V-shaped smile and small twinkling eyes like a doll's, leaned forward and said, "A little further, Cadet. Walk tall!"

He stumbled through the guard of honor, vaguely recognizing a few Collegio members, and, thanks to Leto's tuition, guessing the identity of others. He tried to keep his head high, but his body trembled and he feared his legs would not carry him. At the top of the steps, the Second Apprentice waited, wearing the orange and a triumphant smile. Torbidda stopped at the first step, waiting for instructions.

The new Second Apprentice was adolescent, but he still had a boyish quality. Torbidda knew his name, of course—Pulcher was something of a Guild Hall legend, a first-blood who'd actually lived up to his promise. The chief viper of a generation of vipers, he represented the logical end of Bernoulli's revolution. Naturalism, Empiricism, questions of right or wrong, historic destiny; none of these abstractions troubled Pulcher. He was a kite in the wind, turning whatever way was expedient, with all his thought bent to one ambition: to wear the red. He had a weak chin and watery eyes, and his youthful face was dominated entirely by a cumbersome nose.

Everything receded from the prominent tip, which he thrust forward aggressively with menacing curiosity. He clapped his hands once and the rows came alive. The consuls filed up the steps past Torbidda and disappeared into the darkness. When Torbidda took a step to follow, the Second Apprentice snapped, "Halt! No Cadet may enter here. Those are the clothes of a Cadet."

Torbidda realized immediately what was intended: another shearing. Again he saw beyond the game to its intention. He stripped and stood shivering in the snow.

"Who are you?" Pulcher asked imperiously. He at least was enjoying his part in the ritual.

"I am the Third Apprentice!" said Torbidda through chattering teeth.

Pulcher laughed, "I see a naked lamb." He nodded to the praetorian prefect. "There is no charity here."

The door closed and the icy silence of the night surrounded Torbidda. He looked into the sky, trying to see beyond the falling snow to the stars. They fell together, impossible to tell apart. The world was crumbling, unequal to the stress it bore. The drifting snow was a constantly collapsing curtain in front of the colossal door, a masterpiece of an earlier era. The antique style suggested its creator was Curia-trained. If so, he had paid the Curia back with a parody of the traditional schematic of the hereafter. The Reformation infected everything. The cressets were so placed that the light only illuminated the bottom half. Heaven was dominated by a gentle figure of the Madonna. With surprise and shame Torbidda looked on the compassionate face he had spent so many hours contemplating when he ought to have been fighting.

"You, *here*?" he whispered, tears trickled down his face. He wondered whom he was mourning, Agrippina or himself? For, truly, he was dead as she.

The Virgin looked on in rhapsody at the figures playing among the surrounding clouds. They carried trumpets and long horns and lyres and harps. Plump cherubs chased each another, and these She regarded with special tenderness.

Her gaze led Torbidda's eyes to a particular angel soaring with arms stretched skyward in praise—or . . . was he screaming as he fell? The change was so subtle one could not say where it began. This winged creature was not a saint but a carrion-feeding demon; that singer, a screaming soul. That babe shyly turning was a sly black imp. Cherubs rushed to impale themselves on the long pikes of Hell's black-armored infantry, and so it went, up and up, until one entered another space where soft clouds became jagged stone and twisted metal. The architecture of Hell was eye-cutting desolation. The inverted spires of the ruined temples were the first clue that the World's orientation had changed. Soaring angels became falling souls, and those who survived the spikes and hooks fell into the gaping maw of the swinish creature with greedy, bulging eyes that squatted in the murksome darkness. The door was executed in high relief, but here the goldsmith had excelled himself. The black goddess was wreathed in shadows that nearly obscured her vile drooping teats, dripping snout, curled and broken tusks, her hairy grasping limbs, her sharp hoofs that crushed the damned underneath and her roving hungry eyes—

They fell on him.

Torbidda fell back with a yelp as the door opened. He was unsure whether hours or moments had passed. Behind the row of praetorians he glimpsed the consuls lining the circumference of the crossing under the dome. In the center was a tree-like pillar of glass and beside it was a colossal statue of an angel, thrusting a sword heavenward. The praetorians parted and the Second Apprentice advanced until he stood in the same position and asked again, "Who are you?"

"My name is Sixty."

"A Cadet's name. Yet you wear no uniform. Who are you truly?"

"My name is . . ." He tried to dredge it up, but it would not come. He had lost it somewhere in the darkness—that place where Agrippina's dying eyes were staring, making him dumb.

"Wait, I think I know you—are you not called Torbidda?"

This time he knew the response with certainty. "Torbidda is dead."

"I have not invited you in," Pulcher said as Torbidda began to climb the steps.

"This house belongs not to you but to him we are Apprenticed to: Girolamo Bernoulli."

"Proto Magister, now and forever," said Pulcher, breaking into a smile. "Then welcome, Third Apprentice! Dress and follow me."

A consul came forward, taking tiny steps—the same twinkling-eyed fellow who had whispered encouragement. As he handed Torbidda a yellow bundle, he leaned in. "Well done! Usually this routine goes on for an *age*. Took Pulcher half the night to figure out he didn't need permission to enter."

Torbidda said nothing as he dressed. It felt strange; he had expected some great revelation when he finally took the yellow, but the numbness remained.

The consul stood back appraisingly. "The color suits you. I'm Corvis, by the way. We'll be working together soon. Follow me."

In the center of the nave-crossing, the Second Apprentice stood, apparently suspended on air, in an opening in the glass column. Torbidda felt the consuls' eyes upon him. It was like being back in the Halls. Did they envy him? Despise him? Most likely both—as below, so above, as the late Selector Varro used to say.

As Torbidda approached, the mighty bronze angel loomed clearer and he saw that the sculptor was a more advanced creature than the primitive responsible for the hellish door. All of this titan's forms were noble. It occupied space with the same right any living thing did, and it represented a promise: here was the man of tomorrow, unfettered by defunct morality or doubt or guilt. For a moment Torbidda's spirits lifted—then he read the motto carved in massive Etruscan characters at its base —*Although changed, I shall arise the same*—and found a mocking echo of his own thoughts. These consuls, the smug, smiling Pulcher, they imagined they had evolved beyond antique notions like sin and punishment, and yet Torbidda knew a great abyss lay waiting below their feet.

"Come on. The man in red is waiting," Pulcher whined with youthful impatience as Torbidda joined him in the confines of the capsule with trepidation. "Sorry about all *that* stuff. The First Apprentice takes matters of form very seriously"—a sharp intake of breath—"as you shall presently see."

Torbidda felt his stomach sink as a surge from below pushed the capsule skyward.

"Hell on the stomach, isn't it?"

The circle of consuls dwindled as the floor rushed away below their feet. "It's marvelous," he managed.

Pulcher's lip curled. "I hope you're not *another* devotee of Saint Bernoulli. Reverence is proper in a Cadet, but you've made it now; it's time to put away childish things. We're not supposed to say old Bernoulli died a madman, yet it's true. Even a mind that has reached the greatest heights can fall to the worst depths—and Bonnacio's on the same path, if you ask me." When Torbidda made no reply, Pulcher cleared his throat. "What was the *honorable* consul whispering to you? Oh, you don't have to tell me—but watch out, though. Corvis will make a protégé of you if you're not careful. Since Argenti's death he's been all deferential, but take my word, he's no friend of ours. His great aim is to make Apprenticeship purely ceremonial. Your star's rising, Torbidda. Stick with me and it need never fall."

So it begins, Torbidda thought wearily. *First Corvis, now Pulcher*. There was no graduation from the competition. The politicking never ended; only the faces changed: *as below, so above.*

The coffin carried them up into the grasp of the first dome, which was decorated with a more conventional depiction of the Last Judgment. They passed through the mural and emerged into the second dome, and Torbidda realized with dismay that it wasn't slowing. He had yearned to explore the treasures of the great library, but he did not have long to take it in—though its disarray surprised him—before they left it behind too.

"When we get up there, wait for me to introduce you. Like I said, he's a stickler."

"I've heard he spends every night guarding the lantern. What's he looking for?"

"Madonna knows. The Curia thought the world was the universe's foundation stone, and when they looked heavenward they were comforted by a divine melody that only existed in their imagination. I think Bonnacio still strives to hear it."

"If you're trying to set me against him, forget it."

"Madonna! Who said anything about that?" Pulcher pointed his great nose at Torbidda. "You intrigue me a little. What are you anyway, Empiricist or Naturalist?"

"Neither. The party system is a corruption of what Bernoulli wanted."

"Which was what? Universal love?"

"Just the opposite: every man at every other's throat, all alliances temporary."

Pulcher laughed dryly. "Oh, you'll go far."

The mistral ceaselessly threw fugitive scraps of alpine snow at the First Apprentice. His red robes tumbled around him like a fire too weak to consume itself. The melancholy wind soiled the pristine marble of New City with the dust of the Wastes that fell on the wise and foolish together and maddened both. So long as the wind kept the night sky free of clouds, Bonnacio did not begrudge its blowing. The stars were a book, and he was eager to reach the dénouement. Could He be out there somewhere, born already? No, surely not; the stars would have warned him.

They had whispered to Bonnacio long before he became a Cadet: *Climb higher, we have something wonderful to tell.* So he climbed. And when he finally reached the summit of that mountain of bodies, he realized that the stars didn't whisper: they roared! The Dark Ones who sheltered in the light of a billion turbulent Hells looked upon this chaste blue jewel of water and air as a traitor. Its fidelity to the Old One was contemptible to them. There must be no exemptions from Time's torment. The world must take its place in the universal fire. Bonnacio watched giant Orion stalk stealthily across the horizon. The three kings of the hunter's belt were weak sparks, trembling like a candle harassed by the wind. Some greater mistral assailed the stars and kept their fire from consuming the world altogether. Its source was Him, the Old One.

Bonnacio had seen enough. He retreated below, nimbly navigating the precarious shifting clockwork that served for a staircase from lantern to engine room. The great pendulum and its swooping revolutions circulated the hot, stagnant air. He approached the slate reverently and studied his old calculations, then, with a hiss of disdain, impatiently rubbed them away with his sleeve and began to make new notations, seeking to compare the numbers he saw in the stars with a number he had in his mind. The song was weak yet, but he still perceived its warning.

Behind him the pod slowed and opened with a hiss. Torbidda attempted to step out, but Pulcher restrained him.

From the darkness, Torbidda heard a grating unmusical voice: "Who is this stranger?"

Pulcher rolled his eyes, but answered with formality, "No stranger. Your master is my master."

"Then come forth, Brother."

Pulcher turned to Torbidda and hissed, "Stay here till I call you," before exiting the pod. Torbidda watched him walk toward the great air-slicing pendulum that bisected the long, narrow chamber. Its passage was the rasping breath of a slumbering dragon. A waft of warm, oily air poured over him.

"I hear whispers, First Apprentice," Pulcher said. "Corvis is turning the Collegio dei Consoli against us."

Bonnacio didn't look around. "Our enemies are outside Concord."

This dismissal annoyed Pulcher, who was standing now between two massive tables, one covered with maps of Etruria and Europa, the other with nautical charts of the Tyrrhenian Sea. He picked up one of variously colored markers and threw it down, scattering a collection that represented an army. "Etruria is a land of small cities run by small men. Concord is more than that now: we are an empire. Europa's waiting for a race that knows how to exploit it. Every year we have gone further, gained more land, more rivers, more coal, more iron."

"Every year but this one. General Luparelli's bogged down."

"Luparelli's too dull to make use of a legion like the Ninth. New leadership would shake things up. The son of the ill-fated Manius Spinther, he's only a second-year, but I've heard good things."

"As it happens, I do have another job in mind for Luparelli, but I shouldn't wonder that the Candidate for Third Apprentice—it's his suggestion, I presume—wants to promote young Spinther. They're dear friends."

". . . ah."

"Yes, 'Ah.' Young men must learn patience. If one is hasty, it is easy to overlook the salient details. My predecessor's fixation on Europa gave the states that once composed the Southern League a reprieve. It would take just one city to raise its flag and we'd be facing a two-front war."

"What city?" Pulcher said mockingly. "If you studied politics as deeply as you study the firmament you'd know that the only Etrurian city with a semblance of stable government is Ariminum, and we can buy them off easily enough."

"Fortune's wheel turns fast. John Acuto is assembling an alliance."

"He won't get far with those squabbling fools," Pulcher said wearily.

"Perhaps, but I'm sending the Twelfth Legion on a progress as a precaution. Luparelli may be a blundering fool but the work I have in mind does not require an Alexander. We shall wipe out the last of the condottieri companies, then harry the South and break down the walls of her cities, bring them as low as Rasenna or Gubbio."

"There's more to this strategy, isn't there?" said Pulcher, walking away and approaching the slate. An undulating curve rose and fell between a forest of equations.

"You're a decent mathematician, Pulcher. Follow the steps. We're here"—he pointed—"and descending now faster than ever. The Wave is about to trough. Everything will change in a moment and if we're unready, all this, all Bernoulli's preparation, will be for naught."

"Why don't you just cut up a lamb and be done with it? This isn't philosophy, it's augury."

Bonnacio looked critically at the slate. "Argenti doubted me too. He thought the hollow trappings of power were real. I let him die under your knife for that reason. He would have held back from the sacrifice we must make. Don't forget that the height we have attained only gives us further to fall. All that bears us up is a wind that is about to change. We are but vessels."

"Better king for a moment than slave for a lifetime, eh?" Pulcher said without conviction, then, "Speaking of vessels—First Apprentice, may I present a poor Candidate in a state of darkness?"

"Let the Brother be brought into the Light."

"Come forth, Candidate," said Pulcher portentously as he walked back toward the pod. Torbidda stepped out and reeled as the floor pitched, but he managed to keep his footing. As they intersected, Pulcher grabbed him and hissed, "Didn't think to mention that Spinther's an old chum?"

"He has the requisite skills."

"Oh, I'm sure he's another wonder boy, but it never hurts to have a general in your pocket." Pulcher released him and sighed dramatically. "So now I have you to watch out for too?"

Torbidda said, "I don't want what you want."

"I've heard this tune already; Bonnacio sings it better—he actually convinced me, too. I did all the knifework and he got the red. Let's see what he gets out of you."

Torbidda watched as the pod's doors closed and it descended. Panic gathered around him, but with no retreat left, he walked reluctantly onward, constantly adjusting his step to the tilting surface. He passed between the two massive maps, then had to dart forward to slip past the *whoosh* of the pendulum.

The First Apprentice still stood facing the great slate board, which was dense with chalk notation. The red of his robe was uncannily vivid in the gloom. It was the smoldering color of summer dusk, fresh poppies, oxygenated blood, Agrippina's lips.

The first thing Torbidda noticed when Bonnacio turned around was the fearsome-looking pair of compasses he was holding, and he suppressed a shudder as he remembered how Leto had dispatched the Fuscus girl.

"Behold the man. Come closer."

"Yes, First Apprentice."

Bonnacio was as pale and remote as the stars he worshipped. "Hold out your hand, Brother," he said softly, and when Torbidda submitted he said, "Good; the first rule is obedience." His expression remained wistful as he suddenly grabbed Torbidda's wrist. Holding it tightly, he pricked Torbidda's small finger with the compass needle. As the blood pooled around the point he asked, "Do you solemnly swear to obey the Master, without secret evasion of mind; binding yourself under no less a penalty than that of having your body severed in twain, your bowels taken from there, burned to ashes, and the ashes thereof scattered to the four winds of Heaven, that there might remain neither track, trace nor remembrance among man of so vile and perjured a wretch as you should be, should you ever violate this solemn obligation?"

It The vice tightened as Bonnacio waited for Torbidda's response. "I swear!"

At once Bonnacio released Torbidda's hand, turned back to the board and traced a new circle with the compass. When he turned back, his manner was more businesslike. "You'll spend the next month in the second dome: the library needs urgent cataloging. Count Tremellius has several useful talents, but organization, alas, is not among them."

Torbidda responded cautiously, "With respect, First Apprentice, I didn't come here to be a librarian's assistant."

"You misunderstand. That's an order. Tests and riddles, all that is done. Now you must work. As you ascended, the Second Apprentice asked you to spy on me, did he not? Promised you things? It's all right, you don't have to answer. I remember when I took the yellow how I yearned to wear the orange and then the red. Ambition doesn't merely blind Man, it deafens him. It took time to realize *why* Bernoulli wanted us segregated from the rest of the Guild, why he built so high. It's so we can hear—the stars, they speak to us. I listened until I learned what my unfortunate predecessor could never understand: the Master's return is at hand!"

Torbidda was hot and uncomfortable under Bonnacio's hollow gaze. He said the test was over, but that might be another, more subtle test. Bonnacio was remote, but Torbidda knew that other-worldly manner concealed a mind worldly enough to manipulate Pulcher's feral ambition. He attempted a more servile tack. "*You* are my master, First Apprentice."

"Child, we are but *vessels*. The vessel was once the man called Girolamo Bernoulli, and now it is his Molè. A time is coming when the Molè will be no more. It's not accidental that you're here and not some other Candidate; the hour calls forth the man, his steps ordained by necessity. My astronomy, Pulcher's warcraft, your architecture: men believe they are free, but nothing's free: everything's written and History is a problem to be solved by exegesis. Its treasure belongs to the most penetrating reader. That's why you must go to the library. You must *solve* the Molè."

Torbidda was perplexed: a building wasn't an equation. After a minute went by, the First Apprentice happened to glance around. He was obviously surprised to find Torbidda still standing there and dismissed him with a waved hand. "Attend to it."

Chapter 19

ON THE ORIGINS OF CONCORDIAN GOTHIC

As the dust settled on the mount, Bernoulli drew his plans for the cathedral to be built on the grave of St. Eco's. He understood the Etruscans—their love of the circle, the triangle, the balance of the horizontal with the vertical—and his optical studies gave him a philosophical appreciation of the spectrum, but he rejected all Classical precedents. His vision for what became the Molè Bernoulliana was monochromatic and severe.[9]

With hindsight, it is clear to us that Bernoulli's conception of the Cathedral was more Europan than Etrurian but, when the Curia realized just how iconoclastic the style we call Concordian Gothic was, traditionalist architects reacted with shrill protests.[10]

9. "I hate every line that is not vertical. I hate every color that is not black. History's chains will not bind me."

10. Shrill but ineffective protests. Some were erudite dialogues; more popular were the lampoons that exploited traditional Concordian xenophobia: the

His critics fell silent as the frame of one dome was capped by another and still another. It was clear to all Concordians that the right man had arrived at the right moment to solve the problem that had bested so many. Bernoulli had made his name as a bridge builder, after all, and what is a bridge but an arch, and what is a dome but three hundred and eighty arches? The triple dome of the Molè was more than an answer to Duke Scaligeri's Cathedral; it was proof, for all Etruria, of Concordian superiority—though utterly different from that envisaged by the Curia so many years ago.

slander that Bernoulli's ancestors were fur-wearing northerners originated here. Ciuto Brandini's judgment that "Bernoulli expresses in stone the iron in his blood" was much duplicated in the Piazzetta Bocca della Verità.

PART II:
CITY OF TOWERS

Who shut up the sea with doors, when it brake forth, as if it had issued out of the womb? . . .

Hath the rain a father? Or who hath begotten the drops of dew?

Job 38:8, 28

Chapter 20

One year after the Siege of Rasenna, the Year of our Lady, 1371

The other students never mocked Uggeri's elaborate preparations to his face; he was, after all, a hero of the siege, which had ended with the destruction of the Twelfth Legion and the death of all but the youngest Apprentice. Uggeri made up for his late start in the Art Bandiera with practice and ability. He prepared like the bandieratori of old, and it was quite a thing to watch his prickly dissatisfaction as he picked a weapon from the rack—to hear him testing the flag's snap and the wood's spring, weighing it in his hand, tipping it, letting it roll over the top of his fist with the skeptical look of a man listening to a coin-changer. In any other student Sofia would have called it fetishism, but give Uggeri an enemy and all hesitancy disappeared like dew on sunbaked stones. The Doc used to say sincerity

was as rare in a fighter as charity in Ariminum, but Uggeri did everything with sincerity.

He came at her roaring,

Tok

   Tok

     Tok.

Sofia gave ground coolly. "Pace yourself. Every strike doesn't have
to be a knock-out."

In response Uggeri roared again and leapt for her, twirling his
banner in great red swoops. As Sofia stepped aside her flag did a
great, leisurely rotation, then she suddenly jabbed his left leg.

"Ugh!" He tilted protectively, but declared defiantly, "I'm still
standing."

"Not for long."

She threw the same combination back and this time, balance
gone and footing confused, he tripped himself. Sofia stood over
him, flag aimed at his temple. "Bam, you're asleep. From the
moment you grip a flag you should be thinking. But you're too
angry to think. Find the peace at the heart of the fight and you'll
be unbeatable."

Another student would have been embarrassed to be bested so
easily, but Uggeri laughed and jumped up, eager to try it again. His
approach to Art Bandiera was practical; before he'd picked up a flag
he'd been a fighter. Things that other bandieratori valued—looking
good, style—meant nothing to him, but Sofia knew he loved a good
trick.

His devotion to her was fierce, and she trusted it because it had
nothing to do with her former status. He had given his flag and his
decina to Doc Bardini, but that loyalty did not automatically transfer
to Sofia Scaligeri when she took over the Bardini workshop. Uggeri
became a believer when he saw her fight.

"Go easy on them, Contessa!"

Sofia turned sharply, smiling when she saw who it was. "Pedro Vanzetti! I'll run my workshop my way, thank you very much. You concentrate on running the Engineers' Guild. You left so many half-built churches when you disappeared that I've been thinking of picking up a hood myself."

Pedro held up his hands contritely. "Matters of state; I returned as soon as I could." He wore the same outfit as all Rasenneisi engineers: a sleeveless leather jacket with several pockets, and hose and doublet in sober tones of gray and brown and black, but his long, tangling hood was used as a scarf and was dusty from his travels. He looked better with skin tanned by the sun instead of the furnaces, and not covered with yellow grease and soot. "When's the next meeting?" he asked.

"Tomorrow. I thought you were too busy for us now?"

"I'm trying to remedy that," he said; he'd made a point of attending the monthly Signoria meetings until his responsibilities had interrupted.

A giant condottiere tilted his head into the workshop. "Where is she?"

"Yuri!"

The students leapt out the way as he marched toward Sofia. He picked her up by the waist and held her above his head like a toddler. "Ooof!" His cheeks puffed out. "Getting heavy! Fewer noodles and more exercise for the Contessa!"

While Yuri teased Sofia, Pedro hailed Uggeri warmly, though he wasn't surprised when Uggeri returned the salute coldly. They might be contemporaries, but Pedro represented the city Rasenna was becoming: a city, like Concord, with engineers at its heart. Uggeri took it as a personal affront that the bandieratori were being marginalized. Pedro regretted the animosity, but not the progress Rasenna had made. The coming war would not be won with romantic notions.

"Put me down, you oaf. I need to inspire respect in these boys."

"Who is disrespecting my Sofia?" Yuri let her down and made a lumbering stampede at a cluster of students. "Show him to me!"

When they scattered before him, he turned around with a wave of a giant hand. "See? Respect is restored."

Sofia made a courtly bow. "My valiant knight."

Yuri curtseyed in return and said, "Where's the peddler? Is he getting fat too?"

"No, he's getting saddle-sores riding up and down Etruria, preaching about this league like a wandering mendicant. I'm afraid he's made few converts."

"Levi is good talker."

"Nobody's that good," said Sofia, glancing at Uggeri, "and while you have been away—"

"Don't tells me," Yuri said warily, "the little mices are fiddling. I tell you, Contessa, there'll be no peace until there's war." He lumbered to the door, good-naturedly picking up students and hurling them out of his way as he moved.

"So, what did you learn at Montaperti?" Sofia asked. Pedro had been reconnoitering the terrain between Rasenna and Concord. Montaperti, the site of Rasenna's greatest victory, remained the most likely route Concord would take—though a new offensive was unlikely any time soon if the remaining Apprentice's hold on power was as tenuous as reported.

"Well, I can see why your grandfather picked it. If they come, the pass is still the best place to stop them. I have some ideas to run by Levi."

Sofia watched him as she listened. Pedro was no longer the fragile boy he had once been. He had a hardy strength acquired on building sites, and a solemn, kindly manner. Though he was not yet sixteen, he was growing into a man who reminded the older weavers of the tall, confident figure his father had been before the Families had beaten him down. Sofia was reminded of someone else—a painful memory—but she didn't hold it against him. It was good to have some tangible mark besides the bridge of Giovanni's time among them.

She eyed him now. "That doesn't explain the length of your absence. Your orphans have been missing you."

Pedro became suddenly coy. "I should see how they're doing." The members of the Engineers' Guild were known as Vanzetti's Orphans because of their unsociable hours.

Sofia was about to press him when Yuri's great head reappeared in the doorway. "Sofia! Donna Bombelli, she say come at once to Tower Sorrento. It's time!"

Chapter 21

When Tower Bombelli proved unequal to his growing operation, Fabbro Bombelli built a new workshop which looked exactly like a great palazzo. Rasenna's new gonfaloniere insisted it was no such thing, but it had all the characteristics: thick uncompromising walls to keep the poor at bay, an atrium where petitioners could wait and a capacious courtyard lined with olive trees in large red pots with a fountain bubbling away in the center.

Here Fabbro held court, dealing with supplicants and clients in the morning, conducting civic business in the evening. He'd never been slim, but he had grown even larger in the year since the siege was repulsed. Now he sat drumming his fingers impatiently on his dark banco, which was carved from agar-wood imported at great cost from Oltremare. Its rich, oily scent had come to be associated with debt by a great many Rasenneisi, and with evasion by others.

"If not now, when?" said Levi.

"I don't know, Podesta, but not now," the gonfaloniere said without looking up. "Too much to do."

"I took this job on the understanding that I would be listened to. All I find myself doing is answering for the condottieri."

"Perhaps if their conduct was—"

. "It's no worse than any army!" His voice echoed around the courtyard, upsetting the nesting doves, and Fabbro looked up. Levi apologized. He was used to that.

On the map before Fabbro were coins of different currencies, which he moved around cautiously, trying different combinations. They represented the various sons and cousins Fabbro had dispatched as agents to the cities of Etruria and the frontier towns of Europa. As gonfaloniere, his proper place was across the river in the Palazzo del Popolo, but Fabbro was rich and few will tell a rich man how to conduct himself, and certainly not Fabbro's debtors, a group that included all the priors of all the major Guilds.

Levi was also indebted to the gonfaloniere, for now Rasenna's Signoria paid the Hawk's Company's wages. Levi was still the scarecrow who had first visited Rasenna two years ago, but he moved a bit slower these days. He was still learning to swim in the waters of the city's politics. Like Fabbro, he carried dual responsibilities: in his case, Podesta of Rasenna and General of the Hawk's Company. He had sought neither position, and their contradictions had worn him even thinner.

"John Acuto always said Fortune's not a lady to keep waiting," said Levi. "We'll not have an opportunity so perfect. Concord's in disarray: its nobility are restive and its engineers are panicked and virtually leaderless. No Apprentices have been elected to replace the two who died here and the last remaining is just a boy. Our enemy's tower is tottering."

"Towers don't fall easy," Fabbro said. "Take that from a Rasenneisi."

"Not if they're tackled brick by brick—but a strong wind can perform prodigies. I have personal experience of that."

Bandieratori kept Rasenna free of pickpockets, but the rogue castellans of the surrounding countryside were thieves on a greater scale. These self-styled barons might be pale shadows of the men Count Scaligeri had subdued half a century ago, but their newly-invented tolls were having a chilling effect on trade. In this case, Fabbro hadn't needed persuading to use Rasenna's new army to "free" the contato, and Levi's men had done a thorough job.

"The South's waiting for Rasenna to show leadership, an honor we earned by striking the first blow."

"If we're so well regarded, why did no one accept your invitation to a summit?" Fabbro scoffed.

"Because those Ariminumese dogs refused to take part!"

"Aye, they're too busy making money. If you ask me, those *dogs* have the right idea. Waiting for Etrurians to agree is like waiting for a woman to be silent. Why should Ariminum be the only town to profit from Concord's troubles?"

"Because it won't be long before some strongman wrests the baton from this boy and Concord's legions are ordered back from Europa. Then the small gains we've made will be for nothing."

Fabbro was once known for his imperturbability, but the stresses of power had changed that. Hearing sound profits being denigrated was too much. "Rasenna's gains may seem petty to you, but they pay your wage! You've managed to keep your men in check, I'll give you that, but I doubt they'd be so docile if we didn't buy their beer every night."

Levi ignored the slight. "Another reason to take action. Give us something to do!"

Fabbro looked glumly down at the map as another voice interrupted, "*You* don't give orders to Papa!"

Levi sighed and turned around. "Good afternoon, Maddalena."

A slim girl of sixteen waltzed in the courtyard. Her scarlet satin dress was gracefully tailored to cling to the sharp dips and peaks of her figure. The long sleeves ended in dangerously swinging large green gems. She had a small, elvish nose, wide eyes that could speak across a crowded room and a wide, brazen mouth that was generally set in a pout. For an Etrurian her skin was pale—Maddalena's battleground was the gloomy underworld of wives and daughters who wielded gossip as generals used disinformation and bartered long intrigues and brief alliances—but even so, her cheeks blazed and dulled with her humor. As Maddalena passed by to sit on her father's banco, she smacked Levi's neck with her fan, and not playfully either. She pushed Fabbro's money piles aside and took up a Concordian coin.

"That's *Signorina* Bombelli to you. You take liberties, telling poor Papa what he must and mustn't do. You're a soldier and a foreigner. Rasenna is yet a republic. We shall keep our independence."

"Until it's taken. As podesta, I am obliged to advise on military matters."

"Tactical matters. If we want to capture a convoy, the Signoria will consult you. In matters of strategy, your opinion is neither desired nor competent."

Fabbro sank in his seat. "Maddalena, please—"

"No! You're too soft, Papa. These condottieri like to bully townsmen. We've let them live within our walls, given them their daily bread, and now they presume to dictate terms—"

"That's enough!" said Fabbro and turned to Levi. "I hear you Podesta, just—just let me think on it."

Levi bowed. "That's all I ask, Gonfaloniere."

"Push, Rosa!" ordered Sofia. The girl obliged as well as she could, grunting with the strain. She had gone beyond words an hour ago.

Sofia feared her strength was almost exhausted. She was a pretty thing, but her delicate features were brutally compressed with the effort. Beads of sweat stood out on her red skin and spit foamed through her clenched teeth, reminding Sofia of a racehorse coming toward the last flag. The rhythm of her huffing breath filled the stuffy little room, and Sofia found she and Donna Bombelli were falling into the same urgent rhythm, as if all three were delivering together.

Donna Bombelli held Rosa's hand and wiped her brow. She herself was heavy with child; in just two months she would be in the same position herself. Rosa's cheeks ballooned like a pipe player's, but at last the baby's head breached. Sofia quickly cleared the mucus from its mouth and nose, then ran a finger behind the baby's neck to check the cord hadn't wound around it.

"Now," Donna Bombelli whispered, "one last time, *amore*."

Sofia yelled, "Push!" and Rosa's face went the hysterical red of bellow-blown embers. After a long pause she grunted loudly with release and the rest came out easily enough. The midwives exchanged a quick look of relief and Sofia deftly turned the baby upside down and slapped its back.

"*Mmnwaaaaaaahh!*"

The newborn's first cry filled the room and echoed at every level of Sofia's being. She had heard this sound, vital like nothing else, many times this spring, and every time it shocked her. She cradled the baby, wiping its face again to study its color and breathing. It was a raw but healthy pink, and its little ribcage swelled with surprising power. When she laid a hand on its chest the baby grabbed her finger. "Strong grip, Rosa!"

"And a boy," said Donna Bombelli. "His father will be proud."

The girl's tired, ecstatic smile wilted and she rolled her head into the pillow to muffle her sobs. Sofia handed the child to Donna Bombelli. "Give him to her when she stops crying."

A waft of fresh air and light entered the room as Sofia opened the door and let herself out.

On the other side of the stairway, Polo Sorrento was sitting in the open window, looking down at the traders on the Irenicon bridge. Polo had once been an unsuccessful wool merchant, but he was known now as the farmer despite his soft hands. After the Castellans' towers were torched, he'd bought the vacant land cheap and leased it to the smallholders whose produce filled the bridge market every morning.

Tower Sorrento was just one of the pale new towers lately sprung up in Rasenna. South of the Irenicon they clustered around Tower Vanzetti; on the north side they surrounded Tower Bombelli. Thanks to Rasenna's new breed of engineers, they stood upright in a way that made the old-timers shake their heads—the old towers defied everything, including gravity, and a distinctive curve or tilt used to be prized by owners. The new towers were stouter, too, more akin to palazzi. Height regulations had been relaxed, and those who could not afford to start afresh built superfluous stories until Rasenna's skyline was almost as crowded as the narrow streets below.

Polo turned languidly to face Sofia. "Contessa."

"It's just Signorina Scaligeri now, you know that."

He nodded without interest and said flatly, "Is it done?"

"*Done?* We weren't cooking goulash, Signore. You have a strong, healthy grandson!"

Polo shook his head at such childish naïveté. "How could I have a grandson? My daughter's unmarried."

Sofia acted as if she hadn't heard. "Rosa was good in there. The boy's got a real bandieratori grip. Congratulations."

"For what, raising a whore?"

Inside, the baby's scream was a determined bawl of life; outside, there was another small shake of the head. "No, I have no grandson. Instead, I have a problem—or rather, the city does, until the orphanage is built for this deluge of bastards. I shall place it on the steps of the Palazzo del Popolo. Perhaps some nameless childless family will take it home before it starves, perhaps not. They can throw it in the Irenicon for all I care."

Sofia grabbed his collar and as he flinched away from her bloody hands she said fiercely, "Dog! Your daughter gives you a strong boy and all you think of is your name? I remember when the Sorrentos were the Morellos' crawling manservants."

"And I remember when you were still Contessa. You don't command here anymore."

Sofia slapped him, and Polo flinched so violently that his head struck the wall. Her knuckles slammed into his nose and he sank onto the window ledge, groaning. He wiped his nose, his blood now mingled with his daughter's.

Still holding his collar Sofia tipped him until he was leaning precariously out of the window. She ignored his screams and shouted into the wind, "I'm still part of the Signoria, so jumped-up dogs like you still have to listen to me." She pointed to the dust rising from the construction site beyond the river. "The orphanage will be ready soon enough. You're right: we must do something about all the new bastards. But why stop there? We ought to consider the old ones."

She tilted him still further until he could see the Sorrento family banner dangling from the tower's top story, moving lazily in the breeze. Sofia felt a hand on her shoulder. She turned around to see Donna Bombelli's alarmed face.

She winked and turned back. "Well, Farmer?" she said gruffly. "May I congratulate you on your grandson?"

"Yes!" His voice weak against the wind. "Yes! Thank you!"

Sofia pulled him up and out of the window embrasure. He attempted to stand, but lost his footing and tumbled down a few steps until he managed to stop himself. Sofia watched as he pulled himself to his feet and rearranged himself. He fixed her with a vindictive stare. "Very well, Contessa: I'll give the whore and *it* a roof and bread, but don't ask for love."

"Don't worry," Sofia said. "I don't believe in miracles anymore."

Chapter 22

Levi tipped his hat courteously to the newly married couple standing in the doorway of the church. Popular piety still ascribed the defeat of Concord's siege-engines to the Madonna; the Santa Maria della Vittoria's roofless state didn't reflect any decline in gratitude—it was just one of the buildings begun but never finished in the last two years as an excess of ambition and enthusiasm outstripped the available manpower and money. The usual damn routine of raid, burnout, grief and vengeance was a song grown old in Rasenna; these days fresh foundations and the dust of construction were everywhere.

Levi crossed Piazza Stella quickly, eager to leave behind his inconclusive meeting with the Gonfaloniere. Newly rich northsiders, tired of being shown up by the neighbors, had cleared a grand semicircular space on their side of the Irenicon a year ago. Forty years ago, Count Scaligeri designed the original Grand Piazza in a day: he drew a circle on a map one morning and the towers within that circle were knocked by evening. Such autocratic town planning was, alas, impossible in newly democratic Rasenna. So many families refused to move their towers that the new piazza assumed a jagged star shape, rather than the pleasing half-moon intended.

Fabbro's evasions frustrated Levi, though he was used to them by now. He'd seen similar sophistry in the Palazzo del Popolo. Rasenna had slipped off its Concordian shackles by a series of lucky accidents, and the magnates foolishly believed that their newfound wealth could keep them off. Condottieri traditionally preyed upon such delusions, but the Hawk's Company had linked its fortune with Rasenna, and if it perished, they perished.

As he walked between the plinths at the mouth of the bridge, Levi glanced at the empty one. Soon there would be a full guard of lions. That was another change; Rasenneisi had grown used to these small revolutions since the Twelfth Legion's destruction. After that prodigious feat, nothing could surprise them. Levi looked at the crowds crammed between the stalls; each month the bridge grew ever-narrower as the market grew busier. Even though he'd failed to bring the leaders of the southern cities together, their merchants were in a frenzy of communication, and Rasenna's smart new bridge was the hub. Since it had leapt the Irenicon, the divisions that mattered were between the major Guilds, and their quarrels of precedence were thrashed out in the Palazzo del Popolo and solved the civilized way, by the other river flowing through Rasenna: money. The division between these privileged few and those whose trades were deemed "unskilled" remained unbridged, a gulf wider than the Irenicon.

Levi froze as he felt an arm slide under his; he grabbed it while his other hand went instinctively to his purse.

"You must think I'm terrible," said Maddalena with a smile. Her cheeks were flushed; she must have run to catch up.

"I know you're terrible." He released her wrist, but did not pull his arm free.

She laughed. "Just because I won't let you browbeat poor Papa."

"'Papa' is far from poor, and he can stand up for himself—to everyone but you."

"That's true," she said, unsheathing her weapon of choice. "With me on your side"—she smacked her fan on Levi's chest for emphasis—"you could get your way all the time. You could even be elected gonfaloniere." She paused by a fruit stall and picked up a yellow-green apple. She held it out to him. "Isn't that what you want?"

"I'm sure it'll be delicious, when it's ripe."

"You find the goods *wanting* before you've tried them?" She began fanning herself. "The sample's free, you know." Maddalena was confident that the stall owner would not object—after all, her father supplied credit to every entrepreneur in town.

"Nothing's free, *amore*; you learn that when you're older. Be content. You'll get a fine trousseau when you marry."

"My husband will, and meanwhile my brothers will inherit the lion's share of the Bombelli fortunes."

"Fabbro's still breathing, you know."

"And someday he'll stop. Oh, don't look so shocked, Levi! I can't stand you thinking ill of me."

"I don't. I pity you. If you'd had the luck to be born a man, your father would have given you everything. With a mind like yours, you'd have been magnificent. Instead, you waste your talent on silly dalliances."

"Bad luck indeed, to fall for the only chaste condottieri in Etruria. The rest of your company has been at it like cottontails since they arrived. Weren't you ever that carefree?"

"Once," he admitted, "when I didn't understand the responsibility John Acuto carried. Rasenna's in danger and we can't afford to play games."

"Tell that to your warren."

Levi pulled his arm free, but he couldn't deny the charge. He had only to look at the swollen figures of every second Rasenneisi girl. They'd been locked away in their towers during the long years of hate and now they longed for love. Naturally enough his men were happy to scratch their voluptuous itches—but carousing with the townsmen's daughters was making his soldiers hated, and Levi could almost hear old John Acuto growling, "That's why God invented whores." The old bull would have forbidden any such congress on practical grounds—the price for enjoying respectable women was always too steep. But Levi was no Acuto—who was he to tell men to behave like saints, in Rasenna of all places?

Smiling again, Maddalena said, "With a good man at my side things would be different. We could rule together."

When Levi said nothing, Maddalena leaned close to whisper, "Perhaps if I were a year or two older, like the Contessa, you'd be willing to sample the goods?"

Levi snapped her fan away and cast it into the river. "Hound me all you like, but don't insult my friends."

"*Friend.*" She laughed. "Is that what they're calling it these days?"

Responding to Maddalena's innuendos only encouraged her, so Levi apologized for his temper instead.

"No harm done," she said stopping at a jewelry stall, drawing her fingers sensuously along a row of ivory fans. "I won't tell Papa if you buy me a new one."

"What a scare you gave the farmer. He thought you were going to drop him!"

"I ought to have. Cold-hearted *stronzo.*"

Sofia and Donna Bombelli were walking to the bridge from Tower Sorrento. Piazza Luna no longer looked like an accidental creation; with the new bridge and the rebuilding of the Signoria's meeting hall, the piazza had unexpectedly attained civic dignity, though increasingly new towers were encroaching on its half-moon shape. Rasenna was remaking itself. In every ward, the presiding Guild advertised their respectability and wealth by clearing space for an oversized piazza and decorating it with vulgar fountains and statues.

Only the thoroughfare to the southern gate was kept wide and unimpeded. A steady flow of well-packed carts took Rasenneisi linens and wool south and brought back the Oltremarine spices that Rasenneisi had developed such a taste for of late. Goods from Europa couldn't come via Concordian lands, so the Irenicon was choked with broad-beamed barks waiting to dock. Their clinker-built hulls, bulging with the heavy materials Rasenneisi engineers needed, sat low in the water.

"The farmer's no monster, he's just cheap—who will marry Rosa now? He's got two mouths to feed that will never bring his tower anything but shame."

"Shame! As if the Sorrentos are unique. We've been busy every day this month, and Melissa Tesoro and Lucrezia Abbrescia will pop any day now. There are a hundred girls in Rasenna praying for blood at the end of the month."

Donna Bombelli was surprised at Sofia's vehemence. "I'm just glad I have your help. I'm too old and Rasenna's too big to have just one midwife."

"I'm trying to fill Doc's shoes best I can."

"Well, thank Madonna this one went smoothly."

"She's young. It's only the old ones who have difficulties—" Sofia stopped. "That is, there's more of a chance of—"

Donna Bombelli just laughed. "Stop back-tracking. I've done it enough times to know it doesn't get easier. It wears you, sure as washing wears dye out of wool." She rubbed her hand fondly on the bump. "After this one—*basta*! If Fabbro gets so much as a twinkle in his eye I'm going to chase him from the bedchamber with the broomstick."

The noonday chime made Donna Bombelli's head turn, and Sofia noticed her proud smile. Her husband was determined to leave his mark with his ambitious *Renovatio Urbis*. The new Palazzo del Popolo might still sound strange to her, but the magnificent tower it housed was capped by a clock that counted not only the hours but the phases of the moon, the rotation of the zodiac, and the seasonal ebb of the Irenicon.

Sofia laughed. "I'll let you borrow a banner from the workshop. I never imagined Fabbro such a goat. You should be happy, most men his age—"

"Most men his age work for him," said the old matron with pride, then rolled her eyes. "You know how men are. The more Bombelli business expands, the more Fabbro's—" she giggled like a girl.

"Give yourself a break. Hire a pretty maid to scrub the floor in front of his banco in the mornings."

"Contessa!" said Donna Bombelli with mock indignation. "Such an imagination for such a delicate young lady. Besides, it wouldn't work—even with his pants around his ankles, my husband's a businessman. Bastards are a luxury only nobles can afford. The cost-benefit ratio would make Fabbro wilt before any transaction could be effected."

Sofia avoided looking at the Irenicon as they reached the bridge. The wound still wept, and enough time had passed for her to realize it would never heal. At arm's length, beyond an impassable frontier, Giovanni *survived*, but she could not reach him. He was in another country. When they pressed onto the bridge between the baying salesmen, the Rasenneisi made way for Sofia. The balustrade had been left unmended in tribute to the dead of the Morello revolt, until commerce trumped sentiment; when the foreign merchants complained, the Wool Guild offered to pay for a yearly mass instead, and the damage was now completely repaired. Memory was subject to conversion like every other coin.

Donna Bombelli noticed Sofia's downcast eyes. "Sleeping these days?"

"I'm not dreaming about that boy, the Apprentice, anymore. Sometimes I dream—it's strange—I have my back turned to a ruined city. Don't ask me how I know what it is, I just know. I know like I know that it's forbidden to look at it."

"Let me guess—you look?"

"And the second I do, it crumbles—the whole city, into dust."

"Wonder what that means . . ."

"It means I should find a better place to drink than the Lion's Fountain. You've been a rock, Donna Bombelli, but I sometimes wish the Reverend Mother was around."

They walked on in silence for a space.

"Have you told the little Sister about it?"

"Isabella has her hands full with novices and orphans. I'm not going to trouble her with my fantasies."

But Donna Bombelli wasn't listening anymore. "What *is* that girl up to now?" she said with an intake of breath.

Sofia followed her gaze to the jewelry stall. "Outmaneuvering *that* poor condottiere, by the looks of it."

"Signorina Scaligeri. Donna Bombelli," said Levi with a courteous bow, "your daughter's kindly permitted me to buy her a small gift."

Donna Bombelli eyed Maddalena knowingly. "I hope you haven't been pestering the gallant gentleman. Did you thank him?"

"No, Mama. Yes, Mama." Maddalena performed a slow curtsey to Levi. Then, with the same satirical coyness, she grimaced. "Mama! You stink like a whorehouse. How many times must I tell you: midwifery isn't a fitting occupation for a magnate's wife. We've a *name* now—let someone more suitable take over. Now that Rasenna's got real soldiers"—she tapped Levi's chest affectionately—"the *former* Contessa must needs work. What say you, Signorina Scaligeri? Mama thinks you're a natural. Now that there's no one to raid, your workshop's pointless. I bet you miss that daily fix of horror. So long as your hands are bloody by the end of day you're not particular how it gets there, are you?"

Sofia smiled. "No, I'm not particular. Insult me again and I'll prove it. Your father's this year's Gonfaloniere, but that doesn't make you royalty."

"Ah. Rasenna can only have one princess."

"That's enough," said Donna Bombelli, grabbing her daughter by the arm and marching her back to Palazzo Bombelli. "Wait till I tell your father . . ."

"Madonna, that girl." Levi whistled in relief. "I'd rather face the remaining Concordian legions than her tongue. Did she upset you?"

Sofia was breathing through her nose with a strange look on her face. Her normal olive skin paled and she suddenly rushed to the balustrade and retched into the river. She coughed and spat and rubbed her mouth before looking up. *"Merda."*

Levi patted her back. "Something you ate?"

"Didn't have breakfast."

"Don't let Maddalena get to you."

"Would it be impolitic to break her nose?"

"Sofia."

"I've just got to take it. Great." Sofia looked around defiantly until the curious turned back to their business. "I'm just not used to it, to these—"

"—bitches?" Levi offered.

"They silently hated me because I was free to do things they couldn't. Now that the Families are gone, they feel free to insult me. Come up the tower. We'll get some breakfast."

She rarely called it Tower Scaligeri, though it was hers now. She still half-expected to see Doc Bardini's watchful silhouette on the rooftop, looking over Rasenna and spinning his plans. Everything else was the same—the workshop full of fighters, boys and young men, bandieratori learning the *Art Bandiera*, training with sticks until they were ready for flags . . .

As they climbed the hill, Levi complained in his droll way about Fabbro's apathy. "He doesn't see the urgency. I've never seen him move fast unless there's some gold in it."

Sofia shared Levi's anxieties, but she let him talk. She was still feeling a little queasy, but there was more: she remembered the Doc's informal meetings, where he had corralled consensus. Growing up, she'd never questioned his reasoning—Bardini interests were Scaligeri interests, and so Rasenna's—but now she knew better. The Signoria must speak for *all* Rasenna not just one tower. Finally she interrupted. "Say this in the Palazzo del Popolo. I'll back you." But even that was too much, and she immediately regretted it. Prior agreements rendered the Signoria meaningless. It ended with two parties blocking their ears to each other's arguments, every issue decided by who could buy the most votes. It was still the violence of the strong against the weak, only a tad more civilized than bandieratori fighting it out on the rooftops.

When they reached the tower, Sofia popped into the workshop to check on her boys.

"*Porca miseria!* What's this?" she cried when she found them trading fight stories instead of paired off in tight rows and sparring. She broke the little groups up with a clap of her hands. "You'd think you don't need practice!"

It was still marvelous to Levi. His condottieri were some of Etruria's best-drilled soldiers and he knew the difficulties of coordinating *any* group of men in the twilight confusion of battle. The first time he'd first seen a troop of bandieratori was at the siege of Rasenna: a moving mass of color, swooping in syncopated moves like a great serpent writhing on the dusty battlefield. The discipline of the individual within the chaotic melee had seemed nothing short of miraculous. In the year the Hawk's Company had been stationed in Rasenna, he'd come to understand the thoroughness of bandieratori training, seeing how devoutly the basic sets were drilled, how obsessively minor infelicities were corrected, how reflexes and improvisation were honed as Sofia's boys rose to the challenge. Doc Bardini was gone, but they had her and Uggeri to show them what was possible.

Levi knew it had been a necessary discipline, that without *Art Bandiera*, Rasenna would have destroyed itself centuries ago. Rasenna's beauty was not docile or retreating, and her emblem was no accident: these people were lions. They must scream and howl, break glass and beat drums. Since the day he had agreed to become Podesta, one question had plagued him: his job was to make war on Rasenna's enemies and to keep the peace within her walls—but how long can there be peace between lions and hawks?

Sofia was looking around for Tommaso Sorrento, Rosa's brother, to tell him he'd just become an uncle.

"He's gone to the Lion's Fountain."

"Bit early..." Sofia wasn't annoyed; the boy was entitled to celebrate, and he'd probably cleared it with Uggeri—but where was Uggeri?

"With Tommaso," said one of the boys carelessly, and Sofia froze. Uggeri drinking in the middle of the day? That didn't sound right. Then she noticed that three of the older students were gone too.

She looked at Levi and swore, "Madonna!" She grabbed a flag from the rack and raced for the door. "Levi, I can't wait for you!"

"Don't! Go!"

Chapter 23

An hour past midday, when cats yawn and even lizards find shade. Red-slate-capped towers burn like lynch-mob torches. Men creep home like ghouls, keeping to the dark side of the alleys. For an hour the city is dead, streetside and topside.

The noonday sun reigned in perfect silence everywhere but the Lion's Fountain. There the hours passed unnoticed. The tavern had grown with its clientele, expanding into something more than an unsanitary hole in the wall. Bocca, the proprietor, was a beer-bellied red-nosed cur, known to everyone as the brewer. He was founder and self-elected prior of the Vintners' Guild, which had recently become important enough to merit (or wealthy enough to buy) a seat in the Palazzo del Popolo. Some things hadn't changed; the wine was still wretched and nights in the cramped piazzetta still ended with the customary brawls, only now the fights were not between Rasenneisi but bandieratori and condottieri. The debris of last night's revels—unconscious bodies, broken stools, shattered glass—hadn't yet been cleared when the next wave came for their morning glass: sweet wine for bandieratori, beer and spirits for the foreigners.

Piers Becket had a rusty Anglish look and brute manners to match. He was young and strong and had boyish blue eyes, and he would have cut an impressive figure were it not for the helmet he always wore to cover the patch where his straw-like red hair was thinning. The condottiere was popular with the old inner circle who had set out with John Acuto from the Northern Isles. Like them he was a sailor—or pirate; the distinction was academic—as well as a soldier; military men in Europa, Frankish and Anglish alike, were necessarily both. Tired of starving on small fish, Becket had joined one of the passing condottieri bands that were gravitating toward Etruria and its bull-market of warring states and there he jumped ship again, this time to join the celebrated Hawk's Company.

"I never regretted that decision until now," he said. "If I'd wanted to die of boredom in a town garrison I'd have stayed at home."

"How did we go so wrong?" a fellow drinker burbled.

The question was rhetorical, but Becket had the answer: "Levi. We should have collected our gold and moved on the moment we destroyed the Twelfth. Waiting here, doing nothing, we're not only passing up the cream of the year's Contracts, we're giving Concord time to regroup."

"Concord's done," said a bandieratoro sitting at the next table, "and, as I recall, the Twelfth were destroying *you* until *we* showed up."

"Your flags were a nice distraction, boy, I'll give them that," Becket said genially. "All that noise and color—why, it was like carnival! But don't take credit for *our* victory. That was a battle, not a street fight."

The Rasenneisi table scoffed, but it was uneasy laughter. The absence of a common enemy, and of any objective other than defense, sat uneasily with both groups, who had nothing to occupy their time now but sterile arguments over precedence.

"Congratulations, then," said a different Rasenneisi voice.

"Well, thank you," said Becket looking around. He leapt to his feet, hand on his sword. "What do you want?"

Uggeri didn't frequent the Lion's Fountain, or any other tavern, but more than one condottiere had learned not to cross this born fighter. He coolly indicated the bandieratoro beside him.

"Your new brother-in-law, Tommaso Sorrento, wants to congratulate you." The boy was slightly older, but unlike Uggeri, he was quivering with fury, skin pale, lips tight as the grip on his flag.

"What's this about?" Becket said indignantly, his blue eyes darting around the piazzetta to confirm the proportion of condottieri to bandieratori was in his favor.

It wasn't hard to follow Becket's calculations. Uggeri thumped his stick smartly on the cobblestones. "Keep swords and flags out of this. It's very simple: Rosa Sorrento is waiting. Do the right thing. Give your son a name."

"Get lost before I spank you with the flat of my sword. I came here to drink, not listen to baseless accusations from impertinent boys."

"If you're worried about money, Tower Sorrento's doing well."

"Look, Rosa's a friendly girl—if she said I showed her favor, then I can assure you I wasn't the first. I'm a condottiere. I already have a worn-out saddle. Tommaso here will have to find another rube to marry his slut of a sister." He gestured wide. "Try any of these gentlemen. Their claim's at least as good as mine."

The condottiere's speech had started with catcalls and hooting. It ended in a long silence. Uggeri alone did not look surprised. He stood to one side and gently led Tommaso forward, like a set-dancer swapping position. At Uggeri's touch, Tommaso jerked to life and threw himself roaring at Becket, who, despite Uggeri's advice, was unsheathing his sword even as he fell back in his chair. When he landed, his sword came free, but he had lost his grip. He reached for it, but Tommaso's stick came down hard on his hand with a sound like thickly piled stones crunching. Becket screamed, but Tommaso was on him, using his legs to hold down Becket's arms as he punched his face repeatedly.

Uggeri stood guard in case any condottiere attempted to aid their colleague. One of the three Becket was drinking with made a half-hearted lunge, but a swift parietal-tap dropped him. The other two leaped back, fumbling for their blades, as Uggeri vaulted over the table. He landed with a flourish, using his flag both to conceal his body and confuse their sense of space. Other condottieri tables were getting to their feet; he had to be quick. His foot sank into the first's stomach, doubling him over into the end of a waiting flag. The stick rebounded and Uggeri turned it, catching the base against the second's chin just as he was about to swing his sword.

Three down. Uggeri had always been dangerous, but under Sofia's tutelage he'd become lethal. He glared at the other tables of condottieri. Those already standing exchanged glances and sat down to their drinks; clearly this was a family matter. For a minute there was no other sound in the piazzetta than the sweet, shrill cries of swallows and the wet, heavy rhythm of Tommaso beating Becket's face to pulp.

"Uggeri! Tommaso!" Sofia shouted from a rooftop overlooking the piazzetta. "Flags *down*." Uggeri swore under his breath and watched his teacher nimbly drop from construction hand-holds and window-sills to the ground. As she landed, Levi appeared from a northern alleyway, out of breath.

Uggeri blocked Levi's way.

"Stand aside," Levi said.

"Your man took advantage of a Rasenneisi woman. This is justice."

"Justice is what your Podesta says it is. Stand aside!"

Uggeri's flag went up, but Levi had been around Sofia too long to try a sword against a bandieratoro, or let him get any distance. He pushed the arm holding the stick aside and punched Uggeri hard in the face. The other condottieri had taken courage on seeing their leader arrive and now they grabbed Uggeri's arms as he stumbled back and pinned him to a table.

"Tommaso, *basta*!" Sofia said. The bandieratoro looked up at her, his eyes dull, his face speckled with Becket's blood, and drew back his fist again. Sofia kicked his exposed ribs and he fell off. She took a mug from a table and knocked back its contents as she walked to the fountain. She filled it with water, turned and poured it on Becket's head. Enough blood washed off to reveal the landscape of swollen, broken skin.

She walked over to where the condottieri held Uggeri. "Let him go."

They looked to Levi, who nodded.

Uggeri pulled his arms free and faced Sofia.

"When are you going to get *smart*?" she hissed, "You're not just embarrassing yourself, you're embarrassing Tower Scaligeri—Doc's tower!"

He was shorter than her, but he raised his chin defiantly. Sofia slapped him with an open palm. It was more noisy than painful, but there was enough boy in Uggeri yet to be shamed by the public admonition. With a glance at Levi, she grabbed Uggeri and led him away.

As Levi took Tommaso Sorrento by the arm, he realized the boy was numbed by what he'd done. He followed Sofia, pausing only to tell his men, "Wait for me back at the fortezza. *Dio Impestato!* You've got better things to do in the middle of the day than drink!" But he knew that wasn't true. Just as he knew that an army without a war will soon invent one.

Chapter 24

"Sure you won't take some wine? A little glass?"

Donna Soderini was younger than Donna Bombelli, but she didn't look it. She dressed with the traditional simplicity of a carder's wife, and had the usual pinched, hungry look. She had been a dyer before she married, and the alum and salt steam had wrought the usual damage on her lungs. She spoke in a breathless whisper. "All I ask is that you convince your husband."

"About what?" said Fabbro, coming back into the courtyard of his palazzo.

The two women, who had been sitting at the banco, leapt up. The carder's wife had the look of a discovered thief. "Gonfaloniere!"

"Please, Donna Soderini—how many years have I known your husband? Call me Fabbro and tell me what problem's so grave that you must enlist my wife's help? I must have sinned grievously that you would set her tongue on me."

His attempt to put the woman at ease failed. Donna Bombelli squeezed her hand and answered for her, "It's simple, *amore*. Tower Soderini is having difficulty making ends meet on the money you pay."

"I pay fairly," Fabbro exclaimed. "When Pedro Vanzetti sold his wool contracts to me, he made me promise I would continue paying Guild rates. I'm a fair man so I agreed. What's your complaint?"

The woman took a deep breath before letting the rehearsed words tumble out. "You pay what was fair two years ago—even if bread still cost what it used to, now there are twice as many carders and spinners."

"And four times as much work! The rain falls on everyone."

"But it's not distributed evenly."

"That's my fault? I give work to those who deliver orders, on time and with good quality. Donna Soderini, your husband's a good man—a reliable man. But his operation is, frankly, old-fashioned, and other towers win contracts that he might have. There are rewards for ambition."

The woman's face darkened at the implication that her husband's problems were his own creation. "My husband does things the old way, to the Vanzetti standard. The new towers produce more wool, but the quality's not there. Why should we be punished for doing good work?"

Fabbro almost laughed. "You're looking at it the wrong way!"

Donna Bombelli looked at her husband with recrimination. "Fabbro, you've often said Rasenna's reputation for quality is the only thing that lets us compete with Ariminum."

"It *was* the only thing. Now we have scale." Fabbro's kindly manner was turning hostile. "So what do you want from me, Donna Soderini? More money? Then it comes from my pocket. I suppose that's fairer?"

"Oh, Fabbro! You know quite well there's no comparison. You can trade in different cities according to demand. You can store merchandise until there's a fair price. The Soderini don't have that luxury. They have to sell their work at today's price."

Fabbro was piqued at his wife's indiscretion. "I remind you, my little winter flower, who pays for your wardrobes of elegant furs, the feasts you throw, this palazzo. Would you rather Giuseppe Soderini got it instead? I have sacrificed the crutch of my old age, sending my boys to the four corners of the map to expand the Bombelli banco *and* Rasenna's fortunes. I lose shipments every month, to Tyrrhenian pirates, Anglish routiers, Frankish écorcheurs and Bavarian bandits."

"Fabbro, they're all insured with Ariminumese brokers."

"*Madonna!* Is this my wife or a communard before me? If I paid *your* husband more, Donna Soderini, how long before other towers came knocking? A week, perhaps? A day? No, the wool Guild sets prices, and sets them fairly."

"Fair to you," she said bitterly. "If we carders had a Guild we'd set a different price."

Donna Bombelli turned around to stare at her friend. The silence was broken when Fabbro took a little bell and rang it.

Donna Bombelli took a step closer to her husband and said, "Only the Signoria can create a Guild."

"But only Guild members sit in the Palazzo del Popolo," the woman protested.

"The Signoria can only function if it represents those with a stake in society," said Fabbro paternally. "Come, if every crumbling tower with nothing to lose had a say, how long before Rasenna came to ruin? They'd make decisions on a whim."

"That's what Lord Morello used to say."

Fabbro's fat cheeks glowed like an anvil. "Things are different now! We're not nobles trading on dead names. We're men who prosper by wit and graft."

"—who've cleverly arranged it so that others cannot!"

"Donna Soderini, does your husband know you're here?" said Donna Bombelli coldly.

Fabbro stood and walked around his banco. "I thought not." He took the woman's hands gently. "I suggest you attend to your children. If your husband wishes to, he can petition the Signoria."

"One carder's petition will not be heard."

"Your cynicism pains me, but that's his only option."

A servant appeared. "You rang, sir?"

"Show this *lady* out."

Donna Soderini recognized her escort as a former Morello bandieratoro. Serving the new elite was more lucrative than the workshops.

After she'd gone, Donna Bombelli shot an angry look at her husband. "She went too far with that Guild business, but how shameful to turn her away without a single soldo! That's all she wanted, a little."

"To hell with them! The Small People are suspicious of all wealth except the inherited type. They bent the knee to the Families without a word of protest, but me, because I'm not a Fraticelli throwing away my worldly goods, I'm a bloodsucker! Is it a crime to be a businessman?"

"No, but you're also Gonfaloniere. Tower Soderini isn't unique— how will it look to your fancy Ariminumese friends when they see beggars walking our streets? You used to rail against the Families arranging things in the old Signoria, yet you're deaf to the same complaint."

"Oh, don't be melodramatic. I see where Maddalena gets it."

"Ha! *Your* daughter has been giving herself airs since you were elected. Since the boys left you've spoiled her—it's bad enough how she treats the servants; you should have heard the way she spoke to Sofia Scaligeri today."

"I'm sure the Contessa gave as good as she got."

"I don't know what you have against that girl."

"You don't find it telling who she picked for capomaestro? Uggeri Galati has an interesting résumé: that cherub was one of Gaetano Morello's crew—he tried to shake me down once, have you forgotten that?"

"*Everyone* did things they're not proud of under the Families. Doc Bardini trusted him."

"And that's a recommendation these days? Not all of us go along with Doc Bardini's postmortem beatification."

"He gave his life, Fabbro! Sofia sacrificed, too. If she hadn't renounced her title you wouldn't have yours now." She saw Fabbro frown. "That's it, isn't it? You can't stand owing anyone. Funny that someone who collects debtors like you can never forgive a favor."

"I see Donna Soderini hasn't been the only one whispering in your ear."

"If Maddalena had half Sofia's character we'd be lucky. You spoiled her."

"What are children for?" Fabbro said laughing. He put his hand on her round belly. "I solemnly swear to spoil this fellow too."

"I don't know why you think it's a boy. I tell you, Fabbro, I'm too old for this."

"Nonsense. You're too old to bear them only when you're too old to beget them."

As his wife laughed, Fabbro looked in the direction Donna Soderini had left. "*Amore, why* must you patronize these people? You shouldn't give them false hope just because it pleases your vanity to play intercessionary saint."

Her smile vanished. "Better than playing God and creating enemies for our tower. *These people* are Rasenneisi, and when they quarrel, towers burn. The Gonfaloniere ought to be a shepherd to *all* towers, not just his cronies."

Fabbro was about to reply when the servant returned. "Gonfaloniere, there's been an incident at the Lion's Fountain. The Contessa's man, young Galati, he beat a soldier quite badly."

"Did he now?" Fabbro put on his chains of office while treating his wife to a telling look.

The Morellos' fire-gutted palazzo was just large enough to quarter the Hawk's Company. Where they'd repaired the damage, its walls took on a more military aspect, with merlons and arrow-loops, everything but a moat. It had acquired a new name too: the Fortezza del Falco. The Hawk's Company, unwilling to be fully domesticated, sought to keep the town it defended at a distance. And what exactly was their status? Their general was also podesta, but were they Rasenna's army or its police—and what then were the bandieratori? Until time settled these questions, they lived in dangerous ambiguity.

The stable adjoining the fortezza was theirs too. Levi stored the Company's black powder reserves in its cellar, but after half a year of stationary life, the Hawks did not need extra stables: idle soldiers gamble, and when they lost everything else, they sold their horses. It was lucky timing, because at just this hour Rasenna had need of a dungeon. It was an unpleasant place to spend the night; sleeping over a cellar of incendiary powder inspired nightmares. But all agreed that if it exploded it was better to burn those who owed a debt to society rather than innocent horses.

Sofia was annoyed that Fabbro's daughter had accompanied him to see the prisoners. As for Fabbro, he was still riled by the argument with his wife. When he saw the bloody state of the beaten condottiere he said furiously, "Signorina Scaligeri, your men *cannot* deal summary justice. We have a podesta for that. If you can't support Levi the way Doc Bardini supported Giovanni, then your workshop is a public menace." Though he knew full well Sofia had not been behind the incident, and that she was on better terms with Levi than he, an opportunity to shame the haughty Scaligeri heir was not to be missed. Like many of the magnates, he looked skeptically upon the Contessa's renunciation of her title. Scaligeri trickery was legendary.

The cells still looked like stalls, but the bars and chains were real enough. Most of the current guests were condottieri or bandieratori sleeping off last night's hangovers. Tommaso and Uggeri shared a cell. Neither spoke as their fate was debated.

"They acted without my knowledge. Your wife can attest that I was delivering the baby in question at the time."

"Don't bring my mother into it, Signorina Scaligeri," said Maddalena. "If you can't balance your responsibilities as midwife and workshop maestra, choose one. Neither is fit for a lady in my opinion—but then, I keep forgetting, you're exceptional."

Sofia ignored her. "Gonfaloniere, this problem's not going away. Unless we use them, the Hawk's Company has nothing to do but drink, gamble and whore."

"This is what I was afraid of," added Levi.

Maddalena laughed. "And don't blame my father for your men's incontinence!" She turned to Sofia. "Or your men's indiscipline. Papa's given Rasenna prosperity it never knew before and you have the gall to carp because he attends to trade instead of playing soldiers! The truth of this is too murky for me to fathom but the solution is simple: justice needs to be seen done, and swiftly. Either *this* animal is punished"—she pointed to Uggeri in his cage—"or we give Rosa Sorrento's bastard a father. Doesn't matter which."

"It matters to me," Sofia said. "Uggeri's my man to discipline."

"Very well. Since Signorina Scaligeri is exceptional, the Podesta's man must pay."

"That won't solve the wider problem," Levi said stiffly. "Gonfaloniere, John Acuto always said a soldier with no enemy is everyone's enemy."

"That's your problem!" Fabbro snapped. "My daughter's right. We only need to calm this flap. See that your man does the honorable thing. That'll send a message that Rasenneisi women are not whores to be used and forgotten. Maddalena?"

"I'll follow, Papa."

Inside his cell, Uggeri tipped his cambellotto back from his eyes and yawned, as if he'd been napping this whole time. "Can I go, then?"

"You can stay the night," Sofia shot back. "Next time you want to act for the bandieratori, you come to me first."

"Yes, maestro," he said, and nonchalantly leaned against the wall to watch her leave.

Levi followed to break the news to Becket. The decision would be unpopular, but it was logical. If the company meant to stay, the condottiere couldn't behave like routiers.

Maddalena was left looking down at the two prisoners. With a smile playing on her lips she said, "You're lucky."

"What were you hoping for?" Uggeri asked. "To see me flogged like an animal?"

"The Contessa would never countenance that. She has Levi wrapped up like a parade flag."

"She cares for her men."

"She cares for her prestige, you dumb beast. If it suited her royal prerogative she'd let you hang."

"You're jealous," Uggeri said, calmly and without malice.

Tommaso Sorrento spoke up. "Thank you, Signorina Bombelli. You did my family a great service today. I won't forget."

Maddalena took two coins from her purse and let them clink in her hands. "See that you don't." She threw the coins into the far corner of the cell. "Fetch."

Confused for a moment, Tommaso glanced at Uggeri, then he turned and crawled on all fours to the corner and sat there facing the wall.

Maddalena beckoned with her hand and said softly to Uggeri, "Come here, boy."

Uggeri shuffled to the bars. Maddalena's eyes glittered in the gloom as she watched his awkwardness. He seemed to stumble, but then he suddenly reached out and grabbed her waist through the bars. She gasped as he brutally pulled her toward him.

"I'd like to have seen you flogged," she said, her teeth showing through her smile. "That's the only way beasts learn."

"Shut up," said Uggeri, and pulled her body still closer.

Chapter 25

"Any thoughts?"

"I think it's a good thing I'm not claustrophobic."

Pedro said, "I invited you down here for a soldier's opinion on how we might use it in another siege."

Levi considered it. "Well, the last time the siege ended before it really began. We won't be so lucky twice. If the walls were breached, this might be a last line of defense. But if things got that bad . . . your thinking's taking a dark turn."

"Never hurts to consider the worst that might happen."

"Don't you have to get to the Lion's Fountain?"

"There's time," said Pedro calmly. Down here there was no shortage of time. Down here Rasenna wasn't red and yellow but blue and murky-brown. Down here the air wasn't dry and spiced; it was moisture-laden and iron-stained. The only light came from a flickering lantern, the only sound was the Irenicon's rumble through the miles of stone that surrounded them, buried them, hid them. They were alone. Pedro wound the angel's springs and waited for a heart-beat. He held the device to his ear and listened to the courageous icepick chipping at eternity.

Tik tok tik tok tik tok

He remembered his godfather's stories—strange now to think of Gonfaloniere Bombelli like that—stories that Fabbro had heard from Ebionite dye-traders from Oltremare, of miracle-working Jinni imprisoned in lamps under the sea, in deep caves; surely it was no less miraculous to confine tomorrow's endless minutes in a brass prison, to corral the fleeting moth-winged moments until they piled into millenniums, ages in which all things would come to pass and Natural Philosophers would work miracles routinely.

The annunciator hovered and moved forward, carrying the sway-ing lantern down the dark tunnel, a scout to ensure no gaping holes lay ahead, until it was stopped by the broken engine jamming the tunnel. Pedro wriggled through the confined space until he reached it. The metal was cold and weeping, and the angel cast its light irreg-ularly. He rested his head against the engine and left it there, like a rider letting a horse become accustomed to the presence of its master, then he grabbed hold of the end of the digger and pushed.

After the siege, Pedro had salvaged dozens of these abandoned diggers, the mechanized screws that made Concordian siege-craft legendary. Most were beyond repair, but he had rescued enough for Rasenna's engineers to become familiar with their principle and to duplicate them, at least as far as they had the materials.

"Put your back into it!" shouted Levi, his voice weirdly distorted by competing echoes.

"No," Pedro said to himself, then louder, "It's good and stuck, Levi. The bit's fixed deep in the stone. I'll get the lads down to dig arouuaahh—"

Without warning the ground shifted, and great clumps fell away into the darkness. Pedro reacted instinctively, scrambling back. The digger's back end hung precariously out over the new chasm, but it didn't fall.

Levi grabbed Pedro in case the rest of the floor followed, but after a moment the strange creaks and rumblings subsided.

"All right?"

"I'll let you know when my heart stops hammering."

A wet wave of chilled air rushed up from below.

"How deep do you think it goes?" Levi threw a pebble and waited for the splash. And waited.

"There's a better way to find out." Pedro said, inserting silk plugs in his ear. He pointed the Whistler into the darkness and Levi covered his ears.

BeeeeEE beeeeEE.

Pedro had adapted the Whistler to work in other media than liquid; the strength of the beep's echo revealed distance, but also what type of surface it had struck: rock, soil, ice, water and so on.

"Well?" said Levi with forced casualness. Though he considered himself far more cosmopolitan than most Etrurians, he still thought of Natural Philosophy as a Concordian tool.

Pedro was less superstitious. He might not have a Guild Hall education, but he had the equivalent. Like the Cadets, he'd been raised around machines—in his case, his father's looms—and he had learned the craft from a Concordian engineer with an impressive lineage: Giovanni's grandfather was the *Stupor Mundi* himself, Girolamo Bernoulli (though that was a secret that Pedro knew he must hide deeper than these tunnels).

"These numbers make no sense. This cavern's about fifty braccia deep, but if I didn't know better I'd say that's water at the bottom—*flowing* water." He stared pointlessly into the darkness.

"You mean that rumble isn't the Irenicon? So what is it?"

He looked up to see Pedro smile in flickering light. "Let's find out."

The stars were coming out when they finally emerged from the tunnels and they might have been even longer if Levi hadn't remembered

Pedro's appointment. By the time they got to Piazzetta Fontana, it was thronged with revelers. The blood from this morning's fracas was washed away with vinegar, then forgotten with wine.

He looked around for other engineers in the Lion's Fountain, and when he found none he was both gladdened and disappointed. On the one hand, his men had work to do; on the other, he wanted his engineers to be seen as part of Rasenna. Weird theories about Giovanni's death showed the Rasenneisi suspicion of engineers hadn't yet been exorcised; the very idea of a Rasenneisi Engineers' Guild still made many nervous. That was why Pedro had agreed when they asked him to adjudicate the duel of *li doi Ziganti*.

The crowd made way and watched suspiciously as he tested the table's balance with a spirit level and great ceremony. He measured its dimensions, and made his compass do an elaborate dance across the breadth. Then he put away his instruments, took a piece of chalk from behind his ear and drew a line between the contestants, and an X on either side. The two giants sat opposite each other, backed by their partisans.

Pedro pulled up a stool and stood on it to announce, "As Chief Engineer, I declare this table to be of sound mind and body. Gonfaloniere Bombelli, will you do the honors?"

Fabbro bowed. "All yours, my boy."

Pedro did not demure, but leapt suddenly onto the table and called for a flag. One came flying and he caught it with a graceful flourish—which surprised those condottieri who didn't know Pedro was a flagmaker's son.

"I declare this contest of strength between Jacques the Hammer and Yuri the—"

"Rolling Pin!" Sofia shouted.

"—and Yuri the Rolling Pin ready to commence. Signori, on your marks." The giants slammed their elbows onto their respective Xs.

The condottieri had great confidence in Yuri; the company's cook had bested champions the length and breadth of Etruria. Both men towered over the assembly—Yuri, perhaps, by a few inches more, but his opponent made up for it in breadth. Both men were stripped to the waist, though the bandieratori champion kept on his long-eared leather cap. Jacques the Hammer was an immigrant not long settled in the Smiths' Quarter. He was built like a menhir, concave at both sides. He wore loose, coarse-threaded britches, a soot-gray vest, and a thin leather apron that looked more suitable for a smaller man. His neck thrust forward from between the unbroken curve of his shoulders.

Pedro waved his flag—left, right, then a nice overhead slice—and shouted "Avanti!" as he leapt from the table. Immediately supporters crowded around, baying like hounds.

Yuri's technique was straightforward: push. He strained and turned red, and Jacques' arm tilted slowly to seventy degrees. The blacksmith's strategy of letting Yuri make an all-out effort was risky, the touts agreed. A little bit further and Jacques would find himself at the point of no return. The condottieri pounded the tables rhythmically, shouting, "Hawks! Hawks! Hawks!"

"Hammer! Hammer! Hammer!" the Rasenneisi countered.

"Come on, Yuri!" Levi hollered, "I've got a month's pay riding on you!"

The men were eyeball to eyeball now, and both had stopped breathing. Two towers. Two mountains. Sweat streamed into Jacques' eyes, and he blinked to clear them. His arms weren't defined like Yuri's; they were pillars of knotted muscle and flesh with the mindless endurance of iron. A grin began to form on Yuri's face when, suddenly, a gasp escaped him and he shifted in his seat. His forearm and bottom lip quaked in tandem. He strained. His arm began to retrace its journey, steadily, inexorably, over the halfway point, then downward.

"Ham—mer! Ham—mer! Ham—mer!"

Jacques' forge-scorched face was tranquil. The chant grew louder, more insistent, as the crowd watched Yuri's steadily descending arm, as inevitable as a falling tower. His face rippled with agony. "Aaahieeeeeee!"

Slam!

His fist hit the table and a great cheer went up. Among the crowd that rushed to congratulate the winner was Fabbro. "Well done, Jacques! Been meaning to call in for weeks. How goes it?"

Ignoring the dozens of hands slapping his great back, the blacksmith finished his beer in one long drink, wiped his mouth, and said calmly, "Well. Come tomorrow."

Fabbro offered to buy him another, but Jacques refused. Fabbro was still wondering why later that evening as his godson excitedly related his adventures in the tunnels.

"—then Levi lowered me into the pit—"

"You ought to be more careful, Pedro," said Maddalena. Tower Bombelli and Tower Vanzetti had always been close, and Maddalena still took a big-sisterly attitude to Pedro. She couldn't dominate her real brothers; they were much older. "Let Levi take the risks. That's what Papa pays him for."

Levi raised his drink sarcastically. "Too kind, Signorina."

"Well, what could you see?" Fabbro asked.

"Not much, though I inserted glow-globes at regular intervals. I passed several caverns hollowed out of the tufa, some clearly the work of erosion but others, roughly square in shape, well, they looked manmade."

"How old?" Fabbro asked.

"Etruscan if I had to guess—but that's still not the strangest thing. We didn't have enough rope to go all the way down, so I dropped my last globe. It fell, there was a splash, and then it vanished. A river, Fabbro! There's a second river, flowing *beneath* Rasenna. All this time!"

"How fascinating," Maddalena interrupted. "Pedro, I know that southsiders do things differently, but can't you wait till tomorrow to discuss sanitation?"

The way Pedro reddened reminded Fabbro that Rasenna's Chief Engineer was still a boy. It was easy to forget. Though adolescence lingered on his face, there was hardness too. Life had tested Pedro early.

"Hush, Maddalena," Fabbro scolded. "Since when are you so prudish? The *cloaca* is an endeavor every bit as noble as Giovanni's bridge, and just as necessary."

Giovanni was still alive when Rasenna's boom had begun, and he had warned the Signoria it could be make or break for them. Concord had experienced a similar expansion in the last two decades, and if her antique sewer system, the old Etruscan *cloaca maxima*, had not been still functional, disease would have destroyed the city. The siege of Rasenna had proved doubly serendipitous in this case, for the Concordians' discarded diggers made extensive rapid digging possible.

Few in the Signoria saw the urgency and clamored instead for more public buildings, wasteful vanity projects, needless improvements. Pedro was continually frustrated by losing his newly trained engineers to lucrative private commissions. Their short-sightedness amazed him. Since Giovanni's death, Rasenna's growth-rate had quadrupled: nine months after each new influx—the Hawk's Company, the laborers drawn by work—a wave of babies followed. Children, like men, produce mountains of dung and torrents of piss. The Irenicon could take only so much before it became a festering source of disease.

"Well, let's all turn troglodyte, then!" Maddalena snapped and turned to pester Levi.

After the Gonfaloniere had escorted his daughter home, the traditional grumbling began. Where once the Small People had complained about the Families' exploitation, now they complained about those who sat in the Palazzo del Popolo and kept them out. It was curious: the wider the enfranchisement, the more emboldened the Signoria was to gather taxes. More curious still, the Small People, those without votes, did not complain about the Signoria's greed but that they could not feed at the trough.

Levi and Sofia did not partake in the griping. They drank and listened to Yuri's gruff voice beating an Etrurian dirge into some

Slavic shape in which he found a pleasing melody. He was in fine spirits despite his defeat.

"A night in the stables will do Uggeri good," Levi said.

Sofia was still irked by Fabbro's high-handedness, and naturally defensive of her men. "There's nothing wrong with that boy but the want of a war."

"You look ready to do battle yourself," Levi remarked.

Sofia threw him a streak of silver, which he tried to catch but missed. The coin floated to the bottom of his tankard. When he saw it was Ariminumese, Levi sighed.

"I got that on the bridge today. We're trading with those dogs!"

Levi knew what was coming. "We're going to need them."

"They *sold* John Acuto. They *stood by* as Concord attacked us. What's the point of keeping your company in beer if we—"

"I hate Ariminum as much as you, but do you really want to start a second war when we still have the Concordians to worry about? This town's not big enough to—"

"We're a city now, Podesta," Pedro interrupted. He sat down beside them, pleasantly tipsy.

Sofia relaxed and eyed Levi humorously. Pedro didn't drink often, but when he did he talked like his father. "What's the difference?"

"In a town you know your murderer's name."

"When did you get so cynical?" Levi asked.

"When the Palazzo della Signoria was renamed the Palazzo del Popolo," said Pedro without hesitation. "A sop to the Small People."

"The Families used to ignore them," Sofia said. "Surely that was worse?"

"Was it? Farmers think of spring lambs often, but their thoughts are not kind. They change the name and hope the Small People are too stupid to notice that a body that can't agree on *anything* agrees that every new tax proposed is vital. And if one's repealed, they execute a flanking move and tax the food we eat and wine we drink. The Morello used only to break our legs. At least they left our hearts intact."

"Listen to the communard," Sofia laughed.

Levi finished his drink and said, "Long live whoever wins."

Chapter 26

Isabella woke before the other girls. Her chamber faced east, and the rising sun lifted her gently from sleep. She preferred it so: the night she had woken suddenly to fire was still a scorching memory. While Rasenna slept for a few more hours, she performed her exercises with the gravity of someone far older than thirteen. The fire had taken much, but it gave Isabella the strength to hold the convent together after the Reverend Mother and Sister Lucia were slain; her duty, as theirs had been, was to serve Time, and to divert those who would divert it.

Sofia had become her teacher of Water Style. She took Isabella to the bridge to observe the Irenicon, telling her there was a still-greater river all around, carrying them all into the next hour, the next year and finally, into infinity, and that if she became *aware* of it, she could use it. Like Sofia, Isabella had been raised in a bandieratori tower, so the physical part came easy. Self-control took longer; she only attained it by burying certain memories.

When she felt ready she went to the chapel carrying a jug of water and a glass. She sat at the low table looking up at the depiction of the Virgin and made the Sign of the Sword. She filled the glass with a trembling hand. The water fluttered in the multicolored light of the recently repaired stained-glass window.

. Sofia had warned Isabella that evasion would allow her to progress only so far. The way to get beyond memories, however painful, was to dive *into* them fearlessly. They were waiting: the fear that she would burn with her brothers, her mother and father, and shame that her first thought was saving herself. It took many attempts to pass through the firestorm under the cool surface, but now it was less painful than slowly drifting a finger over a flame.

Below the fire, the water grew precariously cold and viscous, and the pain changed pitch. The deeper she swam, the deeper it cut, until fingers and toes, hands and feet, arms and legs were numb. She had to push on and ignore the ice stabbing her heart until at last she broke through. In the dark infinity below the fire and ice waited the greatest horror: the Darkness. She knew instinctively she must defeat it now, or perish. Its limbs were writhing maggot heads, their touch was intimate, cold and insatiable. Its sustenance was inexhaustible: the hate of the world, the infinity of fear that even the weakest heart contains. Its tight grip pulled her in as she struggled.

Alone, Isabella would certainly have perished, but Sofia had dredged her up and ordered gruffly: "Practice." That was Sofia's way. She was a fighter, and so fought to the point of exhaustion. That came quickly, against Sofia; the Reverend Mother's speed was nothing compared to what Sofia had achieved. Before she landed, Sofia was waiting; before she kicked, Sofia had sidestepped and countered, not just one step ahead but many. Isabella dimly understood from her glimpse of the Darkness the great cost Sofia had paid for that speed, and worked harder.

Day by day she was getting stronger.

Then, a year to the day after the siege, Sofia abandoned her. Was it part of her training? Perhaps this next step must be taken alone, like birth or death—but no, that wasn't it. When Isabella caught Sofia's eye on the bridge, she would turn away. When Isabella visited Tower Scaligeri, Sofia made excuses—she was busy in the workshop, in the Signoria, assisting the midwife. *Something* had changed; something Sofia had not expected. She needed help that Isabella was incapable of providing.

Isabella felt the warmth light on her skin and looked up at the window. "Madonna," she whispered, "you suffered and were not afraid. Give me courage."

She closed her eyes. Alone or not, she must overcome the Darkness: for Rasenna's sake, and Sofia's.

Chapter 27

The Gospel According to St. Barabbas

48   Now King Herod saw rivals to his throne everywhere. He murdered the wives of men; he murdered his own. He murdered the sons of men; he murdered his own; and a great many priests besides.

49   His deeds impressed the Etruscans but disgusted his subjects. The Jews alone amongst the peoples in the Empire refused to worship Etruscan gods. Herod shared neither the religion nor scruples of his subjects. His blood was a barbaric blend and thus he reasoned as barbarians do, that a mighty Empire must have mighty gods.

50   Now at this time there was an upright priest in Jerusalem, a Galilean from the House of David. His name was Zacharias. Of all the priests who served in the Temple, only he condemned Herod's idolatry.

51   But his fellow priests railed at him and said, Zacharias, thou
      art a fool. And this king, though tyrant and pagan, is also a
      fool. Canst thou not see we use him to profit our Nation? Hast
      thou not heard us persuade him that he can buy the Lord's
      favor? Dost thou not know he is restoring the Temple to the
      glory it enjoyed in the reign of Solomon?

52   But Zacharias said, It is thee who are foolish. This Herod is no
      Solomon; he is Nimrod reborn. Dost thou not see his bloody
      hands? Dost thou not know that if the restorers of the Temple
      are corrupt the Temple must be corrupted also? Hast thou
      forgotten the fate of Temples that displease the Lord?

Chapter 28

"Bombelli, you scoundrel! Catch!"

Fabbro deftly caught the purse. "Well?" the street seller said.

"I'm hungover!" Fabbro protested.

"Don't give me that. No amount of drink can make Fabbro Bombelli miscount."

He bounced it in his hands. "Thirty-two?"

"Bravo! You've still got it."

Fabbro grinned proudly and threw back the purse. "Years over a scale, my friend."

"So, where've you been?"

"Book keeping keeps me locked away. Speaking of which, I should get back . . ."

They chatted for a while before Fabbro left, greeting other merchants as he went. The market never failed to lift a black mood; he missed its gladiatorial banter. By the time he reached Piazza Stella he was jolly again. He stopped beside the third lion and looked up at the empty plinth. Instead of heading back to his palazzo, he abruptly turned right and walked along the Irenicon's northern bank.

The northeast of town was traditionally the tanners' quarter. It was underpopulated even before the Wave struck; now it was a jumble of squat houses and sudden towers, apparently built overnight with bricks of coal. A dark cloud hung low over these structures and the river was gauzed in smoke. Fabbro covered his mouth using his hood as a scarf, engineer-fashion. Other fire-working trades had been drawn to the area to the point where it had become a kingdom itself; its cantankerous denizens called it Tartarus. Rasenna once had small need of blacksmiths—masons for towers and weavers for flags answered all the requirements of defense and offense—but of late it had become a pilgrimage destination for metal-workers, just as Concord had twenty years ago. Their ranks swelled further when the Hawk's Company arrived; armorers and sword-makers follow armies as devotedly as whores. These noisy and noisome trades had been herded together so the filth they produced didn't pass through town. The last few empty spaces were filled with the factories of the engineers.

From a distance the factories were a sight to make Rasenneisi blood run cold; closer up, it was clear that the towers were only chimneys billowing steam. Driving northern winds carried the steam and smoke of the tanners and smiths over the city walls, where the whir of mills and the clatter and putter of paddle-powered contraptions competed with the roaring Irenicon. Before the river was permitted to leave town, it was filtered through a mechanical gauntlet—several rows of variously sized paddles, coupled with belts and chains. To Fabbro this combined assault on the senses was beautiful: Rasenna was growing, and every inch was a victory for common sense, a defeat for the turbulent. He entered the foundry yard whistling.

Jacques' was covered in the same black grime as all the other foundries, but everyone knew his was the best in Tartarus. Normally it was full of assistants toiling in its inconsistent gloom, illumined by the ash-bitter glare of cinders and heavy, heaving bellows burping the slumbering ovens awake. Today it was empty, but for a small boy leaning at a wooden desk and tapping a set of greaves with a chasing hammer. Standing silently behind the boy was Jacques. The old waxy sheets on the windows were pulled back to let the morning light visit the workshop's hidden nooks. Red earth was swept up, tongs and chisels stored away. The forge-maestro's work today required only his hands and the world's silence.

Despite its thickness, Jacques' neck was mobile, and he turned and tilted his head as he examined the boy's work. Fabbro had never seen Jacques without his long-eared leather cap; he assumed it was a protective guard against sparks. His permanent squint was intimidating until one got used to it—the sparks were the reason for that, too.

"Jacques! Congratulations again on your victory. Yuri took it well." As they shook hands Fabbro noticed Jacques' hands again: they were crossed and crossed again with searing scars. They must have been from when he was a journeyman—all Tartarus knew that Jacques the Hammer could handle metal until it glowed.

Jacques ignored the compliment. "Come," he said, and Fabbro followed, wondering whose son the boy was. Strange to think he knew so little about someone he'd trusted with so much money. When Jacques appeared outside Rasenna's walls he'd asked who was king here, and when told that Rasenna had none, he had asked for sanctuary, volunteering only that he was a skilled artisan. Of course, he was a Frank, but did he hail from the Isles or the mainland? His Etrurian might be only functional, but his obvious talent soon won respect. That and his physical stature quickly made him a leader, of sorts: Gonfaloniere of Tartarus, if such a thing could be imagined. Jacques had no ambitions, at least as far as Fabbro knew, other than to be left alone. He liked the big fellow, but theirs was a 50 percent friendship, that awkward bluff relationship that exists between contractor and contracted. When business was done, he would know the truth.

Jacques led him to a freshly swept corner bathed in the strong northern light. On a low turntable stood a precariously leaning pillar. It was taller than a man, taller even than Jacques, and covered with a sheet layered with wax cracked like distressed stone.

"Who hunted your assistants away?"

"Later, when I'm pouring metal, I'll need men," said Jacques, looking at Fabbro penetratingly with dark pupils that shone through the thick slivers of flesh.

"Nonsense," Fabbro chuckled. "A good salesman knows the value of suspense. I'll bet every smith in Tartarus is dying to see what's under that sheet."

"Craftsmen are interested in craft."

Fabbro smiled knowingly. "As you like it, Maestro. Well, let me look at it."

Jacques grunted and removed the sheet. He did it slowly, revealing first the smooth earthen clay fashioned into a paw, then a curling tail, a slender torso and finally the snarling jaw. The wooden armature that supported it broke the clay's surface unceremoniously at various points—the neck, the back—but it was easy to ignore this and imagine the final bronze in place on the empty plinth.

Fabbro was gleeful. "This fellow will put his brothers to shame!"

"They are decent sculptures," Jacques demurred, "in the old style."

Fabbro laughed indulgently. "Please Maestro, no false modesty. You know very well this will tear flags all over Rasenna."

Jacques shrugged and gently spun the massive turntable. He doused the lion with a water dispenser as it rotated. Fabbro was right: theatricality *was* part of Jacques' art. Of course keeping the clay from drying was necessary, but a wet surface revealed the subtle modeling nearly as well as would the final polished patina.

Fabbro stalked around, pulling his beard and exclaiming, "Bravo!" in a reverent whisper.

While the other three lions coldly gazed forward, this one would glower over passersby. Its head twisted violently away from a body that trembled with tension and energy. Its scowl pulled ripples of flesh through its muzzle. Fabbro might be no connoisseur but he knew it was not merely the naturalistic rendering but the *variety* of description that made the sweet new style such a break with the past.

He marveled that the old artisans had been blind to these subtleties of contrast: the beast's tense, compacted haunches and bristles of its mane were formed so the former appeared tough as stone, the latter soft as wool.

"Madonna, it's a wonder!" he exclaimed at last. "So what's next?"

"Next I make a shell in which the caterpillar may sleep a while. After the clay dries I'll crack the mold apart and, into the space where the lion *isn't*, pour wax. But the wax is only a semblance of the butterfly; another little death is necessary. I correct the wax's imperfections and, by a similar process, make a coffin more substantial. Pouring the metal's the most difficult part."

Fabbro had never heard Jacques talk so freely. "Tell me when you're doing it. I'll have Sister Isabella say a mass."

Jacques indicated the boy hammering away. "Even if it goes perfectly, it will need a lot of chasing, sanding and polishing." He looked down calmly. "Can you pay the balance?"

Fabbro almost jumped. "You can't have got through the first third!"

"As you say, my studio is empty. I turn down work to give this commission my full attention."

"If it were *my* money, Jacques, there'd be no problem. I *spend*; ask anyone, that's what I do. This commission, however, comes officially from the Wool Guild, a close-fisted bunch who wouldn't thank me if I gave their gold away with nothing to show for it. These men, they know nothing of *art*. They're used to dealing with low sorts—dyers, carders, pullers—and they assume all craftsmen are alike."

"We had Guilds in Francia too. They got rich selling craftsmen's work and taxed them for the privilege."

"My dear fellow, you almost sound like a communard."

"Bombelli, don't complicate things. You're Prior of the Wool Guild."

"That I am." Fabbro laughed. To cover his embarrassment he looked up at the lion critically. "I think I'd prefer if he didn't look quite so *fearsome*. Did I ask for that expression? No, I don't think I did. Who wants to be snarled at on their way to work? We've wives for that. Why not give him a nice smile, regal, pacific? What say you?"

Jacques was watching the boy hammering. He turned slowly back. "I say you paid me fair for my work, but there's not enough gold in Ariminum to tell me how to do it."

"My apologies," Fabbro said quickly, "of course you know what you're doing. I didn't mean to imply—the last two-thirds? Yes, I'm sure I can persuade them."

"Good."

There was an awkwardness now that Fabbro sought to dispel. "What will become of the clay after casting?"

"When I break the first mold, it's destroyed."

"Seems a waste," he tutted.

Jacques inclined his head to one side and then the other, weighing the notion. "Something must die for another to live. Destruction's easy as criticism." And before Fabbro's eyes, he gouged a great handful of the clay from the lion's belly. "See? The hard part's the creation."

He deftly filled the hole with new clay and pressed his palm flat while kneading with his thumb. In a few moments it was as good as new. "But even that's easy if you destroy the right thing."

"Quite," said Fabbro, the implication plain. He bowed. "You'll get the rest today. *Bon lavoro!*" He walked home quickly, eager now to escape the din of Tartarus. The grind of hammers on anvils, the gush and wail of fire, the howl of metal being tortured into uncongenial shapes was an infernal counterpart to the pure note of the baptistery bells nearby.

Isabella poured the water and droned until the cares of the day passed away, as Sofia had taught her. She dived through fire, through ice, into the depths. Darkness came for her and she did—

Nothing. She did not swim nor fight nor even scream as the leather slickness enveloped her. Its dead embrace was worse than drowning. She swallowed *fear* and it was bitter. In the Darkness a blood-caked figure wearing a golden shroud waved its broken limbs. "*Come here, amore*," it mumbled through teeth smashed to slivers.

Then, at the moment the Darkness became total, a voice pure as crystal rang out.

Be not afraid.

These were not vague words of comfort but a command. The fear Isabella felt so overwhelmingly a moment ago was gone and into the vacuum rushed strength. She shrugged off the tentacles with ease and the Dark Ancient shivered a retreat as dawn came plunging from a distant height. The light, pure white to begin, grew brighter yet, though it was nothing to the purity of the voice.

Isabella returned with a gasp to find everything in the chapel exactly as before.

Except the water. As soon as she noticed it, she felt its weight. The water had *floated* free of the glass and hung in swollen drops conjoining and parting in the light's myriad colors. She screamed with effort and the drops fell.

When she had recovered, she limped to the baptistery and studied the murals there, especially focusing on the Massacre of the Innocents—the weeping mothers, the tiny limbs washing through the street on a river of blood. The Virgin had been meek, obedient and forgiving, until the Darkness took Her child—then She sought the consolation of revenge. Perhaps that's why Rasenna had such special devotion to Her.

The mystery now was unraveled: why Lucia and the Reverend Mother had gone so calmly to their deaths; why all three Apprentices had descended on Rasenna during the siege. They all knew something that Sofia herself had only recently realized, the secret to which Isabella now was also privy: Sofia was chosen to be the Lord's Handmaid. The uncharacteristic fear Isabella had sensed in Sofia could mean only one thing: she had accepted the terrible proposition.

Chapter 29

The Gospel According to St. Barabbas

14　Now when Herod had searched all the land from Dan to Beer Sheva for rivals, he commanded his astrologers to search amongst the stars. The wise men from Babylon duly searched and found just what the tyrant had feared.

15　And Herod was exceeding wroth. I have overlooked no tower or palace. Where is this new king born? And the wise men mocked him, Thou hast overlooked the town of David.

16　So Herod sent forth and ordered all the newborns of Bethlehem slain, and though the lamentation of the other mothers was great, there was one who was not content with lamentation. She was a tumultuous Galilean and Her name was Mary of the House of David. She went up to the Temple and beseeched Her father, This cursed king hath slain my child and husband. Wherefore should he live to beget more children? Wherefore should his child live while mine is slain?

17 Zacharias was sore grieved by these words and he enjoined his fellow priests to lead the people into the streets. They answered, Alas, Zacharias, we cannot give your daughter justice. Herod is the Etruscans' man. He hath restored the Temple for the glory of the Lord and our Nation. Wherefore should we rebel against him? For the sake of a few babes? The world has no shortage of those. And furthermore your daughter has sinned grievously by threatening the Lord's anointed.

18 And Zacharias knew Etruscan silver had corrupted them and warned Mary to flee before Herod's agents found Her.

Chapter 30

Like a general, Fabbro oversaw all the preparations, dictating what dishes the servants cooked, in what order, and even how. He made his wife serve the food and Maddalena pour the wine. Everything must be perfect. The idea had struck him as he returned from Tartarus that morning and seen the sun rising behind the towers on the end of town. The Irenicon, striving upward against the land's slope, reflected the light so that the riverbank and bridge looked gilded.

The Mercanzia, effectively a Guild of priors, was another of Rasenna's unplanned births. The night before every Signoria meeting, the Wool Guild met informally at Bombelli's. Their ostensible purpose was to discuss trade, exchange information and to settle debts and disputes. In reality, discussion focused on Signoria tactics. Fabbro might have a salesman's talent for persuasion, but the rest of the Wool Guild were poor orators. Indeed, the tiresome business of making speeches and proposing motions, seconding them and voting, struck them as highly inefficient. Obviously reason and rhetoric were inimical: a talented speaker could persuade the mob to do anything. A little block-voting made everything go quicker.

The priors of the other Guilds soon worked out they needed the Wool Guild's vote to get anything done. The week before every Signoria meeting, Fabbro's palazzo was besieged with visitors, and the Mercanzia came into existence to bring order to what was already happening. It was founded on the sensible premise that if fabrics, spices and precious stones could be traded, so could votes.

"Wait till you see the lion, my friends." Fabbro kissed his fingers passionately. "A marvel!" He had taken every care to make sure his guests were spoiled, but still they looked somewhat discomfited.

"It will raise Rasenna's reputation to new heights," said the brewer, with a strained smile. All the credit for the statue would go to the Wool Guild—did Fabbro seriously expect the other priors to share his pleasure? The brewer's only act of patronage was to have a mass said on the Vintners' Guild's saint-day, and he always haggled with the nuns over the price.

Maddalena filled the brewer's cup. "Do you enjoy art, Signore Bocca?"

"I enjoy all things of beauty, Signorina," he responded, and Maddalena giggled dutifully and cleared away the empty glasses. She left the courtyard with a smile and full tray, which, once inside the kitchen, she thrust at a waiting servant. "*Dio*, why must *I* play serving-wench when these sluts hide here?"

"Nothing makes old men as pliable as the attention of a young lady with prospects."

"Bah. Why's Cook cooking *lampra dotto*? That's peasant food."

Donna Bombelli looked up from the tray of cold meats she was preparing. "Because your father didn't get rich by being stupid. A banquet's like a battle—without clear goals it's doomed to failure. Some feasts are intended to overawe. Tonight, we aim for intimacy. An army of servants would alienate these men. Fabbro wants them to return to their wives talking about how the Bombelli are living beyond their means."

Maddalena raised her eyes. "How very subtle. And you're dying to tell me why."

"It's simple," Donna Bombelli said, walking out with the tray. "Men are never so generous as when they are being condescending."

The conversation had moved on to the price of barrels. The brewer was complaining about dealing with coopers: "It's not the wood, but the price of metal. Of course Concord's always hogged demand, but now I can't get iron for love or money. If you ask me, that's why Concord's renewed its Europan offensive. It pleases our vanity to think they're scared of us but really, what does Etruria offer? A country of feuding city-states with no resources other than blood, bile and water." He shook his head at the world's folly. "Where's that delightful daughter of yours, Donna Bombelli? Not bedtime already?"

"Certainly not! I can go all night," Maddalena said as she returned with more bottles.

Fabbro waited for the ribald laughter to subside before steering the conversation toward his goal. "My friends, a notion struck me the other day that I must tell you about. Jacques will soon cast the lion—but should its pelt not be gold?"

"You mean to gild the bronze?"

"I mean to cast the beast in gold! Let it advertise our wealth as well as our taste—'Rasenna's Golden Lion'—what would the Ariminumese think of that?"

Skeptical, even worried looks were exchanged.

"The Wool Guild can afford *that*?" the farmer asked.

Fabbro looked suddenly mournful. "Alas, no. I've arranged a loan from one of my Ariminumese partners to pay for the bronze. As you can imagine, no one in the Wool Guild's happy about it. I don't need to tell any of you that my colleagues aren't known for their generosity. If I had the courage to propose this finishing touch, I'd be deposed."

"Or exiled," the farmer said.

There was relieved laughter around the room and the brewer swallowed a large mouthful of wine. "But it *would* be lovely," he said, and held up his glass to Maddalena. After glancing around to confirm the other priors were thinking along the same lines, he said, "What if we shared the cost? The gold—how much would it be, Fabbro? Any idea?"

Fabbro played with the plumes of his beard vaguely. "Oh, Madonna. I ought to have looked into that before I mentioned it—I really haven't the faintest. Gold's what, these days? A hundred per troy ounce?"

"Ninety," the farmer said.

"Really? And if casting requires, say, two thousand ounces, it'll cost, oh, one hundred and eighty thousand. The Wool Guild would still pay a third—I must insist on that—and the remainder divided between you six—why, that's just twenty thousand each, isn't it."

The brewer's face paled at the figure, then blushed as the other priors directed looks of recrimination at his big mouth. Fabbro affected not to notice. "It's too expensive, certainly, but *imagine* the prestige it would bring Rasenna. We think nothing of investing in new machines, do we? And prestige is no abstract thing"—he gestured grandly in the air—"for the louder Rasenna's name rings out, the more business comes to the bridge. All Rasenna would profit, but we would profit most."

"But, *Madonna!*—twenty thousand!" exclaimed the prior of the Silk Guild, a dwarfish fellow of Veian origin.

"It just seems so intangible," the brewer said sheepishly, desperately trying to think of some way out. "Art . . ." The word dangled unpleasantly from his lips.

"Nonsense!" Maddalena interjected. "This is *patronage*—a kingly act. Would you not be kings?"

"My daughter would willingly be a princess." Fabbro laughed, then became sternly serious. "No, Maddalena, not one of these good men wishes to be more or less than a citizen of Rasenna. That is privilege enough for us all."

The brewer stood suddenly, swaying doubtfully for a moment. "You've yet to steer us wrong, Fabbro. Let no one accuse us of short-sightedness. But let's also remember that this will benefit *all*

Rasenneisi, great and small. The Small People ought to bear some small share of this burden. The Signoria might impose an excise on some essential—"

"Wine?" said the farmer dryly.

"Salt!" said the brewer with sudden inspiration, "as the Ariminumese do, and the money raised goes to pay some small fraction, two-thirds, say. Then the remainder is manageable enough that the Wool Guild doesn't have to pay extra. Split seven ways, we only pay . . ." He began counting digits.

"Eight thousand, five hundred and seventy-one," Fabbro said coolly, "and change."

"A pittance! The lion's share of glory goes to us, but the pain's distributed equitably."

"I'm all for equality," said the silk prior with a dirty laugh. As others joined in, applauding the plan, Fabbro caught the concerned look on his wife's face. He knew he should stop this before it got too far.

"Papa," said Maddalena with a girlish squeal, "can I unveil it?"

Fabbro looked around at his guests. They too were waiting for an answer. "Of course, *amore.*"

Donna Bombelli and Maddalena were sitting in the courtyard under the open sky, the banquet's ruins lying around them. The older woman had the excuse of her condition, but Maddalena was content to let the servants clear up in the morning; no sense continuing the farce when their audience had left.

"Why's Papa so angry? He got what he wanted."

"Silly girl. The *priors* got what they wanted: a share in the credit at a bargain price."

Maddalena found a bottle with some wine left and poured herself and her mother a cup each. "Who cares where the money comes from?"

"Few towers are rich as ours. With good fortune comes responsibility. People expect us to share our wealth through charity and patronage."

"Why should we squander our money?"

"Oh hush! I'm talking *pennies*, girl. It doesn't break the banco and it buys the love of our fellow citizen, it's a sound investment. Your father understands that, but those other charlatans . . ."

"That dreadful brewer." Maddalena made a sour face. "I can still smell him."

"They think they got rich by their own wits. They think they don't owe anyone anything. Fabbro was making money before you could pick it up off the streets."

"Yes, yes, and I should be grateful for my wonderful papa. I believe you've told me this bedtime story. So what's a little pinch? It won't be much for each tower, and the Small People will take more pride in the lion than anyone. They eat up that kind of vulgarity."

"A little means a lot to them. Since the Signoria shut down the other mints, everything's that much more expensive. We don't see it, Maddalena, but the Small People are living hand to mouth. You should have heard Donna Soderini the other day—"

"Glad I didn't! Those people . . . Mama, don't be such a worrier!"

She looked up at the stars. "You'd do well to worry. You're Fabbro Bombelli's daughter. Our tower stands tall and a little discretion wouldn't be amiss."

"I'm sure I don't know *what* you're talking about."

"You may have secrets from your papa, but nothing's hidden from your mama."

"I don't recall you telling your sons to be discreet. I could tell you stories that would curl the hairs on your chin. Why don't you pluck them, incidentally? Is there a rule somewhere that midwifes have to look like—"

"Don't be naïve! It's different for boys. How would it look, the Gonfaloniere's *unmarried* daughter carrying one of these around?" She patted her stomach.

Maddalena kicked her legs in the air and laughed. "We'd make a pretty pair, wouldn't we? Anyway, I'm not like those dull-witted sluts. I'm in control. I know how to stop before it goes too far."

"That's the trouble, *amore*: when it gets that far, you won't want to stop." Donna Bombelli abruptly lurched forward as if grabbing for something. "Uhh oh!"

"Is it time?" Maddalena jumped up fearfully. "What'll I do? Shall I get Papa?"

"Get Sofia!"

Maddalena tripped over a stool and scrambled to her feet. She was just on her way out when Donna Bombelli called, "Stop, Maddalena—it's not coming. I don't know—I thought it was."

Maddalena sauntered back. "You look *bad*, Mama. You shouldn't be up this late drinking. You'd think you'd be used to having babies after all those boys."

"You were the worst."

"At least you're not getting sick in the street, like Saint Sofia." She tittered, "Perhaps you should've had this chat with your *other* daughter. No, of course not—nobody ever thinks ill of the Contessa."

"Maddalena . . ."

Chapter 31

He was never romantic about materials: "Wood and metal are born, they breathe and finally rot, but stone pretends to be insensible. It is a rebel against the law of universal impermanence. It is happy lying in the earth but I make my quarrymen cut it out. With chisels and rasps and numbers my masons interrogate it until it surrenders to proportions that send it heavenward. Every stone in my Molè must work. It may rest come Judgment."

The Maxims of Bernoulli, *collected by Count Titus Tremellius*
Pomptinus

Another wasted night. Torbidda laid down his quill with a sigh. He rubbed his brow and picked up the metallic egg that now served as a paperweight. Its brass skin reflected the small amount of light in the study. After the Molè's destruction, Argenti had commandeered the Selectors' Tower. Flaccus had not been pleased, but he could hardly refuse the three Apprentices. Now, after returning from Rasenna alone, Torbidda had it to himself. The egg served also to remind Torbidda of his disgrace, of which its late inventor— the traitor Giovanni Bernoulli—had been the cause. Not that any reminder was necessary; not a day passed without some slight or encroachment on his powers from the party of Consul Corvis. This latest was just one more.

"Prefect Castrucco, if Corvis calls a meeting, who am I to demur?"

On the other side of the desk the praetorian prefect adopted what he considered a paternal expression; his battle-brutalized features made the effect rather sinister. "You are the First Apprentice of Concord! My oath is to you, not any consul." He put his hand firmly on the hilt of his sword, as if enemies were all about them. "This sword is yours. Say the word and I'll accompany you *into* the Collegio with my men and any dog that presumes to give you another order we shall leave in pieces on the floor. A show of force, lad! What say you?"

Torbidda managed to keep a solemn face throughout Castrucco's performance. He knew perfectly well that he was being asked to sign his own death warrant. The victims of an indiscriminate bloodbath would most certainly include him.

"Your loyalty is heartening, Prefect, and I thank you for it and your offer, but I must say no. Such violence would only provoke an outcry from the engineers at large. Corvis, for all his ambition, is a moderate. If we quarrel, the Guild as a whole looks weak and our true enemies will be encouraged. I can't put my pride over the interests of Concord."

"I understand, First Apprentice," said Castrucco, grim-jawed and sighing deeply.

"I'll be along presently. Go ahead."

"I shall wait outside."

"I will go, but not with an escort. I will not be seen to fear my countrymen."

"Given the circumstances, I don't think that's wise—"

"—and I don't recall asking. Dismissed!" Torbidda waited till Castrucco left before smiling, enjoying how badly the prefect had managed to conceal his disappointment. The new instability had seeded dreams of power in the most unlikely places. Praetorians were the only soldiers allowed to bear arms in the city; though that law was largely ignored these days, they remained the largest armed body in Concord. Nobles were ineligible to join the thousand-strong division, the idea being the nameless would never be able to make a credible power grab, but ambition is like any plague: proximity makes one vulnerable. No, Torbidda thought, staring despairingly at the pages of inconclusive calculations in front of him, whatever had to be done he must do alone—and it must neutralize all his enemies at a stroke.

He picked up the quill, then dropped it. This attempt was the same as the rest, a failure. He'd started well, then the contradictions, the myriad unknowns and weight of unsupported speculations, all combined to slow his progress to a stop. He scrunched the parchment into a ball, rose from the desk and walked to the window. A web of wires connected the Selectors' Tower to the mist-wreathed Guild Halls below, but otherwise it was isolated. This view had been his first really close look at the Molè; now he watched the snow skitter off the distant mount. It was empty now, but for a few jagged remains of pillars that stood like the charred remnants of a forest fire. This was all that was left of the greatest tower ever built: the lantern, the engine room, the triple dome, all gone.

And the library.

When he recalled the dusty months he'd spent there it felt like the type of nightmare where he yearned to warn the actors to flee, but knowing they could not hear, silently watched them play on as the world crumbled. Argenti had told Torbidda to "solve the Molè"— *that* charge he had taken seriously. The First Apprentice's other warning, that the Molè's destruction was imminent, he'd dismissed as Naturalist hyperbole.

Stupid, stupid, *stupid*.

Ever since the Handmaid had burned down the Molè, Torbidda had choked on a heavy stone of regret. Had he heard the clock winding down, he would have done things differently.

"Hello? Count Tremellius?"

If the elegant exterior of the triple domes reflected the virtues of the Reformation—reason, balance, precision—the eccentric maze within the second dome reflected a mind mired in confusion and contradiction. Its curved walls were lined with thick volumes and the air was heavy with dust. The floor was filled with unwieldy stacks, barricades, cascades, valleys and tottering hills of books. A stench of mold rose from dark nooks while other parts were parched under the direct sunlight streaming in through the roundels.

A winding path led from the pod to a scholar's desk. It too was empty, but Torbidda approached and examined the old-fashioned banner that hung behind it. Suddenly a mound of books nearby erupted and a fat little man emerged sneezing. He squinted like a mole, blinking his small round eyes, before they settled on Torbidda. "Heavens! Our new Third Apprentice! Welcome!"

His attempts to clamber out caused a small avalanche of books, but he rolled out of the wreckage unconcernedly. "Now," he said proprietorially, "let's have a look at you . . ." He waddled around Torbidda, stroking the neat circle of his beard with his pudgy fingers. "I must say the yellow suits you better than it did Pulcher."

Torbidda noticed his gold rings, and that the gown Tremellius wore was more luxurious than your average Guild notary. Leto had always laughed at those nobles who ostensibly conformed to the Guild's egalitarian ethos, all the while taking care to make their more elevated status plain. The rosy glow of his skin was surprising in someone who spent his days buried in a literary crypt. He had an undignified, boyish quality, despite his three-score years.

"My dear boy, we shall make excellent colleagues and more, if you permit me. I will be Aristotle to your Alexander. Oh, I see you're skeptical now, but you'll come to rely on me, as your superiors do. I sometimes like to think of myself as the Fourth Apprentice."

Torbidda ignored his nervous laughter. "Do any of these books concern Architecture?"

Tremellius leapt back as if accused of some impropriety. "Oh! Fully one-fifth deal with nothing else. There are hundreds of volumes, ascribed to Nimrod, Imhotep, Daedalus and Hiram—Madonna knows who actually wrote them. If you are looking for authentic work, there are several I can recommend, by Callicrates, Apollodorus, Anthemius and Vitruvius. There's more recent stuff from the Continentals, men like Abbot Suger and Jean de Loup—though they are a bit dated, frankly. I've been meaning to catalog them, but somehow I never find the time. To be perfectly honest—I feel I can trust you, Torbidda—it bores me terribly. I mean really, if you've read about one damn cloister-vaulted Ionian column you've read about them all! Give me a good History, a Biography, Theology even, anything but Architecture!"

Tremellius rolled his eyes and reeled as if fighting off the awful subject, then stopped as a thought struck him. He looked again at Torbidda. "That's what you're here for, isn't it? Why, just the other day I told the Third Apprentice—that is to say, the former Third Apprentice—that I need help cataloging—you don't mind, do you?—'course you don't, eager fellow that you are. You see! I told you they listen to me. All three do, did—poor old Argenti, I'll miss him, of course, but life goes on and we make the best of it. I envy you, Torbidda. The Molè is a veritable school for a budding Architect. Do you know, besides History, I believe Architecture is my favorite subject?" He paused and grinned shyly. "Have you worked out my library's scheme yet?"

Torbidda looked around the chaotic landscape. "There's a scheme?"

"You mocking rogue, of course there is! It's the world, Torbidda, the world! Here in the West is History, Theology and Etruscan literature, which is a hybrid of Theology and History. In the Eastern Hemisphere there is Prophecy—what's History but Prophecy in reverse?—and works from the once-mighty Radinate. These are the Ebionite translations that preserved the wisdom of the Aegyptians and Hellenes. Bernoulli mined some of his chief jewels here. This brings us to the center, which would make the pod correspond with Jerusalem. Why not? We can go above to Heaven, or below to Hell. And in this unloved corner,

Torbidda, is Architecture. The northeast, the chaos of the Steppe. Your task, dear boy, is to bring order to the unruly tribes of Gog. Whip them into shape with filing!" So saying, Tremellius wandered off, exclaiming with joy as he found a misplaced History volume. He buried his nose in his treasure, ignoring the stacks he knocked over as he made his way back to the West.

The main canal had three separate lanes; Torbidda's gondola traveled in the central one. Only the middle current led away from Monte Nero.

Perhaps, he thought, looking down on the mist-shrouded Old Town passing beneath, *a praetorian escort would have been a good idea.* The Small People had been restive since the Molè's destruction, but after the defeat at Rasenna they'd become positively mutinous. When the terrible news had flooded the Depths, its denizens awoke after brown decades of correct action and thought and celebrated the calamity like a great victory. Little wonder—Bernoulli's Reformation might have created the world anew, but it was a world that excluded them. Some discovered they had exchanged masters only when the new aqueducts blocked the sunlight, months after the event. They shrugged and carried on—what does it matter if the dogma they were required to believe came from the Guild instead of the Curia? They were equally incomprehensible.

Now that the myth of engineer invincibility was dead, the bereaved exalted. Since Rasenna had finally learned to be rational, Concord must learn to be quarrelsome. The Mouth of Truth burst forth with new eloquence. In the Depths bears danced on street corners, prostitutes plied their trade and thieves preyed with impunity on engineers and were cheered on for it. Nobles once more strutted the streets; they expected deference and were ready to duel for it. Who could not applaud such extravagant wastefulness? Fashions became indiscreet and sensuous; flesh heretofore hidden behind walls and barred windows and veils tumbled forth like spring flowers. Saints were invented so that parades could march, with gay songs sung in their honor. And everywhere the rival processions of mendicants went sweating and bleeding, leaving trails of ash in their wake. The noisy Fraticelli were the most popular of the competing orders. The old shrines and street-corner niches, empty for years, were once more occupied by Madonnas—some newly carved, most disinterred from the dusty attics and basements where they had lain hidden for decades. The Rasenneisi had succeeded because of their devotion, so the Concordians would best them in love as they once had in philosophy.

The Collegio dei Consoli moved the Fraticelli on when their sermons disrupted the city's traffic, but otherwise left them alone. It had been a long time since Concord's rulers had considered the Small People as anything other than a resource; so long as it did not affect production, the consuls were tolerant of the poor's religious enthusiasm; it was bound to be short lived as their other crazes. The Collegio's peace of mind was disturbed far more by the newly puffed-up nobility than by the preachers, but Consul Corvis used his growing influence to convince his tremulous colleagues that the Collegio could use the latter against the former. By reinstating a Curial institution, the long-disbanded Office of the Night, they could harness the Fraticelli's puritanism to productive ends. A few burned sodomites—this abomination was the nobility's special vice—were a small price for stability.

Though doubting the wisdom of this strategy in the long term, Torbidda had acceded. Maintaining Guild unity was vital. He looked ahead into the mist and wondered what new insults Corvis had in store for him at the Collegio.

Weeks had passed. The chaos still had the upper hand, but Torbidda felt he was making some progress. He'd separated historical accounts from the mythical and speculative and practical works on tools, technique and materials from the numerous mystical tracts on ritual and proportion. His investigation of the Molè itself went more slowly; there was no obvious route to clarity there. Varro said that great buildings never revealed themselves at once; there must be a seduction first. Torbidda proceeded methodically—haste would only inhibit his chances

of finding the solution. He had a few certain facts and certain intu-
itions, which might lead him into any number of blind alleys—that's
what the landscape of literature around him represented: thousands
of journeys to nowhere. He would not *make that mistake. The next*
step would determine success or failure, so he would move not an inch
until certain of his course.

But too often his patience was overcome by a vertiginous panic,
and the horrible suspicion that the Molè had no purpose except to
waste the lives of generations of engineers set to puzzling over its
purpose, that its springs and levers and dials represented nothing but
the tricks of a desperate fraud who'd run out of ideas.

A melancholy ringing bell brought Torbidda from his reverie and he
turned to see two men in a gondola emerging from the mist.

"Damn it, Castrucco—I told you I didn't need an escort . . ." Torbidda fell silent when he heard other bells competing. Two gondolas
were coming toward him, one on either side. Without warning, the
gondolier on the right side pushed his paddle against the canal wall,
causing his gondola to switch lanes. For a moment, momentum carried the gondola forward, so that it looked as if it would crash into
Torbidda's, but the current of the lane soon slowed it.

Torbidda's gondolier cursed his counterpart's dangerous maneu-
vering. "Careful, you fool!" he shouted, but the other gondolier just
turned his back. As Torbidda realized the way was blocked ahead
and behind, the gondola on the left came parallel. The gondolier and
his passenger, a young praetorian, were masked; those in the other
two gondolas were similarly disguised.

Whipping out a dagger, the praetorian on the left jumped toward
Torbidda. In the moments he was flying through the air, Torbidda
had time to consider several things: it was an incredible leap—
impossible, in fact, unless the praetorian knew Water Style. So if
that was the case, he must assume the others did too. As much as
he trusted his own skills, in Conclave one fought one-to-one. If he
allowed them to attack simultaneously, his fate was sealed.

He rolled onto to his back and kicked up his legs, and the airborne praetorian, unable to avoid Torbidda's upraised feet, found himself hurled over the gondola and into the water of the right-hand lane, where the current carried him swiftly away. Torbidda did not yet spring up. Whoever had organized this would not have taken any chances. His own gondolier, who moments ago had voiced his outrage, was now swinging a paddle at his head, but it was too high; Torbidda let it pass over before standing and jostling the gondolier before he could recover, sending him tumbling over the bow.

A quick glance told him that the rear gondola's passengers were readying to jump, and the gondolier on the boat parallel was in the process of using his pole to vault across. But Torbidda now had a paddle of his own, and he simply tipped the gondolier backward, then jammed his paddle into the aft of the unmanned gondola and pushed it hard into the bounding wall. It bounced off diagonally and charged into the middle lane, crashing into the gondola behind him and overturning both of them. One of the men fell into the current going back to Monte Nero; the other floated in the middle lane.

Torbidda felt the impact as the praetorian from the final gondola, the one in front of him, landed in the bow. He took a moment to bring his paddle down on the floater's head before turning and chopping at the praetorian's wrist, making him drop the dagger. Then Torbidda let him attack: the praetorian's Water Style was rudimentary but still considerably more advanced than any nonconsul should know. Satisfied, Torbidda slammed both fists into his chest. A trickle of blood came from the praetorian's nose and his arms fell limply to his sides, then the rest of him dropped.

Torbidda stepped over his body, sizing up the last man standing in the gondola ahead. The man held his paddle in both hands, ready and waiting. Torbidda picked up the dagger and leapt.

Chapter 32

The Collegio dei Consoli was the most secure part of New City, adjoined as it was by the praetorians' barracks. Torbidda was glad that he had arrived before the other consuls; it gave him time to interrogate Prefect Castrucco about the slain praetorians.

"Who are these men?"

"New recruits . . ." Castrucco looked genuinely at a loss.

"Well, they fought like Candidates."

When Castrucco offered his resignation, Torbidda demurred. "Unnecessary. I placed myself at risk against your advice. Besides, at a time like this, I need good men around me."

He left the grateful prefect at the door and entered. In the center of the rotunda was an empty circular table. The Collegio's many tiers reflected the Guild's dense hierarchy. On the uppermost row, sitting in the First Apprentice's throne, Consul Corvis was waiting. "Keeping my chair warm?" Torbidda said, climbing the steps.

"Precisely!" Corvis was obviously surprised to see Torbidda alive, but he disguised it well. "So glad to see you again, First Apprentice."

"I was a little delayed; I feared I would be late. I'm glad we have this time to talk, Consul."

"Well, thank you for coming on such short notice. The convulsions in Old Town demand prompt—"

"Please. Save the pretense till your audience arrives."

"Excuse me?"

"I know you tell yourself that you never achieved your full potential," said Torbidda. "You think it's a simply a matter of being ruthless enough, of killing all your rivals. That's why you'll never climb higher than chairman of the Collegio. To wear the red, you need to be as hard on yourself as you are on your rivals. The best sacrifice most."

The merry twinkle in Corvis' eye went out like a candle, replaced by something sharp and cold, and his lips narrowed. "By that measure you are truly great. You sacrificed a whole legion."

"And gained something worth all twelve. The Scaligeri girl is the Handmaid Bernoulli predicted," Torbidda replied calmly.

"Madmen's predictions are debased currency these days, but if you truly believe in augury, go out to the Wastes and recruit a mendicant army." Corvis looked down as the consuls streamed into the chamber. "There is *my* army. You'll need something better than threadbare prophecy to explain your inaction to them. I imagine you'd like nothing better than to snap my neck—but then you'd just be a boy in a tower, wouldn't you?"

"And you'd attack me openly if you were certain of your position."

"True, but my position grows more certain every day. Yours, on the other hand—you really think I covet the red? As chairman, I control the machinery of state, and that's better than any color. So enjoy it, and your throne, First Apprentice—while you still have them."

Corvis walked down to the table. Soon the lowest rows of the amphitheater were packed shoulder to shoulder; general assemblies were rare events and Corvis had no need to summon those eligible to put their name in the purse; rumor drew them as surely as the scent of imminent riot drew the Small People onto the streets.

Corvis cleared his throat, looked sternly around with a defiantly set jaw and said, "Today marks the anniversary of our nadir. A year has passed since the Twelfth Legion was destroyed. The Small People, poor sheep, had only just recovered from the burning of the Molè when they heard the dire news. We can hardly blame them for thinking it the death knell of our Reformation—the end of us, my friends."

The Collegio's executives, those consuls sitting at the round table, were stone-faced. The surrounding rungs were more demonstrative. Corvis waited until all eyes had settled on the lonely figure in red sitting in the high chair and the empty chairs on either side of him.

"But let us recall the reason we did not give in to despair in that unhappy hour: our flag was not *captured*. Etruria will remember the siege of Rasenna, but not as another Montaperti. Can we *ever* give thanks enough to Apprentice Torbidda for having the presence of mind to burn the carroccio before he fled the rout? No, there is no limit."

He turned and looked up at Torbidda with heavy sympathy. Torbidda almost regretted not taking up Prefect Castrucco's offer. Better surely to take his chances in a praetorian coup than to endure more of the consul's impudent sarcasm. He let his mind roam back to the dusty shadows of the library.

He stolidly hunted the solution Argenti had bade him seek, even while his hope was fading. He spent long hours crouched in niches, like the statue of some queer saint, silently watching the Molè change with the passage of the day. He used the sun to test the fidelity of its north–south axis; the east–west axis he tested the old, laborious way, with ropes. It was painful to compare the Molè's gloom with the chaotic brightness of the Drawing Hall; the Molè treated light as a slave, corralling it to illuminate a few features but otherwise contemptuously locking it out.

The Molè threw its shadow over all Concord—but how was that colossal psychological effect achieved? He gave the time ungrudgingly, though beginning to doubt that understanding would ever come. Using triangulation, he measured the Molè's three domes precisely; he compared the length of the nave to the width of the transept, to the height of the columns.

And slowly he began to suspect that there were hidden symmetries of proportion throughout. A governing proportion was more than an anchor to keep masons' work harmonious; consistently employed, it was like poison in the blood. His breath quickened, like a hunter who spots his prey. There was one proportion that appeared and reappeared, the famed Etruscan "Golden Section," but it did not perfectly apply to the Molè taken as a whole. It was like an unfinished sentence, or a musical scale that stopped maddeningly short of the final note— and perfection.

He felt his prey escaping. There was something else, something he was missing.

"A year today!" Corvis choked with emotion so patently disingenuous that Torbidda woke from memory to admire it. "This is a time to take stock, to ask ourselves what we have achieved since then. We must not shy from the answer: very little. This unrest in Old Town has disrupted important public works—rebuilding the Molè and digging the sea-corridor. While General Spinther has had some success on the Europan front, otherwise our project is stalling. Just this morning, the First Apprentice was attacked by nameless assassins sent by some opportunistic enemy power!"

Corvis waited for the murmurs to subside. "Yes! By Fortune's grace he escaped, but what if he had not? Our ship would face this storm captainless. We have not even found someone to wear the yellow and orange—why, we have not yet begun the search! A year ago the First Apprentice asked the Collegio for time and we gave it willingly. But our patience is not inexhaustible, and that of the citizenry is at an end."

Corvis turned again to Torbidda. "The question will wait no longer, First Apprentice; it is not *when* shall we replace your fallen comrades but with *whom*? Shall we begin examinations again?

Find two more children, gifted as you, and hope they are as lucky. Or"—he turned away slowly—"should we instead recognize the unique nature of the crises that face us and meet them with experience? Should we instead elect two colleagues from the Collegio?" He made a sweeping gesture to the grim faces around the chamber. "No one's more reluctant to break with tradition than I, but to safeguard Concord—to safeguard the *Reformation*—there is *no* innovation I would not try, no sacrifice we should not be willing to make." He finished by muttering, "The final decision, of course, is yours, First Apprentice."

Torbidda stood and walked down to the floor. As he approached the table, Corvis proffered the Speaker's Mace, but he did not take it. The whispering grew as he reached the door. There he stopped, turned around and spoke in a level voice that carried around the chamber: "Consuls, Concord requires loyal servants now more than ever. That's why I propose to award General Spinther a year's extension."

The old consul sitting opposite Corvis said, "I second that motion."

"Thank you, Consul Scaurus," said Torbidda. "As to the other suggestion, I tell you: there shall be no more Apprentices. I am First, and Last."

A wave of protest crashed against the door as it slammed behind him. Protest and speculation—what did it mean? When the empire most needed direction, had the First gone mad? Others, more hysterical, parsed Torbidda's meaning differently: if there were to be no more Apprentices, then surely the time was at hand for the return of the Master. Corvis stayed standing with a resigned, regretful air and a faint smile he did his best to conceal.

"Consuls, please! Take your seats. Clearly, the boy's still traumatized, and who could blame him? We must give him our support, and ease some responsibility from his young shoulders until he's ready to bear it. It would have been correct to debate the matter, but I commend to the house extending General Spinther's command of the Ninth. The Collegio must show that it too is a friend of the army. So let us go further: the Transalpine Franks are restive, and the last thing Concord needs is an interruption in its coal and iron supplies. I propose therefore that we award command of the Tenth along with the Ninth to General Spinther, with orders to aggressively subdue the Frankish Isles."

In the vestibule outside the Collegio, Prefect Castrucco and his men were keeping back the petitioners. Torbidda spotted a familiar face among the crowd.

"Prefect, earlier today you offered me your sword."

The praetorian grinned greedily. "Yes, First Apprentice?"

"Have your men surround the next man I approach," he said. "Do it quietly."

The withered old man stared at Torbidda like one seeing a ghost, then when Torbidda abruptly turned and approached him, he looked around in alarm, as if assessing the possibility of flight.

"Grand Selector, it's been too long. You appear to have fallen on rough times." Since the state of emergency had been announced a year ago, Guild Hall classes had been suspended. Flaccus, unemployed and homeless, was a shell of his former robust self.

"Ah, we are all reduced, Cadet Sixty."

"You'll address the First Apprentice correctly," Castrucco snarled.

Flaccus stiffened and glanced around and saw he was surrounded by praetorians. He smiled wanly. "But he's not *First* Apprentice. He's just the last."

Torbidda stopped Castrucco from striking Flaccus. "It's all right, Prefect. The Grand Selector and I are old friends."

"Corvis will soon get things in hand," Flaccus said defiantly. "There'll be a proper election and Concord will return to normalcy. The Apprentices have failed Concord."

"You failed *us*. The Contessa of Rasenna defeated the First Apprentice in hand-to-hand combat."

"Nonsense. Rasenneisi workshops don't teach Water Style anymore."

"Nevertheless, she knew it, and at a higher level than you ever taught. Your arrogance left us unready."

"As I heard it, the Apprentices abandoned the Twelfth Legion to its fate. You want someone to blame. I know how good you are at deceiving others, but don't deceive yourself."

"You're right, Flaccus. I *am* looking for someone to blame. This morning I was attacked by rogue praetorians who *had* Water Style training. Do you know anything about it?"

Flaccus paled, but said, "Only that it's a tragedy for Concord that they weren't successful."

"Prefect, take this dog to the barracks and see if you can't bring him to heel. Be creative."

Torbidda let his mind wander as he made his way back, not to the tower but to the Guild Halls. He knew these winding paths well: the arches, vaulted roofs and pillars, the niches that afforded hiding places—occasionally from selectors, more often from fellow Cadets. To hear his footsteps alone was a strange novelty, however. The Guild Halls were cavernous without Cadets, but even untrained hands were needed when the ship of state was sinking.

Was it really sinking, though? During his lifetime the empire had grown; that decade-long run of success had made Corvis and all the rest of them forget how much they gambled on each throw. He had no frame of reference to answer the question on which his life depended, but curiously, he was not worried about the consul's machinations. A greater problem preoccupied him.

He handled it cautiously, fearing that that it might crumble like ash. Many of the library's volumes were so old that his touch was the final insult. Tremellius could take all the precautions he liked; the fire consuming these pages was Time and nothing would stop its progress. The volume was a loosely bound collection of preparatory studies for the Molè; the hand was Bernoulli's. As Torbidda studied it, he realized that many of the designs were for another great edifice, a Molè that never was, almost double the size of Concord's Molè. Torbidda assumed it had been abandoned because of the cost.

In the corner of one drawing, he spotted a tiny scribbled note in a distinctive spidery hand. He took out his dagger and polished it in his sleeve and studied the equations in the blade's reflection. He had seen other examples of Bernoulli's transcription; he normally recorded his calculations in a precise, crystalline manner, the numbers falling like notes on a scale. But this was blotted, convoluted, halting, speculative, like a mediocre Cadet's first attempts at Wave Theory, until finally it petered out into multiple question marks and crossed-out numbers. At the end this afterthought was scribbled in frustration: "The preceding being an attempt, alas unsuccessful, to describe an engine most fanciful, one that requireth a most singular fuel: the Blood of the Lamb. The formula is elusive, though I feel it is possible. Return to this, time allowing . . ."

Torbidda locked the door behind him. The Drawing Hall was empty, but it had always been that way; that was why he loved it. The praetorians' ambition, the rhetoric of the Collegio, the convulsions of Old Town, all fell silent in here. He had taken the largest desk for himself and the crisp light streaming in the window fell upon the vast sheet pinned to it. As he stood there, examining it critically, he found he was still carrying the balled-up page of equations. It didn't really surprise him that he had clenched his fist all day; he had never been able to let go of a problem until he had solved it. He unrolled it, straightened out the creases and began systematically checking the measurements of his drawing against the bizarre results that were coming out in the formulae. The inconsistency was here somewhere. He just had to find it.

It was just like the bridge competition: there was no problem so hard that constant pressure would not crack it. *Labor Vincit Omnia.* He would just wear it down. He smiled to himself at the thought that where Bernoulli had failed he would succeed. As he did so he caught sight of his reflection in the giant mirrors. The red he wore curved and danced on its warped surface like a flame.

A glass dome protected the lantern's flame from the full force of the winds. He had to shout to make himself heard over its howling. "I found Bernoulli's final journal, First Apprentice."

Argenti didn't look away from the stars. "You have questions."

"It's babble. Was he mad?"

Argenti fixed Torbidda with his cold stare. "To the Curia, his work was incomprehensible from the first. What does that demonstrate, his insanity or their inadequacy?" Without waiting for an answer, he continued, "Do you know how many chief architects the Molè had? How many mosaicists, sculptors, painters worked on her? How many lives were spent in its construction. Thousands, Torbidda: a small war. And today we remember the name of only one Proto Magister."

"Please," Torbidda said, "help me understand."

The First Apprentice regarded him sadly. "Ah, if it were that easy! If one wants to reach the heavens, there is no map. Night after night you must study the stars and give them time to study you. When you are ready, if the stars judge you worthy, they will reveal their secrets. It is like the dawn of a thousand suns. I would not rob you of it, even if I could."

He was so tired of evasion. "Another riddle!"

"Yes, and one that only the worthy can solve. The Molè is well proportioned, logical and precise as Heaven, but there is another side to both, chaotic and mad."

"The beast."

"What I did not understand for the longest time was that they are reflections of one another. If you are worthy, illumination will come." He turned away, once more looking raptly up at the heavens. "Leave me now. I have my study too."

Though Argenti had since drowned in the Irenicon, Torbidda believed he now understood his purpose. In making Torbidda puzzle out the Molè's mechanics, by letting him discover the truth—that the pit beneath it was the real wonder—Argenti sought to inspire the same intellectual reverence that he felt when he looked at the stars, all so that when the time came, Torbidda would lie upon the sacrificial altar, humbled and gratified to be a part of this wonderful enterprise.

It might have worked, too. The pit's secret *was* humbling in its grand implications. Man prefers the lie, Varro had told them. The secret was hidden within a great deception. The keystone of Wave Theory was that a space could be designed to amplify other qualities beside sound. A structure with the correct proportions could create, capture and distil the essence of pain. That was how the Wave worked. But the truth was, that world-shattering hammer was just a by-product; the greater part of the groans and weeping that the pit's turning produced was sustenance for the sleeper lying dormant at its heart. The pit was a chrysalis where the soul of its creator could hibernate through the winter of death. The al-Buni test, the selections, Candidacy, Conclave—they were all rituals designed to distract from the truth: that the Guild was a machine with a secret purpose, to ensure that the perfect vessel would be obediently waiting when the terrible spring came.

It had all worked perfectly—all but the last detail. Torbidda did not want to be a vessel.

"Although changed, I shall arise the same," he said, looking over the drawing. He had labored over it since he had returned from Rasenna with the knowledge that the Handmaid was among them. The regret he felt for the Molè's passing was dwarfed by his ambition to show that old ghost who was the greater architect—and not just Bernoulli, but Hiram and Nimrod too, all of those ghosts. He would show the world a tower greater than the Molè, greater than Babel's— and this time God would be powerless to knock it down, for the mortar that bound its bricks together would be God's own blood.

Chapter 33

From General Leto Spinther of the IX and X Legions of Concord,
To the most August and Prudent First Apprentice of Concord,
In the name of Girolamo Bernoulli and the martyrs of the Reformation,

Greetings,

That's formalities out of the way! Things were simpler when you were LX and I was LVIII. I'll never get used to all these titles, not that you don't deserve yours. As for me, the extension of my command was welcome, but the Tenth has so far proved more hindrance than help. They are in as bad a state as my beloved Ninth were when I took charge of them. Luparelli, may he rot in peace, was the worst kind of disciplinarian: an indiscriminate one.

Still, I'm not ungrateful. I've got a good group of captains around me, some of whom fought with my father. My second-in-command is the best of them, and the worst. When Lieutenant Geta (Lord Geta to his friends) is not fighting he occupies himself with drinking and quarreling and scandals as destructive as tower fires. For the moment the wives of my other captains are his fuel, but one day I'm certain he'll consume himself. I'll never understand his popularity with the infantry: the worse he acts, the better they like him. Our partnership's a strange one. I'm not sure whether he hates all engineers, or just me. I suppose it can't be pleasant having a twelve-year-old promoted over you, but if he doesn't respect me or my rank, at least he respects the name Spinther. I tolerate his insubordination because of his tactical ability. He trained in Rasenna, and you can tell. We've had some hard battles up here (almost as rough as the Guild Halls!) and I've seen Geta turn utter routs into victory on more than one occasion. Perhaps this is a foolish thing for an engineer to say, but he's lucky. I can see your blank face now, Torbidda, but on the front luck is as real and as treacherous a thing as the weather. I'll use him as long as I can.

To business. I've just sent an official report to the Collegio, but this letter's just for you. The Collegio's orders were to subdue the Franks. Obviously they're worried about supply—ever since Rasenna, all sorts of rumors have been flying around, and yes, the tribes are more adventurous than usual—but any grunt of the Ninth could have told them that the so-called Regnum Francorum isn't very impressive up close. I may have been stationed here only three years, but remember I grew up in this wretched place. It's no great boast to say I understand the Franks thoroughly; they're not complicated. These rival chieftains may call themselves kings of nations, but as long as they remain disunited, they're no threat. The only thing that could forge these barbarians into unity is aggression. Peace is the worst thing to give them, so for the last few months I've been doling the stuff out liberally. It's working a treat too: succession struggles have erupted throughout the Isles. You may reassure the Honorable Consul that the mines of Bavaria and Bohemia are safe.

By the way, Corvis has been getting his way in the Collegio before either of us was born. Tread carefully. He'll try to provoke

you, but when the other fellow has the high ground, never attack—
maneuver. I know designing an edifice worthy to replace the Molè
has been your focus this past year, but you ignore Corvis at your
peril. Of course this is not entirely disinterested advice: as my patron
and champion my destiny is bound to yours.

Given that association, and current timorousness, I don't propose to ask the Collegio's approval for the venture I have in mind,
but you should be aware of my plans. After Rasenna, other cities might be getting notions, so I've decided it's the right time to
remind our other neighbors that we haven't gone away. I'm going
to raid Ariminum's colonies along the Adriatic's northern coast—
don't worry, I'll leave the Tenth behind to protect the mines when
I lead the Ninth east. We'll hug the coast of the Venetian Gulf, ride
swiftly through the Tyrolean Highlands then down into the Dalmatian March. Again, Torbidda, don't worry: I may not be brilliant as
you, but I understand logistics, and I can read a map as well as any
soldier. I know how easily my lines can be cut in the narrow pass.

Supply's a problem that every army campaigning in this water-
fractured land must deal with. The Ninth's bedeviled by it. Your
bouncing bridge design served its purpose when it got you noticed,
but it's a shame you only got the phase-transition to work on paper.

A self-forming pontoon would work wonders in this terrain and
I'd like to see the plans again next time I'm in Concord, not that I'm
likely to succeed where you failed. Still, this is a problem that engineering can only mitigate. I've been studying the geography of the land
bridge between the twin seas and I believe it can be taken. Speed's
the nub of it; we must not go too slow, but we cannot go too fast
either. The longer we take, the more likely we are to get cut off, yet
if we advance faster than our baggage train can catch up, we cut
ourselves off.

It's a riddle worthy of Varro.

It was Lieutenant Geta who suggested hiring Ariminumese boats
to keep the Legion supplied, and so far it's working. Everything has
a price in Ariminum. It was an inspired solution—I confess that I
would have never thought of it but, if cynical bastards like Geta are

the types of colleagues I must become habituated to, I hope always
to remain

Your friend,
LVIII

POST SCRIPTUM:

Thanks, incidentally, for your last letter. It can't have been easy
to finally tell me what happened in Conclave, but I feel better for
knowing the circumstances of Agrippina's death. At least you got to
kill the bastard who murdered her. She would have been happy for
you, of that I'm certain.

Chapter 34

The boys continued their drill when Uggeri entered the workshop. They were curious to see Sofia's wrath, but they knew better than to make it obvious. Uggeri had his flag returned upon release—or perhaps he'd just taken it. Sofia walked over, her hand out. As he reached forward, Sofia feigned a left, he shifted right and she snapped his flag away from him. Uggeri reached after it, but Sofia blocked him with a stick under his chin. He stopped in time, looked up and saw she meant it.

He stood up straight. "I'm not sorry."

"I didn't ask if you were. All I ask is obedience. I give an order, you do it. This isn't Palazzo del Popolo. Here, I'm still Contessa."

"Got it."

"Fine then," she said and lowered her flag. "Don't go south again without my express permission. I need you here in the workshop. Flags have got slack." She said it loud so everyone could hear. "Doc wouldn't have stood for it and neither will I. You boys expecting someone else to do your fighting? The Hawk's Company? The Sisterhood?"

The answer came clear, punctuated by flags thumping floorboards. "No, Maestro!"

"Every workshop in town's lost its snap. That going to happen here? To Doc Bardini's boys?"

"No, Maestro!"

Sofia lowered her voice. "What about you? You want to fight?"

"*Yes*, Maestro," Uggeri said earnestly.

"Too bad. You're my capomaestro. Train these boys until I can hear that snap again." She thrust his flag back at him.

"What about you, Maestro—want to spar?" Uggeri said with a shy smile, and Sofia knew this was the nearest she'd get to an apology. Uggeri was a physical creature, the way the Doc had been. Perhaps he didn't have Doc's brain, but who did?

"I'm not feeling great. Maybe after this Signoria meeting."

The Signoria's elegant new assembly hall was planned by Giovanni and finished by Pedro. With its distinctive clock tower and bold rejection of Concordian forms, the Palazzo del Popolo was a vigorous essay in "Etruscan Revival." The style was popular in Ariminum and the wealthy southern cities like Veii for political as much as aesthetic reasons; it was this neoclassical execution rather than the dome's modest breadth that impressed foreign visitors most.

The keyhole-shaped plan was rational, but not lacking drama. The old palazzo was often flooded and permanently damp; it had caused the premature death of many elderly parliamentarians. In contrast, the new rotunda was raised to a proud height. At the top of the steps, large bronze doors opened into a lofty corridor lined not with family crests but with the flags of the major Guilds. It led to a cylindrical, light-filled chamber—the Speakers' Hall, which was capped with a barrel fretted with circular windows that supported the shallow dome. In memory of the building it replaced, the dome's apex was open to the sky.

Pedro was standing in the center reading his report on Montaperti. It was dry stuff. Sofia leaned over to Levi. "So how did you break the news to Piers Becket that he was engaged?"

"Down on one knee. I'm a traditionalist."

"How'd he take it?"

"He warmed to it, eventually." Levi saw her skeptical look. "Becket just looks dumb. I explained that the Hawk's Company isn't going anywhere, and that he could do worse than aligning himself with Tower Sorrento. Selling cabbages is a lot more lucrative than being a condottiere these days, and safer. Once he got the idea, he made a handsome apology to the offended patriarch."

"Also on bended knee, no doubt. The farmer won't mind a condottieri captain in the family. I bet Bombelli turns the wedding into a state occasion."

"If I could convince all my men to pair off, there wouldn't be any more bad blood."

"What are you, a matchmaker? This is Rasenna. We'll find a new reason."

The textile Guilds—furriers, silk-makers and cloth-dealers—sat together and voted together, as instructed by the Wool Guild. The Guilds of the Bandieratori, Engineers and Doctors were floating voters. The minor Guilds had neither vote nor seat, but were instead represented by a major Guild, a relationship akin to parents and children, according to the priors. The dyers, pullers and carders did not think their association so benign, but they had no other option. As for those trades too menial to have any Guild status: they were orphans.

Pedro had come to end of his report. He took a breath and glanced at Sofia. "And since we'd gone so far, we decided to go a little further."

"What if you'd been caught?" Sofia said angrily. "Who would lead our engineers? You have a responsibility to people other than yourself—"

"Yuri was with me, and we only circled the Waste—near enough to see Concord's walls, but not near enough to be in any danger. *Dio*, it's a wonder!"

"But what were you doing?"

"Surveying the western canal," Fabbro interrupted. "Maestro Vanzetti was acting under my orders." The gonfaloniere was flanked by Polo and Bocca, the farmer and the brewer. All three glared at Sofia.

"You don't seriously propose to attack it?" said Levi in alarm.

The farmer smiled bitterly. "Of course not. You must be tolerant of us, Podesta, if we occasionally consider other things besides war. It is a weakness of merchants. Rasenna is no further from the sea than Concord. If they can build a canal, so can we."

The old days of waiting for the mace to speak were gone. Levi knew that Polo Sorrento was still smarting with embarrassment over his daughter, but he would not have spoken without support.

Levi ignored the sarcasm; he got it now. "Ariminum has a port so—"

"—we need one too." Fabbro said. "Rasenna can't *really* compete with Ariminum until we become a maritime power."

"Gonfaloniere, I've got nothing against your dreams of empire but the timing. I've been trying to fuse the southern league into a meaningful coalition. Naturally, the other cities are waiting for Ariminum's lead. After Concord, it *is* the strongest state in Etruria. If we it drive into Concord's camp—"

"The league. The league. When will you give up that dream? You know all too well that Ariminum's a slippery negotiator. The more leverage we have over them, the better. Besides, Concord's in no condition to cause us trouble. It's falling apart! And if it ever does regain stability, its ambitions are in the north. The Twelfth's expedition south two years ago was about getting rid of the condottieri; effectively, they did. Times change, Podesta. Commerce and diplomacy will be better shields than any league."

Sofia could stand no more. "Diplomacy isn't an option. Concord means to destroy us!"

"*Tranquillo*, Signorina," the farmer said sweetly, "diplomacy's always an option."

Levi said strongly, "This impasse will not be solved by more letters. It will be too late if you only see the point of a league when Concord acts."

"We sent them packing once; we can do it again," the farmer said breezily. "Friends, we owe the Podesta an apology. The city of towers hasn't lived up to its turbulent reputation." He turned to Levi with a sympathetic expression, "If settled life bores you, don't spare our feelings. Go—take your men too. No one will complain."

There was laughter among the textile priors and their allies. Only the brewer, who made a lot of money keeping the condottieri drunk, didn't join in.

But Levi ignored them. "As the southern league's northernmost city, Rasenna will be first to face Concord's army: you must see that. If and when Concord comes, you'll be thankful for every man you can get. With the Hawk's Company, you defeated a legion that wasn't expecting a fight. How will you fare against several legions who come prepared? If you continue to stand alone, you'll fall."

The farmer applauded slowly. "Bravo, Podesta! The flags, the horses, the alarums and clash of sword and ax! The grand sweep of war! Let's take a breath after all that excitement. Friends, we mustn't hold it against the Podesta that he loves war—after all, that *is* his occupation. But we must remember it when we weigh his arguments. Don't your spies tell you anything? Concord lacks the wherewithal to launch a new offensive against us."

"It's true, Signore Sorrento, that their attempt to subdue Etruria proved more difficult than anticipated. But in Europa, Concord's strong as ever. They have turned away from us only briefly; when they turn back, we must be ready, or we will perish. The Ninth and Tenth legions under General Spinther have made short work of the Franks and"—he paused for emphasis—"I have reports that put him in the Tyrolean Highlands a week ago."

The chuckling abruptly stopped.

As Levi sat, Fabbro stood. "I do hope you pay your spies badly, Podesta. You've just heard that Spinther's legions are advancing into the Dalmatian March, but the lowest bridge merchant might have told you that weeks ago. Our Ariminumese partners complain of nothing else. Even if they did not, we would know it by the inflated price of Oltremarine silks and spice."

Levi's embarrassment showed in his cold anger. "It doesn't trouble you that our enemy has encircled the Venetian Gulf?"

"No!" Fabbro laughed. "The Concordians are racing headlong into a wall—at the end of Dalmatian March there is a little city called Byzant; you may have heard of it. The northern capital of the empire of Oltremare is impregnable. If Concord wakes that giant, so much the worse for Concord. If they go to war, all the cities of southern Etruria will profit, and the Oltremarines will be that much more disposed to do business with us to boot."

Sofia caught Levi's glance. As usual the status quo was winning the day. Not for the first time, she sensed the hidden hand of the Mercanzia.

The notary's confusion as he came to the next item on the agenda drew their attention "A vote on the proposed . . . salt tax? But when was *this* proposed?"

Fabbro was already on his feet. "I took the liberty of amending last session's minutes." He was prepared for opposition. His explanation that this was about equity, a temporary measure to share the expense of an important public monument, did little to console Sofia.

"Let me get this straight: the priors get the glory and the Small People get to pay for it? Think they'll accept that?"

"When we make it law they'll have to," said the brewer.

Pedro responded to Bocca. "Our prosperity is contingent on peace. In the old days, every tower was equally poor. Some towers are higher than others now, but they can still burn."

As the notary struggled to restore order, the point of having a Speakers' Mace became apparent.

The farmer shook his head contemptuously. "We've heard this communard argument from Maestro Vanzetti ever since he sold his towers. He claimed he wished to be free to concentrate on engineering, and we believed him. It's obvious now that he only wanted to be free to look down on those who *earn* their daily bread. The Vanzettis have always been expert in telling others how to do things. All the goods we sell are taxed by the city, and all profit by our low prices. Those same few towers who pay for the Hawk's

Company's beer pay for the engineers' fanciful projects—and are we thanked? No. Do we complain? No. Do we ask the Small People for much? Again, no; we're simply asking for a *contribution*—and for that temerity we're treated to threats of being burned in our beds. Fine gratitude—fine talk in a house built on the rule of law."

Sofia was depressed to hear that same self-serving argument that had dominated the old Signoria, but it was Pedro who responded. "If we ask the minor Guilds and those trades without Guilds to share this burden, they are entitled to ask for a seat in this house."

The notary began reciting, "Only priors can sit in this house, and only the priors of the major Guilds can—"

"The right to form a Guild should be the prerogative of the workers concerned," Pedro declared, "and them alone."

The brewer started to snarl, but Fabbro pulled him down. "Friends, we are family, but families are not democracies. Unhappy families have one thing in common: an excess of freedom, and inevitably it brings them ruin. Wise parents allow children to make mistakes, but a parent who lets his child destroy himself is not wise. The major Guilds do not have the vote because we are *rich*, we have the vote because we are *prudent*. Moderation is a virtue in all things, not least in governance. An excess of freedom is as bad as slavery: we must have freedom, but not too much." He sat down with Pedro in his sights.

Sofia kept her seat and shouted back, "Gonfaloniere, I heard the same argument used to deny you a seat once. You didn't want to be taxed without a say in how it was spent. If you were right then, then you're wrong now."

Fabbro, furious that Sofia hadn't bothered to stand, remembered the contempt Doc Bardini had shown the old Signoria. "It seems to me, *Signorina* Scaligeri sometimes forgets that Rasenna no longer owes allegiances to Count or Contessa. She has voice in this house only as prior of the Bandieratori Guild. The Scaligeri did not rule by consultation. When, I wonder, did she acquire her love of the people? Was it when she realized what she had given up? Was it when she realized that parliamentarians must *persuade* equals, not command subjects?"

"Stick to the point, Gonfaloniere," the notary interjected.

"Very well, it's easily refuted. Signorina Scaligeri does not compare like with like. Yes, I objected to the Families' rule: the city they ran was feuding. The city they ran was poor. The city *I* run is at peace. The city *I* run is prosperous. Enough. I don't have to explain myself to this spoiled girl, whatever she once was. There are other matters on the agenda. Let's vote."

As the notary prepared to read the motion, Levi stood.

"Podesta, you have no vote."

"I know that. I know nobody asked my opinion either. I'm giving it anyway. Some have argued that a wider franchise would be fairer; I don't know about that. But there is the practical consideration of stability. Whatever little you earn you'll lose if there's a revolt."

"Even the Small People know tax is a fact of life," the brewer started.

"That's true," Levi admitted, "but they also know the less of it, the better. And if you insist on raising a new tax, I'd hope it was going to pay for something more useful than this—"

"Like defense I suppose," said Fabbro angrily. "The Hawk's Company is quite enough of a drain as it is. Be seated, Podesta."

The notary called for the vote and the Wool Guild's cascade of ayes led the way.

After the meeting, Pedro caught up with Sofia on the bridge. "Sofia, wait up! I'm sorry. I should have told you I went to Concord."

"You shouldn't have gone!"

"My gonfaloniere ordered me to survey the canal; what was I to do?"

"Refuse! Some people still don't understand that we survived the siege because we had Giovanni, but I know you do. You not only endangered yourself playing spy, you endangered Rasenna."

"I admit it was risky—that doesn't mean the canal's a bad idea. The rest of the priors are greedy dogs, but Fabbro's no fool. Levi's proved that patriotic arguments don't move the Ariminumese. We can't afford to be irrational now of all times. Giovanni never was—" Pedro stopped himself as soon as he saw Sofia's reaction. "I'm sorry, I shouldn't—"

"No, maybe you're right," Sofia said. "I'm just a little tired today."

She left him standing there and crossed the bridge and Piazza Stella slowly. She climbed the slope of the healthy hills, and then Tower Scaligeri's stairway. By the time she reached her chamber she was breathing hard. A month ago she could navigate Rasenna's rooftops without breaking a sweat; now she was earthbound. As soon as she closed the door behind her she threw herself on the bed, pouring her tears on the pillow.

What was *wrong* with her? Pedro might very well be right: she was angry with Fabbro, but that was nothing unusual. Rather than persuasion, he always liked to present the Signoria with a fait accompli. The only thing unusual was that this time, Pedro had gone along with it. She touched her stomach protectively as she raised her head and looked out the window. The sun gleamed on the golden angel on the locker. What else did she expect? The *buio* waiting for her to tell her it had all been a terrible mistake? She wondered sometimes if it had been a dream, but the as-yet imperceptible swell of her belly said otherwise.

Chapter 35

The Gospel According to St. Barabbas

19   To escape the agents of Herod, Mary returned home to Galilee. She fled into the highlands, hiding no longer but searching now. Etruscan legionaries avoided these dry hills for fear of Sicarii. These desperate men, known for their cruel hearts and ready daggers, were led by a great thief, Barabbas. For forty days, Mary searched in the caves and lonely places.

20   When She came upon them, Barabbas said unto Her, Woman, How did you find us, and how is it you are not afraid, for we are desperate men? And Mary answered, Because my murdered husband Josephus was one of your secret brethren. Here is his dagger. I would learn to use it for I too am desperate. Your cause is my cause.

21   So She lived with them, learned their skills of disguise, dissimulation and assassination. She had much practice for in those days many had taken the Etruscans' silver. Her deeds became known from Dan to Beer Sheva.

Chapter 36

New understanding brought new focus. As Isabella's Water Style improved, so did her ability to teach her novices and they improved together. Whatever danger the Handmaid faced, the Sisterhood would be ready to help her.

Isabella sat cross-legged on the chapel floor. The stained glass bathed her in warm light, red and yellow interwoven with slivers of blues and purples. In front of her on the small low table sat the glass. Heavy beads trembled on its rim and on the young nun's forehead. When she inhaled, the surface of the water swelled; when she exhaled, it sagged. Concave . . . convex . . . Her hooded eyes watched the center gain mass, growing round, rising, a drip forming upside down. She huffed like a weight-lifter, her cheeks swollen and red.

"Madonna!"

Attaining greater height, the swelling became a sphere, and now the glass it floated above began to tremble. There was a high-pitched *crack!* and a lattice of jagged lines interrupted the surface of the glass. The unseen arrow loosed.

"*Ahhh!*" Isabella covered her face as shards flew around the room. The water spilled onto the floor. She stood and composed herself, looking contritely at the cracked stained glass. From its fractured tapestry, the Madonna looked serenely at the impatiently hovering angel. "I'm trying. Give me strength."

In the sun-kissed enclosed garden, the ranks of the sisterhood practiced Water Style. There were more than a dozen of them now. They wore white linen gowns with short, practical sleeves. Some were orphans like Isabella, but most were new mothers whose children had died and who had been turned out by their families for disgracing their towers. It might strike outsiders as odd that the novices were older than their Mother Superior, but not them. They knew what Isabella was capable of.

"Enough! Let's see you apply what you've learned. Prevent me from entering the baptistery."

The hitherto synchronized dance became a series of individual sets, faster but still graceful. Isabella was a dark silhouette among the fluttering white; the elaborately long sleeves of her habit stretched after her as her lithe body tumbled in the air, moving across the courtyard like a darting bird, her feet touching earth only momentarily. Graceful as the novices were, they looked clumsy trying to catch her. It wasn't a question of speed, but of fluidity. Her winding route between the novices was preordained as a river's course. She had almost reached the end of the courtyard when a hard-eyed figure leapt out from the doorway. Instantly reacting, Isabella kicked the edge of the door to propel herself backward, twisting so that she landed upright.

The novice fell to the ground with a grunt.

Isabella stood in the doorway and held out a helping hand. "Good effort, Carmella."

The novice stood on her own. "Not good enough."

"You'll get there," said Isabella, then to the group, "just like the rest of you. Back to it. Another hour."

Isabella turned her back on Carmella and walked into the coolness of the baptistery. The novice stared after her with a mixture of admiration and resentment. Carmella hadn't lost her family in a burn-out, or been disgraced like the others. She was one of the orphans created in the siege; Rasenna's hour of glory was her nadir. She was the type of hard-knuckled girl one found in the bandieratori towers: proud, with endless reserves of wrath.

Isabella had to stand on tip-toe to look down into the baptismal font. With a dancer's grace she leapt and seated herself on the edge of the dark water. There was little light to reflect except certain golden gleams from the walls, the brightest point the tip of the Herod's Sword hanging over the font. Isabella involuntarily shivered as she beheld the sacred symbol. Rasenneisi parents held their babies beneath it, that they might became one with He who had died prematurely from an imprudent excess of love.

Isabella looked up. "I was just thinking of you."

"I haven't been avoiding you," Sofia said lamely. "It's this place. I come here and I think of the Reverend Mother and the Doc. It scares me. Even when the Families were at their worst, we had them to defend it. All we have now is an army."

"And you."

"I'm not Contessa anymore."

"You're much more than that. Memories weren't keeping you away. You didn't want me to discover the truth. Sofia, you need to understand there's no escaping it. Soon everyone will know."

"How could I be—?" Sofia began, then stopped in embarrassment. "I've never been with a man."

"I believe you."

"No one else will."

"You accepted the responsibility. Now you must live with it."

"Why?" Sofia felt like a child who finds the rules changed. "I thought that when I said yes, there would be a change in the world as well as me. If I'm lucky, people will whisper behind my back. More likely they'll call me whore to my face. My grandfather made the Scaligeri name famous and Doc died defending it. I had to give up my title—I accept that, and I accept that Rasenna has to change—but why must my name be tarnished? Can't God change the hearts of men? He can open tracks in the desert, move mountains, stop rivers. If this child is His, shouldn't everyone know it?"

"No one can know," Isabella hissed, "and you know why." She pointed to the sword above their heads. "Nothing's changed in two thousand years. The same power that destroyed the Madonna's child will murder yours if It learns of Him."

"But why must I sacrifice my name?"

"It's that or your child. Would you choose differently?"

When Sofia said nothing, Isabella asked, "What did the Apprentice say? The one in red you and Giovanni fought on the bridge."

"Before the river took him he said he was going to tell his Master."

The beads worked in Isabella's fingers, a habit she had learned from the Reverend Mother. "The Madonna was just a woman like you. Herod and Bernoulli were just men, but this child, this child is *more*."

"What if I'm too weak?"

"Then Man will sleep on, troubled by the same old nightmares. But if you are strong enough—O, what a wakening!"

Sofia's voice dropped to a whisper. "I'll give up everything— become a nun; people can whisper all they want."

"There's no safety here."

"Where could be safer than Rasenna?"

"There is refuge only at the World's center."

"Are you *pazzo*? Jerusalem is half a world away."

"You'd sense the water's flow if you still practiced contemplation."

Sofia could not deny it. She'd sought to avoid water since the *buio*'s visitation, but nowhere in Rasenna was far from the Irenicon, and every time she crossed Giovanni's bridge she felt it: a black storm of hunger blowing toward Rasenna, and the river whispering *Run! Run while you can!*

She had ignored it. She had been Contessa and bride in Rasenna, prisoner in Concord and cook in the Hawk's Company; if she must be Handmaid now, very well, but for once it would be on her terms.

The ceaseless costume changes were like some desperate farce and she was tired of it. Most of all, she was tired of running.

"Sofia, war is coming. The longer you tarry, the greater the danger to you, and the worse the destruction visited on Rasenna. Wherever you go now, the Darkness follows. Now that It knows you're in the world, Its agents hunt for you. Stop and It will consume you. There is no safe tower, no friend who cannot be corrupted, no water that will not be polluted."

"I don't believe you."

Isabella cupped her hands in the baptismal font and held up her palms. They were covered in blood.

Chapter 37

The Gospel According to St. Barabbas

22   As Mary grew strong in Galilee, ill tidings came from Jerusalem. When Her father Zacharias had discovered his colleagues were loyal to the tyrant, he railed at them, O worthless priests, corrupt thou art and corrupt is your work. The sacrifices ye offer up to the Lord in this Temple are an abomination.

23   But the priests laughed and turned away, saying, Who is this fool?

24   And Zacharias waxed angry and crept into the tunnels beneath the Temple. He knew the secret sign that would release the demon that Solomon had there imprisoned. No sooner had Zacharias made the mark than a great wind sprang up. In fear he fell back, and when he opened his eyes, a Jinni looked down upon him.

25   Man, it said unto him, I will not kill thee. As you have done me service so I am bound to do thee service. What dost thou wish? Women?

26   No, said Zacharias, I am a priest of the Temple and must preserve my purity.

27   A thousand pardons, the Jinni said. Gold then? Fame?

28   Demon, I told thee I serve the Lord. There is no greater treasure.

29   Truly, Man, temptation is wasted on thee.

30   Demon, I am old and want for nothing. What I ask, I ask on my daughter's behalf.

31   Sore exasperated the Jinni asked, And what is that?

32   And Zacharias answered, Revenge.

Chapter 38

As Sofia predicted, the nuptials of Rosa Sorrento and Piers Becket were heralded in every piazza. Becket was enthusiastic about joining Rasenna's magnates, and Polo Sorrento—though still cold to his daughter—was mollified by the new prominence his tower would gain in the transaction. The condottieri might be nothing more than foreign thugs with swords, but their ranks and military bearing created an air of legitimacy that a bodyguard of masterless bandieratori could never match. Watching how the farmer had turned humiliation to profit, the other magnates considered selling their own daughters before they were taken for free.

A great feast was prepared in Piazza Luna, with tables of meat and drink and entertainments not seen since the night the bridge opened. The ceremony itself was quickly got out of the way in the doorstep of the roofless church, while the bride's mother nursed the baby. The crowd in Piazza Stella was oddly muted as the couple began their procession to the bridge.

They crossed in an ominous hush, and Becket looked over his shoulder at the silent, menacing crowd following them. He was relieved to pass under the guard of honor formed by his fellow captains and enter Piazza Luna, where he led his shy bride up the steps of the Palazzo del Popolo and turned to let the crowd admire them— except there was no crowd. When the guard of honor broke up, they discovered the train of followers was still occupying the bridge, and showed no sign of moving.

The father of the bride looked on in horror as his public triumph became another public disgrace. "Bombelli, what does this mean?"

Piers Becket, equally embarrassed, asked the same question of his commander but, like Fabbro, Levi confessed ignorance. "I'm going to find out though," he said, and grabbed Yuri. They caught up with Fabbro as he reached the bridge. The trio stood between the stone lions facing the rows of weavers and carders carrying the obscure flags of minor Guilds.

"Who's in charge here?" said Fabbro, and to Sophia, "and it better not be you." Sofia wasn't carrying the Art Bandiera flag—that would have been too provocative. She said nothing as the line behind her parted.

"I am."

"Pedro!" Fabbro sighed. "I'm not surprised to see Scaligeri here, but *you* understand what the Signoria means."

Sofia said, "A law needing coercion to be enacted is a bad law."

Fabbro ignored her. "Pedro, is this necessary? It's supposed to be a *happy* day. Why spoil the couple's celebration?"

Pedro was unmoved. "We're supposed to celebrate the condottieri and major Guilds climbing into bed together? If the minor Guilds can't be heard in the Signoria, they're going to be heard here. I'm not here as an engineer. I'm here as a citizen."

"The point of this marriage was to prevent strife," Levi interjected. "Tell him, Sofia."

"I went along with it until I saw its real purpose. The Mercanzia wouldn't have dared propose the salt tax without arms behind them. Yes, that's right, Bombelli; I know about your little parties."

Fabbro looked away from his godson in disgust and settled on Sofia, "I seem to recall you took part in a vote, Scaligeri. If this is how you act when a decision doesn't go your way, why not burn down the Signoria and be done with it? These citizens are subject to the Signoria. We don't rule by their consent; we rule by right. By taking part in this unseemly protest you undermine the law. Sedition's a strong word, but I'm struggling to find a better."

Pedro said, "A Signoria that rules by compulsion is no different than the old one."

"So those bandieratori sitting on their flags over the river, I'm supposed to ignore them? And what happens if I order the Podesta to break up this little party?"

Sofia said, "Don't do it, Bombelli. My bandieratori come from the families that make up the Guilds on this bridge. I won't stop them defending their families."

"What a privileged existence you live, Contessa. You take part in referenda but don't abide by results you dislike. You goad these tower-renting fools to disrupt business, and if I attempt to remove them, you threaten to hinder me."

"I don't like your tone, but that's about the size of it," Sofia said.

"Doctor Bardini schooled you well."

"Doc died defending Rasenna's freedom."

"Yes," Fabbro sniffed, "never mind how he spent the years before that moment—"

"Bardini paid the ultimate price," said Pedro, "as did Giovanni, as did my father. That's why we're here, Fabbro. Rasenna can't be ruled by a few towers."

"How long do you intend to occupy the bridge?"

"Until the tax is revoked."

"Pedro, she's using you!"

"My eyes are open. Aren't the priors using you? They want to create a precedent. We're here to do likewise."

Fabbro pulled Levi back a few steps. "Can you break this up?"

Levi shook his head. "Only if you want a riot. You can't win, not that way. Sofia says the bandieratori will stay clear as long as we do. I say let them cool off for the rest of the evening. They'll get bored—and *if* they start anything, we'll be in the right."

"We're in the right now!" Fabbro hissed. He swore and looked back at the other magnates, waiting expectantly at the palazzo's steps. When he turned back to the bridge he was smiling widely. "Well, I'm not going to let a good feast go to waste because of a few spoilsports. Unfortunately, things cost in life. Stay here and brood if it makes you feel virtuous. Anyone who cares to join us in celebrating this happy day is welcome."

And with that he walked back to the isolated wedding party and ordered the musicians to strike up. The celebrations that began were an odd affair, with acrobats, jugglers and puppeteers performing under baleful eyes from the bridge. The jaunty airs were ridiculous in an empty piazza. No one danced. The condottieri captains drank with the embarrassed groom, while the twice-humiliated bride, ignored by all, wept quietly to herself.

Donna Bombelli gave her a glass of warmed spice wine, then walked to the bridge with a tray.

Sofia and Pedro watched her approach with embarrassment. Instead of reproach, she tutted mildly as if they were mischievous bambini. "Do what you think right. Closing down the market, you've hit on the one tactic that might change Fabbro's mind."

"Because it hits his purse."

"No, Sofia, because the market brings peace. My husband cares about peace more than anyone."

"Because he hasn't figured out how to get rich from rioting."

"Girl, you're just like him: stubborn. Well, take a drink. It'll warm you up." Donna Bombelli was passing out drinks when suddenly the glass was smacked from her hand.

"Keep your charity! You and your husband act like royalty—you're nothing but thieves."

"Donna Soderini! I—I've been nothing but a friend to you—"

The glowering woman stamped on the broken glass. "Where were you when we were thrown out in the street? We're sharing a single floor now with two families in a crooked old tower in Tartarus. And you're going to make us pay extra for our *salt*? My *friend* Donna Bombelli"—she spat at her feet. "You've had a good life—all your sons, your fancy daughter, your money." She made horns with her hands and waved them at Donna Bombelli's belly. "Whatever *that* is, I hope it brings your husband *grief*. He should eat the unsalted bread the rest of us choke on."

Donna Bombelli put her hands protectively over her belly as Pedro stepped in front of the angry woman.

"This is nothing to do with Donna Bombelli."

"You're Vanzetti's boy! How can you of all people defend them? Your father came to grief while Fabbro Bombelli got rich."

Donna Soderini's embarrassed husband pulled her away before she could say more. "She doesn't know what she's saying. Maestro Vanzetti, we're thankful for your help."

Pedro flushed, embarrassed at the accusation, but also vexed at the disrespect shown to the woman who had been a mother to him after his father's death. "Sofia, can you escort Donna Bombelli home?"

Sofia felt the mood getting ugly. She took the midwife's hand. As they crossed the bridge, the crowd parted for her, but treated Fabbro's wife to evil looks and whispered insults. Donna Bombelli was more shaken by Donna Soderini's spite. "I never knew she felt that way."

"Her husband drinks. She's looking for someone to blame."

Piazza Stella, packed with bandieratori, was barely less hostile. Although they all now carried the same red banner, each borgata kept separate; only the disciplined example of the Borgata Scaligeri kept the others from flooding onto the bridge.

Uggeri tipped his cambellotto respectfully to Donna Bombelli. "What's the situation, boss?"

"Waiting to see who blinks," Sofia said. "Your job—"

"Do nothing. I know."

"Keep your flag up. As long as the magnates see flags behind the Small People, they won't push it."

"Levi wouldn't let them," Uggeri said doubtfully.

"Levi's podesta; he must do what the gonfaloniere orders." She glanced at Donna Bombelli. "I know Fabbro doesn't want violence, but the other priors . . . Just keep it cool, Uggeri."

He leaned back. "Got it, boss."

Sofia led Donna Bombelli back to Tower Bombelli. She was, at heart, an old-fashioned Rasenneisi—the palazzo was a place of business, a place to greet the world—but all she wanted now was the privacy of her tower. Sofia had to help her up the ladder to the first floor; towers were designed for security, not for heavily pregnant women. Since Palazzo Bombelli was finished, Fabbro's old counting room in the tower had been used for storage. The camphor bags hanging from the roof had grown stale and dust covered the rusted scales on the old banco.

"I don't feel like climbing any more steps, Sofia."

"You all right? You've gone pale."

"Oh, for goodness sake, I'm not a—Oh! Sofia, oh!"

She sat down clumsily on a pile of silks, smiling as if she'd been caught in a lie. "It's coming!"

Sofia grabbed her hand and kissed it. She cleared a space on the floor, piled up some wool bags and covered them with fabric to create a little nest for Donna Bombelli to rest in. She laid her down gently and started tearing linen strips. "I expect Fabbro will make me pay for these?"

Donna Bombelli laughed. "Only if it's a girl."

"Where's Maddalena?"

Donna Bombelli pointed upstairs. "Nobody told her the banquet's been canceled. She's probably still getting ready. She likes to make an entrance."

Sofia bounded up the ladder, lifted the trapdoor that led to the central stairway and shouted. From a few stories up, a pale, pretty face appeared, "What do *you* want?"

"Maddalena, get down here."

"Excuse *me*, I—"

"It's your mother!"

"It's time? Oh, of all the nights!"

Maddalena marched down the stairs, pushing one servant ahead of her while another followed, fiddling with her elaborately coiled hairdo. She was dressed sumptuously in a yellow gown inlaid with tiny ivory buttons. She swished her dress experimentally as she climbed down, crying aloud, "Better not be another false start, Mama!"

When she reached the last step, she recoiled at the scene. She pulled her gown away from the floor. "Mama, what a mess! Is that natural?"

Sofia kept tearing linens as she said briskly, "Maddalena, find your father, tell him what's happening. You, Francesca, go to the baptistery and fetch Sister Isabella."

"But we haven't even thought of a name yet, have we, Mama?"

"For once, don't make a scene," Sofia hissed. She turned to the other servant. "Angela, fetch three basins of water from the cisterns and heat them. Then clean this up, and keep cleaning if you have to."

Donna Bombelli called Sofia's name like a frightened sleeper. "Don't leave me."

"I'm here."

The hand pouring the water was shaking. All day Isabella had tried to ignore the stone in her gut. She looked up at the window, but there was no comfort there; its rich colors had turned to mud in the gloom. The new crack—was it getting wider? The sun was obscured by clouds, which would not disperse, despite the northern wind. The water before her was quite clear, but she felt an aversion to it as though it were poison. Dismissing her fancies, she began to breathe deeply, then she dived.

This time was different.

The way was blocked by a boiling dark sun, as large as the ocean. In panic, she turned and swam away with all her strength and surfaced in the chapel's dull light with a horrified gasp.

She caught her breath and tried to understand what that *thing* was. It was a wickedness beyond words—the very hunger of famine, the sickness of pestilence. When Sofia had agreed to be the Lord's Handmaid, a seed of divinity had been planted in her vulnerable mortal womb, and now, somewhere, *another* power was gestating, growing like a canker.

A small, snaking movement in the glass caught her attention: a scarlet cloud in the water, swelling with writhing hunger until it filled the glass with a diluted pink that turned swiftly into a syrupy red. It spilled over the lip and onto the table, and with a nauseated cry, Isabella kicked against the leg.

A novice appeared at the door of the chapel. "Reverend Mother?"

"Carmella, the blood! The blood!"

"Blood? Where?"

Isabella looked down. The shards of broken glass were lying in a puddle of water. "I'll clean up the glass," said Carmella, giving her an odd look, "You're needed urgently at Tower Bombelli."

Maddalena tried barging her way onto the bridge and was surprised to be rudely pushed back by the wives and daughters of carders and pullers who usually showed such deference. "How dare you? Get your dirty hands off me!" she cried, and when she realized her threats were ineffective, she strode away in a fury and crossed Piazza Stella to the corner where Borgata Scaligeri had raised its flag.

"You, boy! Uggeri, isn't it? I need to see my father. Those sheep-shearing sluts won't let me through!"

"Whatever it is, it'll have to wait."

"My mother's giving birth—shall we push it back in?"

Uggeri took the news gravely. "*Merda.*"

"'Congratulations' is more traditional, you uncouth dog," Maddalena said sweetly.

"Where's Sofia?"

"Madonna, you really have no tact, have you? Elbow-deep in my mother! Do you want me to draw a picture?"

"*Merda*," Uggeri repeated, then, "Stay here!" He marched to the bridge and the crowd parted before him. A ripple of excitement passed as he crossed the Irenicon.

Over in Piazza Luna, Yuri could see over the heads of the crowd. He nudged Levi. "Flag on the bridge, chief."

"What idiot? Where's Sofia?"

"It's probably the Scaligeri bitch herself," said Piers Becket.

Yuri grabbed him by the collar and lifted him closer. "You're lucky it's your marrying day. Otherways we see how well you outswim *buio* with breaked legs."

Just then a bottle flew from the bridge and crashed at the steps of Palazzo del Popolo, where Fabbro stood surrounded by the priors.

Levi walked to the line. "No more of that now."

But the excitement grew as Uggeri got closer, and though Pedro tried to stop them, the crowd began to surge forward against Levi and Yuri. Other captains came forward to back them up and soon it was a pushing match, with the condottieri shouting, "Back! Back!" and the crowd instinctively reacting to the force by pushing just as hard in return.

Levi shouted over the other voices, "Stop pushing, everyone," and a more authoritative voice within the crowd echoed his: Uggeri. The heaving stopped, and they came face to face.

"What the devil are you thinking?" Levi shouted.

"Where's Sofia?" Pedro shouted back.

"Donna Bombelli is having her baby—"

Pedro's face registered joy, then frustration. "Levi, tell Fabbro and tell him Sofia's with her. Come on, Uggeri."

The heaving stopped after Uggeri left, but with the captains now face to face with the front line, the tension could only mount. When Fabbro tried to pass through, he found it impossible.

"For the love of decency, I need to be with my wife!"

"We can force a way through, Gonfaloniere," said Becket with excitement.

"Don't be stupid," Fabbro snapped, and Levi silently thanked the Madonna that the gonfaloniere wasn't a typical Rasenneisi.

So they waited and listened to the Torre dell' Orologo count the hours' passage. Fires blossomed in both piazzas as evening drew on and the strong men on either side of the bridge kept warm with drink and braggadocio while the Small People shivered and huddled together in the darkness and listened to the unceasing bellow of the Irenicon beneath their feet.

Sister Isabella, her face wan and fearful, came from Tower Bombelli to help the other Sisters on the bridge handing out roast chestnuts and warm drinks. A little girl was crying, and her mother was struggling to distract her from the night's icy grip. Isabella hummed a melody to soothe her, the River's Song, and soon other voices joined in. In Piazza Luna, the brewer stomped his feet to blot out the sound.

"How long are we going to let this farce go on? Know how we look, Bombelli? Weak," he said. "We look weak."

Fabbro stared at the lights of Tower Bombelli across the river. "*Idiota*, we are weak. We've just broken Rasenna in two again."

The music carried to Tower Bombelli.

"Remember the night the bridge opened?" said Donna Bombelli. "You looked beautiful, just like your mother. She was brave like you, Sofia. She crossed the river when everyone else was too scared."

"Brave?" Sofia laughed mirthlessly. "If you only knew."

"Don't be scared. You're going to be a wonderful mother."

Sofia looked around in alarm, but the servants were both asleep. "How—"

"Don't worry. It's not obvious yet but I'd be sore incompetent not to recognize the signs."

"It's not what you think." Sofia reddened.

"I know. You're no fool. Whoever you gave yourself to, he loves you."

Sofia didn't argue. She could see Donna Bombelli floating in and out of consciousness. "Wake up. Are you still in pain?"

"No . . ." Her breath was slow and deep and far apart, but her eyes became suddenly lucid. "Sofia, you're midwife enough to know the trouble I'm in."

"Don't say that!"

The stillness around her was growing. "It's true, and you know it. Promise me something . . ."

On the palazzo steps, Fabbro was surrounded by the priors who, to a man, urged breaking up the protest. He told them it was madness.

"But we have to pay for the gold somehow!" said the brewer indignantly.

Fabbro had hoped one of them would suggest paying for it; instead they kept repeating that simple fairness demanded that the expense should be shared equally. "After all, the lion *must* be gold, and the tax will apply to us as much as them."

"It may be harder to bear for some," Fabbro said, concentrating now on the condottieri captains circling poor Becket. A few drinks on, they were getting rowdy too.

"You know who you sound like, Bombelli? Vanzetti's boy," the brewer said. "Every bit the communard his father was. If that were my boy—"

"What, Bocca? What would you do? At least Pedro has convictions. All you have is greed and an unearned sense of entitlement. You got rich selling beer to soldiers; any fool could have done as much."

"Now hold on—I never said I wouldn't pay my share. That's not the point anymore. It's about the Signoria's standing. If we give in on this, we'll never be listened to again."

As the others affirmed the brewer's sentiments, Fabbro cursed himself for not listening to his wife, for at last he saw that there were agreements he had not been party to; the salt tax had not been a spontaneous idea. The priors *wanted* a confrontation. He had an overwhelming desire to be back in Tower Bombelli with his family and away from these vulgar, ambitious curs.

"I'll pay for the gold! There's no need for anyone to dip into their purse, and no need for the tax."

The priors were speechless for a space. Then Polo began, "But Fabbro—"

"But nothing! Podesta, come with me."

As they walked to the bridge, Fabbro told Levi his decision.

"Bravo," Levi said mildly. "Let's break the good news."

The good daughter keeping vigil was a tiresome pose to maintain. Maddalena reasoned that she might as well get some use out of her gown. She paraded between the fires of Piazza Stella and the hungry eyes of the bandieratori until she found Uggeri in a dark corner. He was sharing a paper purse of warm chestnuts with Carmella.

The novice blushed when Maddalena approached, as though caught in some scandalous tryst.

"Sister? Shouldn't you be ministering to the dauntless heroes on the bridge?"

Carmella curtseyed and left, and Maddalena turned with a wide grin to Uggeri. "Why, Signore Galati, I knew you were a villain but I never took you for a corruptor of young virtue."

Uggeri could have explained that their relationship was innocent—Carmella's tower had been next to Tower Galati while her family had lived—but he knew better than to rise to Maddalena's bait. "How's your mother?" he asked.

"Hard at it. *I'm* in the way, of course. Only the Contessa can do anything! If there's an emergency I suppose Pedro Vanzetti can rig up a pulley system."

"You hate anyone else being the center of attention."

"I just hate being bored. I was looking forward to a fun night instead of this hysteria. I don't suppose your men could do without your scowl for a couple of minutes? With all these excitable fellows around, I need an escort back to the palazzo."

". . . that all?"

"The servants are in the tower hovering around the Contessa— she likes extra attention too—so there's no one around to help me get out of this thing." She took his hand and pulled it to her waist. "It is *awfully* constricting."

After a moment's consideration, Uggeri cleared his throat. "Allow me to show you home, Signorina."

Pedro turned to the crowd with a big smile. "We've won!" Cheers mingled with cries of *Viva il Popolo!* and *Forza Rasenna!*

Fabbro addressed them. "Friends, the food's getting cold and the condottieri are making short work of the wine. You'd better help them, fast!"

Another cheer, and the congestion on the bridge suddenly cleared itself. As the crowds invaded Piazza Luna, the disgusted wedding party retreated to the fortezza. Levi and Yuri took care to herd the condottieri with them. Humiliations like this could swiftly blossom into violence.

Fabbro let them stream past him. He couldn't face joining either party, the feckless would-be rebels or his venal colleagues.

"Thank you, Gonfaloniere," said Pedro, standing next to him.

Fabbro tousled his dark hair fondly. "You only use my title when you're mad at me."

"Thank you, Fabbro."

"*Di nada.*" Fabbro walked briskly over the empty bridge, feeling some measure of contentment that tomorrow it would be full of merchants instead of malcontents. When he reached the other side he saw the final plinth wasn't empty anymore. There sat an effigy of a fat bearded merchant dressed in scarlet with coins tied around his sleeves. It was burning. He felt laughing eyes all around, waiting for his reaction. He marched on, affecting unconcern, but the portent slowed his step and when he reached the ladder of Tower Bombelli, he froze. What if, up these rungs and behind that door, was an irrefutable fact that would destroy his happiness? Must he climb up? Must he open it? Could he delay the revelation, alter it somehow by not acknowledging it, or maybe negotiate some reprieve? It was childish, yet the thought kept his foot fused to the first rung. He might have stayed on the threshold until the sun rose, but for the soft voice he heard calling his name. He willed himself to open the door.

His old counting room resembled the aftermath of a raid, with tearful faces and blood-stained clothes. His mouth opened and he sneezed once, twice.

"*Cavolo!* Shut the door!" Sofia boomed, and turned back to her patient. Behind her Fabbro saw his wife's face, horribly pale, with intermittent pink splashes.

"She's bleeding . . ." Fabbro whispered, feeling the freeze again.

"It's a popped vein. It happens. Come closer, man."

Fabbro knelt beside his wife and sneezed again; there was pepper dust everywhere. A midwife's husband knew it was a bad sign when labor had to be induced, and still worse when those means failed. "I'm here, *amore*," he whispered. "I'm here."

"Fabbro?" Donna Bombelli spoke like one waking. "Promise me something."

"Anything!"

"Find Maddalena a husband."

Fabbro replied with forced hilarity, "There's time for that yet—she's still a girl."

His wife ignored his babble. "Find a *good* man, Fabbro. Without one she'll ruin herself. So long as he's good, it doesn't matter if he's poor."

She was too delirious to see her husband wince.

"I'll write to our sons and insist they send portraits of a dozen eligible bachelors with their monthly accounts. How's that? We'll sift through them together and—if that fails—why, I'll jump on a horse like the old days to search the length and breadth of Etruria and haul them back for your inspection."

"I'm with you, Fabbro, no matter what happens . . ." The inexpressive mask suddenly crumpled into a spasm of anguish.

"You should go now"—Sofia pulled Fabbro firmly by the arm—"but stay close."

He rose to his feet like a much older man and backed away, "Thank you, Contessa. Thank you." His head bumped a low-hanging spice bag and he stumbled into a stack of silver plates. Neither Sofia nor his wife noticed; they were back in the constrained world of effort and endurance.

He stepped out into the dawn's light blinking stupidly and climbed down the ladder. His feet instinctively carried him to his palazzo.

A lamp-candle was lit in the hallway. The servants were standing vigil at Tower Bombelli—his wife was a popular mistress—or over in Piazza Luna, enjoying the party. So who was here? What was that noise from the central courtyard? Theft was rare in Rasenna, but flags had grown slack of late. He picked up the small Herod's Sword that hung inside the door and left the lamp behind, the better to surprise them. The noise became clearer, groans and grunts—lifting something—his money-chest?

A woman's scream—*Maddalena!* Fabbro ran into the courtyard, forgetting stealth or caution.

Writhing on top of a bandieratori was his daughter. Her yellow dress covered them both, but their occupation was obvious. The boy reacted first, his head turning, his hand reaching for his flag at the same time. Maddalena shrieked in mortification and leapt behind the banco, leaving the boy exposed. He pulled his britches up and moved before Fabbro could take another step. He ran at one of the courtyard pillars, then up it, grabbing the low-hanging Bombelli banner and with it swinging to the second-story balcony. He lobbed his flag onto the roof above and followed it with a catlike leap. He scampered over the roof and leapt into the darkness without looking back.

In the courtyard below Fabbro stood before his weeping daughter. "In my *workshop*! On my *banco*! You let others tend to your mother as you tend to your lust with the son of a lowlife like Hog Galati!" He raised the sword.

"Papa, no!"

"Don't 'Papa' me—" In a kind of daze he threw down the blade, grabbed her hair and pulled her to her feet. "Your mother's right. I've been too soft with you."

Sofia's hands were shaking when she came out of Tower Bombelli. The sun was up over the river, the pink light over Piazza Stella throwing long shadows of those revelers who hadn't yet gone home. She hugged her hands under her arms to stop them from shaking and stopped before the small Madonna perched in an alcove on the side-street. It was an oddly humble statue for the richest family in Rasenna. Was it Bombelli's studied humility, a sentimental attachment to the old style, or just apathy?

The servant Sofia had sent returned with her master trailing after her like a captured prisoner. Fabbro went to the ladder's base and looked pleadingly at Sofia.

"I'm sorry." She couldn't meet his eyes.

Rung by rung, Fabbro climbed the ladder and pushed the door open. The long emptiness was filled by the swallows' shrill songs among the morning towers. Fabbro reappeared at the door, stumble-falling down the steps like a drunkard. "Why did you cut her?" he asked with wounded outrage.

"She begged me!" Sofia wept. "She knew she wasn't going to make it. The baby's only hope was—"

With dull eyes Fabbro wandered away from Sofia's explanations: "It—*he* must have been dead all the time. It was a boy, Signore Bombelli. I'm sorry—"

He disappeared into the maze of alleyways.

"The Contessa *regrets*. What consolation!" Sofia turned to find Maddalena stumbling toward the tower. Her gown was torn at the shoulder and her face covered in ugly bruises. Her left eye was black and the other one was completely shut by the swelling.

"Maddalena—who did this to you?"

"As if you don't know! Papa—you sent him—you want to destroy the Bombelli family. We're in charge now and *you* can't stand it. And now you've murdered Mama."

"I loved your mother."

"Do Rasenna a favor and keep your love to yourself. It's poison."

Maddalena glared at the weeping servants. "Get up there and start scrubbing!"

She turned back to Sofia and screamed, "I told you to *go*!" She clumsily lifted the Madonna from the alcove and threw it with a roar of hate. Sofia didn't have to duck; it smashed harmlessly against the cobblestones. "The Scaligeri are a plague on Rasenna. How many Waves must come before we realize!"

Sofia backed away from the hysterical girl, but her screams echoed in the piazza.

"You'll only be happy when we all drown. Wake up, Rasenna, save yourself! *Wake up!*"

Chapter 39

The Gospel According to St. Barabbas

33   The Jinni searched the depths and the secret places of the earth until he found that prize the priest had wished for. Zacharias stood on the mount that all the city might hear, and cried aloud, O Jerusalem, Jerusalem, you that killest the prophets. See ye not all these things? Verily I say unto you, there shall not be left here one stone upon another that shall not be thrown down. Jerusalem, the winds will take you. Even as the walls of Jericho fell, and the pillars of Iram fell, this Temple will fall. The tyrant who built it, he too will crumble.

34   And Zacharias blew upon the ram's horn.

35   And King Herod ordered the troublesome priest thrown down from the mount. So perished Zacharias of the House of David.

36   In Galilee his daughter heard of it and was filled with wrath.

37　But the Lord had heard the horn. He visited Herod and Herod was visited with affliction.

38　The tyrant fled Jerusalem and her troublesome people. He retired to his palace overlooking the Sea of Zoar, and the servants said that his body stank worse than the sea. His privy parts burst forth with maggots and festering wounds.

39　And though he suffered, the tyrant thought himself safe in his stronghold. But the Lord is not denied.

40　Mary and Her band climbed the mountain. They stormed the palace and found him hiding there. For his life he offered gold that Mary took and threw from the mountain.

41　And She said, Now, false king, thou shalt follow thine idol.

Chapter 40

The gonfaloniere's wife was well liked, and Rasenna was unusually subdued in the days that followed. Fabbro didn't notice. He'd tried losing himself in the minutiae of his accounts and when that failed, drink worked.

It was noon, and Maddalena found him three-quarters through the bottle. She sat at his feet saying nothing. His fingers gently touched her hair.

"We used to fight, Maddalena, your mother and I—oh, the most tremendous quarrels! And not just shouting, either—I, well, I never was a bandieratoro, and your mother was a Cassini—I could tell you stories about her father, he was a *real* bandieratoro. But we'd wrestle and slap and scratch until we were quite exhausted, and then reconciliation would be sweet. Our love matured, but I always took comfort that she was as strong as I. Oh child, what will we do without her?"

"I'm here, Papa."

* * *

When the Ariminumese letter came, it was a relief for everyone. Donna Bombelli's death left Sofia friendless, and with a horrible dread that Maddalena had been right: the longer she tarried, the more would suffer. Hadn't Isabella warned her?

"There's opportunity in every crisis." Levi held up the letter. "The invasion of Dalmatia has woken Ariminum from its lethargy. As General Spinther marches, its colonies fall like towers, one by one. Without this hinterland, the Adriatic is no longer a solely Ariminumese sea. Ships clog Ariminum's harbor, ships full of merchants who've abandoned fortunes to save their lives and families, exiles who infect that proud city with fear—fear that has belatedly made Ariminum realize it's part of Etruria too; fear that shows Ariminum Concord for the threat it is. This summit they propose is the first real progress in months. Where Ariminum leads, the South will follow. That's why we must go and make the case for the league."

Though the gonfaloniere looked to be sleeping, he was listening, and he suddenly had an illicit thought he knew must never be voiced: that Rasenna had more in common with Concord than with any of the cities of the South, which was still ruled by lords, families, tyrants; Concord and Rasenna, ruled by men of skill, should be natural allies.

"They address their letter to *The Contessa*," the brewer remarked.

"So?" Levi said quickly. "How should they know Signorina Scaligeri gave up her title? And for that matter, why should they care?"

"If we send her, Ariminum and the other cities will continue with that impression." Grumbled agreement circled the room. The bandieratori's role in the occupation of the bridge still rankled with the priors.

Fabbro seemed to wake suddenly from his stupor. "This summit is to resolve one question: peace or war. We must do *something* with our surfeit of soldiers." He looked directly at Sofia. "Blood follows the Scaligeri wherever they go. Let this one go and preach war so that Rasenna may have peace. Go, Contessa. If you can persuade Him, go with God. If you cannot, go anyway."

Chapter 41

The Gospel According to St. Barabbas

3   In the distant land of Etrusca, the old Emperor Catiline was vexed by reports of the rebellion that erupted upon Herod's assassination. For though a tyrant, Herod had kept the Jews biddable by constant building and murder.

2   Catiline's soothsayers read in entrails the same prophecy that Herod's astrologers had read in the stars; that a new kingdom would soon arise to overshadow all others.

3   Catiline was greatly disturbed, for while Judea burned, Herod's sons fought for their late father's throne and he sent word that henceforth the Jews would have no King and Judea would be a province ruled by an Etruscan prelate.

4   The new prelate was a man named Pilate and he was charged with quashing rebellion. This Pilate sought to do by cutting off its head.

5   He sent his legion swarming over the mountains and lonely places of Galilee. Mary and Her band fled into the southern desert and only in the shadow of Sinai did they stop to rest.

6   The angel of the Lord appeared to Mary in a dream, saying, Arise, Woman, arise and flee into Egypt. Would that Thy husband had done so sooner.

7   But Mary said, My husband was murdered protecting My son. Where were you then with your warnings? Tell your master that henceforth I choose my own path.

8   So Mary led her band into the Empty Quarter. Though the Sicarii were bold men they were sore afraid, for long had the children of Israel and Ishmael been enemies; yea, even in the womb had they quarreled.

Chapter 42

Lord Geta's knowledge of the Depths was such that he could avoid the conflagrations on his way to the Dolore Ostello. He watched a gang of youths carrying rocks chase a richly dressed woman into a dark alley. Although he knew the alley was a dead-end, he walked on. He had no time to tarry—today was Carnival, and Geta must gamble.

He superstitiously averted his frosty cat's eyes from the dark, disquietingly empty sky. All his life the Molè had been omnipresent; in front of him, in the corner of his eye and if he were bold enough to turn his back, its shadow covered him. Now the Molè was gone, and the sky was indecently naked. Although learning to fight in the tumultuous Rasenna of old was the fondest memory of his youth, Concord the day before Lent was a close second. It amused Geta to think of how innocent he had been—harassing strangers for money, pelting rival gangs with rocks, the hurried frantic couplings, the freedom that came with wearing a mask. Though Geta always made a sentimental point to return to the capital for Carnival, he had expected to miss it this year.

Yet here he was.

The spirit abroad in the streets today was undeniably different. Those shouting children were not noble bravos but fanciulli, Fra Norcino's brood of barefoot angels. The preacher assured them that they were doing God's work, so they stooped to any brutality.

"Death to the catamites!"

The fanciulli used to be known by the great noise they made. Now they were known by the broken mirrors left in their wake. They wore white robes because they were young and stainless, and laurels because virtue was triumphant. They shaved each other's heads to contrast their naked purity with the effeminate locks favored by noble youths and paraded through the streets, olive branches and banners and statues held high. Others dragged the accoutrements of Natural Philosophy and the symbols of noble narcissism: astrolabes and compasses, paints and wigs and jewelry: a funeral procession for vanity in its protean forms.

"Woe unto Babylon!"

Great bonfires burned on every square, and in their dancing light all things seemed possible: that Carnival's once-a-year inversion could be rendered permanent, that Fra Norcino could be king. Knowing the Collegio would let the mob do their worst, most nobles kept off the streets, and those who were abroad tried to be inconspicuous—all but Geta. A swordsman could never be inconspicuous. His breast was decorated with war medals and wounds and his face with scars—enough to frighten women, in the right way. From his shining spurs to his bounteous moustache waxed into prongs, he belonged to an age of selfish chivalry. He was in disgrace, and though that was a condition he was accustomed to, the memory of his show trial still rankled.

"Lord Geta, have you anything to say before we pass sentence?"
"I need a drink."

"In your defense!"

"Let's not make this farce more hypocritical than it already is, Corvis. I rolled the dice. Had I won, you'd be giving me a legion of my own."

"What about you, General?"

Leto Spinther stiffened. "I am the one bringing charges against this scoundrel. I don't have to answer your questions."

"Let's just go over it one more time."

Consul Corvis was as smooth as he was patronizing, and the young general looked up to the lonely figure in red sitting behind the assembled Collegio. "Torbidda, is this necessary?"

When the boy did not reply, Corvis continued, "Indulge us, General. When we awarded you command of the Tenth along with the Ninth, we expected more gratitude."

"Expected to dictate strategy, you mean. Do you really want your generals so supine?"

"You're in no position to take this attitude."

Leto's temper flashed. "Torbidda, are you going to let this jumped-up—"

"You will address me as First Apprentice, and you will answer Consul Corvis with more respect."

"Thank you, First Apprentice. Why, General," said Corvis patiently, "did you not seek our permission to strike out into the Dalmatian March?"

Leto waited for his friend to speak up on his behalf and when Torbidda remained silent, he set his jaw and answered, "If I had failed, I would be standing in Lord Geta's place so you could strip me of my rank and replace me with someone more docile. But I did not fail. We overran Ariminum's colonies and plundered their wealth. I don't recall hearing complaints then."

Corvis flushed. "Of course, such unexpected bounty—"

"Nor did I drop everything when you recalled me to the capital for a Triumph. I acted responsibly: before my departure I withdrew the Ninth and established a defensible perimeter in the Tyrolean Lowlands."

"And why was that necessary?" Corvis asked innocently.

"You know full well—" he started, then said more calmly, "My Dalmatian campaign was about capturing the Ariminumese colonies. I took care not to encroach too far beyond it."

"Into Byzantine territory. So you were aware of the risks, and still you gave command to this reckless cavalier."

"War is risk, Consul; you'd know that if you wielded a sword instead of a pen. I will not deny that I lent Lord Geta my baton. Till then the fellow had served me well. I charged him to hold the perimeter and rebuff any attempt by the Ariminumese Navy to recapture their colonies."

"But he had other ideas, did you not, Lord Geta?"

"The Triumph you awarded Spinther was rightly mine—"

"Silence, dog!" Leto shouted, then turned back to Corvis. "I pieced the story together later. After my departure, Geta stoked his jealousy until he had convinced himself and the other captains that they could do the impossible. They rode for glory, plunged once more into the March and on to the frontier. Lust for honor and spoils outpaced what little good sense they had left, they advanced further than the ships could supply them and as soon as they entered Byzantine territory they were met by an army—"

"A host as large and merciless as the sea," Geta cheerfully interrupted.

"Geta, of course, managed to save himself," Leto said, "but the Ninth simultaneously suffered its first defeat and destruction. When the Frankish tribes learned of this, they forgot their differences and united and I returned with the Eighth Legion as fast as I could."

"Too late to save the Tenth."

"They were unready. I returned in time to safeguard the mines; obviously our metal supply is more important than men. I pummeled the tribes into quiescence, then turned east to salvage what I could of the debacle . . ."

Torbidda listened as his old friend described the ruin that had confronted him when he returned to Dalmatia, and his struggle to keep the triumphant advancing army of Prince Andronikos within the Dalmatian pass, and he realized that the enthusiastic boy of the

Guild Halls no longer existed. The battle was done, but its echo was still with Leto. He'd heard war cries give way to sobs of terror, then death rattles followed by the exultant squawking of a thousand carrion birds. His voice was cracking when he finished, "Then I relieved Geta and dragged him back to the capital in chains."

Corvis was partially satisfied. He turned to the accused. "Lord Geta, this is recklessness verging on treason. Byzant is the northern capital of Oltremare—to wake that dragon in this time of crises was madness. Do you know how costly the peace we negotiated was? The humiliating price—all our recently acquired Ariminumese colonies, all our gains, gone in a moment of overreaching vanity. First Apprentice, what shall we do with this fellow?"

"Dishonorably discharged. Consider yourself lucky not to hang, Geta. And you, General Spinther, are lucky not to be demoted. Your Triumph, of course, is canceled."

Torbidda stood up and looked down at the Collegio. "Consuls, we have lost the Twelfth, the Ninth and the Tenth Legions. Morale is low, but let's keep things in proportion: a twenty-five percent reduction is not so great a disaster in an endeavor so fraught with risk as war. Fortune will smile on us again. If that's all, Consul Corvis, I must return to my work."

"Of course First Apprentice."

Another in his position would have slunk from the city, but not Geta. Disgrace became him. He wore it stylishly, just as he covered the standard fine-mesh vest of the legion with a tabard checkered orange and black. This innovation wouldn't be tolerated in a lesser soldier, but one needn't be a vexillologist to recognize Lord Geta's colors. They were well known, as was his contempt for the Collegio's prohibition. Recently many nobles had begun to emulate Geta and wear their colors in the street. The debacle at Rasenna had reminded Concord's bluebloods of something too long forgotten: the engineers were men like them. The Dalmatian March, though a disaster, they saw in a different light, as a chivalrous *jeu d'esprit*, vainglorious, needless and magnificent.

Geta took a different lesson from his court-martial than the one the Collegio had wished to impart. The Guild was weak: they hadn't stuck his head on a spike on the Ponte Bernoulliana, and that was weakness. The First Apprentice sitting mute while that upstart consul ran the trial: weakness. Indeed, Corvis' new prominence was the most telling sign that the Guild's greatest asset, its collective cohesion, was ebbing. Signs of weakness all around. Actors, buffoons, toothpullers and quacks freely roamed the streets. The Collegio of old would never have allowed such scoundrels entry. But the Collegio of late was a fair reflection of the wider Guild: indecisive and divided.

Most scandalous of all were the processions of Fraticelli everywhere. No one could remember the first time they saw Fra Norcino; how long *had* he been around—months? Years? He had become a familiar sight, wandering the Depths like a lost child chased by the rattling stones of city boys, beaten by soldiers for warning strangers to repent before the imminent arrival of . . . *something*. He was just another desperate face in the crowd: tolerated, like the Mouth of Truth. No one could possibly take him seriously. Everyone laughed at the old maids who, after hearing Fra Norcino talk, became anxious for their souls and broke off the heels of their shoes and waddled home to smash their mirrors. But anyone who makes promises in senseless times finds an audience. Fra Norcino promised bereaved parents their children, and orphans parents. He promised remission and absolution, indulgence and youth, and it was madness to believe—so they forgot their sanity and followed him.

As he walked on hurriedly, Geta heard a droning noise, interrupted intermittently by savage wailing and ecstatic moans. It conjured up the drear masses his pious relatives had dragged him to as a child. But those illegal gatherings had been held in attics and basements, never out in the open. Geta had survived battles and duels and not much gave him pause, but *this*—the echoes of outlawed devotion—this made him shiver.

He peeked out into the square, and found himself involuntarily drawing back at the size of the crowd. As Fra Norcino's oratory grew increasingly seditious, so his audience swelled from dozens to

hundreds. Now their attention was entirely focused on the blind Fraticelli perched like an anchorite of old on the stone pillar, the *Umbili-
cus Urbi*, the official center of the Concordian Empire, the point from
where all measurements started.

"Surely no *man* could have burned the Molè?" The voice was
unpleasant, reminding Geta of a soldier's roar-strained squawking
after battle. Could that appalling wreck of a man truly be the notorious Fra Norcino?

"Only God!" they screamed. "God! God!"

"Aye, surely—for if God is master of this world, then surely it was
God. The engineers gave ye an idol to worship, that impious tower,
and in a single night He threw it down."

"O Woe, He is jealous!"

"Consider the fate of the city of vice—consider Iram and Gomorrah and Jericho. Consider Jerusalem! For make no mistake, Concord is a new Jerusalem. As God visited destruction on the city of
Solomon, so he visited it on the city of Bernoulli. Solomon built
his temple by enslaving the wind, just as Bernoulli enslaved *your*
spirits. The Babylonians broke Solomon's temple because they had
learned the awful truth: that *all* towers offend God. Solomon had his
Jinn and Bernoulli had his engineers. Our temple mount is empty,
my children, but you must complete God's work. Tear down every
tower! This time the Jinn are not buried beneath the mountain. They
are within us!"

"Cast it out!" they chanted.

"Only when vanity is exorcised, Children, will Concord be a city
of God. Only then will He grant us victory!" The timbre of his voice
was harsh—his violent screaming had scraped the cords ragged—
but the pain behind the hoarseness wrought the crowd's enthusiasm into passion. "Our enemies' blood will flow: the Rasenneisi, the
Ariminumese, the Veians, all the dogs of the south, aye, even the can-
nibals of the Black Hand. Yea, there will be new rivers. Then we shall
cross the Middle Sea to complete our work in Oltremare. We
shall slaughter the schismatics and the apostates together, we shall
make holy the land again and rebuild the true Temple—"

Geta had heard enough. He turned and hurried away. He had an appointment at the Dolore Ostello and he did not want to be around when this sermon reached its climax.

The circling children carried flagellant whips and they used them on the crowd's backs, turning the circle ever faster, increasing the pressure at the grinding center, who pushed and swayed around the pillar, groaning with animal passion, mirroring the wild undulations of the preacher's voice. Those around the base climbed on top of one another to get closer, to touch Fra Norcino, though they achieved little except to injure one another. The bottom of the pillar glistened with bloody handprints.

Fra Norcino paused and looked fondly through his hollow sockets at the mayhem below.

The groans and cheers of the crowd formed an atmosphere that rose up like smoke and hung like a sticky cloud over the streets and piazzas and canals of New City. The scent of it warned those still sane that the streets were unsafe; the rest it drew like flies to carrion. They forgot their businesses, abandoned wives and husbands and infants and joined the procession of toothless old men, fallen women and starving children down the stairways to Old Town.

Lord Geta muttered a blasphemy and drew his sword.

"Give it up," said the man to his left. "There's no way out of this."

"He's a grown man. I'll take that bet," said the one sitting opposite. "I always wanted an Ebionite sword. Where'd you get it?"

"I took it from an Oltremarine soldier. He didn't mind, since I'd just killed him. And he—well, I assume he liberated it from an infidel in similar circumstances."

"Geta! For the Madonna's love, quit," said the shriveled crone next to him, "before you end up betting your spurs." Madame Filangeiri, the proprietor of Concord's most exclusive brothel, wore a faded low-cut gown that had last been in fashion before the Reformation. The Dolore Ostello offered clients a range of nubile children and games of chance for those who still had money left over. She'd done well lately: Norcino's fanciulli had hunted gamblers from their traditional street-corner haunts into gloomy attics and cellars like this one. Norcino's objection to dice-throwing had nothing to do with the more traditional view that the habit ruined families; rather, that it was vain to contest with God, who had decided long ago how all throws must fall. Normally Madame Filangeiri was content to let her clients beggar themselves, but Geta was an old customer, and as close as she had to a friend.

"Madame, I don't know much, but I know when to leave the table," said Geta. "I am still hot." His self-esteem had been increasing with every draft.

She sighed, and said dismissively, "Don't say I didn't warn you. The wager's three hundred silver and one heathen sword. Who's in?"

"Saint Maria!" they heard from the streets above. "Queen of Concord!"

"I wish they'd shut up."

The basement's wood ceiling bulged with age and was shrouded in an inert smoke cloud; the only natural light came from a narrow little window that showed a sliver of the street through dirty brown glass. Hundreds of naked feet went by: a procession of murky, chanting ghosts the gamblers pretended not to hear.

"Who rolls the Die will tell a Lie,
Who rolls the Dice is full of Vice!"

Geta threw down his cards—the Horseman, the Tower and Virgin—and laughed greedily.

"Porca bestia!" The legionary who lost the bet exclaimed, "To lose to this—this—what are you anyway? You even made centurion yet?"

"Truth be told, I'm not sure *what* my rank is now. They're always tearing off my epaulets or adding more bars, so I don't pay attention anymore. I just do what I do and people follow." Geta proffered his bar-laden shoulder. "What do they mean?"

The other man swallowed. "Um . . . Lieutenant . . ."

"Really? You should probably salute me then, Soldier. That's the protocol, isn't it?" As Geta reached for his winnings, there was a thunderous knocking from above and Madame Filangeiri paled beneath her thickly caked lead paint.

Geta chuckled. "Didn't pay up this month, dear lady?"

"Bribe people who melt gold into bonfires? I'd sooner be fed to the Beast." She kicked her sleeping doorman awake. "Get up and see who's there—and tell 'em there ain't no one here."

As the doorman climbed the narrow staircase, Geta turned his predicament over in his mind. He looked at the procuress. "Don't suppose there's a back door you've never told me about?"

Her eyes never left the ceiling. The pounding stopped. "One way in. One way out."

"A man ought be able to let his guard down here of all places," Geta said sulkily.

The other gamblers in the cellar listened to the footsteps overhead with dawning comprehension.

"Madonna, defend us," Madame Filangeiri whispered and blessed herself.

This was a rarity enough to clear Geta's mind. "What about blades?" he whispered.

"No shortage there—that's what most of my customers end up gambling." She produced a key to the chest behind the bar and Geta quickly distributed the hardware. "Stand up, ye heartless hinds," he cried softly. "Remember: it's a disgrace to die without blood on your sword."

There were muffled sounds overhead: the footsteps stopped, words were exchanged; they heard a curse, glasses broken and crunched underfoot, a struggle—and then finally, a stampede of footsteps down the corridor to the stairs: drums rolling them into war.

Geta smashed a dozen bottles on the bottom steps. His fellow gamblers assembled behind him. The drunks had found a sudden dignity, while the sober were shaking and discovering their hitherto unknown devotion to the Madonna, just as Madame Filangeiri had. Geta pushed the most useless to either side of the door and handed them cleavers. "Wait till the first ones pass, then start hacking. Don't be particular: this won't be fencing, it'll be butchery."

He handed around a bottle of claret and made a speech that despite its brevity covered essentials: "Stop praying and pissing yourselves. We came to gamble, didn't we? I've faced the hordes of Byzant and lived and by God, I'm not about to run from a rabble of ten-years-olds! Ready? Here they come. If you want to live, get chopping!"

The broken glass incapacitated the bare-foot mob's front line, but those behind pushed forward without sympathy and the first bodies provided a damp carpet for the rest as they rushed at Geta and his crew of butchers.

No one counted the dead. Fra Norcino was not interested in reassembling the parts; he waded into the still-warm ashes of the Dolore Ostello and made relics instead. After such a reverse a more prudent—or more cynical—leader would have leavened his preaching with caution, been more vague in his condemnations, less precise in his threats—but Fra Norcino was not a cautious man. "O Children, the Virgin said unto Herod, What you have done to the least of these, so God shall do unto thee. She was the agent of God's wrath. Will you be that sword?"

"Yes! Yes!" cried the crowds as they fought over burned hands and charred feet.

"Pity not your brothers and sisters; envy them. They are not fallen; they are risen! By their fiery deaths these martyrs have escaped hell. Consider their reward: consider the fire awaiting their murderers: the nobles and the engineers, the perverted and the blasphemous, idolaters of mammon, idolaters of reason. O Children—"

Geta's once-soiled reputation shone anew after the Battle of the Brothel. Disaffected nobles flocked to his banner, though he knew these soft hands would make worthless soldiers. Decommissioned officers in the capital were rare—the legions were hard-pressed on the frontier—so instead he trawled the Depths for veterans: scarred old soldiers with elaborate beards that looked buffoonish to modern taste; gnarled elders who nursed their amputations and bottles and muttered endlessly of betrayal, of *backstabbers*. Cast aside after years of service, not good enough even to die for their country? They spat their grievances at Geta as if he were responsible, and he nodded and bought another round. Like Fra Norcino, he made promises: medals and women and revenge, and instead of derision in the eyes of the city, fear! It was enough to make even impotent old men stand tall.

The streets no longer welcomed the bare-footed fanciulli. Rocks were no match for quick blades in the night. Different doors were knocked upon now, and those who answered surrendered not their vanities for inspection, but their children. Those recognized as Norcino's followers were led away into the night. The morning found boys hanging from bridges, girls floating in canals.

From his perch in the New City, Consul Corvis watched the damn progress of Geta's bravos through the Depths. He watched the bonfires relit by Fra Norcino's ragged followers and he realized that in this war of all against all, the initiative had passed from the Collegio. If they were to survive, he must make peace with old rivals.

Chapter 43

The Gospel According to St. Barabbas

7   Now this Pilate pursued the Sicarii to the threshold of the
Empty Quarter. The Etruscans boasted that their sword
overreached the world, but that emptiness gave him pause.
In the desert neither king nor emperor has dominion, but
only the Wind. And Pilate hid away his cowardice saying
unto his men, Come and let us leave, for surely the Ishmaelites will kill these interlopers.

8   This did not come to pass. The Ishmaelites were nomads, dis-
trustful of strangers and loyal to each other, but they respected
skill and courage. They recognized the skill of the Sicarii and
the courage of their leader and made them welcome.

10   They eschewed strictures. Their devotion to God they showed
as they showed gratitude or wrath: artlessly and with full
hearts. In time, Mary learned their customs.

11   Their poetry tempered Her grief and as anger left Her heart, the Lord entered it.

12   He said unto Her, Forgive me, my lady. My warning was tardy because I am not Master of this World. I am as Thou art, a fugitive.

13   But I have loyal servants yet. When Thy ancestors escaped out of Egypt, they begged Me to part the Sea. My servant Water was unequal to that task, and needed Wind's assistance. The Water is My right hand and favored, but the Wind is My left hand and mighty.

14   Mary learned humility and the ways of Water and Wind and waxed great in strength and wisdom. Under Her banner the children of Abraham were reconciled.

15   But Mary had not forgotten Her vow to destroy Herod's seed. When Word came that Galilee was oppressed by Antipas, the tyrant's son, She bade farewell to the desert.

Chapter 44

Levi was one of the few condottieri who hadn't pawned his horse, and now his gray destrier set the pace for the stocky maremmano mounts Sofia and Pedro rode. Although not fast, they were dependable beasts. Rasenneisi weren't natural horsemen, but Sofia had been taught to ride in John Acuto's camp and Pedro was a fast learner.

They rode east, clinging to the Irenicon's banks as long as possible. The further away from Rasenna they got, the more the Irenicon behaved like an ordinary river. It inclined downhill and north while their path was up into the Apennines. Thanks to his years as a soldier, scout and spy for John Acuto, Levi knew the quickest route through the so-called Alp of the Moon. Their small party could take narrow paths and passes that would have been precarious for an army carrying baggage. Even so, it was cumbersome going. The Ariminese side was steepest and they had to dismount and pull the horses along.

The Alp of the Moon, Etruria's rooftop, marked the boundary of the Rasenneisi contato. On the far side lay the great flatness of the Marches of Ariminum. The air was thin and the north wind tireless, and when Levi stopped to get his bearings, the horses huddled together for warmth. The peaks of Monte dei Frati and Monte Maggiore loomed over them like horns. They were the source of the gray-blue Ariminus and the Albula River, which thundered south carrying tons of sediment yellow as amber into the great estuary which ancient Veii overlooked.

Levi decided they would follow the Ariminus, and ford it on the other side when its torrent was spent.

He hadn't left his concerns back in Rasenna. "Can Uggeri keep the bandieratori out of trouble?" he asked.

"Making trouble's what good bandieratori do," Sofia said. "The better question is, can Yuri keep the condottieri out of their way? Who knows? We just have to trust them."

Levi didn't like to be so pessimistic, but the hostility they'd faced in the Palazzo del Popolo was still preying on his mind. "Bombelli told me you were the one who suggested the people's Signoria, Pedro. You still believe in it?"

"It was my father's idea; I just repeated it. 'Vox Populi, Vox Dei.' He believed that, but God help us if it's true."

"I've been around, kid. Rasenna's Signoria isn't perfect, but every other state that's thrown off its Families has replaced them with tyrants. The Signoria makes mistakes, but so does everyone—even engineers."

"The difference is that engineers have ways to spot errors and correct them. In the Signoria it's the loudest voices that get heard, and it's always the rich who speak loudest. That's fine in peacetime, but we're going to war soon, whether Bombelli can bear the thought or not."

"What's the alternative?" Sofia said. "The Families again?"

"We've already tried that experiment."

Levi's eyes narrowed. "Perhaps a government of philosophers?"

Pedro shook his head. "Giovanni told me how that ended in Concord. If engineers took over Rasenna we'd run it well for a while, but eventually we'd begin enriching ourselves at the common expense. Power accumulates like water forms in pools. Give me a practical problem and I can solve it, but there's no solution to that."

"So you're not going to participate anymore?"

"The only thing I'm sure of is that one less voice can only be a good thing."

"Your father trusted Bombelli," Sofia said.

"So did I, once, but he's changed. Fabbro the merchant had to get along with everyone. Fabbro the gonfaloniere is different."

"So you'll hide in your tunnels as the towers fall above you," said Levi. "You know where that ends; there are plenty without your scruples seeking power for its own sake. You think your father would be happy with you letting them take it?"

Pedro stopped and looked around. "Are dreamers ever happy? Besides, you're being dramatic. Things haven't got that bad."

The Signoria's compromises faded with every mile they put between them and Rasenna, leaving space for other concerns. Levi had worn out his saddle traveling the South, trying to put together a coalition of Concord's enemies, but now that was actually a prospect, he was concerned that it was the *right* coalition. "Be on guard," he warned them both. "Whatever else they are, the Ariminumese are not honest brokers."

"Surely the fact they called a summit means they're desperate as us," Pedro pointed out. "It means they will be numbered among Concord's enemies, but they do it anyway. I mourn for John Acuto, as every Rasenneisi does, but continual suspicion is an indulgence, Levi. You've said yourself that a necessary precondition for Concord's defeat is a strong league, and a necessary precondition for that league is trust."

Levi considered the logic of this for a while. "They'll try to dominate it," he said at last.

"Let them." Sofia looked at him. "Someone must lead and the Ariminumese won't submit to Rasenneisi—I dislike it as much as you, Levi, but what's the alternative? We need the league more than any other. To go south in strength, Concord must go through us:

that's a fact. With a league at our back, Concord will have to think twice."

"You've changed your tune," Levi said mildly.

"I'd trust the devil himself if he'd help us defeat Concord."

"If I thought defeating Concord was Ariminum's sole aim I wouldn't care who held the baton. I'm just afraid they've come around to the idea for reasons that have nothing to do with Etruria."

"You mean they want help recapturing the Dalmatian colonies?" Pedro suggested. "So that's why you invited the Oltremarines."

"Whether Queen Catrina will come or not is another question. She's not exactly on good terms with the Doge," Levi pointed out. "But we do need a counterweight."

The talk fell away as they rode on, until at last they saw yellowed smoke bleeding over a hill. Beyond the rise, an avalanche of cloud tumbled over a still further peak, rendering hazy the sharp line of the mountain's silhouette, like an ink-loaded brush drawn over damp paper. Levi moved to the front, but all three were on their guard and wary.

It wasn't long before they came upon the burning mound, where two masked laborers were hacking and coughing as they fed black lumps to the flames. Except for a tall, skeletal tree bent under the weight of a senate of crows the hill was bare of life. The black-eyed birds and laborers paused to watch them as they rode by.

Sofia covered her mouth. "Smells like death."

"The sheep must have the murrain," said Pedro. "The farmers have been complaining about it at the markets."

Levi held his nose and murmured, "The only time you need worry about farmers is when they stop complaining. You know what's over that pass south and yonder? Gubbio."

Sofia felt a stabbing chill at the name and pressed her heels to her mount. They rode quickly past to escape its bad luck and whatever miasma poisoned the air, not stopping until they reached a mountain clearing that overlooked the beginning of the Ariminumese contato.

They'd forded the Ariminus a while back, and now they saw its winding trail eased down the flat slope to empty into the lagoon, its strength spent, with sundry tributaries veering off to the south like deserters.

The last time Sofia had approached this city, she had taken another route from Concord. It was getting dark, and just as then, Ariminum's twinkling lights glowed in the night like an aurora: the burning energy of ceaseless trade, the type of city Bombelli wanted to build, the city Giovanni's bridge had made possible.

As Pedro and Sofia went to collect firewood, Pedro started to talk about Ariminum's famous shipyard, which he was eager to see for himself. "Giovanni would be proud of you," Sofia said.

Their mutual esteem for the dead engineer made them affectionate to each other, but each was weighed down by things unsaid. Pedro had never dared tell Sofia that Giovanni was a Bernoulli—even if he could find the words, what would be the point of adding to her grief?

Sofia wondered if she could ever tell Pedro—or Levi, for that matter—the truth about Giovanni. She had always been vague about the manner of his death, intimating that he had drowned when the second Wave struck. There was no way to make people understand that, in one sense, Giovanni hadn't died. But whatever he was, buio or man, he had sacrificed himself to save Rasenna, so perhaps that was all that mattered. At times she felt his presence, in her dreams, when cold rain struck her skin, when she looked into the undulating, leaping froth of the Irenicon going under the bridge . . .

Pedro picked up the wood and left Sofia to her thoughts and she gazed down at the two horns of Ariminum's harbor stretching wide apart, welcoming the Adriatic, Ariminum's "road" to the great Middle Sea and the infidel lands beyond. To the north lay the great Venetian Gulf—more swamp than sea, to be sure, and cluttered with marsh islands and rocks, but the gulf was Ariminum's back door to Europa, by which it avoided Concordian tolls. Growing up under Doc's flag, Sofia had *learned* Rasenna, from its narrowest alleys to its highest tower-tops. It was a world complete unto itself—an illusion destroyed when she was taken to Concord. Now she knew that Rasenna was but one tower among many. Based on her last experience of negotiating with the Ariminumese, with John Acuto, the summit would be a protracted affair.

This was much more than a positive political development for her, though: the opportunity to escape Rasenna before every fool in the street could see she was pregnant was God-sent. She felt her stomach with mixed dread and excitement: *life*, inside her and growing, like an idea in one's mind, but much more. This was *real*. But the summit was unlikely to last more than a few weeks at best; what should she do when it concluded? Stay until she had the baby then return with an "orphan"? She knew Rasenna; no one would be fooled by that charade. And if Isabella was right, neither option was safe.

But it was hard to consider abstract danger when the prospect of humiliation was so much more real. Sofia had grown up with the boys of Workshop Bardini; she had heard the mockery pelted at unmarried mothers. Some families had a grim solution to the shame: a midnight drowning. There were many Rasenneisi—like Maddalena Bombelli—who'd rejoice to see the proud Scaligeri heir brought low. Even worse than the mockery, she feared the high-minded pity of the matrons. Only now that there was a small chance of avoiding this would Sofia admit to herself how scared she had been.

When she wandered back to the fire, Levi was saying to Pedro, "Don't get your hopes up about the shipyard, kid. We'll be lucky if they don't make us camp outside the walls like last time. Right, Sofia?"

She smiled in acknowledgment. In the silence, the fire popped and winds howled between distant peaks. Levi threw some more wood on. "Tired, huh? Tomorrow'll be easier." He smiled at Sofia. "It's downhill all the way—"

"I'm with child."

Pedro and Levi looked at each other in alarm, then back at Sofia. She stared at them as if ready to fight. "There it is! It'll be impossible to hide soon."

"Contessa!" Levi smiled wanly. "Congratulations!"

"You mean commiserations. You mean who's the father? Well, I won't say but I can tell you I don't intend to return to Rasenna until after. You called me Contessa, Levi, but I gave up that title. The Scaligeri name's all I have now, and if this gets out, I won't even have that."

"You can count on my discretion," Pedro said.

"Thank you," Sofia said, and turned to Levi.

"How can you even ask?" He was indignant. "I'll defend your honor with my life."

"All I ask is silence."

The riding next morning was smoother, as Levi had promised. The ground leveled off into a great green flatness; beyond the city's high walls it ran seamlessly into the sea. An awkward silence had troubled breakfast and more than once Levi caught Pedro looking at him narrowly as he stamped out the fire.

Sofia was riding slowly behind. Levi fell back into step beside her. "Sleep well?"

"Fine."

"Look, that's where the Hawk's camp was—remember?"

Sofia said absently, "Yes."

Levi took hold of her arm. "Look here, damnit! I've never blamed a soldier for having fun when they get an opportunity—a girl just pays a higher penalty, that's all—"

"*Fun?*" She pulled her arm away. "It wasn't like that!"

Levi's face clouded. "Who?"

"It wasn't like that either. It was . . . something else. I told you and Pedro out of respect. Respect my privacy."

Levi nodded quickly. "I understand. Forgive me." He flicked the reins with forced casualness and rode ahead. Pedro looked back as he caught up and Levi saw again the suspicion behind his glance. "How dare you, boy? She's almost half my age!" It was a weak defense; that had never stopped a condottieri before, but Pedro knew the truth when he heard it and apologized.

The road was lined by poplars which overshadowed it like long fangs; the trees were overshadowed themselves by the soaring columns of a ruined Etruscan aqueduct. When Pedro wondered aloud that no one repaired it, neither Levi nor Sofia replied, though either might have told him that Ariminum had no lack of water. As the party rode up to Ariminum they kept their distance from each other and their fears private.

Chapter 45

The Gospel According to St. Barabbas

17 Mary's band, now grown great, returned to Judea. As it was Passover, they stopped and went up to Jerusalem.

18 And the disciple called Barabbas saw the temple. He was angry and said, my lady, we must cast out all those that sell and buy in the temple, and overthrow the tables of the money-changers, and the seats of them that sell doves.

19 But Mary answered, It is too late to make that place clean. Is it not written that My house shall be called the house of prayer; but ye have made it a den of thieves? The time is coming when ye shall see the words of My father borne out.

20 Now the priests heard that Mary was in Jerusalem, and they sought to trap Her. Since they were jealous they believed Barabbas when he said he was jealous and would betray Mary.

21 He led them to a garden on the Mount of Olives where the Sicarii lay waiting. In the fight Barabbas lost his ear, but he thought it a small price to kill those who would betray his lady.

22 After the Sicarii broke out of the city there was uproar. Every man was turned against every other as one brother backed the priests and another, the Sicarii.

23 And the wise remembered the prophets' warning, that every kingdom divided against itself is brought to desolation.

23 The Etruscans lost all patience with the Jews and they laid siege unto Jerusalem.

24 This was the beginning of the people's tribulation, yet only when they saw the temple destroyed did they remember the words of Zacharias.

Chapter 46

Take care around men who are careful when drunk. Lord Geta spoke boldly in his cups, but some remembered that he had not spoken quite so freely before the Molè burned, no matter how many bottles had stood empty on his private table. Bold talk was commonplace now; few thought it likely that the engineers would remain Concord's masters much longer.

"You can't tell me we were all bad or that you didn't want us. We lived for *you.* The mob must work so that a few may dance, write verse, fight duels—we were your hawks; we made the hunt elegant and you gave it all to the dogs. Bad luck, Signori, bad luck."

As Geta warmed to his theme, the older drinkers shook their heads and smiled. The speech was foolish and self-serving, but it was true. It was hardly an unusual subject for a drunken noble to declaim upon, but most suspected that even if it were in Geta's power, he wouldn't change a thing.

"Oh, we had our fun, but you whores encouraged us: you can play coy, but you raised your skirts ready enough." His languorous merriment matched neither his polemic nor his military bearing.

"Give it a damn rest, Geta." The voice drifted through the mingled smoke and body heat that passed for atmosphere in The Rule and Compass.

Geta ignored him. "The noble Senator Tremellius was the Reformation's first casualty. Its second? Glad you asked: nobility itself, no less. So, all equal, all impoverished." He looked around for his long-departed lady companion, snorted a laugh and lazily surveyed the company through the yellow gloom. "Not that ye lice would notice the difference."

A different voice answered this time, a boy's, and the tone was not bantering. "You're the bloodsucker."

The tavern fell silent. Geta appeared not to have heard, but as if remembering some pressing appointment, he suddenly stirred, pulling himself up to his full height with a languid grace that belied his drunkenness. He pulled his heavy cloak over his shoulder and snatched up his hat, setting it at a precise angle, more dandy than soldier, before striding out. The other patrons watched fondly; his proud bearing carried the past with him—a hundred battles, a thousand banquets. Even with his limp, the snapping heels of his long boots and bright ringing spurs conjured stately dances of days gone by—dances to which they would never have been invited. Now nobody danced, the musicians had departed and they called it progress.

It was almost a shock when Geta stumbled into a low table where a girl and boy sat whispering together in low voices under low hoods that covered their faces.

"A thousand, one million apologies, my good—"

"Mind your step, you drunken oaf," the boy snarled, pushing Geta's elbow so that he lost his balance again and fell sprawled on his back.

Lord Geta lay there a moment and sighed loudly. Presently he sat up and said with regret, "Boy, I must kill you for that."

"Lord Geta," the tavern owner began as the swordsman stood and dusted himself off, "just leave him alone—don't you know he's—?"

In a whirl of color, Geta had his sword unsheathed and pointed at the boy's neck. "An engineer? Is that what you're going to tell me?" He pushed the blade forward before the boy could react, though he wasn't aiming to cut. With his blade he pushed back the boy's hood to reveal the numerals imprinted in sepia italics across the side of his shaven skull. "He might have been, if he hadn't insulted the wrong fellow."

The boy was speechless, but his partner spoke up. "My lord, please."

Geta kept his blade pointed at the boy's neck, but his eyes slid sideways. "Take off your hood." He looked at her appraisingly as she did. "You're no beauty, Cadet," he said after a moment, "but you could do a *lot* better than this pug-nosed whelp."

"Please," she said. "He'll—"

He brought the blade down and prodded the boy's gullet. "Pay for my drink? Damn generous of him. I've been running up my slate since yesterday morning and the lady I came in with appears to have absconded."

As the stupefied boy fumbled for his purse, Geta leaned up against the bar and ordered another bottle. "Baldy's paying. *Salute*," he shouted after the Cadets as they hurriedly stood up and left.

He pinched some snuff onto his hand as he kept an eye on the door. A month ago, Lord Geta's only goal had been getting reinstated, but since the Battle of the Brothel a larger prize was in sight. He wasn't about to leave the table, not with this hand, not while he was this hot.

The door opened again, and a fair-haired boy walked confidently to the bar, shooing away a barmaid by saying he was waiting for someone. Geta leaned over and offered some snuff, and when the boy studied him coolly, he affected to be insulted and turned away, pointedly leaving his silver snuffbox open on the bar. The boy sidled closer to whisper an apology and returned the box. As Geta took it, the boy took Geta's hand, turned it over and sprinkled some snuff on his wrist, then slowly brought it to his own nose and inhaled. He held it there until Geta suddenly grabbed his neck, but he didn't struggle as Geta pulled him in, but rather stood on tiptoe and leaned against the swordsman's chest to whisper in his ear.

No one paid any attention: The Rule and Compass' reputation for discretion was well deserved—and anyway, noble perversions had long ceased to be fodder for gossip; in their long twilight and exile from power, bluebloods had little to do but cultivate louche habits. Since the Curia's overthrow, there were no more confession boxes for censorious informants to hide in. Fra Norcino's followers were less liberal, but since the Battle of the Brothel they had troubles of their own.

After the boy left, Geta stayed to finish the bottle and to let the streets empty. The Old City byways used to be thronged at all hours, but not now; those who still walked the Depths at night were swordsmen whose long shadows made victims where they fell.

Geta was an old hand at intrigue; he had recognized the lad's blend of secrecy and earnestness. He had been invited to talk of revolution, but until he discovered whether that invitation came from fools or men of consequence, he must tread carefully—but his interest was piqued by the New City address the boy had left in his snuffbox.

His disempowered generation had grown up amid fevered intoxicating talk of Restoration, and he knew where most plots ended: those that did not collapse though internecine assassination and betrayal led straight to the scaffold. But that was before. Now Concord was up for grabs, whether one dated it from the night the Molè burned or from the day that the Twelfth perished.

Geta was out of shape since his court-martial. He found himself sweating as he climbed the narrow old stairways that led to the Ponte Bernoulliana, where New and Old Concord were allowed to meet. He stopped to urinate and catch his breath at the Piazzetta Bocca della Verità.

A single cresset fixed to the wall above the leering Mouth kept the darkness at bay—only New City was worth illuminating by globe.

With the help of the moon's impartial light, Geta read the latest Truth:

I spit libation for brave Rasenna
Pondering Concord's dire dilemma:
hat cruel fate it was that sent us
boy to be our last Apprentice.

Pinned below, in another hand:

I Say, I say:	*The Twelfth is none,*	*Three is One:*	
	The Tenth, The Ninth,	*What's the point?*	
	Sore subtraction.	*War's eruption*	
	Bound to follow.	*Hard to swallow*	
	One more lie.	*So hang them high*	*Say I, Say I*

Still smiling at that, he scanned the other scrawled graffiti. There were the usual partisan slogans of the Naturalists and Empiricists, and more numerous complaints from those who made no such distinction and denounced all engineers together. But here—yes, he'd seen it in New City too—a new graffito: a Herod's Sword in front of a rising sun, and the legend, *Her Kingdom Come.*

What did it mean? Nothing. Who was drawing it? No one. The children of the city were a new class as far as Geta was concerned: not noble, not engineer, not Small People, but some other thing. He turned away with a bemused smile and found two shadows waiting behind him. Assuming ambush, he raised a quick dagger, but then they stepped back into the light and he recognized the Cadets from The Rule and Compass. Perhaps they'd come here to slander one of their teachers; perhaps he'd interrupted an assignation.

The boy recovered his courage quickly. "Put your knife down, old man. It's rusty and you have no audience here." He was obviously still smarting from the embarrassment the swordsman had dealt him in front of the girl, and the tavern.

"Aye, we're all alone," Geta said softly. The moon reflected in his still-raised blade, then it blinked and became a red liquid eye. A slash of black appeared on the boy's neck, growing as if drawn by some unseen, slow-moving pen.

Geta appeared not to have moved, but for the widening smile underneath his moustaches. His eyes shifted to the boy's companion as the boy attempted to gurgle his sweetheart's name through a fine spray of blood from his neatly severed trachea. A fountain of blood followed, splashing into the dark puddle at the boy's feet. Pink steam wafted from the mingling blood and piss.

"My Lord." The girl took a step back from it and whispered, "I won't say a word."

"Who could you tell? Nobody's listening anymore."

As she turned to flee, Geta grabbed the back of her gown and tugged her toward him into his embrace. As she whimpered, the blade entered and Geta dragged his hand across his weary brow. He considered the merits of dumping the bodies in a canal. The cease-less current would quickly bring them to Monte Nero—the Molè might be gone, but all Concord knew the beast's appetite remained, undiminished. The young couple would not be lonely on their final journey; these days, the canals were choked with bodies, a pilgrim-age of true equality drawn from every stratum. But Geta's romantic mood passed and he left the Cadets where they were lying, not even troubling to destroy their faces—engineers were no longer untouchable, and murder had never been remarkable.

Feeling thirsty again, Geta had automatically turned toward the nearest tavern when he remembered his destination, and swearing, he turned around and raced up the steps, anxious now that he might be late. The labyrinth of stairways and little alleys leading up to New City was crooked as an Ariminumese cleric, the quite intentional effect to separate old and new, ruled and rulers. The nobility's complaint had never been the segrega-tion, which they approved; they simply thought they were on the wrong end of it.

"Concord *needs* you."

Geta sniffed the wine with exaggerated care, then swigged it back and held the empty glass up to the fair-haired boy to refill. Dispatching the Cadets had left him in a sour mood. "*You* need me, but you don't speak for Concord anymore, Spinther."

"I will soon," Leto said with assurance.

The general looked like an insolent boy to Geta, though any youthful élan was fading somewhat. Disgrace plainly did not sit easily with the lad. He might wear his raven-black hair long, like a soldier, but a number was etched on the skull beneath, just like the rest of them.

"You're not confident of that. If you *were* confident you wouldn't have allowed my glass to be refilled three times. If you *were* confident, you'd want me sober instead of agreeable. If you *were* confident, you'd be giving me dates and places and names."

"I'm confident, Geta, just not in you. Before we get to details we need to be sure we can trust you. There's never yet been a successful rebellion, and every *unsuccessful* attempt has one thing in common."

"They were betrayed," Geta agreed.

"I didn't become general at the age of twelve by being foolhardy."

"But it can't hurt having a name like Spinther, not to mention friends in such high places."

Leto ignored this. "The majority of the consuls want to see an end to Apprentice rule: it's inefficient and outdated, and after Rasenna, it needs only a push."

"Getting ahead of yourself, aren't you? If the Collegio wants to overthrow the last Apprentice it's only to take power for itself."

"That's why I am keeping this to senior officers only: control the army and we control the State."

"I'm not an officer anymore. You saw to that."

"That's entirely to do with your lack of discipline, not lack of talent. Besides that, you're a graduate of the Rasenneisi workshops."

"You mean there'll be street fighting."

"Most likely, and if it comes to that—"

"—you'll need someone good at it." Geta was impressed, but he refused to show it. "Isn't the last Apprentice a friend of yours?"

"Torbidda was . . . an ally once. Things change."

"Tell me about it. Look, this is all very thrilling, but you're assuming the legions will follow you, and that's assuming too much. The only thing the generals hate more than the Collegio is each other. I didn't hear any great outpourings of grief for Luparelli."

"Luparelli was a pompous ass. I'm not interested in your analysis; I'm asking you the same thing I'm asking the others: when it happens, that you mobilize for me."

"Mobilize what? I have no men."

"Don't be disingenuous. I have my spies: I'll never fathom why, but you've acquired quite a following in the Depths, and it's in this city, not the swamps of Europa, where the empire will be won or lost."

"What about the praetorians? You have to get through them to get the Apprentice."

"Corvis has Castrucco in his pocket."

"And you have Corvis? Ah, I wondered why you two were snarling at each other so much at my court-martial. I felt quite left out. Very well. Very clever. Let me ask the same thing whoever else you've approached has asked: what's in it for me?"

Leto sighed deeply. "That's a hell of an attitude. Where's your patriotism?"

Geta started laughing. "Madonna, is that all you have? I'm loyal to those who pay. I came here expecting an offer." He stood up and grabbed an unopened bottle. "I'll take this for my troubles. Don't bother me again till you have something real."

Geta turned and wobbled a little on his feet, exaggerating his drunkenness. He stumbled to the door, and then turned around, almost disappointed.

"You're still so young, Spinther. When I said no, you ought to have killed me on the spot. That's how I know you're not serious. When I start hearing stories of generals meeting untimely deaths, I'll start believing. Good luck, Signori."

Leto listened till Geta's footsteps had reached the bottom step, then he cleared his throat. From a dark corner of the room, a side-panel clicked opened. A man wearing a consul's chain stepped out. His eyes twinkled in the gloom as he asked, "Did he say 'Signori'?"

"Yes—it's that Rasenneisi training. Geta can smell a trap better than any officer I know."

"Why don't we just hire a damn condottiere?" said Corvis with sudden distaste. "Geta's only talent is making trouble."

"We need troublemakers."

"Well, he said no."

"Just wait. The situation's getting worse by the day. The worse it gets the better for us. Geta's a wharf rat, he'll jump aboard."

Consul Corvis listened thoughtfully; the Spinther boy understood the legions like he understood the Guild, but Geta brought something to the table neither of them had: Old Town. Corvis was still a little incredulous that the general had even suggested enlisting the scoundrel who had nearly destroyed Spinther's career along with his own. To rise above such a grudge, to ally with an enemy in order to go to war against an old friend? The coming struggle would require such discipline—that, and a great deal of luck. The last Apprentice might be isolated and friendless, but he still wore the red.

How many legions was that worth?

PART III:
CITY OF BRIDGES

Ho, every one that thirsteth, come ye to the waters.

Isaiah 55:1

Chapter 47

THE HISTORY OF THE ETRURIAN PENINSULA

Volume II: The City of Bridges

All Etrurians share one belief: that the Ariminumese are not to be trusted. This prejudice does a great disservice to a remarkable race. The Serenissima is not a city, it is a miracle: a miracle built with refugee prayers using malarial sandbanks for foundations.

By the end of the first century Anno Domina, the Etruscans had taught their pet barbarian armies two things: to love gold and to hate Etruscans. When the Empire's decline began, it was these barbarians who dealt the killing blow. The Etruscan peoples retreated to the safety of hilltops as the peninsula was invaded by successive tribes of swift horsemen with names as strange as their manners.

One group of Etruscans had a different strategy: these eccentrics took refuge in the Ariminumese lagoon, a place favored only by hermits and water-fowl—and began harvesting the salt-fields and pickling fish. A dark, perilous age passed, and when dawn broke, Etrusca had become Etruria and the lagoon had become a city.[11] In the centuries to follow, the Ariminumese were well situated to dominate the trade-routes of the Middle Sea. Today, though her colonies dot the Adriatic coast and her wealth is beyond reckoning, her motto proclaims that she will be virgin, unarmed, unwalled and unconquered always.[12]

11. The first reliable reports of the settlement appear in the fifth century. We must not imagine the exquisite beauty of the contemporary city but a motley cluster of huts wobbling on stilts like insects.

12. *Fortis Iusta Trona Furias Maris Sub Pede Pono*—Enthroned, Just and Strong, I defeat the Fury of the Sea. How then to explain her recent expansion onto Terra Firma and acquisition of the accoutrements of war? Ariminumese diplomats maintain that these are precautionary measures prompted by Concordian expansion. Less biased commentators call it a betrayal of Terra da Mar, the source of her greatness.

Chapter 48

Though it was already outmoded, Pedro studied the famous triple wall out of professional interest.

"It impressed me once," Sofia said as they rode to the gates.

"There's no security in fortifications anymore," said Pedro with a sigh. The Ariminumese clearly had no experience of the efficiency of Concord's sappers.

"Think there'll be anyone to welcome us?"

"Doubt it," Levi said as he dismounted. "You remember last time."

When they announced themselves, a tiny bell rang, and was echoed directly by chiming bells from the mist-shrouded city beyond. The gates lifted to reveal a guard of honor, with a middle-aged man waiting at the end. Levi didn't recognize him, or the court-iers hovering around. "Must have had a change of management," he muttered.

The man was plump and hairless, and wore a turban like an ancient Radinate king. As they ducked under the portcullis, he smiled. "Welcome, friends!"

"Well, this is a good sign," Pedro whispered.

"Or bad," said Levi. "They must be really desperate."

The smiling fellow who introduced himself as the Procurator of Saint Barabasso's Basilica was full of old-fashioned courtesy to Sofia, who had agreed to Levi's request that she resume her title for the trip, but when Levi introduced the procurator to Pedro, he took a reverent step back. "You're the one who blocked Concord's wave?"

"Well, not on my own—"

The procurator waved away his protestations. "A Rasenneisi *engineer*: this is a *sensation*!"

The flattery was designed to put them at ease, but Pedro wasn't fooled; every Etrurian knew that Ariminum had two faces: the newly acquired mask she presented to the land, and her true face, that looked always and hungrily to the Middle Sea.

Sofia had glimpsed a few of the famous canals on her previous visit, but she had had no leisure to pay them much attention. She was therefore both surprised and concerned when the procurator led their party down a side-alley to a dock where a large gondola was waiting in the still water. Pedro had no reservations and bounded in first. Sofia exchanged a glance with Levi and followed.

The gondolier, a silent Tyrolean slave with jaundiced skin, propelled them though a dark maze of canals, over which old tenement houses leaned confrontationally. Often the only thing holding them apart was a small humped bridge, though many of the bridges were dead-ends hanging pointlessly in space like spontaneous eruptions of masonry. Ariminum was a city raised from the waves, and everywhere Sofia looked, seaweed and barnacles knotted the church spires and fish flopped breathlessly on canal banks. Her Rasenneisi sense of direction was based on a topside vantage; after a few turns in this foggy netherworld she was quite lost. At least she now understood why the streets on her last visit had always been empty, except for a few bony dogs: the streets were for foreigners.

Here was Rasenna's dark twin, a city connected by water. There were paths and piazzas like other towns, but here they *flowed*. The "streets" were not uniformly deep: boats glided over one part; over another, people scurried across, getting soaked to their shins. A guideless foreigner would never survive this city. If he didn't drown, the ubiquitous griffins would surely have him—they peeked out under bridges, loomed from rooftops and snarled from doorknobs, rendered in carved stone, cast bronze and beaten metal and embroidered on flags and crests.

The gondola escaped the pressing alleys at last and turned into a wide canal crossed by several bridges, each decorated distinctly— austere Etruscan, geometric Oltremarine, severe Concordian— although Pedro noticed that they all leapt the canal with an identical apogee arch. The bridges were laden with people, and the torches they carried danced with their reflections in the still bright evening.

"You didn't go to this trouble for us?"

The procurator shifted uncomfortably. "Oh, ah—"

"They're not well-wishers, Levi," Sofia said, "they're fighters."

"I'm afraid the lovely Contessa is correct," the procurator said, still a little embarrassed. "This congregation is not in your honor— your visit, alas, has coincided with a rather violent rash of *battaglia di pugni*. But it should not cause any problems to you or any of the delegates, if you avoid certain neighborhoods—"

He saw Levi's scowl and quickly clarified, "Not that the State approves, you understand. We try to keep the peace between the Guilds; but every couple of years the arsenalotti and the merchants— that is, those who build ships and those who sail them—require another forum to thrash out their differences. Afterward the map of ownership is redrawn, each ward gains a few new blocks here and loses a few there." They passed under the first bridge and the procurator looked up and said with condescending admiration, "Look at them. They fight for each inch with such *passion*."

A man with a violently scarlet neckerchief fell, but was caught by another man in a scarlet chemise. The pair were promptly attacked by several men dressed in checkered gray.

"What caused this outbreak?" Pedro asked.

"That question, dear boy, only a theologian could answer. I will say that the lower orders feel more freedom to express themselves when the government's unpopular. But in truth, the Small People are like Stromboli, there's no pattern to their eruption—not a night goes by without an altercation—a drunken first mate and arsenalotti dispute over money, women, what have you—but what makes a brawl turn into a city-wide tumult is beyond the ken of even the Consilium Sapientium."

"Homesick?" Levi asked Sofia. She punched him in the arm, and asked the procurator who typically won.

"They look evenly matched in terms of manpower," said Pedro.

"Each party grows with our commercial shipping and navy respectively—and both are very bloated, I'm happy to report. I don't presume to be a judge of fighters besides Rasenneisi, but I'm told the arsenalotti are tougher."

"The ones in gray?"

"Just so, Contessa. There hadn't been a *battaglia* since I was very young. But we had one immediately after news arrived that the Hawk's Company had saved Rasenna—"

Levi looked coyly at Sofia, and she punched him again.

"Well, everyone hates to bet on a loser, don't they? The Doge wasn't very popular. And now everyone's out of sorts again—perhaps it's this business in Dalmatia, or maybe revolt's in the air—a wicked pollen, floating all over Europa and sowing conflagration where it alights. Watch out!"

Another body tumbled from the bridge and the splash was followed by a great cheer. The victim's fellow Guildsmen efficiently fished him out with long gondolier oars.

"Why do you allow it?" Levi asked.

Sofia smiled at his gravity. He was accustomed to thinking as a podesta now.

The procurator made an anxious face. "We Ariminumese are conservative by nature. We respect the Guilds' ancient privileges—although this one is relatively new, admittedly. It's only been in existence a few centuries. Still, tradition is tradition."

"You mean it's preferable they exhaust each other, rather than join forces against you."

The procurator's laugh was high and innocent. "You have it exactly, Contessa! Plain speaking's a foreign tongue here, so I'm grateful for the opportunity to practice with a Rasenneisi. It is just so: if the Small People periodically require a riot, as long as it doesn't interrupt the good order of the State or—Madonna forbid—commerce, then so be it. We think of the State as a ship: you can't always expect peaceful waters. If our canals were as lethal as your rivers, we'd have to find another way to distract them. No reform is possible, so by necessity we make distraction a fine art. The book was closed centuries ago and now we must play our hand to the end." He pointed to a silver plaque on the bridge they were passing under. "My father was a boy when that bridge collapsed in the course of a particularly boisterous *battaglia*. That motto was inscribed upon it when it was rebuilt."

Sofia read, "*Cam'era, dov'era.*"

"That's how we'd rebuild Ariminum if she burned tomorrow. As it was, where it was. We are condemned and committed to this place and we cannot escape it." He sighed romantically. "And nor would we wish to."

"At least you know you're playing with fire," said Levi. Sofia knew his thoughts were back in Rasenna.

"The *battaglie are* rather messy," he admitted, "but when tension builds up, better out than in—look at what's happening in Concord. Everything's turned upside down just because they are unaccustomed to choppy waters. It defies understanding, does it not, Maestro Vanzetti? Engineers of all people should appreciate the value of a release valve. When one runs into bad luck, *someone* must pay for it." He shook his head philosophically, then cleared his throat. "Speaking of dues, this misunderstanding we had with the Hawk's Company during our last negotiations—"

"There was no misunderstanding," said Levi calmly. He and Sofia had both reconciled themselves to dealing with the man who'd betrayed John Acuto.

"I admit the Doge made a terrible mistake, and naturally, you want revenge. But I hope you realize why handing over our leader would be unthinkable! The Doge *is* Ariminum—"

Sofia and Levi were tight-lipped.

"—oh my, listen to the bells! We must hurry—I do hope they don't start without us."

Chapter 49

The slurred Ariminumese dialect is notorious, but the language of her bells is even more impenetrable. It is a rare foreigner who can distinguish the Campanile's chimes and their meanings, rung out according to various combinations. Some tell the time: the *Nona* marks midday; the *maragona* rings at dawn and dusk. Others report governmental activities, a universal concern; the *trottiera* and the *nezza terza* announce meetings of the Consiglio and Senate respectively. Others announce public holidays; the *malefrico,* for example, announces executions, and when it rings nine peals of doubles an especially rare spectacle is in store.

from The Stones of Ariminum *by Count Titus Tremellius Pomptinus*

They were close to the sea now. Great white gulls made lazy figure-eights overhead and the great canal was choked with barges coming and going to the harbor. The procurator noticed Pedro's eyes fixed on the dark smoke columns.

"I see you've guessed our destination, Maestro Vanzetti. Doubtless you'll appreciate how rarely this opportunity is afforded to foreigners. Much of the work at the Arsenal is secret, but I'll be happy to arrange a pass so you can visit whenever you wish during the negotiations."

Before Pedro could say anything, Levi interrupted, "That may be . . . premature."

The procurator smiled. "Of course, Podesta Levi. You've been very gracious not to dwell on how *poorly* you were dealt with at our last encounter."

"By 'poorly' you mean—"

"—I mean treacherously. That's why I brought you this particular route."

From nearby, a deafening cheer erupted suddenly, followed by cascading cannon-fire.

"Oh, *cazzo*!" the procurator swore. "Damn your sloth, Slave! I'll have you scourged if we've missed it!"

Pedro smelled the familiar tang of foundry smoke, and something else—boiling tar? The procurator berated the silent gondolier to quicken his stroke and as they cleared the last bridge the canal bisected. They ignored the branch to the harbor and took the other, sailing into a solid greasy fog like that of Tartarus multiplied a hundredfold. They glided under a steel arch and between two tall, featureless walls lined with grim sentries toward a great shipyard emerging from the black smoke.

Pedro gasped at the tapestry of dense rigging between the ships, and the hardy workmen scrambling careless over this tangled net like ants: the arsenalotti in their element. The ships they tended were not the fat-bellied cogs that jostled in the harbor, but streamlined and multi-decked men-of-war bristling with shining black guns.

"What say you, Maestro Vanzetti?" said the procurator merrily. "Concord has its legions, but Ariminum has the Arsenale. However much Concord's engineers dissect and prod, they will never understand water; it's our natural element."

"Impressive," said Pedro. From any other, it would have sounded faint praise.

"What does mastery of the seas matter when we have no rivals to contest it?" the procurator said, glowing with false modesty. "But I didn't bring you here to marvel at our navy; I wanted you to say farewell to the outgoing government. Alas, we missed their departure."

Between two galleys stretched a rope, thick as a man's waist, and from it eight naked bodies were hanging. Denuded of their official robes, the old men's withered bodies looked pathetic and sad. As the gondola got closer, Sofia recognized the beak-nosed cadaver in the center; his legs, brown with dribbling shit, were still dancing.

"After Rasenna demonstrated Concordian vulnerability, we had to reconsider our policy."

"You *hanged* the Doge?"

"*Madonna!* The very idea, Contessa! Executing a Doge is impossible. But *arranging* an election, that is a very simple thing, and when we took the corno from the Doge's head and the ring from his finger, his Serenity became a simple citizen once more. He wasn't happy about it, but he understood the ship can always find a new captain. Ariminum is bigger than any one man, any one family. Only *continuity* matters." The procurator had the modest smile of one who has done a great favor.

The macabre spectacle struck Sofia dumb, but Levi was smoothly diplomatic. "Thank you for this most thoughtful gesture."

Chapter 50

VOLUME II: THE CITY OF BRIDGES

The Empty Throne

Besides a talent for commerce, a true Ariminumese has an intuitive ability to navigate bureaucracy. The dense tiers of government are a topic as urgent for foreign merchants as the tides and currents of the lagoon are for sailors. Like any intricate work of art, it takes time and study to reveal its overall shape.

At the top is the Doge, who presides over the Signoria. Unlike the Signoria of other cities, Ariminum's is a ceremonial body with few executive powers. It consists of seven Councillors[13] and the three Heads of Forty, the leaders of the Senate. The Senate is made up of a select hundred and twenty "good" men. Beneath the Senate is a Maggior Consiglio which rejoices in one thousand and one members. Participation in this last

---

13. Typically, former Doges.

branch is restricted to those patrician families listed in the Golden Book.[14]

These ornate arrangements, though certainly picturesque, conceal the reality from foreigners. Real power in Ariminum is invested in a small side-branch of the Senate known as the Consiglio dei Dieci.[15]

14. One can buy one's way into anything in Ariminum, with the exception of the Maggior Consiglio. According to tradition the Golden Book was closed forever in AD 1001 on October 1st at 10:01 a.m.

15. This mundane truth is deeply unsatisfying for conspiratorial Etrurians, and where reality fails, imagination takes flight. The rumor goes that The Ten are subject to another ministry of state, the so-called *Consilium Sapientium,* a three-man body that spends men's lives like days, that has not slept since the city's foundation. The identity of these mythical wise men is a favorite speculation among the cognoscenti.

Chapter 51

Knowing the Serenissima's hospitality would not last a second longer than was expedient, the Rasenneisi did not stop to enjoy their sumptuous apartments, however magnificently decorated they were, and perfectly placed in the heart of the governmental quarter, with the fresh breeze from the harbor and the cooling shadow of Saint Barabbasso's Basilica. Sofia and Levi were eager to explore the parts of Ariminum that had been out of bounds last time.

Pedro was only interested in the Arsenal.

The ship's skeleton was encased and supported by a cage of scaffolding that didn't appear equal to the task. One look at the elegantly carved spars told Pedro that the arsenalotti knew their trade. They were practical men, like him, who had learned their craft from their fathers: how to judge timber, how to spot rot and infection, when to use pine, when oak; how to steam wood, how to harden it, how to cut. The less skillful parts of construction were left to the numerous slaves whose destiny was to later row the very ships they were building.

A chorus of bells kept the arsenalotti dancing in time, but to guess their meaning was as impossible as saying where one ship's rigging ended and another's began. As Pedro watched, an entire galley was assembled in a few hours, and his incredulity turned to respect. He was astounded not just by the workers' speed, but the efficiency with which their labor was divided. Ariminum was like the short-lived corporations Fabbro assembled before trading ventures: an unreal legal entity that sufficed to allow squabbling manufacturers, investors and merchants to work harmoniously for a time.

All these new warships bore out Levi's suspicions too: the Ariminumese had a different conception of this League than everyone else.

The forest of dark ships in the harbor swayed gently on the water as small jetties darted between them and circled like kites, the tillermen unerringly finding the gaps. They heeled hard without ever slowing to bring themselves parallel, needing only a few braccia to execute such maneuvers.

Sofia and Levi got used to sidestepping the heavy ropes thrown from fore and aft of the docking galleys. Opportunistic traders thronged the harbor with gangs of jostling slaves, offering to assist unloading whatever goods the ships carried in return for first preference to buy.

RAT–AT–TAT–TAT

The gangway bounced once, twice, and the slaves continued their work but bowed automatically—they might not know the first man to disembark, but they could be certain he was important.

Most ships were unloading people, not produce—and well-dressed people, not slaves. "Refugees from the Ariminumese colonies on the far side of the Adriatic," Levi observed. "There's what precipitated this summit. The greedy dogs don't care a fig about Etruria; they only want Dalmatia back."

While Levi cursed their hosts, Sofia remembered that day, nearly two years ago now, after she had uncovered John Acuto's part in the Gubbio massacre, when she had sought passage to some distant land where betrayal, lies and blood were not currency. An old sailor bound for Oltremare told her that not even the Holy Land was free from that contagion. *Wherever Man was,* he'd said, *you'll find it.*

She looked, but she couldn't see his battered little cog among the docked ships. She wondered aloud if she might see him again.

"Not likely," said Levi. "Relations with the Oltremarines are especially frosty lately."

Sofia understood theoretically that neighboring states were like neighboring towers, best of friends or deadly enemies. "But what's the point of hating someone so distant?" she asked.

"They share a border," Levi said, pointing to the sea.

"How did they fall out?"

"When someone depends on you, they'll forgive any trespass. After the Oltremarines finally broke the power of the Radinate, they didn't need Etruria anymore. Every foreign merchant was promptly expelled from Akka."

"The Ariminumese didn't take it well?"

"By then most of Etruria had decided that Crusade was a great waste of money; the Ariminumese started a whisper that gave them a pious excuse to abandon it for good."

"What did they say?"

"Oh, the usual: that the Oltremarines had fallen into apostasy."

"That's it?"

"Well, the whisper went that their great victory at Megiddo came at a terrible cost, that King Tancred made a pact with Jerusalem's dead, who gave them victory in return for Jerusalem and the freedom of Akka."

Sofia whistled. "Nice. I'm surprised that Oltremare's not on Concord's side."

"For the time being they're on their own side. Etruria's war is an opportunity for them to consolidate control of the Middle Sea."

"The procurator looked pretty mad when you told him that you had invited them."

"I *was* worried he was going to order me strung up along with the Doge, but he knew it was too late already, so managed to limit himself to a lecture about 'acting unilaterally.'"

"Too late—he already knew?"

"Well, it's kind of hard to miss." Levi pointed to a great ship sitting majestically still on the placid waves, its blue flags roiling and whipping like chained dragons. Painted on each side of the hull was a great blue hand with a single eye staring out of the palm.

Sofia looked blankly from the ship to Levi.

"Madonna, Rasenneisi are a slow breed. That's the *Tancred*! The procurator said it arrived a week ago."

"Then the Oltremarines are in?"

"Conditionally. Queen Catrina is insisting that the summit take place in Akka."

"Oh." The hope that had suddenly lit in Sofia's breast was snuffed out just as suddenly. "Bet our hosts liked that."

"I think the queen sent her flagship just to infuriate them. Any merchant's cog could have carried that invitation here and the envoys back. If that was her intention, it worked; the *Tancred*'s been impounded ever since."

"Isn't that an act of war?"

"Sinking it would be, but they're probably just going to delay them until the *Tancred*'s supplies run out. The cruelest cut of all is that they've forbidden any Oltremarine to disembark. I believe the local courtesans have quite a reputation."

"How inhuman." Sofia examined the great ship. With nowhere to go and no one to do, its crew was occupied with maintenance; she could see them patching sails and painstakingly replacing the running rigging. Boys were diving and cleaning the hull.

One of the young barnacle-scrapers was noisily attempting to haggle with a ragged old sailor who sat thumbing through a book and paying not the least bit of attention.

Sofia looked twice, then cried, "Levi, that's him—the old man!"

"Signorina?" The old man looked up at her voice. "Do I—? Ah, I remember you!" he exclaimed, shutting the book carefully. "The nearly stowaway."

"Where's your little ship?"

"Sleeping soundly on a seabed somewhere off the Levant. You wouldn't think that recommends me as a navigator, but that's what I'm employed as on the good Queen Catrina's flagship."

"The *Tancred*? Why did they let you disembark?"

"I am on good terms with *Tancred*'s captain—we sailed together before he took the queen's silver. Oh, you mean the Ariminumese, *that* prohibition applies only to Oltremarines," he said cheerfully. "Some races are beneath the State's attention."

"You're not an Oltremarine subject?"

"In Oltremare, I'm subject to Queen Catrina; in Ariminum, I'm subject to the Doge and," he said looking directly at Sofia, "if I ever go to Rasenna, I'll be subject to the Contessa Scaligeri."

Levi's eyes narrowed. "You're Ebionite?"

"Don't fret, Signore. I do not bite. Etrurians aren't kosher." Levi didn't smile, so the old man turned back to Sofia. "So, Signorina, what brings you back to the City of Bridges?"

"Same thing as last time."

"Ah, the summit! The talk's of nothing else. It's not drink or women that sailors look forward to in strange harbors, it's gossip. Captain Khoril sent me ashore to retrieve some. I understand that the states south of Concord are making peace with each other."

"In order to make war on Concord," Sofia said sardonically.

"The Prophetess said, 'Blessed are the Peacemakers.' Motivations don't matter, only actions."

"Motivation is clearly something you struggle with. You're the only sailor I see sitting on his ass."

He shrugged. "The *Tancred*'s impounded."

"So are your shipmates. They're working."

"My shipmates are Marian, like yourself. Today is the Ebionite day of rest."

"You people have a fetish for prohibitions," said Levi scornfully. "What if your ship were sinking?"

Sofia glanced reproachfully at Levi, but the old man said with a smile, "Depends on the rate it's sinking."

"Life's to be lived. You really think God cares if you constrain yourself?"

"Self-imposed prohibitions can be liberating. My people know what *real* bondage is like. When we get tired of being slaves, we wandered until we found a land where we could be masters."

"Too bad the Oltremarines had the same idea."

Levi might have been aiming to wound, but he answered cheerfully, "Alas, that's true, and so we are slaves once more. What's worse? My people never had more freedom than in the desert, and all we did was complain. When you settle, the world insists you adopt a role, slave or master; they're equally limiting after a time."

"You'd rather roam and be nothing?"

"I prefer to keep my options open. Wisdom does not come at once, and to those who will not take it slowly, it does not come at all. A good book helps pass the time." He patted the thick volume on his lap reverently. Battered skin covered the yellowed pages.

"That your logbook?"

"In a manner of speaking. It is the adventures of God and His fleet. It's all here—His famous captains, their famous voyages, the storms they survived, mutinies foiled, appalling shipwrecks, warnings of rocky shores, treacherous currents, sirens, sea beasts—"

"*Merda*," Levi interrupted, "It's a book of laws for a race of slaves."

"Sounds more like a storybook." Sofia was annoyed with Levi's fractiousness, and glad that the old man was not taking offense.

"It need not be one thing. This is not a book, it's a book-shelf. A library containing History, Philosophy, Poetry, and a thousand and one trifling fantasies. If you see only one of those things, you don't diminish it—there will be more perceptive readers, after all—you diminish yourself."

"What good is it?" said Levi. "It keeps your people slaves."

He held up his hands like a prisoner. "What good is it? Well, it's riddled with contradiction. The protagonist barely seems to know His own mind. He is obtuse and stubborn. It jumps from precept to commandment that seldom agree. It distorts facts, garbles history. It's inconsistent, wild, undisciplined. In short, it is, like life, a work of genius. So tell me"—he looked up at them—"is life good?"

Sofia declined to answer. "Enjoy your reading, sir. We shall not take any more of your time."

"You cannot *take* my time; I have a surfeit of it, and it's pleasant to talk to a pretty girl and a blunt soldier on a quiet morning. One sees so few these days. When I see you tomorrow, perhaps you'll answer my question."

"If negotiations allow."

"They will," he said with certainty, and returned to his reading.

Chapter 52

Fra Norcino rolled a battered old coin from finger to finger, then held up a second to a shaft of dusty moonlight. The coins were older than Concord, minted when Etruria was called Etrusca, and bore the profile of a forgotten emperor.

"Herod's soldiers were not devils. They were men like you, no worse. They followed orders. Is guilt a link in the chain of command? Do the soldier's crimes tarnish his officer? Do only officers' sins count? Is guilt compounded?" The theme of the oration was an old favorite: the Massacre of the Innocents. He preached with his usual intensity, although tonight nobody was listening; he was surrounded by the sleeping bodies of his closest followers.

Since Geta's bravos and Corvis' praetorians had joined in common cause, the fanciulli were on the defensive. No one knew what part the First Apprentice had in all this—there were rumors that he haunted Monte Nero's summit like a grieving spirit while Corvis

ran the Collegio—but no one was certain. What *was* certain was
that the streets were unsafe, so each night the fanciulli found a new
safe house to stay in. It was exhausting work, yet no one ever saw
Fra Norcino sleep.

"Certainly it was wrong to dash the little ones against the stones—
but compared to the great sin the soldiers committed that day, O
what a trifle. They couldn't know, but ignorance is no excuse! God
was watching, and he struck them down! Everyone! Their murdering right hands forgot their cunning, their lying tongues cleaved to
the roof of their mouths." He stopped and looked around. Snores
drifted around the low-ceiling room. "O faithless generation, is not
one of you awake?"

Footsteps. The thud of soldiers' hobnails. Suddenly the door burst
open to admit a boy, one of his most devoted fanciulli. "Master," he
hissed, "you must flee!"

The other sleepers didn't stir. Norcino raised his finger to his lips
and gestured the boy closer. When the boy came within reach, Norcino pulled him in and clapped a large hand around his mouth. He
whispered in the boy's ear, "It's time to render onto Catiline that
which is Catiline's."

Without much exertion he twisted the boy's head—

Craa aa aa kkkuh.

He laid the body among the sleepers like a mother putting a child
to sleep and placed a coin on each eye. The hobnails were thumping
down the stairs now.

The Collegio's board sat around the stone table in the otherwise
empty chamber. It seemed much larger than it did during general
assemblies. The speaker's mace rested in front of the chairman's seat,
which was empty, like the First Apprentice's throne. Like everyone
else, the members of the board had heard the rumors of Norcino's
arrest.

"Where is the First Apprentice? It's not proper for the board to
assemble without him," said Scaurus, the old consul who sat opposite to the chairman's seat. Scaurus was a veteran of Forty-Seven,

and an opponent of all innovation. He still bore the scars on his skin, which was now translucent, and wormed with tiny blue veins.

The other consuls paid no attention. They whispered among each other until the door opened and Corvis entered, followed by General Spinther and Lord Geta.

"Consuls, please be seated," said Corvis. "Thank you for coming at such short notice. I trust you'll understand in times as disturbed as these the proper channels were too slow—to safeguard our security it was necessary to—"

"*Necessity,*" a voice croaked. "The watchword of tyrants."

"Consul Scaurus, I must—"

"—you must *nothing*!" He stood with difficulty and said, "You arrest this preacher, and then peremptorily summon us, presumably to retroactively approve your actions. Where's your respect for Guild protocol? Due process? For that matter, where is the First Apprentice? And now, the final insult, you enter this sacred arena flanked by soldiers. I remind those who remain loyal to Bernoulli's legacy," he looked around the table, "that there is still one Apprentice, and our allegiance is to him."

"Scaurus, you are either joking or senile. No one could seriously suggest that the Guild still owes allegiance to that *boy*. He's locked himself away in that tower while Concord burns. He's no fitter to wear the red than Bonnacio was. Sit down."

"Your hired thugs might intimidate these children, but they do not intimidate me. I stood side by side with Girolamo Bernoulli against better men than them, aye, and you."

Corvis slammed his fist on the table. "I don't need your approval, any more than the Apprentices or your beloved Saint Bernoulli needed it! I have the praetorians and that's as good as wearing the red."

"You're a fool, Corvis. By arresting Norcino you've exacerbated the situation. Consuls, are we really going to let this outrage continue?"

Corvis took up the mace and handed it to Leto. "Give Consul Scarus due process."

Leto took it and walked around the table to Scaurus. Geta walked around the other side.

"General Spinther, it comes to this?" said Scaurus. "I fought along your grandfather in Forty-Seven. He'd be ashamed to see you a tool of this usurper."

"You don't get it, old man," said Leto, lifting the mace. Geta seized the old man from behind and bent his head down to the table.

"We're—" *CracCK!* "—all" *Sssspraklesumph* "—usurpers!" *sqwelcsh*

The consuls closest to Scaurus were showered in viscera. Leto held onto the mace. "Will that be all, Corvis?"

"Will that be all, Consuls? No other objections? Good. We have a crowded agenda today, beginning with a Motion of No Confidence in the aforementioned Apprentice. Geta, Spinther, probably best you stay till we're done."

The knocking shook the door of the Selectors' Tower and Leto walked in without waiting for an answer. A cold wind entered with him, scattering papers from Torbidda's desk.

"Close the door," said Torbidda mildly.

"First Apprentice, I come with ill tidings."

Torbidda did not look up from his drawing. "I don't recall, Leto. Were you ever sent to Flaccus' office? You always knew how to stay out of trouble."

Leto continued in the same solemn tone, "The Guild has passed a Motion of No Confidence in your leadership." He opened the door again. Outside, Corvis, breathing heavily, was climbing the final steps to the tower.

"The Collegio's consent is not a condition of my leadership," Torbidda said evenly. "I wear the red."

"And you never tire of reminding us," Corvis wheezed. "We have also decided your dereliction of duty amounts to treason. General Spinther has a warrant for your arrest—"

"Enough!" Torbidda slammed his hands on the desk, upsetting a jar of ink. "*This* is more important than anything else in the Empire.

I've tolerated your inveterate scheming for the sake of Guild unity, but if you think I'm going to let you take me away from my work—"

"What makes you think I'll give you a choice?"

"We're alone up here, Corvis. The stairway's the only way up. Your pet general should have told you never to attack someone on such defensible high ground."

"Oh, Spinther's been very helpful." Corvis grinned, and Torbidda saw the direction of his glance. He walked slowly to the window and whispered, "Leto, what have you done?"

Perched like carrion birds on the web of wires binding the Selectors' Tower were dozens of hard-faced children, all armed with bows.

"As you see, I came in strength," said Corvis exultantly. "The class of Sixty-Nine all volunteered to be part of the surprise. It's a reunion! They say the friends you make in school are friends for life. I suppose you're the exception that proves the rule."

"Torbidda, I'm sorry. I have to look out for myself," Leto said, then, with less repentance. "Frankly, in allowing things to get this far you've demonstrated—"

"Don't apologize. I understand perfectly. If you get a chance to cull the competition, you take it. So what's to become of me? Shall I slip on the way down? A tragic accident?"

"I wanted to have you killed on the quiet," said Corvis sadly, "but your old friend here insists on a very public trial. He believes that will set the correct tone for the new Concord: a city ruled by the Collegio, by reason, and by me!"

The dungeon below the praetorian barracks was dark, damp and chill. Norcino's sightless eyes looked up as he heard the commotion of a new prisoner being led in. Vagrants usually escaped with a flogging and the loss of some or all of their limbs, but the praetorians stood respectfully back from the boy in red as he walked in.

Norcino sat up and crawled as far toward him as his manacles allowed. "My king! Is it really you, Majesty?"

"*Tranquillo,* my good Fra. I haven't come to free you. I'm in the same bind you are." Torbidda rattled his chains so that the blind man could hear. The guards opened the cell next to Norcino's and Torbidda calmly walked in. He waited for the guards to leave before turning to his neighbor. "When I heard of this blind preacher disrupting the city I knew it was you. Who *are* you?"

"Never mind that," Norcino hissed. "Do you know the Handmaid's identity?"

"Her name's Scaligeri. She's the one who burned the Molè."

"Then *why*," he demanded, "did you not complete the rite? You know what's at stake."

"I know."

"Then what have you been waiting for?"

"Out in the Wastes you told me I didn't have to be a sacrificial lamb. I didn't climb the mountain to donate my flesh to some tattered ghost. The rite's unnecessary. I can deal with the Handmaid myself. Bernoulli had his turn to run Concord. This is mine!"

Norcino rattled his chains in mockery. "And a fine mess you've made of it!"

Chapter 53

Ariminumese are not a God-fearing race, but the new Doge's most solemn vows at his coronation are to protect the Basilica of Saint Barabbas. Foreigners surprised by the reverence accorded to the Basilica misinterpret its role. This centuries-old institution maintains a depository for private individuals and the commune and has considerable wealth in trusts and landholdings. Its most important function is to advance loans to the government—in the words of Doge Dandolo, "A State without credit can accomplish many things, but no great things."

from The Stones of Ariminum *by Count Titus Tremellius Pomptinus*

They came to forge an alliance, but no venue could be more ill-suited to that end than the green jewel-wearing whore of the Adriatic, the city of gold lacquer, of wine swoons and expensive sin. The unsophisticated principalities of the south—violent, in-bred hill-towns, sleepy under-populated settlements along old Etruscan dirt roads and brash cities of the coast—sent eager ambassadors whose full purses were soon emptied by Ariminum's industrious harlots. And every dalliance, every cup, was spied upon and reported in meticulous detail to the undying Consilium.

The procurator had left in their apartments a list of which cities had sent envoys. It was a depressingly short list.

When Sofia greeted the ambassador from Salerno next morning on the dock outside the ornate basilica she didn't disguise her anger. "Where are the Syracusans?"

Doctor Ferruccio had fought alongside her grandfather at Montaperti, and had visited Tower Bardini from time to time when Sofia was growing up. He still wore the deep-blue ermine-lined cape she remembered. It was fretted with stars and had seemed as large as the sky on his great back. With his hoary white beard, wild hair, big, oft-broken nose and pendulous lips, he would have been ugly, if not for his gap-toothed smile and unassuming manner. He radiated the quiet confidence one often saw in old fighters; hard-won experience remained, even though that strength was gone. After the Wave struck Rasenna, Ferruccio had allied himself with the Doc because he was Sofia's guardian, and because he was a fighter too.

"They refused to participate on grounds that this is purely an Etrurian matter. I suppose that's technically—"

"They won't even talk? A year ago they were all for attacking Concord. They volunteered to lead the vanguard!"

"To be fair, Contessa, those were heady times. They had never seen Concord defeated. Few of us had. We thought anything was possible."

Taranto, the most southerly city attending (no one even thought to invite the Sybariates), took a similar attitude: this was a northern Etrurian matter. Geographically and politically, Veii was somewhere in the middle, favoring vague treaties of mutual support rather than a league with a combined army.

"Concord *is* on the brink of collapse," Levi said stoutly. He too was disappointed at the poor turnout.

Ferruccio grinned. "You don't hunt, then, Podesta? The quarry's most dangerous when wounded."

Before Levi could answer, the procurator appeared behind them on the steps. His hairless dome reflected the rising sun. "A special someone wishes to make your acquaintance this morning. If you'll follow me . . ."

In contrast to its clean marble exterior, the Basilica's interior was smoky and cavernous. Although it was dark, Sofia could see the Ariminumese had adopted the Ebionites' bizarre geometric iconography and fetish for golden ornament.

"There he is!" said the procurator brightly. "What's that you've got?"

The "special someone" was the city's new Doge, but the round-faced boy plainly found greeting guests less interesting than torturing his black-and-white puppy. At the procurator's prompting he mumbled a formulaic welcome, then sulkily retreated to the bishop's throne in front of the Eucharistic tabernacle to pull the puppy's ears. Next, the procurator introduced the basilica's board, a perfunctory smile passing from one pale, dour face to the next. Sofia's eyes skipped to the end of the row, to the looming figure waiting with muscular arms crossed over his bare black chest.

The smile on his smooth ebony face was unfeigned and terrifyingly wide, like some ever-hungering fish of the deep. He wore pristine white baggy pants with a high waist, with a dagger tucked inside his belt and hanging from it, a double-pronged blade as large as a Europan broadsword but curved like an Anglish longbow. His open silk undershirt was a fiery orange; the wide cuffs were visible under the short sleeves of his white jacket. He was bedecked like a war stallion in rings, earrings and necklaces, and the effect was vulgarly virile. His wide shoulders were covered by a light cloak that fastened around his bull-like neck with an oversized ornamented pin.

"Lastly, I give you our new admiral, the honorable—"

"Captain Levi and I have already been introduced."

The ambassador from Pescara had paled at first sight of the admiral. He turned on his heels and stalked out of the Basilica, muttering in outrage.

"*Shalom aleikhem,* Azizi," Levi said. "It's Podesta now. I see you still have the same effect on tender hearts."

"*Aleikhem shalom.* So I am informed." His deep voice had the timbre of creaking ropes, and an ebullient mockery. "Forgive me; I hesitated to congratulate you on your promotion, no doubt richly deserved, before I had opportunity to offer my inadequate but heartfelt condolences for the way you came by it. At least the old bull gave the Twelfth a hiding on the way out, eh?"

The Moor was close to six braccia from the smooth dome of his head to his sandals. His skin was blacker than any Sicilian's, blacker than boiled tar, but there was a captive rainbow in its oily depths; in one light it had cold crocus hues, in another, the appetizing brown of scorched chestnuts. Though his Etrurian was faultless, he spoke as though reciting strange verse. He paused at odd times, emphasizing words without concern for context or meaning, as if each sound had a flavor to savor.

"When John Acuto bet, he bet big." Levi clicked his fingers as if he'd just remembered something. "Come to think of it, didn't *you* once make a bet with him—?"

"That promise died with John Acuto!" The Moor's anger dissipated as quickly as it had fired up. "But for what it is worth, I didn't return voluntarily. I grieve for him truly. He was a born condottiere."

"He was a knight," Sofia interjected.

The Moor threw back his head and laughed: *Haw Haw Haw!* His teeth were like stars in a black sky, too many. "A knight! Capital! Little girl, I have hunted mermaids, and the dragon of the Middle Sea has hunted me, but even I do not believe in *knights.* John Acuto never did a deed that did not profit John Acuto." The Moor examined Levi again. "Don't tell me you've become a knight too? That would be too great a shock."

"In another venue," Sofia said seriously, "I'd make you regret that."

His smile disappeared, but his teeth remained bared. "And if you were not with child, I should give you the beating you plainly require. Rasenna must be short of men to send a round-wombed girl to fight for it."

"Ariminum must have the same problem," Sofia retorted, "to promote a filthy galley-slave to admiral."

At this the Moor laughed again, but as Sofia maintained her composure, she wondered if this barbarian was especially observant, or if her condition was now obvious to all and only a barbarian was ungracious enough to mention it.

Presently he stopped laughing and bowed low. "Forgive me, Contessa, for teasing. Of course I know who you are. Now, if you'll excuse me, I have some galley slaves to promote."

He stalked out, trailing rumbling laughter, followed by two soldiers. Sofia suspected their job was not to protect the admiral. The grim fate of the last Signoria made it clear that Ariminumese loyalty was a mutable thing.

Levi turned to the procurator with fire in his eyes. "That pirate will betray you the first chance he gets! What are you smiling at?"

"Forgive me," the procurator said stifling a giggle, and there was a brief silence in which only the yelping puppy was heard. "Surely you see the humor of a condottiere giving lectures on loyalty?"

"*Former* condottiere. And no matter how many doges you strangle, we won't forget that you're the ones who double-crossed the Hawk's Company. What did the Moor mean, that he didn't return here voluntarily?"

"What the Contessa said about making a galley-slave an admiral was impolite, but not altogether inaccurate. He arrived on the *Tancred* wearing chains." The procurator's teasing manner vanished. "Believe me, Signore, we're not naïve. It's because the Moor's loyalty *is* for sale that we trust him. His fidelity's guaranteed because no one pays as well as we."

"If you give him your navy, you might as well give him the keys to your treasury while you're at it."

The procurator shook his head. "We must agree to differ." He rang a tiny bell and announced, "Esteemed guests, before we dive into the sordid details, let's turn our minds to more elevated matters and pray for a fair wind in this venture. In the name of the Father and of the Mother and . . ."

After the morning's formalities, there was an adjournment. The Rasenneisi retired to their apartments. Pedro carefully lined up the annunciators on the windowsill while Sofia and Levi conferred.

"Who was that impudent black?" Sofia asked. "A condottiere?"

"A company captain, the only one who never learned the rules."

"Rules?" she said archly.

"I didn't know there were regulations concerning pillaging," Pedro added.

Levi took their mocking well. "*Steps*, I should say. The dance of the condottieri, march and counter-march, until one side runs out of gold or the other makes a better offer. Nobody danced it better than John Acuto. The Moor wasn't interested in dancing, or even in money; he loves only gambling. We made it our business to keep Etruria divided, to keep the States balanced against each other, but the Moor upset the whole racket and everyone agreed he had to go. The captains of other companies wanted to unite our armies and crush him. John Acuto had a simpler solution: he would do it alone, for a fee. And the other captains needed to pay him only *if* he got the Moor to leave."

"Sweet deal."

"Very sweet. He offered the Moor a wager: the loser would leave Etruria to the other. The Moor couldn't resist. He forgot that John Acuto was Fortune's favorite."

"Did he keep his word?"

"Yes, but after that John Acuto was never again lucky."

"Maybe he used up his luck in that one throw," Pedro said, aiming his whistler at a distant galley and taking a reading.

"Maybe," Levi said. "Where are you going, Sofia?"

"Down to the harbor. I want a clear head for this afternoon."

* * *

The old sailor's talk of the desert yesterday had reminded Sofia of Isabella's warning. She wanted to speak to him, alone this time. Levi, like most Etrurians, was hostile to Ebionites; even though the Curia was a memory, the polemics that had launched the Crusades lived on.

He spotted her from the *Tancred*'s prow and trotted down the gangway.

"I came to apologize for my friend the other day."

"Forgotten already. Each day we start afresh," he said with a bow. "My name is Ezra. What is yours, Signorina?"

"I think you already know," Sofia said carefully.

Ezra glanced around and said in a hushed voice, "I don't wish to be indiscreet, Contessa. Last time we met, you were running from your name."

"I'm no longer Contessa, but I've stopped running."

"I expect you have, in your condition. At the risk of spoiling my record for discretion, I see you've got a stowaway on board."

Sofia blushed.

"Congratulations! But as before, I assure you that all my hours are accounted for in my logbook. So if you're looking for the father . . ."

"I'm not." She patted her stomach. "This one's father is a most inconsistent fellow who promises much and delivers little."

"You mustn't be vexed with those you love. Is he looking for you?"

"No," Sofia said, "but someone else is. His father has enemies."

He looked at her keenly. "Ah. Then it isn't true that you've stopped running. You're in good company. God is a fugitive in this world. He must race on the winds with the jinn and in the depths with the buio, where none but the righteous dare follow."

"Why must we do all the work?"

Ezra laughed. "Little sister, in this war we are only flag-bearers. There are armies clashing behind the night, in the cold vistas between the stars. We cannot hear them, but this battle raged before we came and will continue after we've gone. The stakes are immense, and a more prudent general would not hesitate to sacrifice us like pawns."

"God is not prudent?"

"When it comes to His children, God is downright prodigal."

The procurator was waiting in the Basilica to welcome back the ambassadors and show them to their seats. The tiered arrangement suggested how Ariminumese expected the league to operate; the basilica's gray-eyed board entered last and sat above the ambassadors like a row of judges.

"I trust there are no objections, but we've taken the small liberty of rearranging the agenda," the procurator began. "We rather hoped to skip immediately to the Dalmatian situation—"

As he was speaking Sofia stood and noisily turned her chair around. When the rest of the ambassadors followed suit, the procurator bleated objections. Without turning her head, Sofia shouted, "We can't hear you from up there. You'll just have to come down and talk to us as equals."

At this the Moor erupted with deep laughter. He walked down, carrying his chair, and joined the newly formed circle.

It took a while, and a separate round of negotiation, threats and pleas, but eventually everyone had a place, though Count Grimani, the Veian ambassador, proved especially hard to please. Veii's and Salerno's relationship was marginally less fractious than Concord and Rasenna's—but not by much.

"The Contessa's trying to impress us with her equalitarianism, I expect, but we're not blind," Count Grimani said aggressively. "Ariminum and Rasenna have been fighting for precedence for the last year." The count was young and ambitious, with a sharp nose, bulbous eyes and a shrill voice designed for objecting. The summit's grand venue had inflated his self-importance. "Well, I didn't come here with preconceptions; I came here to question the whole premise of the Southern League, so-called. To start with, you're all Northerners to us. The way we see it, you'll both have to give up something if you want peace. Procurator, Dalmatia is gone—accept it. Move on. And Contessa—well, I know peace is a dirty word in

Rasenna, but the South's not going to let you drag us into a war. The Concordians have lost face; that's all this is about. Give it back, and we can go on with our lives."

"Your lives are going to change, whether you like it or not," Levi retorted, "and that's why we need a league. Concord has built a canal to the sea, and you can bet they're already building a navy. One thing they do well is plan. If Concord launches that navy, then the whole peninsula is vulnerable. No Etrurian city is far from the sea."

He looked at the ambassadors of Veii and Taranto. "You won't have the luxury of Rasenna or Ariminum fighting your battles when Concord can simply sail past us."

"All the more reason to make peace," Grimani insisted.

"How can there be peace when Concord considers Etruria its property and every Etrurian its slave?"

"I've heard of Rasenneisi, Salernitans, Tarentines, Concordians and Ariminumese, but I've never heard of this strange creature, the Etrurian. Pray tell, where can one be found?"

"Look around you, fool! No city can stand apart. Concord won't rest till they've broken Etruria. It doesn't want allies, it wants vassals—but you're right, our unity's too fragile to survive without allies." Levi straightened and cleared his throat. "That's why I propose we accept Queen Catrina's offer and send a delegation to Akka. Too long have the Marian peoples been divided. We have common cause, and reinforced by Oltremare, we can win!"

The procurator interrupted frostily, "That alliance is out of the question. Oltremare competes with our eastern trade, steals our colonies, taxes our merchants and blockades our galleys."

"And you do the same to them," Doctor Ferruccio remarked.

"Oltremare is as great a threat to us as Concord is to Rasenna. No, I must—" He paused as a notary whispered in his ear, then announced, "Signori, I'm afraid we'll have to adjourn early today."

"Oh, but we've just started," Count Grimani complained.

"Another ambassador has arrived."

Sofia was delighted to hear it. "From where?"

The procurator attempted to be casual about it. "Concord."

Chapter 54

As they left the basilica, the Moor fell into step with Levi. "I'd have told you that involving the Oltremarines was impossible, had you asked."

"But I didn't. I know the Ariminumese never forget a slight, but the Oltremarines might not be so short-sighted."

"Your information is some decades out of date. These days, Oltremare desires one thing only from Etruria, and that's to keep her sea-lanes free of its pirates."

"I dare say your knowledge isn't out of date," Levi remarked.

"I haven't been idle since your late employer persuaded me to vacate the premises. God despises sloth. You'll be pleased to know the principle of contracting works as well on Terra da Mar as Terra Firma, with the minor difference that a condottieri in a boat is called a *privateer*. The skills transfer wonderfully."

"You were a natural, I expect."

The Moor beamed. "I was! Until a year ago I commanded a small fleet, and we were paid a hefty fee to not pay a visit when we passed a city. The Oltremarines got tired of paying me, so I was obliged to plunder the queen's shipments. Most unfortunate."

"And I bet you collected a nice bursary from the Ariminumese for your trouble."

"The very suggestion! The procurator would be outraged." The Moor laughed. "It's nice to be paid for doing what you love, but eventually I tired of it. There's nowhere to spend a fortune at sea. Like you, I want to settle down. I had my eye on a fertile strip of Barbary. Alas, my dream proved to be just that."

"The natives objected?"

"On the contrary, they worshipped me. It was those damn Oltremarines. In the saddle, on a ship, one can always flee when faced with superior odds, but when one has a throne, one is obliged to sit on it. I lost my fleet but not, God be praised, my life. The sailors I had so heavily taxed rejoiced in the expectation of seeing me hang over Akka's harbor, but Queen Catrina is singularly intelligent, for a woman. My activities were a minor nuisance compared with her trade-war with Ariminum. All maritime empires are rivals but they have one thing in common—"

"A fondness for pirates?"

"You mock me." The Moor sighed wistfully. "I have been many things, but never a diplomatic gift. That heartless bitch had me trussed up like a pig and sent across the water for the Doge's delectation." His sudden anger cleared. "But in all her calculations, Catrina never suspected that her counterpart would be awaiting execution. The new Consiglio saw my activities in a more tolerant light." He saluted the Basilica reverently. "Instead of a noose, they awarded me an admiral's baton."

"If Queen Catrina is as dispassionate as you say she won't give a damn, because what I said in there is true: a Concordian navy will ultimately aim at her throne. The Oltremarines don't know it yet, but they're going to be involved in our war, like it or not. This is an opportunity. If we make the case to them, they'll help—I'm sure of it."

"Rasenneisi were ever dreamers, and alas, Levi, you've gone native. Politics tire me. Come! Let's watch the *battaglia* in the glass-workers' ward—it'll be great betting. No?" The Moor bowed. "Then I will pray that you recover your wits. Farewell."

After the first day's negotiation, Count Grimani invited some of the other ambassadors to dine on the Veian flagship. The Rasenneisi were not invited.

The Veian was dismissive of the whole venture. "*You believe this navy business? I don't.*"

"*The Rasenneisi are just trying to scare the Ariminumese. Can't blame them. For them war's unavoidable, for us it's optional. I tell you candidly that if I signed up to this league, my job wouldn't be the only thing I'd lose when I got back. I presume you are under similar pressure?*"

"*For form's sake I'm allowed to offer a few troops, nothing more. Look at it from their position—a few years ago Concord could march to our door unopposed, unless we bankrupted ourselves with condottieri. We were the ones agitating for the league then.*"

"Who's that?" Pedro whispered. "Is that the old fellow from Salerno?"

"Ferruccio, yes. Shhh!"

"*That's history. Should we just ignore the fact of Rasenna's resurgence? They are effectively a wall between us and Concord: in the unlikely event that Concord ever gets strong enough again to march south, the Rasenneisi will dull the force of the blow.*"

"*Lucky for us that the Rasenneisi are too pig-headed to think about making peace.*"

"*The Ariminumese, on the other hand . . .*"

"*I don't trust them. How much did they pay you—?*"

Pedro took off his earpiece. "We're not hearing anything we didn't already know."

"We're on our own with Ariminum unless Salerno joins us," said Levi.

"Ferruccio would if he could," Sofia said.

"I'm more interested in what our hosts are planning. If Rasenna and Ariminum agree, the southerners will fall in. Can you get the annunciator up to the sixth floor?"

"Should be enough power," said Pedro, "though we won't be able listen for long."

Sofia was looking out of the window at the Veian galley in the harbor. As Pedro operated the controls like a puppeteer, the little golden cone rose from its porthole perch and dropped silently toward the sea, falling in an arc, a chink of sunlight lost in the reflected evening ripples. They heard an argument of sounds: wind, water lapping, boatmen calling, gulls' screams, horns and bells from the dock, and then different voices as the annunciator rose up the basilica's many stories.

"The sixth floor's where the Consilium Sapientium meets," said Levi, whispering, even though the annunciator broadcast only one way, "if I can trust my Ariminumese informants."

"If you can't trust an informant," said Pedro, "who—?"

"Stop!" Sofia said. "Did you catch that? Drop it back to the third floor."

Pedro checked the annunciator's ascent and expertly brought it to rest on a windowsill, where it was helpfully concealed by a lace curtain rippling in the wind.

A familiar deep voice: *"Are you offering me a contract?"*

"I could use someone like you." The voice of a much younger man, level, serious.

"You couldn't afford me, boy. Ariminum's larder is well stocked. I intend to stay here and eat my fill."

"You're working for *Ariminum. Work for me and I'll give* you *Ariminum."*

"Work for Concord, you mean."

"The army won't be subordinate forever. The Guild isn't the power it was."

"What of the Apprentices?"

"There's just one left and he's . . . I'm a patriot. As long as the triple-headed beast provided stability, I was content. That's changed. Consul Corvis has taken charge."

A tutting sound. *"One defeat and you act like Heaven's falling."*

"I'm negotiating with my enemy in a city I should be dictating terms to. A government that let that happen does not command my loyalty. If I'm going to change things, I need strong men behind me. I need you, Admiral."

Levi stared at the annunciator as he waited to hear the Moor's answer. Finally it came: *"It's uncanny how closely patriotism resembles ambition. Although it is a sin, I've grown inordinately fond of the local wine. Why should I gamble that for your advancement? Good day, Spinther."*

The sound of footsteps and a door slamming was followed by silence and the duplicated cries of the gulls.

"I'm glad the Moor didn't go for it. I don't care to bet against him again."

"Should we leak it?" Pedro asked. "Let the Collegio dei Consoli know their best general's plotting a coup?"

"So they can make plans against it?" Levi was smiling. "Spinther's just one boy. If we get him executed, the legions remain. But if he rebels, it'll split the army. No matter who comes out on top, Concord will be weaker. The only thing to do with news as good as this, Pedro my boy, is to sit on it."

At the beginning of the next day's meeting, General Spinther was invited to address the delegates. Sofia took him in: a rather dark southern complexion for a Concordian, tall and clear-eyed—just a boy, but his youth, like everything else, was deceptive. They picked them for intelligence and trained them in the art of war, so they had all the vim of youth but none of its rashness; all the wisdom of age and none of its doubt.

"My Lords, I will not speak long. You know me as a soldier, but today I'm a dove. We have spies in your cities; you, in ours. Your spies' work has never been easier, for Concord's problems are no secret. I assure you we do not *want* peace, but we *need* it. The Collegio dei Consoli respectfully invites the Contessa of Rasenna to Concord to discuss terms."

The general paused while the southern ambassadors whispered to each other, directing skeptical glances at Sofia, until the procurator rang a bell. "Enough! This isn't a music hall. General Spinther is obviously under the misapprehension that our league—putative as it is—is bound to be led by Rasenneisi. I assure you—"

"Not at all, Procurator. Any viable Southern League would rely on Ariminumese money. That's why we're here today in your exquisite city, instead of Montaperti's killing fields. If war comes, Ariminum *will* be dragged into it, but the fact remains that it will not be *your* war." The Concordian looked suddenly and with unexpected tenderness at Sofia. "It is *ours,* Contessa."

Sofia's hand went instinctively to her side and grabbed—nothing. Levi was right to say it would be undiplomatic to go armed to a negotiation, but without her flag, she felt naked.

General Spinther looked around the room. "Doctor Ferruccio, you were alive to see it, but the rest of us learned from our grandfathers of the terrible war Concord and Rasenna fought, how it eventually involved the whole peninsula. We're on the brink of another such cataclysm. Peace doesn't interest me, but a period of stability does. Ask your spies: they'll confirm that Concord has been plagued by schismatics since the siege of Rasenna."

The procurator smiled. "On the northern frontiers, you've had reverses too—"

The general took this jibe personally. "The Europan war does not concern anyone here! The war you've been discussing these last few days concerns all Etruria—for make no mistake, that *war* is what you mean when you say *league.* Today, I have placed my person in your hands. I only ask the same gesture of trust of you. Thus are bridges built. Leap the chasm, Contessa, and the day may come when *our* grandchildren look on each other as friends and not enemies. Peace is worth the risk."

Not waiting for an answer, he bowed and strode out, spurs ringing, heels smartly snapping on the marble floor. The ambassadors
were silent until he left, though Sofia felt their eyes on her.

Doctor Ferruccio spoke before the procurator could. "Now, everyone take a breath and don't get hung up on details. If Concord wants
to talk, we should talk. The boy's right. I *was* at Montaperti. *Anything's* preferable to that. Even at our most optimistic, no one expects
a war to end in anything better than stalemate. What do we have to
lose by talk? 'Tis fitting that they ask the Contessa. Her grandfather
fought the first war—so how magnificent if she could stop this one.
Friends don't make peace; enemies do. The Scaligeri and Bernoulli
broods have been—"

Stunned at Ferruccio's matter-of-fact betrayal, Sofia blurted, "I'm
not Contessa anymore. I've given up my title."

Levi was shocked at Sofia's public admission, but the Tarantine
ambassador waved her announcement away dismissively. "Then
why are you here? Gonfaloniere Bombelli's no fool. Whatever you
call yourself, you're a Scaligeri. It's in your blood."

Levi interrupted with exasperation, "You're all taking this seriously? The Concordians mean to trick us. The Contessa escaped the
belly of the beast—would you ask her to return? Whoever goes will
never come back."

"Yes!" cried Count Grimani in exasperation. "A thousand times
yes. Would you ask us to go to war for you? We are each of us repre-
senting our people; thousands of lives depend on our decisions. For
peace," he said portentously, "no risk is foolhardy!"

The procurator stifled a giggle into a handkerchief and hammered his gavel. "On that we can agree. Let's adjourn. We all have
some considering to do in light of this offer."

Sofia was first out of her chair.

"*Tranquillo*," said Levi. "We're not at war yet. Are you all right?"

Sofia stepped back from the table, knocking her chair. Her feet
didn't work anymore. She was falling.

Chapter 55

Levi carried Sofia back to their apartments and laid her down. In whispers he told Pedro the Concordian offer, and finished, "It's a trap, a damn good trap. Spinther knows full well Sofia won't go, and that if she doesn't, this league will collapse before it's even begun."

"You're being irrational—what would they get from killing one girl? Call their bluff and go. I know it's not easy to trust them, but maybe it *is* worth the risk. Giovanni was Concordian. They're not *all* bad."

"If Sofia goes, they'll just keep her till they're strong again. The war's opening salvo will be her execution."

"Water . . ."

They both looked down at Sofia. Levi poured a glass and handed it to her. She took a long drink, placed the glass on the locker by the bed and looked at them. Her face was wan, but she spoke with certainty. "Pedro, Levi's right. War's coming, no matter how we dull our ears to the thunder. And Giovanni wasn't a Concordian."

"He may have died for Rasenna but that doesn't change his nationality." Pedro gathered his courage and said, "And he wasn't just *any* Concordian. Sofia, you need to know: Giovanni was Girolamo Bernoulli's grandson."

Pedro expected a furious denial, but she didn't blink. "I know who he was."

"I don't understand—since when?"

She took his hand and placed it on her belly. "Pedro, this is all I have of Giovanni."

Pedro pulled his hand away. "I'm an engineer, not a doctor, but even I know that's impossible. Giovanni died two years ago. I miss him too, Sofia, but—"

"No. *Listen* to me: the person we called Giovanni wasn't human. He was a buio."

". . . impossible . . ."

"—but true. The Reverend Mother knew it, and died for it. It wasn't an accident that brought Giovanni to me. Whatever Girolamo Bernoulli ripped apart in Nature is trying to heal itself, and I'm part of it now. The child I carry can restore things to their right track, and that's why I can't go to Concord. This isn't some stratagem, it's bigger than that. We burned the Molè, but not the beast incubating in the pit below it, and it's getting stronger as I get weaker. Whatever makes the Irenicon flow, that power is in me now." She pulled herself to her feet. "If my baby dies, it'll be for nothing. I have to run!"

Pedro looked at Levi. "She's delirious."

"I've seen Sofia do things I can't explain."

"Don't ask me to believe that. Giovanni, whatever he was, made me an engineer."

Sofia held him, her eyes full of pain. "Stand back then. I haven't done this lately—"

She took the glass of water, turned it over in a fast, fluid motion, and—slowly—pulled the glass away from the water. Pedro stared dumbly, a child once more, and Levi tensed, though he'd seen this sorcery before.

Inside the mound of water, bubbles appeared and swirled, getting faster until they were boiling as Sofia spoke. "Giovanni Bernoulli died a decade before you met him, in the killing fields of Gubbio. The man we knew was a buio cursed to live in his place."

In moments the water had dispersed into wreaths of vapor. "I will never get the same water back into the glass, but it hasn't died. Water never dies."

Sofia fell back exhausted and waited for Pedro's decision.

"What are we hanging around for?" Pedro said. "We're not captives—not yet. Our horses can be saddled in an instant—"

"Where can I go? When I leave, Concord will withdraw the truce offer and all Etruria will blame me for destroying the peace. There'll be no welcome for me in any city south of here, not even Salerno—you heard Ferruccio."

"Home, then."

"No! If I return to Rasenna, disaster will come, not just to me and my baby, but to everyone around me."

Levi swore. "There must be somewhere."

"Not in Etruria," said Sofia.

Pedro looked around as a flashing green on the side of the annunciator caught his eye. "Hold on. There's someone still in the basilica." He adjusted the control boxes and the shriek of feedback turned into something recognizable: the procurator's smooth voice.

"*Of course we know you tried to bribe the Moor.*"

"*Can't blame a chap for trying.*"

"*Not at all, General. We believe in the Free Market.*"

"*Then you don't object to a Concordian harbor?*"

"*Ha ha, you're pushy. What does Concord need a navy for, to sail its rivers? Come, we both know that the sea-corridor was just a ruse to scare us. Our spies tell us it was barely begun when work stopped.*"

"*Many things have been disrupted of late. If it were a ruse, I would hardly admit it, would I?*"

"*That true. It's also the main reason we're hosting this summit. We have no long-term interests in petty Etrurian quarrels. Without Ariminum, the Southern League's no danger to you. So how's this? We'll give you the land if you leave us the sea.*"

"*Divide the world? You ask a lot. The Tyrrhenian is large.*"

"*And the cost of war is high.*" A pause. "*Your offer to the Rasenneisi, you realize they won't accept it.*"

"*I know that. If you can convince the other delegates to go home, Concord will give you anything that you want. What is that, Procurator? The corno?*"

"*Bah, none but a fool would wear that cap. We'll let you have your way with Etruria if you help us invade southern Oltremare.*"

"*That would isolate Byzant, but as you pointed out, we're not a seafaring people.*"

"*No, but when it comes to siege-craft, you have no equal. No point sailing all that way unless we can take Catrina's coastal cities. Akka especially will be a tough nut to crack . . .*"

Darkness was falling in the harbor, and the pale lights of the boats were briefly an adequate mirror for the stars. They reached the end of the dock and found the old sailor sitting there, still reading, as if he hadn't stirred since yesterday.

"Ezra, you said you're close to the *Tancred*'s captain," Sofia started. "I need passage to Oltremare. How much?"

"You once boasted of being a good cook if memory serves—that'll do. But I hope you're not expecting to go anywhere soon. We're locked down."

"We need to go tonight."

"Forget it. Captain Khoril isn't authorized to start a war."

"Too late for that," said Pedro. "The Ariminumese mean to ally with Concord."

Ezra didn't look very surprised. "The *Tancred*'s fast, but one galley can't outrun several. You'd want at least a day's start to be sure. And that's not the real obstacle."

"So what is?" Levi asked.

Pedro answered before Ezra: "The chain. It's designed to keep enemies out of the harbor, but serves as well to keep us in."

"Ram it," Sofia said.

"The arsenalotti know their trade," said Pedro. "Even if it was possible, there are a hundred eyes on the harbor. We'd be boarded before we even got close."

"Then we're trapped," Sofia said, a black knot in her stomach.

"Not necessarily," Ezra said. "See that white line creeping up from that east? Feel that moisture in the air? By Vespers, there'll be a fog so thick you won't be able to see the color of your own flag."

"Unless a wind comes."

"It won't. I know a thing or two about winds."

"That still leaves the chain," said Levi flatly.

"It's suspended from towers on either side of the bay," said Pedro. "Which is the control-tower?"

"The southern one," said Ezra. "There's a watchman, but something tells me you're a lad good at solving problems."

"He can't go alone!"

"If I don't go alone there's no point. Be rational, Levi. Sofia can fight better than any man, but not in this condition. She needs you. If I get the chain lowered, there'll be no time to wait. I'll return to Rasenna— it's where I need to be if things are about to get worse anyway."

". . . if you're certain," Levi said after a moment. "I don't like the idea of Sofia landing on strange shores without a friend, but I'm still Podesta."

"Yes, and your job is to *protect* Rasenna. It won't survive without allies, and there are none here. Concord's going to get stronger, and then it will turn south. The league's failed before it's even begun. Our last hope is that the Crusading spirit is still alive in Oltremare. You have to persuade them."

"We will, Pedro," Sofia said. "Tell Isabella I'm going where she told me to."

"This is all very touching, but we should get going," said Ezra. "The fog's rising."

Soon the fog had thickened so much so that walkways and canals became indistinguishable. Pedro's pass got him into the Arsenal district, but in the misty conditions he took first one wrong turn, then another, and he had to return to the main canal to get his bearings. Another *battaglia* was under way, more chaotic than before. The hump of each bridge was burdened by a brawling mob, and the air was filled with war cries, challenges and flags. Men tumbled into the canals, and some were fished out, others lay floating where they fell. The people on the boardwalk pressed toward the bridges, eager to join the fight—or gamble on it. Pedro, trying to go against the traffic, found his way blocked by a well-dressed young man.

"*Permesso,* Signore."

"Whose form do you like, boy? The reds?"

"I'd bet on the arsenalotti. Signore, I must—"

"Ah, a working man? Of course, I knew I recognized you. You're the Contessa's pet engineer. Count Grimani, at your service."

Just as Pedro realized this encounter wasn't accidental, strong hands pulled him into an alley. None of the passersby answered to his shouts for help—only the *battaglia* mattered. Grimani's swordsman bundled Pedro into a gondola waiting at the other end of the alley and the count leapt in afterward. "You, search him; you, get moving." While the swordsman patted Pedro down, the gondolier pushed off and soon they were cruising down another canal under similarly thronged bridges. Dead and unconscious bodies floated by, and pairs of swimmers struggled together, trying to drown one another.

Grimani's swordsman took an annunciator out of Pedro's satchel and held it up with a blank expression.

"So that's how you've been spying on us," the ambassador tutted. "Give it here. Maybe that's how you do it in Rasenna, but in Veii we consider eavesdropping"—he smashed the annunciator against the side of the gondola—"very rude! I don't know what you're up to, but it's no good. Perhaps if I give you to the Concordians, I can negotiate a wholly different league, with Veii in charge."

"You'd betray Etruria."

"So you're another who thinks there's such a thing as an Etrurian. Tell me, how can one be a traitor to a nation of traitors?"

A falling body created a massive splash that set the gondola swaying. Grimani looked up. "Insolent dogs! I could have you all strung—"

Suddenly a falling body crashed into the gondola and Grimani's swordsman was knocked overboard. The body stirred, and Pedro realized it was draped not in gray or red, but in a fur-lined cape the color of night and lined with stars.

"Ferruccio!" Grimani hissed, whipping out his sword and retreating to the gondola's prow. The old man ignored him and turned to the gondolier, a more pressing danger, but Pedro had already grabbed his oar. Ferruccio's blade rammed home, then he turned to deal with Grimani.

"I have diplomatic immunity—you really don't want to start a war with me, Count. Don't come nearer."

"As you like," Ferruccio said. He crouched and began rocking the gondola from side to side.

"What are you doing?" Grimani bleated, trying to keep his balance. "No, stop—I can't—Ahhh!" He fell into the water screaming, spluttering until he found a body to cling onto.

"Hand me that paddle, lad," Ferruccio said.

"Don't be hasty," Grimani said, trying to paddle away as the gondola approached. "Look, we can make a deal! We can—"

Grimani was still begging when Ferruccio lifted the oar over his head and brought it down on his head. Ferruccio turned to Pedro. "Where's Sofia? Count Scaligeri saved my hide at Montaperti and I'm not about to let his granddaughter be sacrificed. She needs to get out of Etruria, now."

"She's leaving on an Oltremarine galley tonight."

"*Bene.*" Ferruccio steered the gondola toward the dock "What do you need?"

"Time. I have to get to the chain-tower, and they must be long gone before anyone notices."

"Right. I'll keep these sham negotiations going as long as possible."

"And what about him?" He looked at the body in the water.

"Who? This never happened."

After Pedro climbed onto the boardwalk, he turned back. "You knew the Concordian's offer was a trap?"

"From the first. I'd be a poor hunter if I didn't. Go on now, lad—do what you must."

Khoril, the *Tancred*'s commander, was a short hairy Levantine. He gave them a warm welcome—he was furious with the Ariminumese, and blamed the Moor for their confinement. The enmity between the two ex-pirates was obviously personal. Khoril had been looking forward to seeing the Moor dangle in the Arsenale, not running it. Still, when Ezra told Khoril the plan, he was skeptical.

"It's true," said Ezra. "The *Tancred*'s spooked them into Concord's arms."

"Queen Catrina never learned to tread gently," said Khoril. "Look, if this were *my* ship, in a heartbeat I would do it."

"You wouldn't have this fine retirement home if I hadn't helped you outrun the Moor so many times."

"If I sink this galley, Queen Catrina will set me rowing in another, and you beside me."

"And if you let the Moor scuttle it, she'll give you the freedom of Akka? Let's keep her Majesty out of it. This is between you and me."

Pedro's pass got him through the Arsenal without arising further suspicion. The tower—a Rasenneisi would never call it that; it was more like a stubby lighthouse—sat on the very precipice of the southern horn. Its low, thick walls were built to take heavy pounding, and the chain cast to defy cutting—each link was as big as a child. It hung across the harbor in a shallow arch just above the water's surface, attached to a huge wheel in the top story. The northern horn had vanished in the fog, so it looked as if the chain was suspended in nothingness: a bridge to oblivion.

Pedro remembered the rope bridge he had made—was it really just two years ago?—the day he met Giovanni. A cascade of conflicting emotion assailed him. Giovanni, his friend, the man who taught him engineering, was not a man, but *water*. Certainly it was implausible, but could he really say it was impossible? Giovanni himself had told him that Wave Theory was the realm of paradox and shifting definitions. Pedro had seen one buio that thought it was a boy. The only difference was that Giovanni's disguise had fooled even Giovanni himself.

Pedro gathered his courage and knocked on the door. He heard uneven, stumbling footsteps on a stairway before the watchman opened the door slot and grunted, "What is it?" A hot waft of alcohol came from his breath. "Oh. Maestro Vanzetti, isn't it? What brings you out here?"

"Just out for my passeggiata."

"Aye, s'lovely view."

"Bit chilly, though. Can I come in?"

Even drunk, the watchman was wary, "I ain't supposed to—"

Pedro interrupted genially before he could shut the latch. "Oh, I understand." He dropped his voice to a conspiratorial whisper. "I don't suppose you have anything to warm a fellow up instead?"

The watchman smiled through a trough of rotten teeth. "That's the boy! I have just the medicine."

He left the slot open as he turned his back, Pedro dropped the Whistle in and pulled the slot closed. The shrill beep ricocheted inside. After a second, he pulled the slot open and saw the watchman on his knees, holding his ears. Then his eyes rolled back and he fell over. Pedro reached in to open the door from the inside. The tower's upper story was open to the chill of the night, and the watchman had apparently been warming himself by a little stove. A jug of grappa was heating there.

Pedro examined the chain and the wheel by the light of a smoky cresset. Without help, raising the chain would be impossible—but he *could* slacken his end. Hopefully that would be enough—the *Tancred*'s displacement didn't look to be as profound as the new Ariminumese galleys he'd been watching the arsenalotti build.

The moment he released the lock, the chain unwound with a thundering that made the whole tower shudder. The hot metal hissed like a great serpent as it hit the water; Pedro prayed that at this hour, this far from the city, it would not be heard.

He cut the dangling end of his hood off with his dagger and soaked the rag in grappa. Then he took his last annunciator from the satchel and tied the rag to its base before beginning to wind it up. He tilted the arms so that it would fly straight up when he released it. The burning rag was the signal the *Tancred* was waiting for. He prayed that they could see it through the fog.

A distant horn sounded.

"Grazie Madonna!" He took a swig of the grappa, then climbed down the stairs and poured what was left on the unconscious watchman and closed the door behind him. He would wake tomorrow with all the symptoms of a bad hangover; with any luck he might not remember Pedro—and if he did, hopefully nobody would believe him until it was too late. Sofia and Levi needed all the time they could get, and he should get going too: Rasenneisi were about to become universally unpopular.

Chapter 56

THE HISTORY OF THE ETRURIAN PENINSULA

Volume II: the Land across the Water

The thoughtful Reader will ask what place a Levantine kingdom has in a history of Etruria, but the very question, reflecting our generation's theological amnesia, is its own answer. In the centuries since Jerusalem's destruction, our 'native' religion has so altered that we forget it was forged in that holocaust. To the common Etrurian, perhaps, these scorched foundations are an irrelevant footnote, but this volume is meant for scholars.

Since the removal of the Curia's dead hand, it is hardly controversial to observe that our "Madonna" is a composite figure. After scraping away those characteristics borrowed from Etruscan mythology,[16] we excavate the woman who led the First-Century

---

16. If you can ignore its plodding prose, *The Bifurcated Goddess* by Duke Spurius Lartius Cocles competently demonstrates that the Madonna's iconography and supernatural powers are almost identical to the Etruscan fertility goddess, Thalna (virgin consort of the Sky God, Tins). Likewise, the Madonna's

Jewish rebellion that precipitated the rise of the Ebionite Radinate and the fall of the Etruscan Empire.

That fall was cataclysmic, yet our peninsula was reborn in and renewed by its new Marian faith. Although we have since abandoned all superstitions,[17] it would be unwise to forget that its light led Etruria out of the Age of Darkness and that its values continue to shape our history, for good and ill.[18]

short-lived child, Jesus, was equated with the wonder child, Tages (son of Thalna). Etruscan shrines to the fertility goddess were converted into Marian baptisteries throughout the peninsula.

17. By "we," the Author means Post Reformation Concord; Etruria's other cities have retained their primitive idols with a grip as tenacious as it inexplicable.

18. The worst of these values find their fullest expression the Curia of the last Century, the best, in the empire of reason founded by their successors.

Chapter 57

Several home-bound Ariminumese barges rang their bells as they passed the *Tancred*: their masters might be on poor terms, but the sailors exchanged the usual courtesies. Over Khoril's objections, Ezra didn't steer the *Tancred* along the coast—the open sea might be more hazardous, but it was faster. Weather allowing, it would take a few days to escape the Adriatic's confines, and Ezra wouldn't be easy until they had passed out of the grasping Hands of Helen and into the Middle Sea. From there the swift trade winds would carry them East.

They made good headway—Ezra claimed the Bora wind owed him a favor—and a cheer from the nervous crew rang out at the first sight of the outstretched thumb of Etruria's so-called hand. Normally the *Tancred* stopped in the Tarentine port of Brindisium, but not today—by now their escape was surely known, and the Ariminumese had doubtless set out in pursuit.

Ezra told them it was better to think of something else. "At sea, what matters most we control least. All we can do is do our work as well as possible."

It sounded like something Doc would have said, and Sofia wondered what *he'd* make of her now, abandoning Etruria on the strength of a few bad dreams. She kept telling herself that her flight was Rasenna's best hope, in the hope that she'd start believing it.

Levi's respect for Ezra had visibly grown as he saw his expertise at the tiller, and how the crew relied on him. The Ebionite's work might keep him at the stern, but nothing escaped his keen black eyes. He watched the fog, stubbornly hugging the Etrurian coast, but his weather-beaten face felt the wind changing and the color of the sea, changing from cold green to dark blue, told its own tale.

Sofia had never sailed before, but discovered happily that it did not make her ill. Ezra inspired confidence; she found it fascinating to watch him work. As he checked the ship's course against the stars and corrected it, he told her, "Wind and water are alive, and like us they change their mind ceaselessly. The stars alone are constant."

"I'd like to be that way," Sofia said.

"Hush, girl," said Ezra, making horns against ill-luck. "That's wishing for death."

The sails barked and rippled complaint and jealously held on to the last of the day's wind. Sofia looked up at the bloated silhouette of the sail and saw there a portent of how she would be in a few weeks. By then she *must* have found safety. She was cold, and tired of running.

Ezra noticed her yawn and sang to the waves, "The day ends and even the sea's paths darken. Time to sleep."

Khoril had donated a small sternward cabin to Sofia. As she let her cot's gentle rocking lower her into sleep, she looked though the portside hatch at the coast. Fog clung to it like snow. To assuage Pedro's doubts, she had manipulated water—but doing so meant exposing herself to the Darkness. Now, even as the distance between her and Etruria increased, she could *feel* the hunger at the heart of Concord. The beast grew strong; it would consume Rasenna,

Ariminum, Veii, Salerno and finally all Etruria. Giovanni had saved
Rasenna from the Wave, though the price was annihilation. If her
fate was to die for her child, she swore she would not be found
wanting.

Hours later, when she woke from her usual dream of the abandoned city that must not be looked upon, she left her cabin and
found Ezra leaning on the stern rail contemplating the stars that
were fading before the dawn. The splashing waves disintegrated into
foam.

"What's it like, Ezra? The Holy Land? I've never seen a desert."

"You're looking at one now, child. Don't you know what makes
a desert?"

"Sand?"

"Emptiness. There's none greater than the sea. In all deserts the
wind is master, holding life and death. See, it molds the waves as it
molds the dunes. That is why one who travels deserts must know the
winds, learn their names so that he can negotiate with them."

"Haggle with the wind?" Sofia said wryly.

"Certainly. Sailors harness the wind with sails just as your engineers funnel water with weirs."

"It's your slave then."

"It could drown us in a second! There is a great difference between
using the flow and forcing it. One must never force Nature."

Sofia looked down at the receding water. She felt its strength taut
like the muscles of a bandieratoro and shivered. "You've heard of
Girolamo Bernoulli?"

"I live on a boat, not under a rock. Who hasn't heard of the Stupor
Mundi?"

"He was my grandfather's enemy. He forced water to do awful
things. He tortured it into a deadly Wave; he raised a great tower in
Concord with it."

"I heard that tower was burned," Ezra said, looking at her keenly.
When Sofia said nothing he said, "He will not forgive that."

"I'm safe from him at least," Sofia said with a smile. "He's dead
some twenty years."

Ezra kept looking at her. He began to say something, then stopped. He turned around and swore.

Three silhouettes in the early dawn.

A moment later, a voice from the rigging above announced that the ships were Ariminumese.

Captain Khoril came to the stern to see for himself. "Damn. Damn. Damn."

Levi joined them. "We have a good lead," he said optimistically.

Neither Ezra nor Khoril looked away from their pursuers. Their heads shook simultaneously. "That big bastard in the middle is the *San Barabaso,* the Moor's flagship. It has one more deck than us. He'll chase us until our rowers are completely exhausted, then the other two will board us. Listen! The drums are changing. If only we'd had a few more hours' lead . . . *damn.*"

"What about making a break for the Thessalonian Hand—that's Oltremarine territory. We could get lost in the islands—"

"Too far, too little time. I'm sorry, Levi. We're well hooked."

In a quarter of an hour, the *San Barabaso* was within hailing distance. At the helm, Leto Spinther stood quietly beside the Moor as he hollered, "Captain of the *Tancred,* prepare to be boarded."

"The hell I will, you black devil!" Khoril returned. "I don't care what title they've given you, you're still a pirate by my reckoning. Board this ship in open waters and Oltremare will consider it a hostile act. You authorized to start a war?"

Large swells buckled the waters that divided the two galleys. The two other Ariminumese ships were still some distance away.

When the Moor didn't answer immediately, Leto grabbed his arm. "Do it! I'll back you."

The Moor pulled his arm free and gave the Concordian a gentle shove. Leto hadn't got his sea legs and stumbled. "General Spinther, I let you aboard at the Procurator's insistence, but if you issue another order on my ship you'll spend the return voyage in the brig. I'm well aware it would suit Concord to see Ariminum at war with Oltremare, but I answer to the Doge." He turned back to the *Tancred* and cupped his hands. "Captain Khoril! I give you a minute to turn around. If you do not allow me to *escort* you back to Ariminum I cannot answer for your safety."

Leto watched the Moor turn a small egg-timer. A minute passed with no answer. The Moor's face was blank as a death-mask until the last sand grain dropped. Then his features twisted into those of a gleeful demon. He ordered his marines to prepare for a hostile boarding.

Then with a muttered oath, he said, "Wait—listen!"

A small bell rang humbly across the waves, and the *Tancred* slowly turned around.

"Stand down, lads," the Moor called, then, with a tight smile, "another triumph for diplomacy. Piracy's so much easier with the force of the State behind one's sails."

Leto could feel the Moor's disappointment that the *Tancred* had not elected to fight. His experience with Geta had taught him about gamblers. "Something amiss?" he asked innocently.

"I thought Khoril had salt," the Moor remarked bitterly, and gave orders for the other two vessels to fall behind the *Tancred,* "—in case he finds some."

Chapter 58

VOLUME II: THE LAND ACROSS THE WATER

Roots

The dream of Crusade was first dreamed in Etruria, so the tragedy that follows might best be described as a family history. Like winter before the monstrous vitality of spring, the Etruscans retreated before the Ebionites. Maritime trade entirely collapsed. The Middle Sea became a Radinate lake for a millennium and the imperial pillars[19] tumbled into a vacuum that created new wars and new rivals. The first city-state to throw off this doddering parent was Ariminum.[20]

---

19. The only pillar to survive the cataclysm was the school of cardinals based in the northern city of Concord. The vigorous new faith was a light the Curia shielded against the gathering gloom.

20. Ignore chauvinistic propaganda of "Manifest Destiny"; Ariminum's early start was but the accidental consequence of taking refuge in a singularly defensible lagoon. The interested reader can track Ariminum's evolution more precisely in *The Southern Principalities,* an earlier chapter in this volume. It would be remiss not to mention *The Stones of Ariminum,* a highly regarded cultural study, also by the present Author.

The Etrurian[21] peoples who had retreated from the coast to the more defensible vantages of northern heartland, the hills and mountains took longer to rise.

There followed the Age of the Castellan, when every lord was fundamentally a land lord. These mounted thieves preyed upon the isolated towns and sought, with onerous tolls and outright robbery, to inhibit trade—an inherently unchivalrous activity. But slowly and irrefutably the market developed until the towns became cities strong enough to overthrow these parasites. With the aid of a more welcome breed of parasite—bankers—Etrurian mercantilism expanded until the Middle Sea again beckoned, a siren call, a call to arms. In one of history's more ironic reversals, the old Radinate, now a fractured realm, faced an invasion from a West that was unified, vigorous and murderous.

21. As the postimperial Etruscans become known. The interested reader may consult Appendix 23 for a detailed survey into the predictably chaotic etymology of this period.

Chapter 59

The *Tancred*'s return voyage to Ariminum was uneventful. Back in the harbor, Captain Khoril took his time tying up and gathered a crowd by hollering over the rails about "diplomatic repercussions." When the Moor ordered him to lower his gangplank, he protested, "Board my ship without permission and you violate Oltremarine sovereignty."

"I'm admiral of this harbor. If I have grounds to believe you're carrying goods on which duty has not been paid, by maritime law I have not only the right to board you, but the right to repossess any contraband I find and impose a commensurate fine."

"Once a pirate, always a pirate," Khoril muttered.

"Just drop it, will you? We both know what we are."

When the gangway was lowered, General Spinther was waiting to board.

"What's that Concordian doing here?" Khoril said. "Having trouble remembering who you work for, Azizi? Suppose it must be hard to keep track."

The Moor's patience was running out. "I might add, Captain, that if I find evidence of contagion aboard I have a right, nay—a *duty*, to burn your ship to ashes. Speaking of which, you look a pale, even for a white man. Running a temperature?"

Still grumbling, Khoril made way for the Moor's men. They searched for an hour until Leto finally announced, "She's not here!"

As he fulminated and threatened, the Moor bowed to his counterpart. "Nicely done, Captain."

Slow smoke columns rose from the Old Town like great seaweeds as Fra Norcino's children ran riot in an orgy of puritanical destruction. Their tantrum would continue until their master was returned. Bare feet crept up the old, unguarded stairways and small hands hurled stones that shattered the blue orbs, letting the lithium Jinni escape and darkness rush in. The fanciulli stalked for the first time through the streets of New City, knocking on shuttered windows, whooping with glee at the wonderful sound of shattered glass. They never got tired of it. The praetorians and Geta's bravos beat them back down the stairways, but with each passing day the pressure grew.

But that was not the worst. Since General Spinther had left Concord, not a day went by without the murder of a consul, sometimes several. More terrifying to the thinning ranks of the Collegio than these violent deaths was the implication: the consuls were all former Candidates; each one should have been proficient enough a fighter to survive a fanciulli mob. The organized assassins picking off consuls in backstreets, in brothels and in their beds were obviously a more sophisticated threat than barefoot children.

And Consul Corvis was able to do nothing to stop it.

He called himself "Barabbas" because he was one of Fra Norcino's first followers, though he was a little too old now to run with the pack. Since the preacher's arrest he had become a vagrant. His stubbled face was covered in scars and scabs. He fought and spat at the guards as they pulled him along, but when they released him outside one of the cells, his expression of fury changed to trembling reverence.

He leapt forward, grabbing the bars. "Master! You're alive!"

The guards—there were three of them and a boy—tried to pull the vagrant away, but he struggled violently, throwing his body into spasms until they threw him down and kicked him senseless. When his fingers finally came free, the guards did not drag him away, but instead opened the door to Norcino's cell.

Norcino smiled and called to the occupant of the cell next to his, "Wake up, my king—they've come for us!"

Torbidda opened his eyes and yawned. "Cadet Fifty-Eight? You took your sweet time."

"You're welcome, Cadet Sixty. We need to move quickly," Leto said as he knelt to unlock the preacher's manacles.

Norcino's breath was hot and foul as he whispered in Leto's ear, "These soldiers, boy, you trust them?"

"Of course. They are praetorians," Leto said confidently, omitting to say he had bribed them generously. "Now, I need you two to swap clothes."

The vagrant, though subdued from his beating, had breathlessly followed the exchange. He began stripping with enthusiasm. "Anything for the master!"

Norcino pulled off the rags that clung to his emaciated frame and paused to kiss the naked vagrant. "Barabbas, you shall be rewarded, if you never deny me."

"I could never!"

While the swap was effected, Leto unlocked Torbidda's chains. Rubbing his wrists, Torbidda nodded acknowledgment to Castrucco—the praetorian prefect was proud to be included in the deception—then turned to Leto. "What about the Scaligeri girl?"

"On the way to Oltremare I'm afraid."

"Damn it, Leto—!"

"*Tranquillo,* we'll catch her."

"Don't worry, there's time yet," said Norcino. "Now I shall rally my followers and we'll take the mount and hold it while you complete the rite!"

"That's the plan," Torbidda said with a tight smile at Leto, who struck the preacher hard on the back of the neck. He collapsed like a pile of bones and Castrucco caught him and produced a baggy hood, which he pulled over Norcino's head. He passed the unconscious body to one of the praetorians.

"You mustn't!" The vagrant fought against his chains. "Leave him be! Traitors! Blasphemers!"

Leto didn't need to give any more orders; everything had been arranged in advance. Prefect Castrucco entered the cell and drew his dagger.

"Sorry. Sorry. I—I don't know that man," the vagrant pleaded. "Do what you like to him, I'll never tell! I saw nothing!" He tried backing into the corner, but the manacle constrained him. He screamed when the blade struck, then fell to the ground still promising silence. Castrucco quieted him with his hobnailed boots. When he was done, the vagrant's cheekbone showed through the ripped skin. He looked at Leto. "Enough?"

"Madonna's sake, harder! We get one chance at this!"

A minute passed, with the repeated squelch of flesh pulping and skull cracking, and when it was over the vagrant's jaw hung at a ridiculous angle and Castrucco was breathing hard.

"For God's sake." Leto pushed the third praetorian into the cell. "Take over."

The young man swallowed, entered the cell and tapped his exhausted commander on the shoulder. When Castrucco turned around, a dagger jabbed in and out of his chest. With a look of disappointment he sat slowly beside his victim, wheezing, and patiently watched his blood splutter around the wound, sluggish and black, until he died.

"He tried to sell me on another double-cross," Leto said in response to a look of inquiry. Torbidda tutted.

Castrucco's assassin knelt down, pulled the dagger from the vagrant's side and sank it into the wound already in Castrucco's chest. He placed the prefect's hands on the handle so that it looked like a particularly determined suicide. He stood back to examine the scene critically, then looked back to Leto for approval.

"The preacher's blind," said Torbidda.

"Yes, First Apprentice?"

Torbidda pointed at the vagrant's ruined face. "So scoop out the eyeballs—they didn't grow back!"

After that detail was attended to, the party left with the unconscious prisoner. They were discreet, not that it was necessary: the Small People knew it was unwise to pry into praetorian business.

"I'll go and find Corvis," said Leto, taking his leave. "You'll be all right."

"I'll follow you shortly."

Torbidda led the way through the Guild Halls, then through the tunnels and secret vaults he had discovered while poring over the old plans. The fire that destroyed the Molè had no more affected the beast than the mountain that encased it, though it had lately been starved of prisoners. They deposited Norcino in one of the top cells and Torbidda watched through the cell door as he woke up.

The blind man sat up, instantly aware that this was not merely a new cell but a new prison; he cocked his ear to the echoes of dripping water and groaning metal, feeling the cold moisture in the air. "I should have expected this. More and more you impress me, boy. Truly you will make a worthy vessel for *him*."

"I am no one's vessel—not yours, not Corvis," and least of all *his*."

"Then what now, your Majesty? Are you going to kill me?"

"At some point. You don't have to die yet to be useful. We'll announce your martyrdom to your followers and find a constructive use for all that grief."

"What will you tell them?"

"The facts will speak for themselves. On Corvis' orders you were slain, and afterward the assassin patriotically ended his life in the vain hope of preventing more bloodshed."

"Very good." said Norcino. "Obviously, you can't leave this pair alive."

Torbidda hit a switch, and Norcino's cell flooded with blue light. He collapsed into a twitching heap. Torbidda turned around and took off his cloak. "Obviously."

The two trembling praetorians drew their swords.

Corvis shuffled through the papers stacked around him as if the answer could be found there, but finally gave up. "What can we do?"

Geta sat in the chair formerly occupied by Consul Scaurus; his boots on the table partially covered the brownish stain left by the late consul's brain. Geta ignored Corvis, as usual. The consuls around the table were ominously silent as well. The Collegio's tiered rows were mostly empty—fear kept them away—but Consul Corvis imagined that they were full of men sitting in judgment of him. He was a shrunken man: the weight he had been so eager to bear was crushing him. "Geta, if I didn't know better I'd say you were enjoying this chaos. The time's come to restore order."

Up until this crisis, the spectacle of Corvis coming apart had been mildly entertaining. "You're getting to be a right old nag," Geta snapped. "I told you already, I don't have enough men to keep the peace."

"When this is over you will have questions to answer."

"You can't court-martial me twice. Why don't you do something if you're so worried? The praetorians are at your disposal. You've made the First Apprentice toothless, so it falls to you. Go on, win your spurs! A bit of blood on your sword will win you some credit with the Small People—unless you bungle it, of course. In heaven's name, don't show this weakness in front of praetorians. They're men, after all."

It was time for Corvis to act. He walked to the door like a man going to the gallows, but as he reached it, the door opened. "Spinther, you're back! Thank goodness—Geta's good for nothing but drinking, and his men are only interested in looting," he started.

"You really can't blame Geta for the riot out there. You're the one who let those animals loose on Norcino. What a mess they made."

Corvis wilted. "I—I did no such thing—"

"Well, he's dead and so's Castrucco, and they're blaming you for it."

"*Madonna!* Can't you do something?"

"I can't resurrect the dead."

Corvis returned to the table, recovering his composure by the proximity to his memoranda. "General," he said imperiously, "for what do we give you these armies, if not to safeguard us?"

"Consul, I shouldn't even be here. You can't propose to take the legions away from the Europan Front so soon after securing it." Leto looked around the table. "I know things are bad here, but if we lose the mines, all's lost. I'm as powerless as you."

"The great Leto Spinther," Geta said, "mortal after all. Glad I lived long enough to see that."

Leto stiffened, "If you have any suggestions—?"

Geta waved the bottle. "Little drinky?"

"I have a suggestion."

Corvis, who had buried his head in his hands, looked up suddenly, clearly considering flight, but he mastered himself. "First Apprentice! How good to see you. I see you've extricated yourself from prison—how clever of you. Look who it is, General."

"I have eyes," Leto said casually.

Corvis was betrayed, but he carried on, as if ignoring it might make it otherwise, "Well, boy, what is your suggestion?"

Torbidda walked to where Geta was seated. "May I?"

Geta leapt up. "Be my guest, First Apprentice."

"Thank you," said Torbidda, sitting down. "Consuls, nothing will satisfy that dog-pack but blood. I propose we let Corvis supply it."

Neither Geta nor any of the board leapt to Corvis' defense, or argued with Torbidda's reasoning. Corvis saw the glances exchanged and understood their import. "Why not your blood, First Apprentice?"

"Come, be logical. You've made yourself prominent at my expense; I wouldn't sate their appetite."

"I second the motion."

"And I."

"And I."

Corvis showed unexpected resolve as the floor caved in beneath him. "So, finally picking up the baton, First Apprentice? Finally remembered your responsibilities? Not before time. I fear, however, that you've misjudged your strength. These cowards might do what you say, but I need only stamp my foot and the praetorians will cut you down. The rank-and-file engineers still side with me—not out of love, you understand, but because they know that without me, the nobles are back in charge."

"I beg to differ. The engineers can smell the meat cooking on the bonfires as well as you can. They're more concerned about surviving the week than preserving your powerbase."

"Geta, are you going to let this continue?" Corvis shrieked.

"I think not," said Geta. "Guards!"

Two burly praetorians entered and Corvis meekly sat back down, his hands automatically sifting through the memoranda in front of him to find some directive, some loophole through which he could escape. There was nothing.

"Lord Geta?"

"Take Consul Corvis to the dungeons and scourge him. I'll be along shortly."

They dragged him away screaming, "Traitors! They'll come for you next, Geta—Spinther, we had a deal!"

Torbidda gestured for Leto to take the empty seat. Geta, sobering up rapidly, pondered what this meant for him as he watched the changing of the guard. He gave a little jump when Torbidda addressed him. "Lord Geta, what Concord needs now is stability and unity of command. If the last few months prove nothing else, it's that when engineers and nobles squabble, Concord grows weaker. Are you patriot enough to put country before ambition? Spinther's men hold the frontier. Yours hold the capital."

Geta burped and straightened up. "Not for much longer they don't, not without reinforcements. My men can crush a riot, but an outright rebellion would sweep them away."

Torbidda looked at Leto.

"I can spare some," Leto said, quickly adding, "Not many. Think you can you convince the rest of the Collegio to accept the new order, Torbidda?"

"If sweet reason fails I'll show them Corvis' whipped carcass before throwing it to the fanciulli."

"That should do it," said Geta lightly. "I've always found mortal danger clarifies things enormously."

The clatter of hoofs rang on cobblestones and a rider in a black cloak galloped across the Ponte Bernoulliana, leading a second horse, but he had to bring both to a swift halt when the guard at the gate didn't stand aside.

"What's the meaning of this?"

"No passage in or out. General Spinther's orders—"

"—obviously don't apply to me." Geta pulled back his hood. He had no way of knowing whether he'd been proscribed yet. He'd have to risk it.

The guard noticed Geta's second horse, breathing hard. "What's in them bags?"

"Nothing to do with you; my business in the north is urgent."

When the guard still hesitated, he snapped, "Madonna! Check with Spinther if you must—and explain to him why the Eighth Legion was lost while you're at it."

Chapter 60

"Idiota!" Leto slapped the guard with his glove and walked back over the bridge in a dark mood. He'd been rather looking forward to putting Geta on the rack.

"Cadet Fifty-Eight!"

Leto pulled up short. "Who said that?"

"Up here, General!"

On either side of the barbican's archway were gibbets. The gibbet on the left was older, and the wicker had worn away, leaving a rusted outer frame and a tattered skeleton; the prisoner had outlasted his prison, but freedom no longer interested him. The gibbet on the right was still functional, and the prisoner within likewise, although the unnatural tilt of his shoulders revealed he had been treated to the attentions of the strappado, and what was left of his strength had been broken on the wheel. Leto scowled—he disapproved of prisoners keeping their tongues. "How do you know my number?"

"I gave it to you."

"Grand Selector Flaccus? Well, I never. You've moved up in the world."

"And you, General! Congratulations on your promotion."

"How did you end up there?" Leto said politely, but without much interest.

"Your talented friend saw to that—but I'll be out soon. There's some justice in this world. Sixty is languishing in a dungeon now, if Corvis hasn't had him killed."

"Ah. No, sorry. He's First Apprentice again."

"Oh . . ."

"Well, I must be going. So nice to see you again."

"Stay for a while and I'll tell you what really happened to Agrippina. I don't suppose Sixty ever told you the truth."

Leto looked puzzled. "I expect he killed her. You really thought I'd give a damn? Dear me. No wonder you stayed a selector all your life."

Geta raced through the Wastes and did not look back. He'd always boasted that he knew when to leave the table. The one stop he'd made before leaving was the treasury, making full use of his authority to take what he wanted without explanations—another gamble, but necessary. Whatever city he stopped in couldn't be an ally of Concord's and he'd need to make friends quickly. He should perhaps have squirreled away a cache outside the capital, but he did not regret it: a true gambler never hedges. To win Fortune's favor one must be faithful—but because of his fidelity he was destitute, with only as much gold as two horses could carry and a question: *Where to?*

There was nothing in the north but legions loyal to Spinther, so south then.

Geta didn't begrudge the First Apprentice's success—he only wished he had seen it coming. The boy had played a bad hand brilliantly. He and Spinther had obviously prearranged the assassination campaign to discredit Corvis with the Collegio; they'd decapitated Norcino's mob, and, since Spinther had been dissimulating all along, the army was his too, and Concord was his again. He deserved it. Geta's motley militia was the last loose end, and he expected they'd all be dead before nightfall. Shame really: nice lads. Obviously the First Apprentice had expected their leader to nobly stand by them, hence the appeal to Geta's patriotism. That had been his one miscalculation.

The gruesome spectacle of ex-Consul Corvis' public flaying was a timely lesson that served to forestall any more Collegio conspiracies and cool Norcino's followers. Geta's bravos, abandoned by their champion and offered the choice of joining Corvis or reinstatement in the army, all chose reinstatement. Though Old Town was not yet fully pacified, the First Apprentice promptly returned to the isolation of the Drawing Hall. Throughout Corvis' power grab, Torbidda had been directing Leto's movements, while the rest of his brain chipped away at the other conundrum. It was challenging, but no more than the simultaneous chess games they used to play in the Guild Halls. Corvis was dealt with, but Torbidda's confidence that the other problem's solution would dawn on him, given time, had not been borne out.

He needed to return to first principles.

For the first few revolutions, prisoners in the beast were fed a recycled mush, the origin of which was best not speculated upon. The beast was like a mine-shaft, and the fuel it mined was agony, so prisoners must be capable of producing it for as long as possible. Once cells reached a certain depth, feeding stopped; Torbidda had seen the relevant formula in Bernoulli's notebook. It was bad luck if all the upper-row cells were full; a lower cell whose occupant had died prematurely would have to be found.

For the last week, along with food, Torbidda had been punctiliously administering the excruciating blue light, until the preacher was ready to talk. "Whatever you are, you're no mendicant. Who is your master?"

Words spilled from his drooling maw. "The king of the world. Ages ago my brothers and I conquered the Worm, that we might serve Him forever."

"Who are you?"

". . . Melcior? Or was it Balthazar? I've forgotten."

Torbidda reached for the lever. "Don't lie. No one forgets his name."

"Was that not the method by which you won the red?"

"That's different."

"Is it? Perhaps it is. I get so confused." He crept closer to the door. "Go easy on me, child. You're still so young. You don't know about *the years*. There's no end to them! They bury you unless you keep moving. After the Bethlehem . . . *incident*, my brothers and I did what we always did and parted ways to wander the world's dark paths, listening to rumor, watching the stars, following the winds where they led us, to the courts of strange kings, majestic huts built on jungle canopies, caves fretted with rubies and blue ice, hide-skin tents that rumble over the steppes like ships, and always we asked the same questions: is the new Emmanuel born? Are you the new Herod? It was an endless search, but I took comfort that I was not the only one searching. Back in Babylon, we three do not have your wonderful lenses, so we learned to *walk* among the Stars in our minds. It proved a useful skill in the wandering times. No matter which of the world's deserts we were lost in, my brothers and I could confer."

"These are a madman's fantasies," said Torbidda.

"They may be, for surely I am mad, the years have seen to that." The blind man's face trembled with painful grief remembered. "Then, a few hundred years ago, I lost contact. In my dreams I no longer heard their whispers; I could not sense their passing in the world. They were gone! I pondered to myself: was the work done, the war won? Had the Old One surrendered, finally resigned his claim on this world? If so, the Magi were no longer needed. My brothers had perhaps heard the good news sooner than I and taken their sweet reward."

"What's that?"

". . . sleep . . ." He savored the word as if describing the sum of the world's treasure. "I took me to a desert I knew well and found there an old pillar, strong and tall, and all that stood of a temple of a god whose name I have forgotten. My plan was to let the sun and wind and rain consume me together—each had as good a claim on my bones. I sat there for—oh, a century at least, getting thinner, retreating from the world. Whenever a stranger happened by, once a decade or so, I'd ask, more out of habit than curiosity, to what king was he a subject? Finally there came a day when a man—he was an engineer like you, child—told me a thing I had never heard in all my wanderings: he said he had no king!"

The blind man shook his head with dissatisfaction. "I insisted that all men have a king, but he insisted that he was subject to Reason alone. So I *pried* a little, asking who taught him this novel dogma. With a reverent manner he spoke of an artful man of war who'd enslaved the Water even as Solomon enslaved the Wind."

Torbidda looked down at the dark pool at the bottom of the pit, felt the *hunger* biding there. "Bernoulli."

Inside the cell, the blind man leapt with such excitement that he nearly tipped over his slop bucket. "*I knew!* Herod was among us once more, and where Herod is, Emmanuel is near. Oh, I was frantic! I'd weathered millennia, but now time was short. I searched between the stars for my brothers, in *deep time*; I sailed on the burning winds between suns until at last I saw a pair of shifting shadows on the bloody skin of a dying star: two wrestlers. I raced to intervene—Oh, but the vacuum is vast. When I reached the star, the hurly-burly was done and only a smoldering husk was left of what had been my youngest brother."

For a time Fra Norcino said nothing, just sat humming and cooing to himself.

Torbidda leaned in to examine the shivering sobbing wreck.

"My elder brother has fallen into apostasy," Norcino confessed quietly. "He is Magi no more." Suddenly he reached out, and Torbidda flinched instinctively, but he was too slow. Norcino pulled him to the bars, babbling in his ear, "*You* are the last Apprentice as I am the last Magi! When I returned to my body, my skin was raw and blistered and a buzzard was feeding on my eyes. I did not blame the creature; all things need sustenance. I sucked it dry and threw myself from the pillar, and after my bones healed, I limped toward Etruria. On the way, I fell in with some pilgrims—"

"Yes, I remember," Torbidda said, struggling to free himself.

"—but when I came to Concord and learned that Girolamo Bernoulli was long dead, I feared that I was too late. I launched my spirit once more into the stars, to search out my King. I did not look long. It's *close,* Torbidda, closer than ever before. The Darkness waits behind the rising sun to swallow the world at last. It told me to tarry in the desert until the temple burned; it told me the vessel would soon be ready. Then you found me."

"I told you before, I'm no lamb." Torbidda's hand blindly searched for the switch.

The blind man's breath was the rabid panting of a predator about to pounce. "Seek your heart: you know you have a great destiny, if only you will stop running from it. Torbidda, you were born to slay God's son!"

Torbidda's fingers found the switch and the cell was flooded with crackling blue light. The current passed to his body from Norcino's and when his grip fell away, they collapsed as one on either side of the bars: prisoner and jailer; courtier and king.

Chapter 61

VOLUME II: THE LAND ACROSS THE WATER

Crusade

Before broaching this perennially thorny subject, a brief review is necessary of the Holy Land from the expulsion of the Etruscans to the eve of the Western invasion.

The desert has been always incontinent with prophets, but in the first century a flood of holy fools doused the land. Each heralded a new kingdom; each had a vision that bloomed as briefly as desert flowers, beautiful and inconsequential. The Prophetess' message was different, and not merely in the sense that she preached with a dagger. In the great fire that consumed Jerusalem, she reforged Judaism into a proselytizing creed. She turned an inchoate resentment of Etruscans into nationalism. In a remarkable few decades, waves of fanatical armies erupted from the desert to envelop the Middle East and beyond.[22]

22. Inevitably, this success was seen as proof of God's favor, but as detailed in Volume I, the late Etruscan Empire was beset with internal and external problems. Specifically, the attempt to use devalued currency to pay the legions, already

After the Prophetess' death, and under the guidance of her apostles,[23] power migrated to the more refined coastal cities; the capital shifted north to Tire, then south to Alexandria before meeting halfway in Akka. The nomadic fighting spirit of the desert was lauded ever louder as the Radinate became more cosmopolitan. The Melics' belief that this savage hinterland would always save them in time of peril was about to be tested.[24]

exhausted and demoralized after the prolonged Sassanid war, prompted several mutinies at exactly the worst time. Absent this chaos, the Radinate could not have won so much so quickly.

23. Barabbas was the first "Rightly Guided" Melic. Following the Schism, Saul derisively described Barabbas' followers as "the Poor Ones." Barabbas responded that, before God, all were poor. Thereafter *Ebionite* became an honorable appellation among the Jews.

24. The nomads' contribution to the Radinate is similar to that of the Romans to the Etruscans. Also analogous is their equivocal attitude to the sybaritic excess of their respective capitals—the Radinate's decadence prior to the Crusades had attained new depths.

Chapter 62

As the fogbank on the Tarentine coast thinned under the morning sun, a small skiff emerged, drawing on silent oars. Only when the *Tancred* and her escort were out of sight did Sofia dare speak. "What now?"

"Now we run," said Ezra. He set the jib opposite the mainsail and goosewinged it, to put some distance between them and the watchful shores of Etruria. The streamlined little boat's cutwater sank like a dagger into the waves and released an arterial spray that misted them. After a few hours, they cleared the strait and felt the welcome chill of the northern trade wind that would carry them south.

The course Ezra plotted would take them by Crete, then they would hug the Anatolian coast until they reached Cyprus and then finally to Akka. The first crossing was the longest, but they were lucky: Ezra didn't share the traditional sailor's dread of the open sea. It was imperative they escape the sea-lanes where all the traffic was

Ariminumese. The Bora had brought them swiftly down the Adriatic; now the hardworking Greagale was hauling them across the Ionican. "Once we get beyond Tessolonika, we'll be in the Meltrimi's delicate hands. I hope she's in a good mood this time of month."

"'Course she'll be," said Levi, "winter's passed."

"Spring brings forth more than turtle-doves, lambs and blossoms. The dark gods wake from slumber; war banners and pestilence stalk the land. The eastern Tyrrhenian can be cruel this time of year." He glanced at Sofia. "But we've been lucky so far."

Sofia felt the wind against her skin and an instant later heard a fierce crack as the sail caught it. "That's the style of it!" said Ezra.

Levi had proved a surprisingly adept fisherman, so Sofia, feeling useless, asked Ezra to teach her how to trim the sails. It was harder than it looked, but she got the knack eventually. Now she felt the tension and the creaking strain of the running rigging striving against the wind. In flag-fighting, one created these snaps—the Doc insisted they were the mark of a *real* bandieratoro. Now she felt the canvas, billowing slow and regal, pulling the ship with it.

"You've become a serviceable sailor, and just in time," said Ezra, "for tomorrow comes the bride at the end of week. Time to rest, and ponder and dream . . ."

The city had been elevated above all other things in the land, and its pride had drawn the wind's wrath. What hands had carved and gilded and mortised and encased, the winds worked ceaselessly to undo, rounding away all memory of Men's busy fingers, and now the heavy stones lay everywhere, a sea of caved-in houses, characterless pebbles on a forgotten beach, so featureless that the returning families—if ever the prophets' promises of resurrection came true— would never be able to pick out the homes they had once lived in. The sand moved of its own volition, pouring with tireless curiosity into doorways that led nowhere now and creeping up walls, only to tumble back on itself again and again and again. It moved on and settled and moved on. The cobblestones of old paths appeared for a moment before the grains rushed between them and buried them again. The winds charged through the city's forgotten quarters and drove each other to new peaks of outrage.

On the southern hill that faced the city the wind shredded hollowed olive trees into chips. Gravestones trembled like leaves; the carved names were damned illegible. Sometimes, in the shifting dirt, Sofia glimpsed white smooth things: elongated, thinning shells of some extinct creature. The winds harried them into fragile meshes connected by calcium bridges and the desert's jagged teeth did the rest until the last trace of Man was swallowed. The tombstones were finally ripped up and thrown with gay carelessness into the maelstrom, exploding against each other. Their owners, who had thought to be first, would find themselves nameless and forgotten come Judgment. And, if this was Judgment, the wind was a pitiless judge.

And everywhere, in the midst of the dull, incessant rage, floated pages crammed with dense scribbles. Even if she could translate the language the prayers were written in, they disappeared faster than her eye could read them. The lower quarters on the city's periphery suffered least; whole hours would go by before the sands would barge through the streets and make them impassable again. But at the city's heart, the howl of the storm was constant and overwhelming. A defiant section of a great wall circled the mount, the source of the prayers, which bled out between the wounded stones. On the plateau, lightning cracked between burly clouds. Storms condensed into tumbling balls of yellow air against a rumble like great stones being hauled up. The storm was made of grains of sand and scraps of paper. Most of the prayers begged for life, for love, for money, for power, but only prayers begging for annihilation had been answered.

Sofia opened her eyes and quickly closed them. Ezra was already up. Through half-closed lids she studied him. It was odd that she had never seen him sleep. This morning his eyes were not on the sails but buried in the old volume he carried always. He read it aloud with a melancholy melody, half song, half speech, and as if on command, a strong wind sent the skiff skipping over the water.

Without looking up, he said, "The joy of the Sabbath to you, Contessa. It's bad luck to wake a sleeper, but I was tempted. You had a bad dream, I think?"

"I slept fine." Sofia yawned to cover her embarrassment at being caught spying. "Shouldn't you be checking our course?"

"The wind will look after us. It knows I must read."

"You must know it by heart now."

"Even God must continuously study. Study alone keeps back the Darkness." He slapped the wood in front of him and the ship creaked in complaint. "It is a difficult art, requiring nerve and skill. You must wait for the letters to form words and the words to gestate without prematurely imposing meaning. If you can do that, truth springs upon you."

"Sure, sure: *be detached, go with the flow, nothing's real*," Sofia said. "I've heard it before."

Ezra sat up. "Oh no! You must be *attached* to the world. Constant awareness is necessary. God is in every*one*, every*thing*, every letter. Every word in this book spells His name."

"Sure," Sofia said.

He held up two pages then a third against the morning sun and shifted them until the first letters on each page lined up. "What's it say?"

Sofia said, "I don't read squiggle."

"We must rectify that. What about you, Levi?"

Levi had obviously been pretending to sleep too but he sat up and yawned ostentatiously before reading where Ezra pointed, "J–A–H"

"You see! His *Name* is all around, if only we look for it."

"Since when do you read Ebionite?" Sofia asked.

"Condottieri pick up more than exotic rashes in their travels," Levi said defensively. "What's that supposed to prove, old man? With enough letters you can spell anything."

"Each letter is connected to every other. On Sinai for a golden moment Moses saw all connections. When diligent readers relink the letters, the words rejoice. They dance and ecstatically couple and new meaning is born."

"Immediately, or nine months later? Come on, old man," Levi said, "no race can beat the Eebees at fooling themselves. Torah's out of date. You think the scribes who wrote it knew anything about Natural Philosophy?"

"The Concordians say there are atoms and the void and nothing else—a useful philosophy for burrowing rodents. It's true that the scribes were ignorant as we of tomorrow. What of it? I do not care about tomorrow or yesterday. I study to understand *today*. To one who understands this moment, all vistas—past, present and future—are open. He is free, free even to disagree with God."

Sofia had only been half-listening, but here her heart skipped. "God can be *overruled*?"

"I told you even God must study. Torah belongs to all. No one has the final word. Scholars argue to become wise, and when two sincere students differ in their interpretations, their dispute is a journey to truth."

The wind was turning against them, so Levi lowered the sail and secured it against the lifting yard. He yawned, and lay down. "Madonna, it's too early for philosophizing. Wake me up when the sun's over the yard-arm."

"You want a bedtime story too?" said Sofia.

"Sure, why not? How about it, old man? Any good stories in there?"

Chapter 63

The Acts of the Wrongly Guided Apostle

5   Now at this time the Etruscans were besieging Jerusalem and all Judea was in uproar.

2   Mary's fame had spread until even a tent-maker from Tarsus knew Her name. This Saul was a Jew and also an Etruscan citizen. His countrymen's eagerness to join the revolt amused him. Why, he asked, do the Jews always wait for prophets? Can prophecy enrich a man? If this prophetess is true, her prophesy will come to pass; if she is false, it will not. Since most prophets come to grief, it is better to have nothing to do with them. Thus meditating, Saul rode to Damascus with his wares.

3   He was worried about encountering bandits in the desert, but he considered the market worth the risk. Perhaps the road to Damascus was bad, perhaps the horse, perhaps the rider,

perhaps all three—Saul fell and was injured. His horse ran away, taking Saul's purse and waterskin with it. Saul lay there roundly cursing his fortune until some riders came along: it was a tax collector and his servant, and a centurion with a pair of soldiers.

4 Saul begged the tax collector's help, saying, Brother, I am a fellow citizen. The Etruscan laughed at him, saying, Jew, what have I to do with thee? Saul wished to curse him, but stayed his tongue—the tax collector's servant had a rude look. The centurion rebuffed Saul also, saying, Jew, the Emperor is far from here.

5 The party rode on laughing, but the tax collector's servant tarried to give Saul water. He said unto him, Brother, despair not. Trust in the Lord and He shall deliver thee.

6 Weeping, Saul thanked the servant and asked his name, That I might remember thee in my prayers. As the servant rode away, Saul wiped his tears, drank deep and pondered. He knew the servant's name, but knew not how.

7 As the sun grew higher, Saul's water grew lower. It was gone by the time another rider approached, a merchant from Jerusalem. Saul cried aloud, Help me, for are we not Jews and brothers? The Jerusalemite said, If I tarry I will miss the market and if I miss the market I will go hungry. Surely thou wouldst not wish thy brother to go hungry? And so saying he passed on.

8 Presently another Jerusalemite, a priest, came along. When Saul begged for water, the priest refused, saying, Away thou sinner! The Lord God sees all. He would not permit a good man to fall as low as thou hast fallen.

9 Saul wept.

10 He watched the Jinn turning in the distance, and cursed Jerusalem and its citizens and priests. Presently Saul bethought he saw a babe drifting across the sand on the wind, with swaddling bandages flowing behind. And he heard a voice that said Saul, Saul, Why dost thou doubt Me?

11   Now, Saul spoke Greek as well as Etruscan and could there-
       fore reason. This vision was obviously a fever brought on by
       the heat. He buried his dry lips under his robe and only when
       the sun was low did he lift his head.

12   He saw a rider coming from Damascus. As the rider drew
       closer, Saul saw that it was the tax collector's servant.

13   The servant was alone. He dismounted. He did not speak, nei-
       ther did he seem to see Saul. He quickly lit a fire and baked
       bread, and as he did so, Saul studied him. His loincloth was
       torn and marked with blood. When the bread was baked,
       the servant looked at Saul and said, Forgive my ignorance.
       I am no philosopher. How can a Jew be a Jew and a citi-
       zen of the Etruscan Empire? Surely no man can serve two
       masters?

14   Though the question was politely asked, Saul was sore afraid,
       for he knew the custom of the desert: that the servant had not
       offered bread because he was considering killing him.

15   Saul summoned all his eloquence, and said unto him, My friend,
       just as all men are born stained by Adam's sin, so I was born
       a citizen of that Idolatrous Empire. My father was a usurer
       who in accordance with the Law lent only to Etruscan sol-
       diers. They are, thou must know, filth who think nothing of
       cheating a Jew. My father believed that Etruscan Law was
       like our Law, fair and blind. He purchased citizenship so
       that he might prosecute defaulters in Etruscan courts; a vain
       hope. It is well said that the sins of the father are visited on
       the children. My people think me a traitor and the Etruscans
       think me a fool; thou sawest how thy companions mocked
       me.

16   They will not trouble thee again, said the servant.

17   Now Saul remembered where he had heard the servant's
       name: this Barabbas was one of the notorious disciples of
       Mary the Galilean. So Saul informed Barabbas of his vision,
       gilding it and claiming that the babe said, Arise Saul, and
       persecute those who persecute me!

18   Barabbas was much impressed, saying, You must be he that
        my Mistress sent me to find. She said I would find an eloquent
        man on this road who would help spread the Word. Rarely
        have I heard a man who could lie so skillfully.

19   Then Barabbas gave Saul water to drink and bread to eat, and
        went to sleep with his hand on his dagger.

Chapter 64

Levi had caught enough fish the previous day, and Sofia found she hardly had to touch the sails, so with nothing better to do they partook of the peace of the Sabbath. The wind carried them onward as Ezra read. Sofia half-listened, thinking of the wind-racked city and the startling idea that one might gainsay God. Next morning, Ezra was back at the tiller, and his tireless adjustments to the sail were justified in the speed and distance traveled that day. It was evening when Sofia noticed something amiss.

Ezra was standing still, though the sail was flapping, bleeding wind. Levi was merrily murdering a condottieri song—something about stealing a dead comrade's boots—when suddenly Ezra turned around. The look on his face made Levi fall silent.

Ezra mumbled something as he took in the sail and the wind abruptly ceased, then he turned back to the water.

Sofia said quietly, "What is it?"

He put his fingers to his lips and whispered, "We're hunted."

Sofia and Levi looked behind them—if the Moor was following, then surely they should sail for the nearest shore, and quickly? But Ezra was looking down, into the cold depths of the wine-dark sea. Abruptly he pointed, his finger traveling slowly over the surface.

"I don't see anything," said Levi, but Sofia felt her skin crawl as the foul shadow of *something*, a great fish or worm, crossed their path below, followed by a wafting stench of dead, sodden flesh, worse even than the burning sheep mound near Gubbio. A minute passed before the wind took up again.

Ezra quietly raised the sail. "It's gone, but we must be on guard."

Levi announced that in his considered opinion, Ezra and Sofia were sun-touched, and he was going to take a nap.

Sofia found Ezra looking at her. "You've tangled with that old fellow before?" he asked.

"Only in dreams. This is the real world—"

"There are places where they are one. We're in the sea's hands now. The dark place that fellow came from wants to keep you from your destination."

"Those tales you read us yesterday—you believe them? That Mary's son could have made everything better forever?"

"Oh, not so long as that," Ezra said. "Even Messiah is not once and for all. Messiah is the spring that must come when the earth has grown old. For hundreds of thousands of years the seasons of Man have rotated: after summer comes winter, the heat retreats from the land, rivers dry up, the deserts grow, the earth shrinks. Good deeds become rare, charity a myth, cynicism prevails. And then, at the darkest hour, a new voice cries out and all who hear it remember there were once such things as honor and love, and all the wickedness of the world loses courage and retreats into the Darkness."

"But God let Herod kill him."

"Who told you God is master of this world? The disaster that befell the Madonna was His disaster as much as ours. Her grief is everyone's. We see its results all around us—corruption and deceit, revolution and civil war spreading like plague until all hope is gone."

Pedro escaped Ariminum before the alarm went up. On the way back to Rasenna he halted briefly near Gubbio. Where the burning sheep mound had been was a black patch of grassless earth that stank like a wound. The men were gone, the tree empty. Hereabouts Giovanni had died, and hereabouts a second Giovanni had been born. The carrion was too decayed even for scavengers, and the rot in the air made it hard to think clearly. He hurried home.

His first stop in Rasenna was the baptistery. He remembered visiting Giovanni here after he'd almost drowned—had Giovanni himself begun to suspect then? In the light of Sofia's revelation, Pedro felt duty-bound to reexamine all his assumptions. His initial reaction had been doubt. Engineers were skeptical of theory and faithful to experience, but Giovanni hadn't been an ordinary engineer; and his grandfather certainly wasn't. The Concordians had pulled the mechanical arts to a frontier where it was not measurable phenomena like Gravity or Friction that mattered but the unquantifiable: Faith and Love. Pedro had helped to create the transmission that had stopped the Wave during the siege, so he knew the mathematics it was based on, backward and forward. It was as solid as a gear-shank.

As he tied up his horse, the unfinished orphanage next to the baptistery seemed to reproach him. Inside, he circled the cool interior looking up at the stages of the Madonna's life. The fanciful story was familiar, of course, but its meaning had always been remote. He had never even considered that it might be taken seriously, let alone literally.

"Do you believe in Her?"

Pedro turned and found Isabella standing at the doorway.

"I believe in things I see."

"You saw the Wave."

"That's no more miracle than a flag is. It's a weapon made by men."

"Understand a thing and it ceases to be miraculous?"

"I suppose. The Wave was created by amplifying a particular harmonic sequence. We stopped the Wave by creating a signal that was its counterpoint."

Isabella glanced at the aged Madonna of Rasenna in a corner niche. "Like throwing a cloak over Rasenna."

Pedro said nothing; the image from the old Rasenneisi prayer was eerily apt. Perhaps his failure was one of language—call it "Love" and an engineer is suspicious but call it "Harmony" and it can be measured and amplified, dissected and destroyed.

"Sofia told me everything. She told me that Giovanni was one of them—a buio . . ."

Isabella didn't even pretend to be surprised. "Is she safe?"

"More than she ever could be in Etruria. She's on the way to Oltremare."

"*Grazie Madonna!*" Isabella sighed in relief, then looked at him. "That wasn't all she told you, was it?"

Pedro looked around in embarrassment. "I don't know what to believe. Nothing generates spontaneously, especially life. There must be a cause—"

"There is, and someday you'll understand that miracle too. Right now all that matters is that you helped her escape."

The tiered circles ground against each other pitilessly and the echo of the tortured metal was amplified by the pit. The beast carried on its excruciating revolutions, though now it was a prison with only one prisoner.

Fra Norcino scrambled to the compartment before it closed and grabbed the bowl. He threw the food in the corner impatiently and placed the bowl under a drip. His shit-bucket was under another drip, and it was getting fuller. He listened merrily to the tapping, and when the bowl was filled he poured it into the bucket. The water was still below the brim.

"Nuh!" he grunted, unsatisfied.

He stood astride the bucket and made up the missing inch with a steaming stream of greenish-amber piss. He fell to his knees like a worshipper and inhaled the textured vapors of the noxious brew with delectation. "Perfect," he said, blowing upon the surface.

* * *

After Pedro left, Isabella stood on tip-toe, looking down into the cool water of the font.

"Come out, Carmella."

The older novice appeared from the dark corner of the baptistery where she'd been hiding. "I'm sorry, Reverend Mother. I was cleaning when the young engineer came in . . ." She stopped, seeing that Isabella didn't believe the lie. Carefully, she said, "What he said about the Contessa—is she really—?"

"—I expect your discretion."

"How long have you been hiding her sins?"

"You *heard* nothing, and you will *repeat* nothing, Carmella. I would be alone now."

"I—Yes, Reverend Mother."

The novice left hurriedly. Isabella waited for her composure to return and studied the still cold water below. Her mind drifted, and she let it, leaving behind her frail body—it was too heavy for where she needed to be. She was a bird, traveling through the soft froth of clouds, seeing the white feathers of her outstretched wings, making minute adjustments, the better to catch the wind. She felt the bird's hunger, and sensed the change in temperature as it traveled beyond the land, where the air chilled still further. In the calm sea below her she *saw* a tiny skiff. A tremor passed on the distant surface below; electrical tension in the air; drops of unseen rain danced on the water of the font.

Sofia watched Ezra warily. The old man had been surveying the sky for an hour now, though she could see nothing of interest but a single seagull. Ezra sniffed suspiciously as the sails filled with wind, and the breeze, gentle till now, suddenly grew stronger.

Levi woke with a start, like Sofia, gagging at the foul stench that suddenly surrounded them.

"Damn you, not here!" Ezra cried as the skiff suddenly lurched to the side.

Mumbling through his cracked lips, Fra Norcino stirred the foulness clockwise, and it kept spinning when he removed his finger. Far below his cell, in the lake at the bottom of the pit, the water's surface was alive with changing forms, cubes and cylinders and disproportionate disembodied limbs that clawed the air and fell apart.

A sudden wind blew the dust through Rasenna's streets and burst the baptistery doors open. "You have *no right!*" Isabella screamed, seeing—*feeling*—the maelstrom growing in the Holy Water.

"We're being tugged from below!" Levi shouted. "Ezra, what is it?"

"The current," Sofia said. She could feel it in her bones.

Ezra was shaking his fists at the black clouds that had eclipsed the insipid sun. "You may not harm her. You can only point the way!" His voice was small against the howling wind.

Norcino's cackle echoed in his cell. "You broke the Law first by helping her flee. No prohibitions bind us now."

"Who the hell's he talking to?" Levi asked. "Old man, you need to get us out of here!"

"I'm sorry, Levi," Ezra said with terrible regret. "We cannot outrun this."

Isabella plunged her hand into the font and pushed against the current, but it wriggled between her fingers.

Suddenly the boat shifted as whatever had been dragging them released its grip, and they were carried forward by the wind. The spiraling motions of the sea slowed and then the maelstrom collapsed into a dozen smaller counter-twisting currents. The skiff wandered drunkenly between them.

Ezra's smile was manic. "Thank you, little sister!"

"What—?" Norcino began as he felt the water stop turning. "What amateur work is this?" Giggling, he plunged his hand back into the bucket.

Isabella screamed as the blind man grabbed her hand and pulled her down toward the water. Her feet left the ground, her arm sank in up to the shoulder and she struggled to keep her head from following it by grasping the side of the font.

Bobbing wildly, leaving the shattered maelstrom behind, the skiff climbed wave after wave, high as hills. While Sofia struggled to take down the sail, Levi bailed furiously. "You've *got* to be kidding me!" He could not believe Ezra's response to their calamity.

The Ebionite was reading: *"The Lord answered Job out of the whirlwind—"*

Levi saw Ezra's eyes widen as a great waterspout rose from the heaving water. "Well, that's not good."

The spout danced on the waves like a great arm connecting sky and sea, pulling them together. When the spout came closer to the skiff, Ezra raised his voice: *"Who is this that darkeneth counsel by words without knowledge?"*

The spout retreated.

Isabella felt two arms around her waist, pulling her back. She opened her eye under water and saw the pale hand grabbing her wrist. The air in her lungs escaped in a gasp. Then, feeling darkness edge into her, she steeled herself. She released the rim of the font, grabbed the hand holding hers, pulled it toward her mouth and bit down hard on the thumb.

"Whooaahahaa!" Norcino howled and ripped his bleeding hand out of the shit bucket.

Carmella roared with effort, and all at once Isabella's body came free. They fell on the baptistery floor together. Isabella spat out the shriveled yellow thumb—like something belonging to a corpse—and lay there, half-drowned in a puddle of blood and water. Carmella reached out and took Isabella's hand and began singing the Virgin's song. Isabella, her eyes rolled back in her head, joined in weakly.

"Look!" Sofia cried.

The waterspout wobbled wildly, and the base turned a violent red. In seconds the polluting color had reached the sky. It hit the cloud with the explosive rush and crack of a forest fire. Spears of lighting fell as Heaven purged itself in a damn monsoon.

Norcino howled and kicked the bucket against the door, mumbling in the forgotten tongue of Babel.

The water shot up from the font in a great pillar and struck the baptistery's golden roof so hard that the mosaic shattered. Water and gold rained down on the two girls.

And Ezra's eyes returned to normal. He looked suddenly older. "I'm sorry, Sofia. He found us. Wind failed. Pray water does not."

Like a great flag buckling, the sea's whole surface writhed under the electrical scourge, and wave after wave struck the boat, coming from all directions.

Sofia screamed as the sea enveloped them.

Water screamed louder.

PART IV:
CITY OF GOD

O God, the waters saw thee; they were afraid: the depths also were troubled . . .

Psalms 77:16

Chapter 65

The first assembly on the bridge since Piers Becket's wedding inevitably evoked old memories and new tensions. Yuri allowed few of his men to attend. Giant though he was, he lacked Levi's standing with the condottieri—they'd been restive since the *real* podesta left. A small podium had been set up beside the towering mass of the shrouded statue. A somewhat enervated Sister Isabella opened proceedings with a prayer, then Fabbro rose. Standing together, Pedro and Maddalena watched Fabbro climb the podium. He looked older since his wife's death. When he reached the top he looked around in mild distress and after a moment climbed down. "It is pointless making lofty speeches in front of friends."

Maddalena rolled her eyes to Pedro at this obvious bit of theater, but it generated few smiles among the still sullen crowd. Pedro was already eager for the ceremony to end. Since his return, he found Signoria business increasingly distasteful. The orphanage—a dyke to

prevent the flood of unwanted bastards from drowning Rasenna—
had become more pressing than the cloaca, and he willingly lost
himself in the practicalities of the work.

Fabbro carried on as if he had received an ovation: "Friends, I see
you standing there like so many separate towers and I realize what
our problem is." He held up a golden coin. "Money. It makes people
crazy. In hard times, poor families stick together, but as soon as they
get a little money, the quarreling starts. Quarrels aren't the worst
of it, either. There's no one so prone to bad taste, bad investment
and bad behavior as new money. Well, friends, I have a confession:
I'm new money. We're *all* new money. Rasenna has never been so
wealthy. Mistakes are natural—but if we make mistakes, let's make
them together. If we stumble, let's stumble together. A tower divided
must fall. If we are to succeed, it can only be together, as one tower.
The Signoria speaks for *you*, minor guilds as much as major. Our
interests are one. We must put the same trust in our government
that we do in our walls and flags. We must be a tower in which no
part can further its interests at the expense of the others. In a world
where a cold northern wind is blowing, it is all we have. In Concord,
in Ariminum, these institutions are failing, each tower, each class,
each person against one another. Let not Rasenna go that way! Let
there be harmony. From today, let there be one tower."

Fabbro's smile was laced with desperation as he waited for
applause to erupt naturally here. A scattering of polite clapping came
from the priors. "Rasenna, I give you the fourth lion!" With unde-
feated enthusiasm he pulled away the sheet—he'd been around flags
long enough to get a snap from it. This time the cheer was not forced,
and Fabbro beamed like a new father to see the last lion finally in
place with his brothers. Its golden pelt was blindingly beautiful.

"From this day forth, a full watch is kept. Safe at last, my friends:
at last the bridge is safe!"

After a round of handshaking, Fabbro searched among the
crowd for Jacques. The blacksmith stood at the back of the crowd
in his apron and long-eared cap. Fabbro wasn't surprised that the

blacksmith had not dressed up for the event, but it was odd that he looked so displeased.

"A wonderful job, Jacques! Rasenna is grateful. I'm grateful. Your hands have wrought something truly beautiful."

The blacksmith gave an almost imperceptible headshake. "The bridge was better without it," he said abruptly and stalked back to Tartarus with his trailing apprentice. This was more than an artist's false modesty, and Fabbro was briefly taken aback—but he forgot it as another round of backslapping commenced.

When the party was under way Maddalena whispered to Pedro, "Too bad the Contessa had to miss this."

"Don't be unkind," Pedro said mildly.

"You've become *so* virtuous since you set out *so* bravely to Ariminum, carrying all our hopes and dreams. A little bird told me Saint Sofia was carrying more than that."

"Maddalena, if you know what's good for you—"

"I hardly think you should threaten me, little brother, after you bungled the negotiations so badly. No wonder she was so desperate to go. I've heard the whores of Ariminum are so numerous that they have a guild."

Pedro knew Maddalena was no model of chastity, but instead of calling her a hypocrite he walked away.

"Well, now I know it's true!" Maddalena laughed.

The condottiere on watch that night decided it was best to call his superior.

Piers Becket yawned. "What is it? Has the invasion started?"

"I—it's—Well, I thought you should see this."

He climbed up, and leaned forward to get a better look at the rider below the wall, waiting patiently at the North Gate. The banner he carried belonged to Concord.

"Do you think he's mad?"

"Maybe," said Becket, "but he's wearing the uniform of a senior officer."

Ten minutes later, he and Yuri were escorting the unknown soldier into the city. Yuri insisted that the stranger conceal his banner, "For your safety."

Becket noticed that the Concordian rode alongside, instead of trailing them. "You know these streets, Lord Geta?"

"I should think so. I studied under Maestro Agnolo Morello."

"Really? Can you handle a flag?"

"Well enough, though I doubt I'll have occasion to—I can see the rumors are true. Rasenna's changed for the better. I congratulate you, Podesta."

Yuri looked at him coolly. "Rasenneisi changed by themselfs. No can force these peoples."

"I'm well aware of that. I mean, for finding a town to take you in. There's no demand for condottieri in Etruria anymore. I can't think of a better place to retire."

"Don't be envious," said Becket with bitterness. "Settled life's no fun for a soldier."

"There's women and wine, isn't there?"

"Plenty. Trouble is, you have to pay for it."

"You always do," said Geta solemnly.

"That why you come?" Yuri demanded. "Concordians not so popular here. Perhaps you remember this too?"

"Rasenna's grievance is against them who sent the Wave. I'm willing to fight *against* the engineers."

"Another sword, just what I need."

Geta smiled at Yuri's goading; he knew the look of a soldier out of his depth. The giant was desperate for an excuse to deny him sanctuary. "My rank's higher than yours, Russ, and I didn't get it by being *just* another sword. You need to think beyond your immediate problems and old grudges. I can help."

"Sure. By turning around." Yuri snorted and rode ahead, leaving Becket to gossip with the foreigner.

Pedro and Fabbro were discussing the imminent completion of the orphanage when Yuri showed up with the Concordian. Pedro rolled up his plans and left. If Fabbro shared Yuri's suspicion, he didn't show it. Yuri followed Pedro out. "Is wise to let them alone?" he asked. "This one has shiny tongue."

"Don't worry, so has Bombelli. He knows what's in Rasenna's interests." Pedro looked down at his plans. "I'm too busy to be a tour guide."

"Who's your guest, Papa?"

Fabbro looked up, wondering where his daughter had popped up from so suddenly. He bowed to the inevitable and introduced them. "Maddalena, this is Lord Geta of Concord. I was just explaining our delicate situation, and telling him that he's welcome to stay, on condition that he keeps a low profile."

"Gonfaloniere, I specialize in delicacy. I'll be quiet as a lamb, gracious as your fair daughter—" He smiled at Maddalena.

"We've heard Concord's deluged by fanatics," said Fabbro.

"The last Apprentice thinks he can control them. He's wrong. Unless I misjudge, Concord's about to tear itself apart. When that happens, someone will have to take charge."

"And that would be you?" said Maddalena with amusement.

"I'm flattered, Signorina, and accept your nomination with gratitude." He bowed low, and turned back to Fabbro. "You have nothing to lose by sheltering me, and much to gain."

"Yes, I see that. Is that *all* you need, shelter?"

"I wouldn't say no to a glass of wine." He kissed his fingers, glancing at Maddalena. "I was always fond of the local variety."

Initially the patrons of the Lion's Fountain gave Geta a frosty welcome. No one had suffered as Rasenneisi had at Concordian hands, but the Hawk's Company had suffered its share too. Geta appeased them by making it clear that he hadn't fought at Tagliacozzo, and that he thought Luparelli better off dead. The officers of the company recognized Geta as a plain fighting man, as flexible and opportunistic as them, and he won over the rest by the simple expedient of buying their drinks, round after round. The brewer was delighted—Geta paid in silver that was much purer than Rasenna's increasingly debased coinage. His brash charm, his familiarity with Rasenneisi dialect and mores and—above all—his unfeigned scorn of engineers impressed the bandieratori too. By the end of the night, Piers Becket wasn't the only one following him like a puppy.

"To Lord Geta!" he proposed. "If every Concordian was like this son of a bitch, we'd have nothing to quarrel about!"

"Madonna forbid!" Geta gave an exaggerated shudder. "Then we'd have to work for a living."

Chapter 66

VOLUME II: THE LAND ACROSS THE WATER

Millennium

The turn of the millennium was a moment of great hope, hope that drowned in disillusionment when the Messiah failed to return. Etruria's impatient masses turned to the secular world for salvation. This turning, a challenge to Concordian hegemony, was tied to the demise of the Castilians. The Curia had restrained their excesses and fostered the growth of the towns,[25] but once the Castilians were ousted and the other city-states began to grow in confidence and wealth, Concord's claims of moral authority began to chafe.

The Curia, now widely seen as a parasitical encumbrance, sought a distraction, and a mad melic obliged by initiating a vicious persecution of Marian Pilgrims to the Holy Land.[26] In the centuries

---

25. This was not altogether selfless. Larger urban incomes meant larger tithes could be collected.
26. That is, he increased the tolls on roads and bridges along the pilgrim trail.

since the collapse of the Etruscan Empire, the Radinate and Etruria had coexisted by a simple but effective policy of ignoring each other's existence.[27] Etruria's role was essentially passive.[28] It did not contest Radinate dominance of the Middle Sea. It stoically endured raids by Ebionite pirates.

That defensive stance changed as the Curia employed orators to proclaim the duty of all good Marians to free Jerusalem from the schismatics. Deus lo Volt! resounded from the marshes of Ariminum to the towers of Rasenna. Etrurians, briefly, had common cause.

27. There were some tragic exceptions—in the eighth century, an ambitious but naïve Frankish king initiated a correspondence with the renowned Ebionite melic Haroun al Raschid. Since Charles the Great was illiterate, al Raschid replied with a wonderful clockwork toy. The delighted king played with the musical menagerie until the birds fell suddenly silent. When he wound the clock it exploded. Later preachers cited this as clear evidence that all Ebionites were duplicitous and intent on killing Marians.

28. The *Reconquista* myth dies hard, but the collapse of the Ebionite occupation of southern Etruria in the ninth century was a result of rivalries back in Akka more than any effort by the occupied. See Chapters 3 to 5.

Chapter 67

Water lapped her feet. Gulls shrieked insistently. What was so urgent? Sofia lay there with half her face submerged in water and an overwhelming desire to go back to sleep. The water was tepid and the air was cruelly hot.

Then she distinguished another sound behind the tide: a breathless, huffing laughter. She opened her eyes and found herself looking at a strange feral dog with stripes like a cat. It smelled terrible. It was panting and padding a circle on the sand around her, getting closer with each circuit. It had a thick neck and powerful shoulders, but judging by its poking ribs and the way its long teeth emerged from slaver, it hadn't eaten for a while. It reacted to her return to consciousness by sinking abruptly on its hunkers and preparing to jump.

Suddenly a stone splashed into the water beside it, then another skimmed its flank. It hopped up indignantly, before bolting away, laughing miserably.

Sofia rolled onto her back and found a shadow standing over her: a dark-skinned youth, not much more than twenty. His hand rested on the dagger in a broken sheath in his belt. The blade was the only distinguished thing he wore, but his carriage was noble. His face was lean and boyish, though a few curled hairs stood out on his round chin and there was a thin attempt at a moustache under his heavy nose. His thick, expressive brows were ebony-black, like his knotted long hair, which was loosely wrapped in a shawl. Behind him, two dusty camels moaned and butted their massive heads together, making a sound like empty cork.

"Are you alive?"

Though Sofia was surprised to understand him, she played dead until he took a step toward her. Then she wound her legs around his and twisted, taking him off balance. As soon as he hit the ground he rolled, pulled his dagger free and pressed it—gently—against her neck. All else was hot, but the steel was cold. She flinched from it, amazed that she had been caught—he was *fast*.

"So you *are* alive," he said.

"And you're a lousy aim."

"I wasn't aiming to kill. It was only being a dog." His language was some barbaric variety of Frankish, mixed with an archaic version of the Ariminumese dialect. Sofia was grateful for the smattering of Europan tongues she had picked up during her time in John Acuto's camp.

"Where's Levi?"

"I've seen no other bodies. This Levi, he was your husband?" His voice was calm and even; if the attack had angered him, his manner did not betray it.

"A man I was traveling with."

He slowly took the blade away. "Your husband must be a trusting fellow, to let a woman in your condition travel, or a great fool."

"I didn't ask for your opinion, heathen. Is this Oltremare?"

"Technically, yes. But many parts of Oltremare are not safe for the *Franj*."

"I'm not a Frank."

"And I'm not a heathen. I am Ebionite; my name is Arik, son of Uriah."

She noticed the piercing, restless eyes under the thick brows. They were the eyes of a bird of prey: a light-as-honey brown flecked with amber; little mercy in them perhaps, but no cruelty either. He held himself loose, yet poised and fully present, like other hunters Sofia had known.

"We were bound for Akka. There was a storm."

"Yes, the winds were strange last night. You've bypassed Akka by many leagues, but it's a day's journey if you go by the coast along the plain of Sharon."

"Who is your master?"

"God is my master, and yours, but I am employed by the Queen of Oltremare. Whom do you serve?"

Sofia looked around at the wreckage—a torn sail, some splintered wood. Had Levi and Ezra washed up on another shore, or been swallowed by the sea? She took the sail and rolled it up. She saw the Ebionite watching her skeptically. She tried to straighten up, but assuming a queenly bearing was difficult in her bedraggled state. "I am the Contessa of Rasenna."

"I never heard of it." He coolly appraised her. "Perhaps you're a runaway slave. I could sell you . . ."

"I'm an ambassador of the Etrurian league." That was stretching the truth, but she needed to convey that he could get more by ransom than selling her as a slave. "I come offering an alliance . . . Arik."

He frowned, "A tribe's allies are its neighbors, as are its enemies. You come from *Ereb,* a land of darkness far from here. Amity or hostility is equally meaningless with countries so far away."

"Unless you are the queen's adviser as well as her slave, I don't propose to discuss it. You will bring me to her. The queen would not thank you for keeping me waiting."

"The queen does not thank anyone. I am not her slave, or yours," he said.

Sofia got the impression that Arik was the patient type. She gritted her teeth and tried a smile. "I would be most grateful if you
would escort me."

He shrugged in resignation. "I am going to Akka. You may come
along. If you can ride a horse then you should not have much trouble." He led the smaller yellow camel forward and patted its neck
with rough affection. "This one's name is Safra; in the past he has
displayed great tolerance with idiots."

He made the camel kneel and showed Sofia how to catch the
pommel with one hand and place her knee into the saddle. She tried,
unsuccessfully, until the camel started to grumble, then she swore
and said, "Oh, just give me a leg up!"

He took a step back, keeping both hands at his sides. "I cannot.
It is forbidden."

"I didn't ask you to make love to me."

He laughed, but still he would not assist her. Grumbling about his
prudery, she finally managed to get her knee into the right place, but
as soon as the camel felt her weight, it began rising, hind legs first,
and she just managed to throw her other leg over the saddle in time.
She held on with difficulty as the jerking pitched her forward, then
back. She watched glumly as Arik simply pulled down his camel's
head and placed a sure foot on its neck. As the camel raised its head
again, he slid gracefully into the saddle. Arik led the way, and Sofia
noticed that he rode kneeling rather than sitting.

They had gone a while when she spoke. "You said Akka was
north."

"Yes?"

"We're going east."

"There's a sizeable band of Sicarii—bandits—somewhere along
here. I was tracking them when I happened upon you. Anyone they
capture who is not Ebionite they kill."

Sofia felt a dart of fear for Levi. "I can fight," she said.

"That is obvious. Also obvious is that you need rest. I am your
escort now, and honor-bound to keep you safe. Our route will be
longer, for we must retreat a good distance from the coast before

turning north. Then we go through Ephraim and Manasseh and by the Megiddo road into the Jezreel Plain. *Hut hut!*"

They rode on in silence as the terrain gradually climbed. Sofia experimented with different arrangements of her feet around the hump, finally deciding that all were equally uncomfortable. She had not been ill at sea, but she found herself dizzied and sickened by the rolling gait and the untiring wind.

"The Sharav comes from the southern deserts," Arik remarked. "It is the last wind of winter; it blows for sixty days and fills men's tents with sand and their souls with melancholy." From a satchel he dug out two filthy pieces of cotton, the seed-heads still attached. "Here. Block your ears from it."

There were no marks of Man's living presence in any place they passed, though there were many desolate graveyards half-buried beneath the shifting sands.

"The earth fills quickly," Arik said. "The Dead are territorial."

"Where are the towns?"

"Nothing can live out here," he said, then corrected himself: "There were many towns once, then the Great Drought descended, twenty or more years ago. Jordan ran dry. It hurt the tribes much, the coastal dwellers less so. The desert people were once known for their generosity; the strong clans had good springs and fertile palms, but these exist no longer, and honor too has vanished. Scarcity makes locusts of those who remain." The heat went out of his anger and turned to resignation. "But God wills it. He punishes with water, by sending too much or by withholding it. Blasphemy to question Him."

"Is that who taught you to ration it so stingily?"

He threw her the waterskin. "Keep it. I've never met one who drank so much."

Sofia suspected Arik's casual act was just that; he could not have calculated on taking this long route back to Akka, nor having a companion unused to the desert.

The voracious sun warped the sky as wind disturbs a lake. Its light was like the moon's, turning all colors bone-white. The heat came in waves that broke over the endless sand ridges. She concentrated on breathing, but the air on her dry lips was pitiless as fire. Etruria was a warm, wet land and its humid air had a palpable weight. Here the absolute lack of moisture made it insubstantial as a fairy feast—you could eat and eat and never be sated.

Arik promised she would grow accustomed to it, as she had already to the brackish water, and so it proved. She learned to pay attention to the little he said—and to what he did. She noticed he let his camel eat the few shrubs they came across, so when her camel started edging toward a small clump of thorny yellow flowers, she did not stop it.

"Safra, No!" Arik yelled, and Sofia's camel turned obediently. "*That* flower is deadly."

"It's the same one you've been letting your camel eat!"

"Not the flower, fool! Look at the air above."

She did, and saw, many braccia above, yellow petals whirling slowly in the air, apparently drifting freely, but always over the flower—trapped.

"It's a *zar*—a most stupid Jinni that sleeps all day, but deadly to any creature that wakes it. Come away."

They rode on until the land was spiked with rocky hills, a desiccated version of the rolling contato around Rasenna. To the east, the plain elevated precipitously, and a strange cloud of dust circled its highest point. Inside the distant storm she glimpsed man-made forms: broken buildings, walls, and towers scattered around a truncated mountain. Here Arik turned them north.

"What's—?"

"Nothing to concern you," he said, tapping his camel on. "*Hut, hut.*"

Sofia let her mind wander, listening to the metronomic slap of the camels' feet. If Arik spoke truly, the Great Drought had occurred when Bernoulli loosed the Wave on Rasenna. She was startled out of her ruminations by a sudden cold wind—the day's heat had abandoned the desert quickly—as the sky flushed purple and the sun turned over like an old man going to sleep.

"We'll stop here," said Arik, hopping down. "In Akka—if you are who you say you are—they'll give you a bed grand enough for a princess, and your dreams will go no higher than the ceiling. Here, they will reach to the stars."

"Huh," Sofia said. "All I remember from sleeping outdoors is waking with a sore back." She urged Safra on. "I'll be back in a moment; I just want a closer look at that cloud."

In an instant Arik had reached for Safra and grabbed her around the neck. "No!" he cried, then, "The place is cursed, understand? Those who go there do not return."

Arik tied up and watered the camels while Sofia went to find kindling—there was little scrub, but other travelers had stopped here in the past and the old, bleached camel dung left by their beasts was good fuel.

When she returned, she noticed Arik kept his back to the strange spinning cloud. She studied it surreptitiously, as though he had forbidden even sidelong glances.

"This isn't what I expected of the Holy Land," she said at last.

"*Holy Land,*" Arik repeated wryly as he added some twigs to the fire. From one of his goatskin bags he took a few ounces of flour and a little salt, then added a little water and kneaded the dough before dividing it into several little balls, which he flattened between the palms of his hands. He scooped out a bed in the sand, laid some hot embers in, then put some rocks on top. He placed the rounds on the rocks, buried the lot with a thin layer of sand and scattered more embers on top. This done, he rubbed his hands together, looked up and asked, "What did you expect?"

There was no simple answer. The names of the mountains and rivers were the prayers of her childhood; in her head it occupied the same mental plane as Purgatory, Heaven and Hell. Just to be here was disorientating. Isabella spoke of a fairy-tale haven, but what a bleak world if this desolate husk was its center.

Sofia smiled. "Milk and honey?"

The Ebionite laughed. "Sand and fire, more like. My people came through the desert to get here and now the desert has caught up. I sometimes think the fate of *that* place will be the fate of my people."

"What's it called?"

He poked the fire critically. "Its name is too cursed to say. My father called it *The Place where the Jinn Consult*."

His evasions didn't impress Sofia. "It's a city."

Arik pulled a stick from the fire and blew upon it. The glow illuminated his face. "It *was* a city, like Iram of the Pillars, like Jericho, like Gomorrah, like Sodom. Wars were fought over such places— and now the desert has taken this one too, and it is welcome to it. You asked its name: once it had a thousand, and the wise men said, 'That great number was evidence of its greatness.'" He cleared the embers, dug up the bread and set it aside to cool. Then he looked over his shoulder at Sofia. "One of its names was Jerusalem," he spat.

He handed her some bread and she ate in silence. It was warm, and dry as dust. He gave her water, but took none himself. When she protested, he said they would find a well early tomorrow; until then, her need was greater. As Sofia drank, she pretended not to notice the wild dogs that chuckled and chattered in the dusk. They were just out of reach of the fire's heat, but not of Arik's sling.

Sofia had not just been searching for kindling; now, with the sail she had rescued from the beach, she started fashioning a combat banner. As she tested its snap, she wondered about Ezra, and whether he had drowned with Levi.

"Curious weapon," said Arik, breaking into her reverie. "Highly impractical, I imagine."

"A chivalrous weapon, unlike your sling."

His hand kept spinning and his eye never left the darkness. "Chivalry, yes—Queen Catrina mentions it frequently. It's another layer of armor for knights. They murder the *fellahin* freely, but when they are captured they wish to be ransomed. Chivalry doesn't limit war's horror; it makes it endemic. *Yah!*"

Arik made the bravest of the dogs howl with a stone in the haunch. His accuracy in such poor light impressed her, but instead of complimenting him, she complained of riding pains.

Arik chewed a date, grinning. "You have not been *riding*. Safra is *carrying* you."

"Perhaps." Sofia laughed and looked though the fire's dancing flames. The infinite night lay beyond the reach of its light. "Do you want it back, Arik?"

"Jerusalem? Cities have brought only grief to my people. I want for nothing. Sleep well."

"Golden dreams."

They had dates and sugared tea for breakfast. Sofia found the journey more comfortable this time. She looked back before the abandoned city was out of sight: dust-devils spun lazily, making slow circles around the outskirts like sentries.

They rode though a steep-sided wadi. Sofia thought it a strange place to look for water: the smooth pebbles underfoot showed that a river had run here once, but there wasn't a single shrub nor a trace of green now, and jagged rock-salt bled from the dried earth. At the end of the wadi was a boulder. Arik leapt down confidently. "There's a cave here, and a drip at the back known only to my father's people. You will not like its taste, but it will keep us alive."

He came out a minute later with his waterskins still empty, looking subdued. As he mounted his camel he said quietly, "It was choked with sand. I dug it out, but . . ." He was obviously disconcerted. "I've never known it to run dry."

Before she could say anything he'd pulled up and was staring westward. She followed the direction of his eyes. "What?"

"Between those blue mountains. The dust."

"Riders?"

"Five Sicarii, coming fast."

"I'm slowing you down," Sofia said.

"Yes," he admitted, "and even if we could outride them, without water you'll die. Since you're a woman there's a chance—small, admittedly—that they will sell you."

"They'll kill you for certain."

"Yes."

"Then go—leave me."

"I cannot." He smiled. "And even if it were permitted, I would think twice."

Sofia grinned. "I'm ready to fight if you are."

"If we must, we must—but we can at least choose better terrain than this."

They climbed up out of the wadi and dismounted, and watched the men approaching. Arik had been right: there were five of them, and when they saw they were observed, they slowed their pace. At their head was a cheerful-looking villain with curiously white teeth and a long beard knotted with dirt.

"*Shalom*," he called.

Arik occupied himself straightening his saddle-kit before looking up and saying casually, "*Aleikhem shalom.*"

"Truly that Queen found a loyal slave in you, Arik Ben Uriah."

"I'm no one's slave," said Arik coldly.

"You are a thorn in your brother's foot. He yearns to see you again." These were the compliments of a butcher praising a calf. He turned to the youngest of the party. "Tell Yūsuf that we've found his dog of a brother, and another *Franj*." Without a word, the boy turned and rode off to the west.

Arik said, "Then you found someone else near the wreck on the beach?"

"He tried running. Not a bad swordsman."

"Levi!" Sofia said, then looked at Arik. "What is it?"

The boy had not gone far; now he stopped and started warily backing away. As Arik and the Ebionites watched apprehensively, suddenly rider and camel both shot into the air and tumbled there for a few seconds as if weightless before crashing down with a dismal, abruptly terminated roar. A cloud of enraged dust erupted like a swarm of hornets and the Jinni approached at an impossible speed: a tall column trailing a swirling dust-cloud at its base. Arik grabbed his saddle blanket and threw himself over Sofia, shouting, "Get down!"

Sofia squirmed under his weight. "Get off me!"

"Be still, woman! I'm trying to save you—"

Daylight ceased and they were enveloped by a throbbing like the collective scream of battle. The sand-laden wind wept and battered against them rhythmically and Sofia gritted her teeth while Arik chanted, "No God but God, no God but God, no—"

They heard hoarse screams, and mangled oaths as the howl shattered into shrieks and then—all at once—they were gone. Arik moved fast, whipping off the cloak, pushing aside the sand that had almost buried them. It was hard to see; the air was heavy with dust. One of the Sicarii had the same idea, but his legs were buried, and he could not avoid Arik's dive, or his dagger. The dying man grabbed hold of Arik's hands.

A second Sicarii, the one with the long beard, was up now. He saw Arik struggling and stepped stealthily over Sofia—who thrust her flag between his legs. He bent over, groaning, and she got to her feet and followed up with an overhead blow to the back of his neck. The sharp crack made Arik turn and he nodded at her. "The others? There were five."

One they found still sitting on his camel, ready to ride. Sand filled his mouth and nostrils, his ears and eyes. The man's camel opened its eyes and moaned despairingly. It shook the sand from its ears and the body slumped and fell off. "He was too slow," Arik said dismissively. He scanned the sand carefully, stopped at a slightly raised spot and plunged in his hand. He pulled out a foot. "And this one, unlucky. It might have been us, but now, God be praised, we have water."

Sofia ignored the outstretched waterskin. "Let's get Levi."

"Folly. Drink before you collapse. Besides, they will not keep a Frank alive."

"But there's a chance! Your honor wouldn't let you abandon me, so I cannot abandon a friend I know is alive—do you understand?"

"Drink," he said.

"Say you'll help."

"You've already proven your courage. This is only demonstrating stupidity. Which would you water first, a horse or a camel?

You come from a land where water hangs in the air; you've been shipwrecked, riding and fighting. Drink . . . and we shall find your friend."

Sofia drank. It was warm and briny, but she had never tasted better water. At last she wiped her mouth and gulped air. "So let's go."

Chapter 68

Now it was Sofia who rode ahead. No aches or sore muscles now; there was a chance, however small, that Levi was alive and nothing mattered but that.

After an hour Arik insisted she stop again to drink, and as she took the waterskin, she said, "That bandit back there: he said Yūsuf wanted to get rid of you."

"My brother, may God blacken his face."

"Why are you not with them?"

"I would not disgrace myself," Arik said haughtily. "Our father was Uriah ben Sinan, leader of the Issachar. We were the most powerful tribe in the Sands, until the Akkans decided to make an example of us. They called a conference. My father was not a credulous man, but he trusted them to respect a truce—mistakenly, it turned out. Most of his men were slaughtered."

"The other tribes did nothing?" Sofia said.

"On the contrary." Arik's shoulders shook in a joyless laugh. "You saw how hyenas treat their wounded last night? That is Ebionite solidarity. The Issachar who escaped the massacre died by the blades of the Gad, the Zebulun, the Benjaminites, the Napthtali; of all my father's sons, only Yūsuf and I survived. We went to the caves and slowly collected together what was left of the Issachar. My brother called them his 'Sicarii.' You know this word? They were the Prophetess' most devout—"

"I know the Gospel," Sofia said angrily.

"Peace! I scarce know what you barbarians believe. In any case, all my brother's band has in common with the true Sicarii is a name. Their hand is against *every* man."

"Why did you leave?"

"Experience made my brother suspicious, a useful trait in a bandit—"

"—if not a king. If the Sicarii are the remnants of the Issachar, then surely they owe you allegiance as much as your brother?"

"True, but irrelevant. No king's siblings survive long when he views them as a threat," said Arik. "Besides, I do not want anyone's allegiance. The prophet Samuel was right: men are better off without kings." He slapped his camel's neck. "This is the correct throne for Ebionites, better than any gilded chamber pot. It gives me speed to outpace my enemies, vantage to survey the terrain, and when I am weak, its blood gives me succor . . ." Arik's proud speech dwindled to silence.

"What is it?"

"Truly the *Franj* are blind as babes. Look beyond that hill."

"The buzzards?"

"Come on! We may be too late. *Hut! Hut!*"

The dusty plain before them was littered with hundreds of bodies, and the carrion birds were already busy.

"A battle?" Sofia said.

"Hardly—a raid, or rather the end of one at least."

Sofia didn't need to ask who was winning; that was obvious. Those Sicarii who were not going down fighting were scattering over the hills in every direction. Most were dressed like Arik, in robes of flowing black, but some wore ragged loincloths and turbans with long, trailing tails.

Sofia watched in fascination. The Sicarii fought like Arik, leaping and twirling, fleet-footed as the wind. Their opponents, fighting under a banner with a blue-handed icon, were equally skillful, but different; they used some variant of Water Style. It was not skill, however, but sheer numbers that had decided the day for the Queen's knights. They were like an army of ghosts: each had a crude death's head painted on his helmet mask. Underneath their long white cloaks, the knights wore green surcoats emblazoned with a stylized Herod's sword. The surcoat covered reddened chainmail, that didn't appear to slow them at all. They were as deft as fencers with their light axes in close combat, and they threw with amazing accuracy. Half were fighting the last Sicarii hand-to-hand; the other half were mounted on white chargers and held in tight formation. Occasionally the one who looked to be in charge would bark an order, and a few knights would break away and set off to chase down straggling Sicarii.

As the last one dropped, the leader raised his banner and shouted, "Queen Catrina!"

The knights took up the cry lustily, brandishing their axes.

"Let's go," Arik said. "*Hut!*"

Sofia was a little surprised not to be challenged as they approached; the knights obviously recognized Arik. As she looked around for Levi, scanning the corpses as well as the living, she was a little unnerved when the knights kept their cumbersome masks down; normally the first thing a knight did after battle was to throw off his helmet, gasping for air.

Arik led her through the ranks and called, "Fulk!"

The two knights standing on either side of the kneeling Sicarii looked around together but their reactions were very different: the one holding the large ax delightedly exclaimed, "Arik!" but the other knight, the one holding the prisoner, barked, "You're addressing the Grand Master, Slave!"

"Seneschal!" the Grand Master said chidingly, "our friend deserves a better welcome. You *will* apologize," His voice was rasping, but young, and Sofia noticed that he did not have to raise it to get attention.

"Quite all right," said Arik evenly. "Bad-natured camels bite, they cannot help it."

When the Seneschal glared at Arik, Sofia saw that he had only one eye, and that was pale as milk. He snorted but did not retort. "Fine then," the Grand Master said after a moment, "one moment, if you please."

The arms of the Sicarii kneeling before him were bound and his face gleamed with sweat and blood, but his taunting smile was manic. "Enjoy this day, Akkan dog. Your days as masters of this land are at an end. The Old Man has woken from his slumber and returned from the mountains. The first to feel the sharpness of his knife will be the traitors"—here he glanced at Arik before turning back—"then he will unite the tribes and push you and your whore of a queen into the sea."

"If it happens, you will not see it," the Grand Master said calmly and nodded to the Seneschal, who jabbed the prisoner's side with the point of a dagger. The man stiffened, and with one blow the Grand Master took his head off. He bowed to the corpse, then handed his ax to the Seneschal. "See to the rest, Basilius."

The Grand Master turned to Arik and Sofia. "Glad to see you yet among the living, Arik."

The two men clasped arms in a warrior grip. "How did you find them?" Arik asked.

"I sent a small forward party with a long-enough carriage train. Greed drew them to it." Sofia noticed he did not describe the successful ruse with glee or knightly braggadocio.

Arik shook his head. "They forgot all caution? Sicarii indeed! Truly they are dogs and sons of dogs."

"It was nothing wonderful; you saw how many escaped. But where were you? You were long delayed. Dhib's been pining for you."

Sofia was following their exchange. "Who's Dhib?"

The men exchanged looks. "A falcon, my lady." Fulk's voice betrayed amusement.

"Oh," Sofia said lamely, puzzled by her proprietary feelings for an infidel.

Arik, for his part, looked equally baffled. Then he recovered his composure. "Allow me to introduce the Contessa Scaligeri of Etruria. Contessa, this is Fulk, Grand Master of the Lazars. The Contessa came across the water just to see Queen Catrina."

"Consider me at your service, Contessa. I shall be honored to escort you to Akka." He gave a courtly bow, then turned back to Arik and said seriously, "Look here, what's all this Old Man business?" He pointed at the decapitated bandit. "He wasn't the only one raving about it."

"Don't panic. The Old Man's return has been imminent for decades."

"Sorry to interrupt," Sofia said, "but did you find another like me, a Frank? A man? Tall, thin?"

"Impossibly handsome?" said a familiar voice.

"Levi? Oh! I thought I'd lost you too!"

"No such luck." He limped toward her, wan and much the worse for wear—but alive! Sofia screamed in delight, *"Grazie Madonna!"* and they embraced, much to the embarrassment of both Arik and Fulk.

They left the heads piled behind them. Levi slouched weakly in the saddle as they rode for Akka, and Sofia knew she was in not much better state. Fulk seemed like a decent man but the Lazars were an army unlike any she had ever seen. If Arik had not been with them she would have feared for their safety. They were solemn and silent, and they rode their white horses in close formation across the plain, making a collective thunder that kept bandits lurking in the hills under cover. Their fluttering cloaks glowed eerily, like the wings of moths under the rising moon, which was high in the night sky by the time the white walls of Akka rose out of the sands. The chill night air carried the scent of the sea that lay beyond the city. A single figure, a woman, stood on the walls, watching as they approached. She raised a hand and, as one, the Lazars saluted.

As soon as they entered the city, Arik disappeared. Fulk led Sofia and Levi up to the wall to meet the queen.

"Contessa, we are privileged to welcome you to Akka."

Sofia had grown up in the Bardini workshop; she knew how to size up a man. With women, the dance was more subtle, and she usually found herself confused, clumsy and awkward. It felt natural, however, to evaluate Queen Catrina as she would a band-ieratoro, and the queen—whatever words of welcome she said, however warm her smile—was doing likewise. She looked as if she could take a punch, and throw one too. She was tall as a man, wide-shouldered, thick-necked, wide-hipped and magnificently bosomed. Sofia's first impression was that there was *more* of her, that she was constructed of materials more robust than mere skin and bone and muscle. Her voluptuous curves were enmeshed in a gown that glistened like the skin of a reptile, made of small, dark jewels bound together like chainmail: a lapidary armor of a thousand unblinking eyes.

"In times past the Scaligeri and Guiscards were great allies," the queen said. Under her deep voice was the great lazy certainty of a king. "We shall be great friends. You must have suffered terribly. The Sands are a wicked place, fit for Ebionites and Jinn, but not human beings. Tonight you shall sleep in a comfortable bed."

"I'm most grateful," Sofia said, feelingly.

The queen's ladies dressed in a strange blend of antique Etrurian designs and flowing eastern sensuousness, acres of luxurious materials that concealed as much as they suggested, at once conservative and decadent. Even if she had not just arrived from the desert, Sofia knew she would have felt a ragged beggar beside them.

"Akka has no fear of surprise attacks?" said Levi.

"None," said the queen. "Like a gerbil my city sleeps with one eye open. My Lazars man her walls so that all within may dream golden dreams without fear."

Chapter 69

On the north side of the bridge, the swordsman stood, head tilted meditatively, before the maimed lion. Everyone diverted their gaze so as not to see the Concordian or the terrible object of his study. No good could come of either. Yuri was a good man, but the Podesta of Rasenna needed cunning more than virtue. What Doc Bardini would have done, the old men said, was to publicly blame some drunkard for this crime so that the real culprit would think himself free of suspicion. Afterward, the Doc would have administered justice privately.

A soft voice whispered in Geta's ear, "An art lover as well as a traitor?" He spun, and captured Maddalena's hand before she could retreat.

"The first charge is just, but you'll find no one more loyal than I."

"The First Apprentice wouldn't agree."

"That shows the quality of my patriotism." Geta raised his head high. "The engineers have brought Concord's name into disrepute with impious weapons that render knightly virtue irrelevant."

Although Maddalena well knew that the late Captain Giovanni had those very virtues, she did not contradict Geta but listened to him with a skeptically arched brow.

"Perhaps it's no longer politic to say it, but nature has a hierarchy. Discard it, and you invite anarchy." He gestured at the subject of his scrutiny as evidence. "A serf cannot match a knight's courage, but give that serf an harquebus and a handful of shot and courage is irrelevant. And what knight—or gunner, for that matter—can stand against a Wave that levels all? In my youth, I fought for glory in the legions until I realized there was no glory in serving slaves." Geta slowly pulled her closer and she allowed him. "But I needn't tell you this, Signorina Bombelli. Your breeding speaks for itself."

Maddalena laughed. "Then you have wax in your ears. My father's a merchant. Bombelli blood is common as any of these peddlers." She gestured at the noisy hawkers on the bridge.

"You shock me." This was a lie. Fabbro's cajoling manner obviously came from the streets, and Geta had studied in Rasenna; he knew perfectly well which families had been entitled to sit in the old Signoria. He kissed her hand. "If it's true, I earnestly hope you marry *up*. Strange—" He licked his lips. "You don't *taste* common."

Maddalena snatched her hand back and playfully slapped him. "You impertinent cad. I prefer my men strong and silent."

"As you like—it was you, however, who disturbed my ruminations." He clicked his heels and spun back to the defiled statue. It had been cleanly decapitated in the night. Most of the mane had come away with its head, leaving its torso a great open cavity. Around the wound, precious viscera, ribbons of gold leaf, trembled in the wind.

"And just what are you ruminating upon?"

"Guilt," he said. "Your father believes that poor Kitty here was desecrated by bandieratori."

"My father thinks with his heart. It's what makes him a good peddler—he could persuade even you that all you need to set off your uniform is a pretty corset. But he doesn't understand that most men are not like him. He tolerated years of condescension from the

Families who took loans from him because he knew that one day he'd be looking down on them."

"Smart." Geta knew a thing or two about money-lenders.

"Most men value pride over bread."

"If you're hinting at something, I beg you, be plain. I have the most ghastly hangover this morning."

Maddalena walked to the lion, gesturing for Geta to follow her. "This wasn't an insult directed at the Signoria. See how neatly it's been severed? It's downright artistic."

She turned until she was looking in the same direction as the lion, across the piazza at Palazzo Bombelli. "This was an insult from someone my father blunderingly offended. Somewhere there's a trail to whoever did it; you just have to find it."

Frowning, Geta examined the cut. It was indeed a neat job. Maddalena was halfway across the piazza when he turned back. He was admiring her suggestively undulating carriage when she looked over her shoulder and pointed skyward. He looked up and saw the gray smoke soiling the sky, and followed it to its source: Tartarus.

Becket and the other condottiere held their manacled prisoner by his forearms, pulling him along like a rabid dog to the steps of the Signoria. Geta held one end of the rope that was tied in a noose around his neck—naturally, the Concordian had taken charge. At any other time, Fabbro would have feared for the soldiers' lives—even chained, the blacksmith was capable of pummeling them—but when Geta turned and grabbed Jacques' arm, he flinched.

"Behold the man, Gonfaloniere."

Fabbro ran down the steps. Bruises, cuts and burns covered Jacques' face and body, evidence of the great damage a few drunken soldiers could do in a few hours. "Lord Geta, there's been a terrible mistake. Jacques *made* the lion."

"Infanticide's not unheard of. We have it from his own tongue."

"A man will confess anything if he's tortured." Yuri was angry at Geta for commandeering his men, and at his men for their willingness to follow someone who allowed them to give in to their worse impulses. "You're just looking for a scapegoat!"

"If I were, would I pick a man like this? I assure you, he didn't start out this docile."

"Then why?"

"Testimony. If you think women are jealous, try artists. His own apprentice informed on him."

"I still can't believe it."

"Believe it! He spat in your face; now he's laughing at you." Geta snatched off Jacques' hat. His ears were cropped, and there was an ugly circular scar incised into the flesh around his skull. "Believe now? These are old scars. The man's a communard."

"We don't know that!"

"I admit it, Bombelli," Jacques growled.

"Good boy. Now tell the nice man where you got those scars."

Fabbro knew Jacques' Herculean strength, but this task seemed too much for him. At last Jacques met his eye and he started back from the hate he saw there.

"You asked me once if I remembered the market of Champaign. Of course I remember it! All Europa was there. We were happy and prosperous. We would have caught up with Etruria, if not for princes and kings. First they spoiled our coinage to pay for their endless wars with the Anglish—but even that wasn't enough. They needed more, more, *more*. They taxed the market out of existence."

"They were your betters," said Geta, as if that settled everything.

Jacques cowered and went silent—then some ancient anger took him and he looked directly at Fabbro. "So we should let ourselves be ruined by them? We rebelled! That was just what the king's men wanted, and they fell on us like wolves, filched our purses, spat in our faces and called us rebels. They set me to work in my own forge, fashioning crowns for the ringleaders. And as they crowned us, each in turn, they hailed us: Jacques le Roi! The rest died, there and then. Me, they locked away until—"

"I don't care about that," Fabbro shouted. "Why hurt the lion? I *paid* you—"

"You lied!" Jacques said with venom. "I came here because you told me Rasenna was free, a town with no kings. But you're just a new kind of king."

Fabbro struck him. "How dare you! Take this fool away."

"What shall we do with him?"

Fabbro looked up the steps of the Signoria, where the farmer and his peers stood looking down, judging him as he gave judgment. He wheeled around suddenly. "I tried to give Rasenna a symbol to unite behind. It's going to get one."

"We're behind you, Gonfaloniere," said the brewer stoutly.

Only Yuri protested. "Bombelli, you'll make it worse. Jacques' popular—"

"Fine talk from a solider!" Geta interrupted. "How do you punish insubordination, Russ? A spanking? Gonfaloniere, take the advice of one who's learned the hard way: you'll win nothing with kindness but contempt."

Two dozen smiths, the so-called Guild of Fire, bolstered by the same mob that had protested the salt-tax, were spilling onto the bridge.

"It's always northsiders," Fabbro said disgustedly. The Morello had taught the southern towers the habit of obedience, but Bardini's unruly spirit still possessed the north.

Whatever his misgivings, giving into the mob would be worse. Yuri ordered his condottieri to push the men back.

"Hang the foreign dog!" the brewer shouted.

Jacques' head was bowed, as if he was not aware of the mania growing around him.

Fabbro looked down on the man. Jacques had betrayed him, but he took no pleasure in the thought of revenge. He was about to give the order when Geta tugged his sleeve and whispered, "Perhaps a degree of clemency *would* be wise?"

Fabbro looked at the Concordian with gratitude. "Yes," he agreed, and ignored the jeering crowd, ordering them to take the prisoner to the stables. Jacques didn't struggle, even as the harness was fastened to his face.

The condottieri waited for Geta's order. Geta looked to Fabbro. "You did the right thing, Gonfaloniere, but listen to that mob. If you spare his life, you must ensure he won't be able to spread any more mischief."

"Do what you have to," Fabbro said in a dead voice.

Jacques' bottom lip was clamped so that his jaw could be lowered with a screw. Now his tongue was grabbed between a pair of tongs and yanked forward. The small spiked lever turned, forcing his jaw shut again, and Jacques groaned as his tongue was pierced, thick blood spluttering from his lips.

The mess made Fabbro queasy, but the baying crowds were making it hard for him to concentrate; all he could think of was the humiliation, the *ingratitude*. "It wasn't his tongue that destroyed the lion," he said at last. "This fellow's no orator."

Geta laughed. "That's the idea!"

At last Jacques fought as he realized what they intended, and condottieri piled on top of him, hanging onto his limbs while others tightened the chains until he was too trussed-up to struggle.

"Let's do it properly," said Geta, and started heating a blade, ready to cauterize the wound.

Geta asked for volunteers to wield the blade, and when Becket at once backed away, muttering, "Not I—my life would be worthless!" Geta realized everyone was fearful of revenge during the dark nights to come.

"Podesta!" he cried, "this is your honor."

"Yuri! Yuri!" they called, in a paroxysm of relief.

Yuri took the ax in silence, as if he himself were the condemned man. Jacques started up at him, proffering his neck, his eyes eloquent: *Kill me, but do not do this.*

Silently pleading too, Yuri looked at Fabbro, but like the priors behind him, his jaw was set. The ax struck the ground with a ringing note and sparks flew, dying, hissing, in the heat of the blood. Before Yuri raised the ax a second time Jacques had passed out.

Geta expertly sealed and wrapped the wounds as the smell of cooking flesh filled the cell. He looked up at Yuri with a friendly wink. "Clean work, Podesta."

Chapter 70

THE LAND ACROSS THE WATER

Jerusalem

Before the second millennium was a century old, Jerusalem was wrested from Infidel hands. Until we appreciate this achievement we cannot appreciate why the crusaders' children consider themselves a chosen people. Consider the Radinate as a whole, enveloping the Middle Sea in a great crescent, from the harbor of Alexandria to the redoubt of Byzant.[29]

True, it was beset by rivalry, but what empire is not? The skepticism of cosmopolitan Ebionites can be well imagined when the strange soldiers of a strange sect came rudely claiming Jerusalem as their birthright. This amusement turned to horror when they saw the Crusaders fight. The Curia had schooled the crusaders

---

29. Whether part of the Radinate or Oltremare, this famous city bestrides East and West. While the Bosperous prevents encroachment from the East, the Dalmatian March prevents encroachment from the West.

in Water Style,[30] an art the Ebionites had no means, initially, of combating.[31]

The Crusaders promptly founded a kingdom, stretching initially from Jaffa to Bayrut, called Oltremare.[32] Its official capital was Jerusalem, but Akka, with its magnificent harbor, was its true heart. The military invasion was followed by one of civilians: Ariminumese merchants traveled from Akka[33] into Ebionite territory and beyond to the bejeweled cities of Asia, trading wool and saffron[34] for silks and precious stones.[35] Trade and the drudge of administrating their patchwork kingdom doused Crusader fanaticism, but the sectarian spark soon found other fuel—the people they had enslaved.

30. The ancient martial art the Curia had preserved since Etruscan times.

31. The Old Man of the Mountain is credited with reviving the Wind-based martial art of the Sicarii.

32. This Europan interloper rudely bisected the Radinate. Alexandria became the capital of the southern Radinate and Byzant, the northern capital.

33. This was but one front on which the insatiable race advanced. Ariminum had long sought access to the trade routes that ran though Byzant and, when they solicited the now-isolated city with fresh entreaties, the previously haughty Byzantines proved receptive. In Etruria, this scandalous alliance with an Ebionite power drew down a long-threatened Curial interdiction on the Serenissima. The Ariminumese attributed this excommunication more to Concordian jealousy than piety. It was, in any case, a small price to pay for Byzant's friendship and the wealth it brought.

34. The sensual peoples of the East will pay ridiculous sums for spices unknown to them.

35. Account-books breathlessly list "jacinths, chrysoltes, emerauds, and pearls as large as peeled onions."

Chapter 71

Usually Sofia rose with the sun, but it took a screeching gull at the window to wake her on this morning. She had been too exhausted last night even to look around her chamber; she did so now. The window opened onto a balcony, covered by a long lace curtain that trailed onto the colored marble floor, reminding her of the wedding dress she had never worn. All the furnishings were made from the same rich, oily wood as Fabbro Bombelli's banco, and carved in the most intricate shapes—Akka did not lack for labor; that was obvious. She wondered first what hope her mission had, and then what species of a sin it was to try to draw this prosperous realm into a distant war. Perhaps it was hypocrisy to pretend that she had fled for some reason other than saving her own skin.

Clothes had been laid out for her on a red cabinet beside the bed. Sofia didn't care about fashion, but she knew the importance others placed on it. Donna Bombelli, and Levi, too, had often counseled that matters of form were not trivial in diplomacy. Sofia picked up first a headdress and veil, then the flowing, pale-colored silks, looking at each with equal skepticism. She disliked the foreign style, but her old clothes had exhausted their powers of expansion.

"Courage, Sofia," she told herself, and went to work. After she had donned the pieces in roughly the right order and the right way around, she stepped in front of the long mirror—she hadn't seen one since Ariminum—to examine herself. The change just a few weeks had elicited an involuntary gasp. No silks, however flowing, could conceal her condition now.

Plaintive bird cries drew her away from her terrifying reflection and she pulled the curtain aside and looked upon Akka, its bay, its churches, its high walls . . . The city was built from a pale yellow stone that intensified and reflected the sea's harsh light into nooks and alleyways, places that ought to be veiled in a decent darkness. Rather than tolling bells, a clacking like an army of crickets sprang up from the white-domed churches, calling the Marian faithful to prayer.

Unlike Ariminum's cramped but efficiently organized harbor, Akka's chaotic sprawl had room to expand indefinitely. Some of the ships were fat-bottomed merchant haulers along the lines of Ezra's old cog but there were strange small galleys with protruding mizzens and narrow hulls that narrowed into dangerously long bowsprits. With their slanted lanteen sails, they looked fast and predatory besides the staid Europan boats. Smaller vessels along similar lines, flimsy but elegant, maneuvered among them like swallows around towers, and little tugs towed heavier ships into their allotted places like boys leading truculent bulls around. There were a few galleys in the *Tancred*'s class, though not quite as big; they docked further out and small skiffs ferried their passengers to and from shore. Akka had been the Oltremarine Empire's temporary capital, until they abandoned all pretense of rebuilding Jerusalem and that status became official. As the Oltremarines started serving their own interests and not Europa's, Akka blossomed like a deep-smelling steam-house orchid.

Sofia opened the door and found a blank-faced Ebionite servant standing there. As he silently bowed, she wondered if he had been there all night. She walked down the winding marble staircase, feeling the cool stone through her silk slippers, into a long, spacious corridor that felt more like a crypt. The walls were decorated with geometric patterns, interrupted intermittently by huge slabs of marble that rippled with dark veins like a shroud. On slender plinths in the middle of these slabs stood white ovals that Sofia at first assumed were marble portrait busts. It was only as she came closer that she realized with a sudden chill what they were: this was an Ancestor Room. The Akkans had preserved traditions that had long since died out in Etruria. The rows of peaceful faces looking down were the death-masks of Queen Catrina's predecessors. The names and dates inscribed beside bold Etruscan mottos on the plinths were unnecessary: the progression was obvious.

The men, to begin with, were muscular, brutish Normans, with scars and broken jaws and a commanding intensity that survived even sudden death. The women were Ebionites with aquiline noses and docile, intelligent expressions: slaves with haunted, youth-frozen faces who had lived hard lives quickly. As Sofia progressed through the generations, she saw the ruder, softer characteristics being weaned out: the men became less brutish and died younger while the women became less docile and lived longer. They gradually mingled to the type Sofia had seen perfected last night in the cold, superior face of Queen Catrina. This panoply of ghosts had probably watched Catrina's first uneven steps, had seen her fall down the stairs a dozen times. She must have learned early on that there was no sympathy from this audience. Now those same empty eyes glared coldly at Sofia, interrogating her motives.

She found Levi on a balcony, already eating. He was dressed like an Egyptian slave, and they teased each other about their costumes. The view from his floor was not as lofty as hers, but from it they could see the considerable breadth of Akka's walls. Last night they had seen how the city was fortified against the desert; now they saw how the sea was kept at bay.

The walls were patrolled by the Lazars, who carried long, heavy axes, like the one Fulk had used to behead the Sicarii. The lighter battle axes were slung at their hips. In the light of day the Lazars looked more Ebionite than Europan; over the centuries their uniform had become a fusion of Occidental and Oriental that was offensive to all sensibilities.

Sofia looked back at her companion. "Arik couldn't understand why the Sicarii didn't cut your throat when they found you."

"You know me: my tongue's my best weapon."

"You're Ebionite, aren't you, Levi?"

"Me!" Levi scoffed. "You clearly got too much sun out in the Sands."

Sofia didn't press him. She looked out at the sea. It was less pristine than it had appeared from her room: drifts of scum and rubbish sat on the water, swarming with hovering flies.

Levi stood up and leaned on the banister. "My mother taught me early to pretend I was born Marian. She crossed the Middle Sea on an Ariminumese galley, in chains, and pregnant with yours truly. My father was some dog of a slaver. A fisherman from Syracuse bought her and let her earn her freedom. All she ever wanted was to get back to this place—can you imagine? The day she died, I left for the mainland to join a Company. I didn't want to be pushed around anymore."

"You don't have to keep pretending."

"Oh, I think I do. Ebionites are even less popular in Akka."

"This alliance was your idea."

"Rasenna's my country now," he said testily. "I'm no more Ebionite than you."

As they ate their breakfast of dates, nuts and bread with yogurt and sour milk, they watched a gang of local children playing on the walls. The knights ignored the children as they took turns diving fearlessly from the walls into the sea. Neither the height, nor the filthy water nor the jagged rocks below the surface bothered them, though they had to time their leaps with the tide's flow to avoid breaking their necks.

A slave pounded his mace to announce the queen's entry and Sofia and Levi rose as Catrina walked in, followed by her retinue of veiled beauties.

"Good morning, your Majesty," said Levi. "We're admiring your leapers."

"Don't worry; it's not terribly infectious," the queen said cheerfully, then laughed at Sofia's and Levi's confused reaction. "Oh, you meant the *children*! Leapers, lepers—I thought you meant the Lazars!"

"All your knights are *lepers*?" Sofia said in disbelief.

"Yes indeed—but as I said, one has to make a special effort to catch it. The Lazars are very careful; they have their own baths and laundries. They're as jealous of their disease as the rest of us are disgusted by it."

"If it's not so contagious, how do they all come to have it?"

The queen's smile thinned at Sofia's question. "Etrurians never understand that holding a kingdom together in this land entails sacrifice. We are surrounded by a people who dream of pushing us into the sea. My ancestors devised a means to push back. The Ebionites dug up the old name of Sicarii to stupefy us with terror, so we responded in kind. The Sicarii consider themselves the only pure Ebionites. They are hypersensitive about cleanliness, so touching the dead is anathema to them. For such an enemy, lepers are the perfect foil."

The queen threw herself onto a couch and took some grapes from one of the silent servants holding trays of fruit and sweetmeats. "But never mind that. Come, let me admire you, Contessa. Now: is that not a more becoming costume for you? And I *love* how you have made it your own. If any of my ladies were so pretty, I would allow them not to wear a veil too. Let the world see you; why not?" The queen's retinue's obligatory tittering had a dangerous edge that reminded Sofia of the circling dogs in the desert.

Levi was eager to discuss the Etrurian situation, but the queen mocked his haste. "This is not Etruria, Podesta. There is nothing but time in Akka. I insist you allow yourselves to fully recuperate before we even think about the future."

Levi, seeing she was used to having her way, gracefully acqui-
esced, suggesting instead that he explore the walls' perimeter. Sofia
accepted the queen's advice, that she visit the markets, out of the
abrasive sun.

The listless air in the bazaar did not stir even the pale sheets overhang-
ing the narrow passages. Sofia had grown accustomed to checking the
wind's direction by its touch on her skin and its force by the moving
clouds, but here there were no clouds, and her sweating skin detected
no breeze. Perhaps the air had been fresh when the first Crusaders
breathed it, but it was stale now; it was the sun that reigned over this
captive city, bleaching the cobbled streets the color of old bone.

A bawling donkey shoved its way through slaves carrying baskets
on their heads; black-eyed children ran between their legs. The roar
of the sea echoed over the crowd's shouting. It would be easy to get
lost here, Sofia thought. In Rasenna, before she had grown heavy, she
could have climbed the walls to escape, but even walking exhausted
her now. The queen was right; the desert had drained her more than
she had realized.

Akka was less a city than a collection of warehouses, like a
magnificent multiplication of those streets in Rasenna owned by
the Wool Guild. In place of the damp, mannish odor of wool was
the scent of spices and luxurious silks. Most of the merchants were
Ebionites, and their customers were the senior servants of Akka's
noble houses. They emulated their mistresses' haughty manners
and haggled aggressively. Every servant was shadowed by a guard
who carried their shopping in one hand while the other rested on
a sword, lending weight to the haggling. The Akkan women preserved their pale Norman skin with masks and veils—or faked it
with ash-colored powder; Sofia, with her bandieratoro's tan, looked
more like an Ebionite. But all the women, high or low, Ebionite or
Oltremarine, wore veils.

The language sounded comprehensible at first, but Sofia found
herself more and more confused. A fishmonger advertised his wares
with a sign of an open book; a tavern with an egg-timer; outside a

candlemaker's shop hung a birdcage, with a skeleton perched on a swing inside. Like Akka's language, the skeleton was a mangled composite: a falcon's streamlined ribcage, an owl's porous skull, the dainty wings of a swallow. The connections were illogical, perverse and arbitrary. Clearly, there had been a realignment of meaning, and everyone but Sofia understood.

The street corners had niches like those found in Rasenna—but the statues within depicted a skeletal maiden in royal apparel instead of a generously smiling donna. Stacked below the niches were faded shards of plaster—gothic noses, broken lips and empty eyes that stared forever. Sofia avoided looking at the shattered death masks; Akkans paused only to spit on them.

No one paid her much attention either, and when they did deign to notice her, they simply cried, "Move!" If she hesitated, overzealous guards pushed her aside. After it happened once too often, Sofia pushed back, and sent a well-dressed elderly woman tumbling into a fruit stand. The lady's red-faced guard quickly stepped in, shouting, "Ebionite whore!"

When Sofia grabbed his beard he grunted in surprise and reached for her face. Sofia tilted back, grabbed his thumb and, holding it, turned in a circle, at the end of which he was on his knees and Sofia behind him. She rammed her knee between his shoulder blades and he fell face-first to the ground.

The sympathies of the staring crowd were obvious and she quickly backed away, followed by a barrage of hurled insults and fruit. The guard picked himself up, even redder now, and started after her, with the crowd behind him.

In rising panic, Sofia turned a corner which led to an intersection: one path on the left was a dark tunnel leading downhill, the other led up—up, Sofia reasoned, to the palace. She had just turned right when a man stepped out of the shadows of the dark tunnel and called, "Contessa?"

Sofia was ready to fight, then she recognized the voice. "Fulk!"

"This way." Fulk might be Grand Master of the Queen's Guard, but his rank would not slow a mob in pursuit of what they imagined to be an uppity Ebionite whore. He led her through the dark alley to a sloped street which ran red with a stinking stream of blood. The stalls on either side were hung with the skinned carcasses of lambs and calves and imbecilic-looking goat heads lazily attended by swarms of blood-drunk flies.

"Nobody comes this way if they can avoid it," Fulk said. "What happened?"

"He called me a whore," Sofia said.

"And?"

"That's not sufficient explanation?"

"Well, I'm not surprised—you're not wearing a veil. None of the queen's retinue warned you?"

"It was the queen who suggested I go out."

"Huh," Fulk said, and quickened his pace.

Sofia sensed his annoyance. "I wanted to thank you for saving Levi yesterday."

"That was my duty," he snapped, then, more gently, "It requires no thanks."

"And this?"

"My pleasure. We'll have to go the long way back to the palace, I'm afraid."

"That's all right. Is all the tour this scenic?" she asked, swatting away the flies.

The Lazars protected Akka, but the citadel was the type one saw only in garrisoned towns: a thick-walled fortress built to separate the population from the soldiers. The main part was a tall hexagonal building standing on a forest of thick pillars, and beyond these pillars were several dark but airy chambers used for storage. The largest was set aside for Lazar training, and they spent an hour there watching the men spar under the seneschal's instructions. Ignoring Sofia, Basilius asked Fulk if he'd care to go a few rounds. It was an intense exhibition, though Fulk was the superior fighter. Throughout it and afterward, he kept the blank mask of his helmet down; only the redness around his eyes and the huskiness of his voice hinted at the corruption beneath. Though the chamber was cold and sparse, Sofia felt at home for the first time since she'd arrived in Akka.

Fulk was obviously proud of his men's prowess. "Akka would perish without us. The Radinate may have been shattered, but the tribes remain."

"Do they coordinate?"

"None of them trust each other enough for that, thankfully, and if any come close to settling their feuds, Queen Catrina knows how to get them bickering again."

Sofia made no comment, reminded of the way the Families, and lately the Signoria, ran Rasenna. After the training session, Fulk took Sofia around the rest of the citadel. He showed her a workshop where coffins were stacked, to keep ahead of the ceaseless demand. The carpenters were either wounded, or cripples of various sorts. A younger Lazar read Scripture aloud as they worked.

"These brothers are close to God. They can't fight anymore, but they can help the Order in other ways. It is a good way to prepare." One knight was clearly very "close to God." He was not an old man, though he moved like one. His hands were horribly twisted, and shook with a kind of palsy. One foot was completely lame. The coffin he was making was nearly complete, but he frequently paused to catch his breath. Strangely, the atmosphere of the place was not morbid but peaceful. Cold air and the sound of running water came from a large open trapdoor, down which another advanced case was sweeping away the off-cuts and sawdust.

"Standing armies cause problems," Sofia said, thinking of the Hawk's Company back in Rasenna. "They're expensive, they grow too powerful—"

"—unless they're kept apart from the society they protect."

"That's obviously not a problem here," Sofia said, keeping a neutral tone. "How do you keep numbers up? Slaves? Prisoners?"

"No one's infected against their will."

"You're all here voluntarily?" Sofia said doubtfully. Surely no *real* man would bow his head to the ax so slavishly.

"A few people get accidentally infected—we call them conscripts. Their parents bring them to the citadel in sealed coffins, while volunteers walk in. Within the order there's no discrimination—we all leave in the same way, after all—but conscripts consider themselves unlucky."

"I bet."

He saw Sofia's look and shook his head. "Unlucky, because they could not voluntarily make the sacrifice that ennobles our souls even as it corrupts our bodies."

"That's crazy!"

"Chivalry must be dead in Etruria. A knight's life is his lord's, to spend at his discretion."

Sofia remembered Arik's dismissal of chivalry and snapped, "You call that living?"

"We live through Purgatory," Fulk said calmly, "that we may reach Heaven sooner."

The knight Sofia had been watching laid down his tools and called for another brother's assistance, and as they lifted the coffin to the edge of the trapdoor, Sofia saw there was a slanted chute down into the fast-running water. The sick knight climbed in, lay back and crossed his arms over his chest. The other brother placed the lid on top, painted a black Herod's Sword on it, then hammered it shut and pushed the coffin off.

The coffin slid neatly down into the darkness. A soft splash, and it was gone.

"Where does it go?"

"Out to sea."

Sofia wanted to ask Fulk if he was a volunteer or a conscript, but the question seemed horribly indiscreet. Instead she said, "Aren't you afraid?"

Under his big cloak, Fulk shrugged. "Death is the one journey all must take. As the Ebionites say, God wills it."

When she returned to the palace Sofia found the queen conversing with Levi on the balcony. He was complimenting Akka's defenses.

"And you, Contessa, how did you enjoy the market?" the queen asked, sharing a look of amusement with her smiling retinue. Sofia decided to say nothing of the fracas, and instead remarked that she was surprised that Ebionite merchants were allowed access to the market.

"Alas, Contessa, when the West abandoned us, we abandoned ourselves to the East."

"So that's why there were no pigs in the butchers' quarter?"

Levi looked at Sofia with reproach, but she was unapologetic; she was rattled, and she wanted to probe the queen's controlled veneer.

But the queen gestured to the priestly figure hovering beside her. "Allow me to introduce the venerable Patriarch Chrysoberges. Perhaps you'll enlighten our guest, your Beatitude?"

The patriarch was a ponderous specimen. His beard, a rusty column flecked with gray, was carved with straight edges like a topiary block. His sacerdotal vestments were an elegant but sun-faded black, and the tight layers wrapped around him like ivy. He was tall, but somewhat hunched, and Sofia thought that with his long sleeves, he made a great lugubrious T that might have slotted perfectly into the patterned wall behind him. His circular flat-topped hat trailed a flowing cloth that covered the sides of his head and reached to his shoulders. His face was a small, pale island where nervous eyes hid under cover of bushy eyebrows.

To hear him talk was as surprising as spring growth on an ancient tree—but talk he did, holding his psalter tightly with the white-knuckle grip of a strangler as he launched into a tedious account of their adoption of Ebionite dietary strictures: "Although the schismatics obviously miss the larger truth concerning the Virgin's nature, they did preserve some salutary traditions that the Etrurian Curia, in its arrogance, has forgotten. With the light of truth to guide us, the Oltremarine Church has perfected the Marian Faith. In time . . ."

Levi's polite smile concealed his boredom, but Sofia didn't even bother to feign interest. Her eyes wandered out to the children, still diving from the walls. She knew why they never tired of the danger; she had once played similar games.

The queen noticed her indifference and interjected, "To put it simply, Contessa, we were outcasts when we came here. If our children ever returned to Etruria, they would be outcasts again."

"Are all those children Oltremarine?" asked Sofia.

"Of course," the queen laughed. "No Ebionites would dream of diving in."

"Some Ebionites have the courage of lions," Sofia said.

"Or any other beast, I'm sure," the patriarch said coldly, annoyed at being interrupted midsermon.

"It's not for lack of courage," the queen said. "The Ebionites believe it would defile them. They call it *Lordemare,* the Sea of Filth. Admittedly, it is polluted from the royal slaughterhouse, the fish market and the refuse of the citadel"—her eyes flashed—"but our children are made of sterner stuff."

"Besides," the patriarch said, "we don't permit our children to play with slaves."

The queen dismissed Chrysoberges and said, "You mustn't think that all our prohibitions mean we don't know how to put on a feast. You'll see what we're capable of tonight."

Levi bowed. "You honor us, your Majesty."

The queen's ladies tittered and she hushed them. "Forgive me; it's not for you. My Uncle Andronikos, Prince of Byzant, is coming to visit."

After the queen retired, "to let them rest," Levi turned to Sofia. "That's why she didn't want to talk. She was stalling."

Chapter 72

THE LAND ACROSS THE WATER

Degeneration

After Jerusalem's capture, most Crusaders left for home on the next available galley, sick of the desert, the violence, the faction. Those who stayed were either especially devout or especially quarrelsome.[36]

While Oltremare's self-styled nobility frittered away their initiative with internecine power struggles, the ruptured Radinate slowly recovered from the first body blow.[37] The Rabbis anathematized any Melic who traded with the interlopers and, inspiring their shaken people with the example of the Maccabees and the Sicarii, they preached Holy War.[38] It took a century, but finally

36. The scandalous history of Oltremare's first century suggests it was the latter.

37. The Khazarian *Reconquista* is outside the scope of this work but the northeast quarter recovered sooner.

38. The Author is no theologian but the Curia's doctrine, that the Ebionites were schismatics who had corrupted the one true faith, is obviously simplistic.

Jerusalem was retaken. Oltremare, crushed between the southern and northern Radinate eager to recombine, sought aid from the Mother Country.

Etruria responded by launching a new Crusade.[39] This time most of the "knights" were criminals sentenced to "Pilgrimages of Atonement," a sentence that ill-disposed them toward their Motherland. The land across the Water was now Etruria. As Crusade followed Crusade, these exiles created the polity full of dangerous innovation.[40] The king's power was limited by a parliament in which he was obliged to listen to talk of Rights and Privileges from self-styled "Barons," men who had been little better than serfs in Europa.

In many ways, the Rabbis retain a purer version of Mary's message. Few Concordian scholars would dispute the Ebionite characterisation of Etrurian Madonna-worship as idolatry.

39. Met by a remilitarized Radinate, the Second Crusade failed. This was to become a wearingly repetitive pattern.

40. The innovative mood extended to religion. Intermingling flavors of heresy made Oltremare's Faith a strange stew. The cult of death, epitomized in the grim *Madonna Muerta,* outrages both Ebionite and Etrurian sensibilities.

Chapter 73

Some familial dynamics are a mystery to an only child or orphan, and Sofia was both. Even so, she marveled that the queen tolerated her uncle's overbearing manner.

The patriarch's eyes followed Andronikos with patent alarm, as if expecting the prince to assault his beloved mistress any moment. The queen lay back on her cushions, playing with her infant cousin—Andronikos' daughter was a spirited baby—while her uncle stalked back and forth like a great cat. His long purple cape was fastened around his bull-like neck with a gaudy brooch; like his loud manner, it ill-fitted the sluggish, decorous ambience of Catrina's court. With his barbaric matted moustache and dirty spurs, Andronikos might have just come from the field of battle—in fact, he practically had, as he spent the previous night's feast proudly recounting how he had destroyed Concord's Ninth. The party had been quite ruined by the behavior of the prince's retinue. Instead of using Lazarus Knights as bodyguards, he retained a gang of axmen from the ice-burdened lands across the northern seas. Sofia was unsurprised that Andronikos failed to discipline them—he was no less boorish than they, dressing in their furs and matching them drink for drink—but she found it odd that the queen did not protest.

Catrina was more interested in how Andronikos could absent himself from Byzant. "However did you find someone suitable to leave in charge?" she asked.

"Don't worry. Prince Jorge may be very young, but he is quite capable. Popular with the men, too."

"A popular prince! *Madonna,* now I am worried. Do you *really* think you'll have a city to return to?"

Andronikos laughed heartily at this. "Jorge doesn't have the lineage to be considered a rival. Everyone calls him 'Prince' but he wasn't born to the purple. Oh, he has a drop or two of decent blood, but he won his fame and his title racing chariots in the Hippodrome."

"I see," said Catrina. It was clear that she found Byzantine manners as strange as Sofia did.

"But come, Catrina, this is dry stuff. Where's the light-hearted niece I used to play with?"

"Alas, Uncle, she grew up. But you know how glad I am to see you. I have need of wise counsel; tell me, what do you make of our guests' request for assistance?"

Sofia was surprised: Catrina was shrewd, and whatever the prince's qualities, wisdom was obviously not among them.

Andronikos didn't pause to consider his response. "Bah! What concerns us Etruria? In our hour of need, their assistance was niggardly. Now that they need help, the ambassadors they send reveal the contempt in which they hold us."

"Ouch!" said Levi, pulling an imaginary dart from his chest. "Hard not to take that personally."

"Come, Podesta. Condottieri are men of the world. The princes of Europa use Oltremare as a dumping ground for their family scandals."

"I'm not sure I follow," said Levi, less equably.

"Then I'll explain as I would to a child. In the desert, gardens must be protected by walls or the Sands eat them. Someone scaled this *lady's* walls. Only she can say if it was trespasser or guest."

Levi's sword would have taken the prince's head off had Fulk not parried it. The prince's axmen looked on stupidly.

"Back up," Fulk said with deadly calm.

"*Tranquillo,* Levi," Sofia said.

Levi put away his sword, and the prince backed away with a scared laugh.

The queen was merely annoyed. "Uncle, don't be so rude! The Contessa came a great distance at great personal danger to warn us," she said, coaxingly. "Our fathers won this land from infidels—and what are Concord's Godless engineers if not infidels? If they gain control of Etruria, and the Contessa says they will, our duty is clear: our fathers answered the call. How can we do less?"

"Because the Old World is far from here. You don't understand their politics, Catrina. It's foolish to let ourselves be entangled in their quarrels just when our kingdom is on a firm footing."

Sofia noticed how the "our" made the queen's nostrils flare, but Andronikos carried on blithely, "If we turn our back on the Radinate—"

The patriarch snorted, "We've nothing to fear from those gerbil-eaters. Their government is a thing without structure or foundation, like the tents they live in. Abraham's children have become children once more."

"And any one of those children will cut the other's throat for a few pieces of silver," the queen finished.

"Fine," said Andronikos, "but the Concordians—the men you call infidels—were enemies of the Ariminumese until this summit drove them together. That makes them potential allies, as far as I'm concerned."

"Allies!" Sofia interrupted. "Last night, you treated us to a vivid description of a Concordian legion marching to the walls of Byzant."

"Perhaps you slept through the end of the story, child: we saw them speedily off. Geography is the reason no Europan State can threaten us militarily—the Ariminumese plague us in other ways, stealing our markets, underpricing us. They've made a pirate into their admiral. Need I say more? Let the Etrurians fight between themselves. Why search for infidels abroad?" he asked, glancing at the slave fanning the queen. "We have enough of those at home."

"You're right about one thing, Prince," said Sofia. "You *don't* understand Etrurian politics. The Concordians covet territory like the Ariminumese covet gold. If the Concordians get access to the Ariminumese navy, Oltremare will be faced with a new Crusade, a Crusade that will supplant you."

The prince's child shrieked in delight and the queen looked up with a smile. "*My* kingdom's strong enough to see off *any* pretenders." Sofia knew that this boast was for her uncle's ears—and so did he. Embarrassed, he made his excuses and stalked out.

Unperturbed, the queen kissed the giggling baby's stomach. "Where's Papa gone? Where's he gone?" After the last of Andronikos' retinue filed out, followed by Fulk and his men, she turned lazily to the patriarch. "Your Beatitude, what say you?"

Chrysoberges pursed his lips with great solemnity. "Since we have subjugated heresy so thoroughly here, the Evil One is trying to flank us. Our duty is clear: Etruria and Oltremare are one. Your uncle talks of commerce"—a shudder shook the old tree—"and makes arguments of expedience, but there can be no compromise with apostasy! Evil must be vanquished wherever it manifests itself. The engineers of Concord deserve harsher treatment than the Ebionites. Abraham's children languish in the old dispensation, but at least they fear God. The engineers worship an idol called Reason." He added mournfully, "If that poison were to gain purchase in people's hearts, where might it end? What beastliness could not be justified in Reason's name?"

"Considering the sins committed in God's, I tremble to imagine. Get to the point—should we go to war?"

His fervent manner changed entirely. "A more delicate question, Majesty. However just the cause, war's not to be rushed into. Our long-term security rests on controlling the Middle Sea."

"And our fleet is old . . ." the queen said, musing. "Thank you, Chrysoberges. You may go. You too, Podesta. I will speak with my sister queen."

The queen waited till all the men were gone, then rolled her eyes. "I do apologize for Andronikos, Contessa. Do you have siblings? No? Consider yourself lucky. Uncle means well, but he has always been an ambitious dreamer. That's what brought my ancestors across the sea: a dream of a heavenly city. When they found a pointless rock in the middle of a dry nothing, most of them went home. The ones who stayed were weak, weak and divided. Oltremare was several states, then. Impossible to do anything, impossible to agree." This was ancient history, but the queen appeared to take fresh umbrage at it. "They warred with the Ebionites, and with each other as well. The Ebionites took sides in our feuds, and year by year they won back more territory. Within a century, they retook Jerusalem. We could have stopped them if the nobles had united behind the crown. Jealousy almost destroyed us—my uncle knows this!"

Sofia attempted to look sympathetic.

"Oltremare was doomed: friendless in Europa, enveloped by the Radinate, divided internally. The conversion of Egypt reprieved us for a few decades, but my grandfather Tancred was the real miracle worker."

"I've seen his mask in the Ancestor Room," Sofia said neutrally. She remembered a cruel, scar-matted face.

The queen apparently remembered something more admirable. "Ah, Contessa, there was a king!" She mooned like a love-struck girl. "He broke the nobles' power and consolidated the crowns, and faced with our unity, the Radinate collapsed and we took Jerusalem once more." She whispered, almost as if speaking of an absent lover.

"According to the traditional steps, we should have waited until the Ebionites stopped fighting each other long enough to expel us, then begged the princes of Europa once more to save us. But King Tancred had a new dance in mind." The queen's eyes flashed. "If we could not have the rock, no one could. The Ebionites had proved false witness. So Tancred exiled the people and destroyed her walls;

forbidding any entry. And if further proof was needed that *we* are God's chosen now, the Sand Devils did the rest. Then Grandfather looked around and saw a kingdom that might be as great as the Etruscans: we already controlled the trade routes to the east, and we had slaves aplenty to man our galleys. The Middle Sea is a better prize than Jerusalem, and if that put us in competition with the Europans—so what? We have prosperous cities along the coast, while the once-great metropolises of the Radinate have been eaten up by the Sands that spawned their impious race." She grasped Sofia's hand suddenly. "We are *queens,* are we not? We see off *all* challengers." She slowly composed herself and became reserved once more, "Contessa, I understand time is pressing. But we will consult with our ministers."

"Of course." Sofia bowed and retreated with a feeling of new optimism. Clearly, there were powers in Oltremare that viewed an Etrurian war as an opportunity to acquire territory from the weakened states in the aftermath, but the queen impressed her as more clear-sighted: Catrina understood the existential threat Concord represented to her throne.

Chapter 74

It was getting dark when Jacques woke. In the half-light, he examined his wrists for a long while, then—quite calmly—dashed his head against the wall. If he had not been so weak, that blow would have been sufficient.

He woke the following day in a worse state. In front of him was a bowl of tripe stew. He looked at the stone wall, splattered with his blood, and his bandaged wrists, then back to the bowl and considered whether he had anything to live for. After a moment, he crawled forward on his elbows like a dog and lapped up the cold stew.

Next day his jailer stood before him with a fresh bowl. "If you had chosen to die," Yuri said, "I would have let you."

Blankly Jacques nodded. He *had* nothing to live for—no name, no freedom, no hands. What kept him breathing was something else. As Yuri fed Jacques, he told him how his apprentice had been discovered, how his ankles and wrists had been smashed with Jacques' hammer; how his chest was branded; how the letters that formed the word *TRAITOR* encircled the hole where his heart had been cut out; how the organ was cooking on the forge beside the body. He didn't mention the melee on the bridge, or the curfew subsequently imposed. He left after cleaning Jacques' wounds and changing his bandages.

The next day he returned with Pedro. The engineer examined his wrists and took some measurements. Jacques made a sound, the first attempt he'd made to speak: "—meeewhuuu?"

"I can't give you back your hands," said Pedro, "but I can give you something else."

Lord Geta finished briefing the priors—they'd come to consider his advice as both impartial and indispensable. With the swagger of a gonfaloniere, he descended the steps of the Palazzo del Popolo and smiled to see who was waiting.

"Haven't you done well?"

He bowed. "I can't take all the credit. It was your suggestion that led me to the villain."

Maddalena rapped his arm with her fan, not playfully. "I didn't mean *that*, stupid! That was elementary. I meant having Yuri carry out the sentence."

"You liked that?"

"My dear fellow, I loved it. The good Podesta is only a stand-in. The magnates support him only as long as he can keep the peace. I should think his flag's worn pretty ragged in bandieratori eyes, and that there are plenty of condottieri who'd prefer a leader less even-handed."

"So I understand. Personally, I don't see why the bandieratori are still allowed such latitude. The Families are gone."

Maddalena shuddered irritably. "The same reason for every foolishness in Rasenna. You can't step on the street with soiling your shoe on some time-honored tradition. We're faithful to nothing here but the past."

Geta's eyes twinkled in amusement; he saw what was expected of him and harrumphed accordingly. "That must change. Now that

Rasenna has both an army and an engineers' guild, the old way will not serve. The engineers will abuse any liberty we allow them—see how Maestro Vanzetti absents himself from the Signoria, yet no one reproaches him."

"He's playing nursemaid to that traitor."

"Currying popularity with the Small People, more like. The engineers may act like artisans, but don't be fooled: they're soldiers. If the army taught me anything—"

"Besides how to gamble and whore?"

"Besides that—it's that soldiers need discipline. Without it, I fear Rasenna will go the way of Concord."

Maddalena put her arm under Geta's. "You don't need to convince *me*. My father needs to hear these arguments. Just remember he has the same weakness as most selfish men; he can't admit to being one. That's why I like you, Lord Geta. You're different."

"You're too generous, Signorina."

The crowd studiously ignored them as they walked across the bridge together. Maddalena surveyed the stalls with a proprietary air. "Believe me; Papa's as nervous of Pedro Vanzetti's intentions as the rest of the magnates. He's just too guilty to admit it. You must form your argument in terms of what's in Rasenna's long-term interest. Put it like that and he'll go along with *anything*."

"I don't understand how such a fool got to carry Rasenna's flag."

"Papa's no fool; he's just got a blind spot." Maddalena brushed away a fly dismissively. "The chief engineer's father, Vettori, was Papa's partner. He was an agitator."

"Like the good King Jacques," said Geta thoughtfully. "Well?"

"Signore Vettori didn't prosper. Papa did. Success is unforgivable to the Small People, and Pedro's not above playing on Papa's guilty conscience. The engineers have been granted unlimited funds with no oversight, but when a tax that doesn't profit them is proposed, they protest. They say they're taking the people's side, but I'm not fooled."

"Hello, what's this?"

Ahead of them the crowd abruptly parted to reveal Uggeri, flag in hand.

"*Madonna*, Uggeri," Maddelena sighed, "don't make a scene."

"The Signoria has charged us bandieratori to keep cut-purses off the bridge. Hands off, Geta. That's not your property."

"I take it this boy is one of those over-mighty bandieratori you mentioned, Signorina? We have rock-throwing children in Concord too. I know how to deal with them."

"I'm no boy."

"You're an impertinent dog and this young lady is unmarried; you have no claim."

"I apologize for his barking, Lord Geta." Maddalena glared at Uggeri. "He's been off the leash since his harlot mistress fled the city in disgrace."

"Stand behind me, *amore*," said Geta, drawing his sword. Of course the boy had been Maddalena's lover; she was using him to make the boy jealous. He didn't mind—this was just what was needed.

"You're not a boy, eh? Then what say we settle this like men?" He dropped his sword.

Uggeri said, "Suits me," and bowed to place his flag carefully on the ground.

Geta knew a Rasenneisi would never just drop his flag, and before Uggeri could rise, he dived at him. His weight knocked the boy over, but Uggeri punched him in the jaw and neatly rolled him over. His strong fingers locked around Geta's gullet and squeezed.

Instead of fighting, the Concordian pulled out a short boot-dagger and pressed it to Uggeri's neck. "Decide," he croaked. "Live or die. Either suits." A lie: the last thing Geta wanted was a dead Rasenneisi on his hands—like this anyway.

Uggeri's rage was stronger than his prudence and he kept squeezing, even as Geta's blade cut deeper.

Geta's eyes darted briefly to Maddalena and he whispered, "Think she'll grieve long?"

"Don't get yourself killed on my account."

Her derisive laugh penetrated Uggeri's anger and he released Geta, grabbed his flag and leapt to his feet. He was breathing hard, and looked embarrassed. "Next time we meet, Concordian, I'll hold onto my flag."

Geta bowed. "I look forward to it."

Uggeri walked toward Maddalena, who stepped back nervously. "Lord Geta!"

Geta did nothing. If the bandieratoro hurt the Gonfaloniere's daughter, it would only be to his advantage.

Uggeri grabbed a pair of long silk gloves from a stall and flung them at her. "Here. Whores are supposed to wear these."

Maddalena regained her composure as Uggeri walked away and called, "That must be a new law. I don't recall seeing them on Signorina Scaligeri."

"Oh, I forgot to pay," Uggeri said, taking out a few coins.

"A gift, Signore, a gift," the terrified glove-stall owner said, but Uggeri wasn't talking to him. He sprinkled the coins in front of Maddalena.

She slapped him, hard. "Stop embarrassing yourself."

Uggeri smiled to see her angry. As he sauntered off, he said at Geta, "If you stick with that harpy, better watch your back."

Geta wondered whether this was a threat or a warning. He looked at Maddalena's murderous scowl and decided it was both.

Chapter 75

THE LAND ACROSS THE WATER

Deus Ex Machina

In the last century the scale of corruption in the Curia and factionalism in Oltremare had made the word "Crusade" something of a bad joke. Critics observed that the First Crusade was launched to save Jerusalem, not Akka, and that successive Crusades had served only to impoverish Etruria and unite the Radinate. Shunned and friendless, the beset kingdom was left to die.

Only a miracle could save it.

Though the Curia thought it a fool's errand, they still permitted Saint Francis' voyage to Egypt.[41] The Sage of Gubbio, however,

---

41. The Fraticelli had by now been domesticated and enfolded (smothered, some would say) within the cloak of Mother Church. The movement had given the declining Curia some much-needed creditability, but perhaps the cardinals believed that Gubbio's holy fool had reached the end of his usefulness and that a suitably pathetic martyrdom would restore faith in the discredited cause of Crusade.

was confident: he had persuaded carrion birds, wolves and wool merchants to adopt the one true faith; how hard could it be to convert a benighted Melic? Contrary to all expectations, he succeeded.[42] Overnight, Oltremare's territory doubled. The conversion restored hope to the Oltremarines, but it alone would have been insufficient to break the stalemate with the Radinate. That required a third party.

42. This prodigy may owe more to Alexandria's long-standing rivalry with Byzant than to the Saint's powers of persuasion. Whatever the truth, possession of the Egyptian bread-basket saved Oltremare from extinction.

Chapter 76

They waited for the queen's decision. And waited. And as they waited, Sofia's belly grew rounder. She had always taken her body for granted. A bandieratori sweated and suffered in the workshop so that whatever else betrayed him in the streets, it would not be his body. The bovine, lumpen, achingly slow thing looking back at Sofia in the mirror was base treachery.

Since she refused to go veiled, Akka's streets were barred to her. She objected to the restriction, though she had no wish to return there. The air down in the bazaar was adhesive, hopeless as sap oozing from a fallen tree. She found herself thinking fondly of the cleanliness of the desert, where the wind never ceased and the sun consumed all shadows. The wind lost its roar in the labyrinth of streets soaked in Oltremarine art, which, with the exception of the Madonna Muerta, was an inhuman vocabulary of geometrical ornament. Motifs that began as stylized plants became abstract patterns,

intellectually brilliant, but lacking all warmth: clockwork flowers.
The sea's thunder penetrated her dreams in the same way the salt
corroded the Lazars' armor. She was out there, in the middle of the
unbounded water again, with Ezra roaring at the heavens as the sea
sank beneath them and a wall of spiraling water surrounded them.

It wasn't just her; all Akka was on edge. By now Sofia was used
to the near-panic that overtook the poorer quarters as everyone
rushed to buy provisions on the eve of Sabbath. But tomorrow was
not Sabbath, and there had been a nervousness in the air all week.
The people milling in the streets were dressed more somberly than
usual, and that morning she and Levi had watched the seneschal
leading Lazars out of the main gate. It was almost as if they were
evacuating the city. Levi went to investigate—no part of Akka was
closed to a man.

Sofia circumnavigated the wall and found Arik perched on the
east side, watching his falcon's shadow sweep over the dunes. He
held his arm out and called her.

His back was turned to Akka; his spirit also yearned for the freedom of the Sands. The patriarch was leading a procession through
the streets below. Dolorous chants competed with the din of clashing
cymbals. He was followed by a sumptuous train of Akkan ladies, all
veiled, of course, but dressed in black instead of their usual vivacious
colors. They cast ashes on their heads, weeping. In the midst of them,
four slaves carried a float with the Madonna Muerta, wreathed in
incense and sprinkled with black petals and desert thorns.

Sofia asked, "Where are all the Lazars going?"

The bird landed on Arik's gauntlet. He deftly replaced its hood
and fed it some meat. "Ask Fulk."

He was ill-at-ease in the city, but also with her—she was just
another Frank now.

"I'm asking you."

"It's a show of force while the Festival of All Souls lasts." Seeing Sofia's confusion, he scornfully indicated the procession below.
"This blasphemy. Today's the Day of the Innocents." Arik's face didn't

usually reflect his feelings, but today his disgust was obvious. "It's a warm-up for the main event: tomorrow is the Day of the Dead."

Knowing Akka's chauvinistic citizenry, Sofia was sure the Day of the Dead would be a somber memorial to the fallen, followed by vows to revenge them. "What if a tribe attacked the city during the festival?"

"That's what the Lazar patrols are for. But it's unlikely; my people give Oltremarine cities a wide berth at this time. I myself am going to sell Dhib in Nazareth. You're welcome to come—but if you stay, however much they press it on you, don't wear a mask. Stick by Fulk."

"He's staying, then?"

"Someone has to stay sober."

Sofia followed the procession through the streets from her vantage point, watching as the intensity of the mourners mounted, culminating in the women ripping off their veils and tearing their hair and scratching their arms and cheeks. Suddenly there was a clamor from the streets, shouts and yells, and the Lazars patrolling the walls started descending as fast as they could move.

Levi came running. "Get to your chamber and lock the door," he cried.

"What is it?"

"Prince Andronikos tried to kill the queen!"

A scream from below cut the air and the patriarch and the women scattered, diving to either side as several riders burst through them. The slaves carrying the statue could not move so fast—they and it were smashed under horse hoofs: the prince's axmen, with Lazars hot on their heels.

Confusion reigned in the palace. Accounts varied: Prince Andronikos and his men had apparently stormed the throne room, cutting their way through several slaves, and Fulk and the queen herself had kept them at bay until more Lazars arrived.

"I gave him something to remember me by," said Fulk grimly.

That's when the fight had taken to the streets: the prince was counting on popular support, but he had seriously misjudged the city. The bawling of his daughter filled the throne room, an incongruous sound against the sight of corpses being hauled away. The queen did not appear to notice either; she paced and wrung her hands. "No sign of him?"

"He can't be far—probably hiding in the Ebionite quarter,"

"I saw a lone rider leave the city," said Arik, "going south."

"He's fled, the dog!" Fulk rasped. "He tried to take advantage of the festival, Madonna curse his blaspheming eyes. When I find him—"

Arik glanced at Sofia. "No, Fulk, you should stay. Akka needs you tomorrow. I'll bring him back."

"You can't go alone," Sofia started.

"I'll go too," said Levi. "Two of us should be enough."

The queen gathered herself. "Podesta, I will not forget this. Arik, I charge you now: bring my uncle back alive, that I might show him clemency. I will not let my kingdom be again divided."

After their departure the queen clapped her hands and her ladies-in-waiting and slaves retreated. Fulk was reluctant to leave her, but she insisted. "The sun will not slow on our account, Grand Master. You have preparations to see to." She picked up the baby and bounced it roughly in her arms. Though clearly upset by the attempt on her life, she tried to conceal it with gaiety. "I am *so* looking forward to tomorrow. As King Tancred made me, so Count Scaligeri made you. We owe them everything. To loan them our limbs once a year is a small price. What's one day, after all? You'll take part, of course?"

Sofia remembered Arik's counsel and politely refused.

"Are you sure? You can use one of my Family masks—no? Well, suit yourself. If I could persuade you by telling you what it's like, I would, but the truth is, I never remember. Imagine being sated after a great feast, without remembering the feast—for a few hours, someone else takes charge of your body. Though the dead are legion, they have one thing in common: they are not alive. Perhaps the patriarch would explain it better, but let me try: the pleasures of flesh are obviously greater ecstasy than Heaven can offer. The dead are famished, and we live in a land of plenty." She held up the baby. "Don't we, chubby cheeks? Yes, we do! Yes we do!" She turned to Sofia. "Would you like to hold her?"

"Certainly."

"Look at you! You're a natural mother. Contessa—*Sofia*—it's just us girls now. There is something I must ask you." Her eyes dropped. "Who's the father?"

"You'd think me mad if I told you."

"I see—an unsuitable person? The world is full of them."

"You could say that."

"I shall not press you. You've found sanctuary here. From questions, from whispers, from fear."

Two hours before sunrise, clappers and cymbals called Akka's remaining Lazars to mass. They had been fasting since yesterday, but they did not appear fatigued. The chapel was small—only the funeral of a man who owed no one money could have been held in it. The walls were limed white and decoration was absent, but for a faded fresco depicting two angels drawing back a drapery with the satisfied expressions of clever schoolchildren. The rather unconvincing effect was saved by the wonder they revealed: here was the sympathetic Madonna Sofia knew. It was surprising that the Mother of God was depicted as a corpse everywhere in Akka *but* here—but no, not surprising at all—death cannot inspire reverence in those who live in its shadow. The queen had given Sofia charge of the prince's daughter, and she laid her cheek on the downy crown of her head and said a prayer for Levi and Arik.

Before dawn, Fulk did a final check of the city, then retreated to the walls. Stairs were barred and ladders drawn up. He was still enraged at Prince Andronikos' treachery. Sofia understood loyalty; this was something else. He was taking it personally. When she asked about the festival, he was hardly less impatient. "They wear a death mask for a day as a joke. Great fun for them, a security nightmare for us."

* * *

While their masters howled through the Day of the Innocents, the Ebionite servants were busy preparing for the Day of the Dead. They rearranged the death masks in the Ancestor Room, laid out great banquets and then fled the city before the sun went down. The next morning, family members performed their ablutions and then tied blindfolds on each another. One by one they entered the Ancestor Room, and when they came out they were someone else. Nubile girls emerged wearing the faces of bearded soldiers, old men with the faces of beautiful boys. The great feasts vanished in minutes, and afterward, other hungers were sated.

Fulk and his skeleton crew patrolled the walls as the mayhem let loose. Sofia tried to keep the infant calm, but the changed atmosphere was palpable.

"You don't partake, Fulk?" she asked.

"With *this* body? It would be unjust to the dead."

Sofia didn't believe his selfless act; he, like Arik, was obviously disgusted by the festival, but his fidelity to his queen trumped everything.

Sofia asked, "Are they *really* possessed?"

"Does it matter?" he said, then, softer, "Forgive me. I'm just—For the first few hours it's play-acting, as far I can tell, but after dusk . . ." He whistled dryly. "Then it gets rough. To start with, everyone's just delighted to be alive, but later they weary; they feel themselves slipping away. Some go down fighting, and occasionally you get a really strong personality. They always bring a few back. You'll see."

They followed the prince's tracks for several miles until they came to a place where the soil gave way to shifting sands and Arik swore and confessed that they might have lost him. He held his hand out and called, "Dhib!"

The falcon had been following so long that Levi had forgotten it, but now it swooped down and landed on Arik's outstretched arm. He whispered some words to it and it took off again.

"Now what?" said Levi.

"Now we wait. Tea?"

Arik poured the water onto a mint leaf and piled in several spoons of sugar. As he handed Levi the cup, he muttered, "לחיים"

"תודה רבה" said Levi as he took the tea, then looked up guiltily.

"Yes, I thought so," said Arik. He did not wait for confirmation. "When you were taken by my brother's men, did you hear their plans?"

Levi sipped the tea. "I understood enough to know they were excited. They kept talking of the Old Man of the Mountain. I was surprised."

"Surely you've heard of him?"

"I always thought my mother had made him up to convince me the Ebionites once were more than slaves."

"My father also told me stories. The Old Man was the greatest. He could cajole the cautious and tempt the greedy and inspire the timid. He united the tribes and *almost* pushed the Franks into the sea— almost. But he is gone, and they remain, too powerful. Too many."

"They said he had returned."

"Ha! Yūsuf must truly be desperate to feed them such fantasies—" Arik suddenly looked up and Levi did likewise, but he saw nothing but empty sky.

Then a cry came from above, and a distant speck became the silhouette of a bird.

Arik swallowed his tea and leapt up. "Come. Dhib has found something."

That night Sofia slept on the walls, keeping the child warm against her own body. Bad dreams were interrupted by cries as the knights fought back half-hearted invasions of the lecherous dead. After the third such attempt, Sofia gave up any hope of sleep and sat up to watch the carnival. One of the Lazars, a young recruit, was badly bitten and she bandaged his wound. When the baby awoke, she was careful to keep her faced away from the city.

The streets were awash with drunken revelers and the alleyways with frantic couplings as long-dead lovers sought each other out with no regard to who or what their host might be; prim matrons pressed spread-eagled against walls, mothers and sons copulated, fathers and daughters; hardened sailors sweated with priests, tight-fisted merchants wept with joy as their slaves straddled them ... This night Akka's walls were a pen that kept the dead from spilling into the desert and the sea.

Sofia noticed some of the younger Lazars watching the proceeding with prurient interest: so not everyone was as committed as Fulk, as fully convinced that they had chosen wisely when they doomed themselves to corruption, isolation and chastity. She watched Fulk moving between these regretful souls throughout the night, bolstering their sagging spirits.

The carnality of the dead was insatiable. Although they only had new faces, Sofia could hardly recognize courtiers she saw every day, for their movements were at odds with their bodies: girls quivered arthritically and leered at mincing old men. Sofia was shocked to hear the queen's voice among the moaning throng. She was lying on a stairway, grunting passionate imprecations as the patriarch's head bobbed between her legs, gnawing away like a pig eating old vegetables.

They followed the bird's shadow across the dunes until they came to a place where the sand gave way to rock. Arik promptly found the trail in the moonlight, but he was obviously puzzled. "He's this way—but this is a different camel to the one he set out on. This one is near death. See, how close together the footprints are."

When they caught their first sight of him, the prince's camel appeared to be wandering aimlessly.

"Looks like he's sleeping in the saddle," Levi remarked, puzzled.

When they got closer the camel turned, braying plaintively, and Prince Andronikos tumbled to the ground. His throat had been cut and the smell was enough to tell them he'd been dead a while, though they had found him before the vultures could do much damage.

"Sicarii," said Arik. "They wanted us to catch him, but not this quick."

"What's going on?" said Levi uneasily.

"Get back on your camel." Arik handed Levi his waterskin. "Drink."

"What's the rush?"

"We don't stop until we reach Akka. They mounted a dead man on a thirsty camel that knows this area. There's water on the other side of this wadi. Don't you see? They wanted us to follow the camel, but we caught it too early. Look: on either side of the slope, see those rocks at the end of the wadi, in the shadows there?"

"An ambush?"

"And one we've not escaped yet. Are you ready? *Ride!*"

When the sun dawned, hundreds of discarded masks littered the otherwise empty streets. Naked, half-dressed citizens stole homeward, limping and bow-legged, their bodies left stiff, bruised and bleeding by their temporary occupants. Usually at this hour the bazaars would be filling with merchants preparing for the day, but all was quiet as the city slept off the previous night's orgy.

Sofia woke to see Fulk and his men quietly descending from the walls. "Where are you going?"

"I have to check for deserters. Stay here: this is when it's most dangerous."

"No way. You watched my back all night."

"I don't have time to argue."

"So don't." She gave the infant to the injured Lazar and joined Fulk's troop. Fulk unclipped his ax as he stepped onto the street. "People lock up when they get home so it's easy to find the deserters. They make lots of noise. If you hear anything, get behind me." He divided his men into fours and sent them out across the city.

Fulk glanced at Sofia. "Feel the air?"

"It's clean," she said in wonder, "like the desert."

Fulk inhaled with relish. "Enjoy it while you can. Hello, who's this?"

Just inside the mouth of an alleyway stood an apron-wearing hulk. The blood on the apron wasn't his. He wandered up and down, mumbling to himself. When he caught sight of the Lazars he went mute and statue-still, like a child, hoping to hide in immobility. Fulk nodded to his men and checked Sofia was behind him. "Don't be scared," he murmured. "The hosts are the ones in most danger."

Soon the butcher forgot his purpose and started mumbling again, arguing with an unseen other. "I'm not going back," he insisted in a girlish lisp. "I said *No*. It's cold and it's dark—"

The Lazars came closer, dragging their spurs in the dust, when suddenly the butcher brandished his cleaver and screamed, "I said NO!"

Fulk stood his ground as the butcher charged. His men on either side waited patiently and when Fulk took a step backward they stepped forward, slamming their shields into the blundering mass. The cleaver flew up as he tumbled down and the knights fell upon him, pinning his arms.

Sofia caught the cleaver and smiled at Fulk's disapproving snort. "What? You've got an ax!"

Fulk didn't have time to argue; his men were struggling with the butcher. He sat on the man's chest, gripped the mask on each side and pulled. An unearthly dual voice emanated from the butcher's scabbed lips: "Nnnnuuughghgh-gh-ga," he groaned, while the girl within him screamed like a harpy, "SAID NOOO!!!"

The flesh clung to the mask as Fulk pulled and at last it came free with a ripping sound. There were bloody lesions on the man's cheeks and forehead, but he was already snoring. Fulk held the mask like a dead rat—it belonged to a girl with a high forehead and a pouty, sulking mouth. He threw it against the wall under the nearest Madonna Muerta statue. The fragments fell to the pile of other would-be deserters from the Land of the Dead.

"When a mask is broken—" Sofia began.

"They can never return. She knew the rules."

They walked on. Among the occasional discarded mask lay the bodies of dogs and cats and goats. Once they came upon a partially eaten horse. "Supposed to lock the stables," Fulk tutted. He looked at Sofia. "Folks who starved to death tend to have an appetite."

"No kidding." She threw the cleaver in the air and caught it, getting used to its weight. It took an hour to circumnavigate the city, then Fulk sent his men out on a final random sweep of the backstreets.

Sofia accompanied him back to the citadel. A young knight standing outside greeted Fulk with relief. "Grand Master! Thank the Madonna—inside—I don't know how they got in. All the doors were locked—"

"How many?"

"Two, I think."

Fulk sent the Lazar to get some backup. After he ran off, Sofia slapped Fulk on the back and flipped her cleaver nonchalantly. "Two? We can handle that."

They walked down the corridor, which was lined with empty coffins. At the end, it split into two; to the left was a dark corridor, an ossuary, the piled bones feebly illuminated by thin shafts of morning sun. A dry musk filled the air. The other way led to the training hall, a large chamber illuminated by big circular windows. A pair of deserters were wrestling in the middle, though it was a clumsy affair: both parties were frantic with hate, but neither was used to their temporary body.

"Old grudge?" said Sofia.

"Looks like. It's better that they're focused on each other." Fulk advanced with confidence. "Stay here. I'll handle it."

Sofia snorted and began to follow, when she heard a lapping sound to her left and paused. She saw a shadow—a white face—scramble by a shaft of light at the end of the dark corridor, and mocking laughter.

One of the wrestlers pulled the other to the ground and pulled his ear off, but he didn't appear to notice. Fulk risked a quick glance behind him. "Contessa?"

He was about to go and look for Sofia, but instinct made him turn again—just in time to see the two wrestlers coming for him, their quarrel forgotten. Fulk backed away as the pair charged, shocked: this kind of coordination between deserters was unheard of. He slapped the first in the face with the broadside of his ax and as soon as the porcelain mask cracked, the host tumbled over soundlessly, already asleep. The other was more nimble; he dived at Fulk, grabbing his ax hand. Fulk hit the ground heavily with a grunt and winced as his ax skidded across the slabs. The dead man's clumsy, insistent hands found his neck and began to squeeze.

Down the other corridor, Sofia heard Fulk's call, but didn't dare answer for fear of alerting her quarry. She crept slowly from pillar to pillar, listening hard. A drip-fed pool was streaked with undulating trickles of blood. She walked around it, following a dragging trail to the end of the corridor. Between the shelves of dusty bones were side-vaults, stacked with grain-bags and barrels. The chuckling reminded her of the dogs that had encircled Arik's fire in the desert; it echoed in the darkness between the uneven tempo of the dripping liquid.

Steeling herself, Sofia turned into the last side-vault. A girl was kneeling before a niche on the far wall. She had arranged something in the niche; Sofia could see a veil, but she couldn't make out what it was attached to until she took a step closer, and suddenly gagged when she saw what it was. The body belonged to a dog, pregnant to judge from its heavy teats and pink hairless belly, but the bitch's head had been replaced with a sow's and painted with merry, garish cosmetics.

The girl turned around slowly, her arm held straight out. She held a small dagger in that hand. From her body, Sofia judged her to be about Isabella's age, but her mask was that of a purse-lipped older man, a cleric or a notary, maybe. Her skin was beaded with sweat.

"*Porca Madonna! That's you, Scaligeri! How could you be the Handmaid? You're not pure. You're not obedient.*" The guttural voice was full of mockery, the words it spoke a collage of syllables awkwardly hammered together. "*You're a selfless bitch who's let everyone who ever loved you die to save yourself.*"

"Go back to Hell," Sofia said.

"*You'll abandon that piglet in your belly, too, when the time comes, won't you? 'Course you will, dirty pig. Why don't we save some time and let me cut it out? The way you cut Donna Bombelli!*" She threw herself at Sofia, knife shaking a little, nails clawing.

Sofia sidestepped and the girl rolled over neatly, chuckling.

Fulk came upon them, out of breath and limping. He took in the scene and lowered his ax. "If you remove the mask, you can go home and come back next year—"

"*Liar!*" the girl hissed, retreating into a pillar. "*Fuuuulk,*" she crooned as she rubbed her back against it, "*take it if you want, Fuuuulk. You needn't abstain.*" The voice dropped to a whisper: "*I won't tell Catrina . . .*" She untied the front of her chemise. Her small breasts were bruised and scratched from yesternight's entertainment.

"You know you have to go back," Fulk said in the same soothing voice. "Take the mask off."

"*I will if you will. You sound so sweet. I want to see your face.*"

When Fulk took another step, she screamed, "*Take the mask off!*" She put the dagger to her neck. "*Show me, or I'll take her with me into the Dark.*" A drop of blood formed around the dagger's point.

Fulk turned to Sofia, eyes begging.

She understood, and looked away as he lifted his visor.

"So *beautiful,*" said the girl, lowering the knife and reaching out to touch him with her other hand.

He suddenly bellowed

"Fulk!" Sofia shouted as he turned, but she was frozen at the sight of his face: a knot of tangled crimson ropes.

The girl took advantage of the pause, expertly kicking the back of his legs and bringing him crashing to his knees. She held the knife to his neck and glared at Sofia. "*Give me the piglet or I'll kill him.*"

"Sofia, get out of here," Fulk hissed. The claw-marks on his cheek were just a more vivid red in a mass of matted blood.

Sofia stepped back. "I can't do that."

"*He's coming back, Scaligeri! We hear of nothing else in the pit. He grows strong, like your piglet. I'll tell him and my reward shall be great. Wherever you run, he'll find you.*"

"Tell him I'm ready," Sofia said, and threw the cleaver. It turned over and over and over, and the handle struck between her eyes. The mask cracked apart neatly and fell, shattering as it hit the ground, followed a moment later by the sleeping girl's body.

Chapter 77

The servant who opened the door of Palazzo Bombelli made Pedro wait in the atrium to be announced. This pretentiousness would have amused him once, but Pedro was fresh from attending to Jacques in the stables. Still he did not let himself show his anger, not when he'd come to try to bridge the gap between the engineers and priors that had opened since Geta appeared.

"Is that Pedro?" Maddalena called from the stairway. She pattered down the steps, her smile luminous. "I'm glad it's you. You *should* be the first to know."

"Know what?"

"I'm engaged!"

Pedro had only just come from Piazza Stella, where he'd seen Uggeri's crew loitering as menacingly as they had in the old days. Uggeri had so far kept the peace Sofia had charged him with, but he hardly looked festive. "Congratulations," he said, hiding his confusion. "I wish your brothers were here to celebrate."

"I've always considered you a brother, you know that, and I pray you'll agree to be my husband's best man. Lord Geta thinks highly of you too."

"Geta!"

Maddalena's smile twitched. "But you must have heard! I know how fast gossip leaps between towers. What's the matter? It's wonderful news. I'll be a *lady*!"

Pedro struggled to be polite, "It—I—It's only a little unexpected, and a little hasty—I mean, in so short a time, how well can you know this—this foreigner?"

Maddalena's brow clouded. "I see. It's inappropriate because he's Concordian. But, of course, the Contessa Scaligeri can slut around with Captain Giovanni and then Levi, a condottiere from God knows where, and nobody says a word."

"That's not true—Sofia didn't—Oh, never mind that. I couldn't give a damn about Geta's nationality. He's *noble*, Maddalena. You're not naïve. We've only just thrown off the Families. Your father's one of the most important people in town. If your mother—"

"How *dare* you! You're the naïve one, little brother, repeating the communard trash that got your father killed. Perhaps you'd see a little clearer if you weren't burrowing holes all day. Perhaps you'd realize that Concord's nobility are our natural allies against Concord's engineers. I don't know if Geta's a good man—I gave up that search a long time ago—but I know he's strong."

"And what about Uggeri?" Pedro said quietly.

Maddalena stiffened. "What is that *boy* to me?" She turned and stomped up the stairs.

Before she could reach the first landing Pedro called after her, "You know very well!"

That she could discard Uggeri so easily galled him. Uggeri was no saint, but Pedro knew his worth. He *had* heard the rumors about Geta, but he had dismissed them, assuming Maddalena would know better than to get mixed up with such a person. But apparently not.

When the servant haughtily summoned Pedro, he was irked enough to ask, "Do I approach on my knees, Gonfaloniere? What's the etiquette these days?"

"Don't tease, Pedro!" Fabbro laughed. "I'm still training them. Visiting dignitaries expect certain formalities. Obviously they aren't necessary for Rasenneisi; I'll have a word." He was happily rearranging the items on his desk, obviously unable to contain his excitement at the engagement. The apology was a formality too, and Pedro felt a perverse need to puncture Fabbro's complacence. "Doc Bardini didn't care for formalities."

"Because he was a hypocrite," Fabbro retorted with sudden aggression. "Surely you're old enough to see that now? Or do you still believe everything that comes from Signorina Scaligeri's lips? The Doc died for Rasenna, but let's not forget how he lived either. He needed to pretend he didn't rule, but I don't have to dissemble. I'm the elected Gonfaloniere. When someone else is elected, I'll support them." He regained his composure and sat down. "Please, let's forget the past, I want to concentrate on the—"

Pedro tilted his head back to the door. "I heard."

Fabbro clapped his hands together. "Isn't it wonderful! It was my wife's dying wish to see Maddalena married, but I'd given up hope. My sons are quite useless; they haven't found anyone remotely suitable down south and—well, it just happened in the wave of a flag. I only wish Vettori had lived to see it."

He knew he should play along and broach his concerns later, but Fabbro's mention of his father so soon after Maddalena had disparaged him made Pedro suddenly furious. "He'd be appalled! Your daughter should marry one of the Small People, not a noble! The gonfaloniere bears the flag. All Rasenna looks to your example, from the lowest bandieratoro to the mightiest magnate. Etruria's watching too, to see how long our republican principles last. You're becoming awfully autocratic with your formalities and servants."

"Oh, Madonna's sake—"

"For all we know, the man's a villain. He's clearly an exile. He's emptied his purse paying off the tabs of the Hawk's Company."

"If he's right for my girl, I don't care if he's a pauper."

"No, all you covet is his name. How will it look, after so many Small People died to overthrow the Families, when our Gonfaloniere sells his only daughter for a title?"

Fabbro flinched as if from a blow. The question hung unanswered for long enough for the silence to grow ugly. Fabbro stood up slowly. "I never knew you were so politically aware. How sad that you don't share your insights in the Signoria anymore."

"I've been busy. You know that." That was all he was going to say, but a reckless spirit goaded him on. "The Signoria *is* the people— that place across the river represents only the magnates."

"Pedro, you're very brilliant, but very immature, with a boy's shallow understanding in many ways. The Small People weren't the only ones who sacrificed to overcome the Families—far from it."

"Don't give me that line. Maybe you've forgotten what the truth sounds like. I warn you—others won't be so understanding."

If there had been any chance that Fabbro might unbend at that moment it disappeared. "I've been threatened by bandieratori before. They don't frighten me. Flags can be easily bought."

"Towers can easily burn."

His face hardened. "Best leave, *boy*, before you go from insubordination to treason."

Wine, as usual, was served at the meeting of the Mercanzia, but such were the times that Fabbro was forced to open a second crate.

Polo Sorrento was no orator, but anger made him eloquent. "War. War. War. I've heard of nothing else, ever since the siege, but I've yet to see a single drop of blood spilled. You don't hear them gossiping in the street about the blockade, but it's costing everyone here. We can't get wool from Europa, not by land, and now that the Concordians have Ariminumese ships patrolling the Gulf of Avignon on their behalf, not by sea either. Ariminum was our doorway to the east and now it's shut. Costs are rising. We *must* lower wages or raise taxes but we know how the Small People will react. We're in it together, as long as times are good, as long as they get everything at yesterday's price, as long as we *deficiente* make up the difference." He held his hands out like a beggar. "I'm just a simple farmer so someone explain it to me: we're being impoverished by a war that hasn't started, that we can't win, that we don't want. War brings ruin, they say. Well, this peace is ruining me, and the entire wool guild besides. We need a real peace or a real war. This counterfeit is worse than either."

When the rumble of agreement subsided, Fabbro turned to his prospective son-in-law. "What do *you* say, Lord Geta?"

"I know you are suffering, but bad as it is you'll remember this peace fondly when war does come," Geta said. "I hate to say it but your Chief Engineer and Podesta are right about one thing—you can't avoid war, and like it or not, it's a war you cannot possibly win. The arithmetic doesn't require a Guild Hall education: you have too few men. You defeated a legion, by the Madonna's grace. Concord never expected Rasenna to have competent engineers, but a surprise only works once. Can you defeat two legions? Three? Five? If you seek honorable deaths, stay the course, my friends." Geta paused and the sound of wine being gulped was like a chorus of frogs.

"But, if you would not be martyrs, there is an alternative."

"Please, Lord Geta," the farmer said irritably, "we wish to live, obviously. I have a new grandson to care for, and my colleagues have similar dependents. What must we do?"

"Understand your enemy. Engineers are not passionate men. Revenge means nothing to them. If they can retake Rasenna without a fight, they will. Think back. Was Concord's yoke so onerous? Times were bad, but was that because of the Tribute or the Families? I know the engineers; they know me. I can negotiate a just, lasting peace. I can ensure that there is no garrison, which would only become a flashpoint anyway. But I cannot do it without your support."

The brewer stood and declared formally, "I move to elect Lord Geta Podesta."

"Sit down, *idiota*," Fabbro said testily. "This isn't the Signoria."

Pedro and Uggeri—who had Sofia's seat—sat in isolation with Yuri on the other side of the chamber. "Maybe they will awards me medal?" the Russ said dryly.

Pedro locked eyes with his godfather across the empty Speaker's Circle. Fabbro broke away first. The purse was handed around the chamber. Each man had a black and a white pebble. When it came back to Fabbro he added his white pebble and tipped out the contents into a silver tray. Two black pebbles in a mound of white.

"Captain Yuri, the Signoria thanks you for your services," Fabbro said. "You are dismissed. I hereby appoint Lord Geta Podesta of Rasenna, with all attendant privileges and powers. May the Madonna's cloak shield him."

The door opened, and Geta strode in, going straight toward Yuri. The Russ had seen his fate coming, but still he was slightly dazed. He stood to attention, handed Geta the baton and marched out with dignity, followed by Uggeri.

Pedro watched Geta as he hefted the baton in his fist. "Signori, I'm honored. I consider this a homecoming. In Rasenna I learned the art of war. My first lesson wasn't demonstrated by my workshop maestro but rather by the birds of the air." He smiled, looking around the bewildered faces of the magnates, and finally settled on Pedro. "I mean, of course, those audacious cuckoos who nest in the towers. They grow big as their siblings languish. They betray the fools that nurtured them. The Madonna has always watched over the City of Towers. I believe she brought me here to give you a timely warning. The Signoria has a duty to protect the people from monopolistic practice. You, who have so lately thrown off the tyranny of the Families, be mindful not to nurture another. The engineers have far too much power to be allowed the independence afforded other guilds. Engineers are weapons. To let a weapon decide how it's used is not merely bad policy, it's suicidal. If there's a lesson to the Concordian Reformation, that's it. Therefore I move the Engineers' Guild be broken up and that engineers be hereafter considered part of the Guild of Fire, with similar status to, oh, blacksmiths for example; no longer should they have a seat in this house."

Pedro didn't even wait for the pebbles to be counted.

Chapter 78

PUBLIC ORDINANCE
By Order of the Podesta.
Banners may only be used in workshops;
banners are prohibited in public;
NO EXCEPTIONS.

Geta's decree was posted on the doors of the Palazzo del Popolo in Piazza Luna and Santa Maria della Vittoria in Piazza Stella and on each of the lions' plinths. The injunction was aimed directly at Tower Scaligeri as far as Uggeri was concerned. The bandieratori guessed what his reaction would be, and they were not disappointed.

"Flags up!"

He marched to the river with his men, all bearing flags. Standing at the decapitated lion's plinth he tore down the decree and cast it into the Irenicon, then he silently raised his flag. On the other side of the bridge the Small People and other guilds looked on with watchful eyes.

"Doc Bardini taught us to take up this flag. If we hadn't, the Twelfth Legion would have destroyed Rasenna. Should we throw it down because a corrupt Signoria in thrall to a foreign dog says so?" He looked around as if he were genuinely uncertain, then he rolled his banner across his knuckle and caught it in a combat grip. "Should we look for leadership from those who only care to profit themselves?"

"No!" the bandieratori answered as one.

"Damn right! This Signoria taxes us without our consent. This Signoria made a noble our podesta. As long as every Rasenneisi can defend himself, Rasenna is safe. Give up that right, allow it to be taken, and Rasenna is in peril. If Geta wants my flag, he can take it from my cold, dead hands!" He caught sight of Geta crossing the bridge. "Behold the man. Taking down names, Podesta? Mine's Uggeri Galati. I'm not hiding."

The crowd turned with malevolent intent to Geta and those who stood beside him. One of them—the Russ—grabbed Geta's arm. "Podesta, no good comes of this."

Geta threw him off, but Yuri persisted, "They are just throwing tantrum, like children, yes? Let them shout and wave their flags. Who harms it?"

Geta ignored him and marched forward until he was standing face to face with the first ring of bandieratori. "Small People, go home! As for you bandieratori, this is an illegal protest. Anyone bearing a flag is liable to be arrested."

Dozens of flags suddenly popped up among the milling crowd and dangled from the windows of the surrounding towers.

"Hear that?" Uggeri taunted. "Now he says we can't freely assemble. That's how tyranny starts."

Geta turned away in exasperation. Many of the condottieri were eagerly waiting for the order to advance. This fight had been a long time coming.

"Can't let them laugh in our faces," said Becket.

Geta looked at him. "It's better than the alternative."

Yuri relaxed a little, and Geta smiled slowly. "*Keeping* the peace isn't something I have much experience with. What do you advise, Russ?"

"He *wants* a fight, that boy." Yuri shrugged. "Let him talk. Let them march. They get tire soon."

When Geta's men retreated across the bridge, there was loud cheering, cries of *Forza Rasenna!* and *Small People*. The crowd proceeded to occupy the bridge and, when the condottieri didn't stop them, they grew bolder and spilled into Piazza Luna to assemble in front of the Signoria.

Watching all this from behind the fortezza's crenellations, Geta spoke seriously to his fiancée and future father-in-law. "Best you two stay southside tonight. Mobs do things individuals would never think of."

"Fine thing," Fabbro said bullishly, "a gonfaloniere afraid of those whose flag he bears! I'm going home. The day I need protection from Rasenneisi, I hope they do kill me."

"I'm coming with you, Papa."

"Your place is here." Fabbro took her hand and placed it in Geta's. "With your betrothed."

The dark night that followed was tense and full of wind and alarums. In spite of his bluff façade, Fabbro was shaken by the aggressiveness of the bandieratori in Piazza Stella, and he instructed the servants to allow entry to no one but family. The storm damped the enthusiasm of the demonstrators, and as Yuri had predicted, they soon returned to their towers.

In the crisp morning light, Bocca came calling at Palazzo Bombelli, eager to discuss the situation with the gonfaloniere: the brewer wanted to know when he could open his tavern again. He was surprised and somewhat alarmed to find the palazzo's great door open and unattended. He crept in to the atrium, treading lightly and feeling like an interloper, but he felt a wave of relief as he entered the courtyard and saw Bombelli's bulk sitting at his banco.

"Counting money all night's a capital way to ruin your eyesight." He walked cheerfully up and slapped Fabbro's shoulder. "Nothing can buy that back—unh!"

Bombelli's head lolled back. Pushed into his eyes were two Concordian pennics and a bandieratori dagger pinned a large promissory check to his chest. On it was scrawled a single word: *TRAITOR*.

The brewer backed away, too scared to scream. The sensible thing would be to quietly alert the Podesta, but on his way out Bocca tripped over the butler's body. It was the last straw. He scrambled to his feet and ran across the bridge screaming, "Assassins!"

By the time Geta arrived the palazzo had been thoroughly ransacked and the treasures of the workshop stolen. The looters fled from the condottieri, spreading their madness all over the northern city. Pedro was working on the orphanage when the riot erupted, and when he heard what the spark had been, he threw down his tools—the Sisters could defend themselves better than most bandieratori, and his engineers had nothing to interest a mob—that and a lingering suspicion would keep them safe. As he ran to Palazzo Bombelli he saw the chaos and entered the gutted palazzo in trepidation. It was *impossible*. How could Fabbro Bombelli be still? He of all people? His Godfather had been the one person *alive* when Rasenna was at its deadest. There was no force able to affect so great a change.

But there he was.

Pedro was surprised that the first thought that struck him was that Fabbro had become remarkably fat. In life he had never seemed so ponderous. Carefully, Pedro removed the pennies and closed his staring eyes.

"You've come to rob us too?"

Maddalena's hair was streaked and wet, her skin glistened with sweat, her glaring eyes were ringed with dark shadows. She stalked around the banco, looking at him like a rabid animal, hatefully, fearfully.

"Maddalena, I'm so sorry."

"What for? You've sought this all along."

"How can you say that?"

"That knife is Uggeri's."

"You can't be su—"

"And you helped put it there! Out of my house! Get out! *Get out!*"

Uggeri found the mood in Piazza Stella dangerously festive. The gonfaloniere was the city's flag-bearer, and until someone else took up

that flag, there was no law. The north smoldered and the south sank
into silence. Geta's men were discreet, at least, forbidden to venture
over the river. Some northern magnates fled across the bridge, valu-
ing their lives more than their towers; the most prescient had already
made plans for this day and moved their assets south immediately.
Those who hadn't, and who didn't like donating their life savings
to the Small People, barricaded their tower doors and hired flags to
protect them. Though the loyalty of these masterless bandieratori
was questionable, the magnates gambled it would never be put to
the test—and it was a good bet, for the mob was looking for easy loot
and soon moved on to undefended towers.

Scaligeri Borgata did not take part in the mayhem, but neither
did they quell it.

Pedro discovered Uggeri obstinately looking down on the revels
from Doc Bardini's old perch on Tower Scaligeri. "You think Sofia
would be happy with this?" he asked. "If you don't put a stop to it,
Geta will. And he'll be justified."

"Let him try. The magnates have been profiting off our sweat for
too long. Why shouldn't the Small People have some fun?"

"This is not fun. This is chaos." Pedro didn't mention Maddalena, though both men understood this was about her. Uggeri
kept his back turned. Pedro began to climb down the ladder, then
he stopped and pointed at the mountains to the north. Somewhere
in those snowy crags was the pass of Montaperti. "The Concordians will come soon, you realize? All you're doing is making their
job easier."

Uggeri looked at him silently.

"Damn it! Say something! I know you did for Jacques' apprentice,
but surely it wasn't you who killed Fabbro? At least tell me that."

Uggeri stood slowly. "Leave it at that, Vanzetti, if you want to get
to the bottom of this tower using your legs."

As Pedro hurried back to Tartarus he saw that there was no looting in the old Bardini territories, and that the Sisters had kept the
peace around the baptistery and orphanage.

Sister Carmella was helping the novices hold their nerve. Isabella had a pale, unearthly look.

Pedro noticed the purple bruise on her arm. "Who gave you that?"

"A sinner. Listen to me, Pedro, even if civil war doesn't break out today, it will soon."

"Maybe. Wherever Sofia is can't be this bad."

"I pray you're right. However this madness ends, the Concordians will shortly arrive at the gate in greater numbers than before, and they will find Rasenneisi at each other's throats."

"Maybe I can—?"

"No, you need to stop thinking like an engineer and start thinking like a fugitive." She looked around to her flock. "We all do."

Piers Becket did not smile. Glee would have been inappropriate in front of the Gonfaloniere's mourning daughter. "You're *Podesta*, Lord Geta. You must restore order."

The Concordian held Maddalena in his arms as she wept. "Don't you ever get tired of being a fool, Becket? If we venture south, Uggeri will take it as a challenge and riot will turn to war."

"Is last thing we need with legions on march," said Yuri. The giant was subdued after Fabbro's death, but he was impressed that Geta was keeping a level head.

"I don't know what we *can* do," said Geta, "but we can't sit here and let the mayhem spread across the river."

"We go talk," said Yuri. He held out his hand to Geta. "I stand with you."

"Sure, *talk*," Becket scoffed, "Ask them if they'll put Bombelli's gold back. I'm sure they'll oblige."

Yuri picked up Becket and flattened him against the wall, a giant forearm across his chest. "You so hungry for blood, I give you taste."

"Yuri, put him down," Geta said, strapping on his belt. "He's just frightened—we all are. Becket, get the company ready to come north in strength. Madonna willing, it won't be necessary, but who knows what control that boy has over the situation?" He kissed Maddalena.

"If I don't come back, leave Rasenna—go south. Salerno's strong. It'll probably be the last to fall."

"You'll come back," she said. She shot a warning look at Yuri. "Make sure."

Yuri saluted. "Yes, Signorina!"

The unlikely pair mounted up and rode out of the fortezza's gate together. Instead of swords, each carried the red banner of Rasenna. They rode slowly onto the bridge and stopped halfway across. The bandieratori of the northern towers were assembled in Piazza Stella, each company separate from the next. The heads of the bandieratori towers stepped out and Uggeri, acting head of the guild, led them onto the bridge, flags up. Yuri dismounted and Geta followed suit. Towers on either side of the river watched the bandieratori approach and come to a halt in front of the condottieri.

Uggeri glanced at Yuri with silent reproach, then barked at Geta, "Who gave *you* the right to carry that banner?"

"The Gonfaloniere of Rasenna, when he made me Podesta."

"Bombelli's dead," said Uggeri.

"Wash your hands afterward?"

Uggeri's flag spun; the tip hovered an inch from Geta's chin. The Concordian didn't budge. "If I came to fight, you'd know all about it by now."

"*Tranquillo.*" Yuri slowly pushed Uggeri's flag away. "Whoever's responsible, Bombelli is dead, but law is not. Uggeri, what's happening—*this!*—is wrong. I know you know. Sofia, she would not have allowed it."

"And you know she wouldn't have allowed this thief into Rasenna, not in a million years."

Geta glared at the boy. "I don't need to steal anything."

"Is done!" Yuri roared. "Sofia put trust in *you*—in your sense. Levi did same to me. Geta was elected Podesta fair and also square."

"How could that Signoria do anything fair? He stole that too."

Geta said through gritted teeth, "What are you, boy? Reformer or revolutionary? You don't change people's minds by assassination."

"You dirty—" Uggeri stopped, remembering what Pedro had said. Sofia wouldn't have put her pride above Rasenna's security. "Look: if I get my people indoors, we're not going back to the old Signoria. The Signoria has to be like the red banner, for *all* Rasenneisi."

"I'll keep my men north," said Geta.

Yuri smiled. "Good then. Let's get everyone tucked up in beds, and tomorrow—"

"Tomorrow you had better have some ideas on how to give the Small People what they want, or I'll lead the bandieratori across the Irenicon and take it. I've seen the condottieri fight on a battlefield, but the street's *our* natural terrain."

Geta was about to retort, but Yuri pulled him back. "Let us gets through one night in peace. Tomorrow we talk with flags down and cooler heads."

Rasenna lay in exhausted silence that night. The natural reaction to the riot would have been brutal reprisal, but instead, there was a plea for peace, and the mob assented, storing their loot in safe nooks before going back to their towers. It was always surprising how quickly crowded piazzi could empty. Uggeri studied those Rasenneisi left on the streets. The bonds uniting bandieratori were frayed; spurning the Signoria would mean returning to the old way, tower against tower. He was a simple fighter, but he knew his heart's dark byways as well as he knew Rasenna's alleyways and rooftops. There was a throbbing within him that *wanted* that, that yearned to test itself in the damn mayhem Sofia and the Doc had grown up in. And since Maddalena chose Geta it had grown so much stronger.

The virile roll and snap of tower banners as the swallows returned home for the evening was the only sound competing with the roar of the Irenicon. Uggeri listened to the night, thinking how *easy* it would be to give in, easy as making a fist. The moon hid behind dark clouds and a light mist wreathed the balustrades of the bridge so that the river's roar was without origin. Uggeri unclenched his fist and rubbed his eyes. Sofia and the Doc had risen above that base temptation. He could do no less.

Across the river, Geta and Becket were waiting by the fortezza's entrance. Yuri trotted across the piazza, returning from a patrol of the southside streets.

Geta walked to him and patted his horse's flank. "Well?"

"All quiet. Northside too, by the looks. Let's hope it keeps."

"Let's hope," said Geta. He unhooked the girth of the saddle, put one hand under Yuri's boot and with the other shoved. The loose saddle slid sideways to the ground, carrying Yuri's massive bulk with it. His head struck the cobblestones with an audible *crack!*

Becket rushed forward, drawing his sword, and thrust it at the fallen giant. Yuri grabbed the blade in his fist and held it there as he got to his feet. His other hand shot forward and tightened around Becket's neck. The smaller man punched pointlessly and Yuri squeezed tighter—then released him as a bloody rapier-point poked cleanly through his chest. The giant dropped wordlessly to his knees. Geta pulled his head back and cut left to right, working deep, like a butcher. The hapless Becket was doused by the spurting arterial spray.

"Madonna wept. All that juice." Geta shook his head. "Drag this *deficiente* inside and get them ready. Five minutes." He glanced at the sky. The moon was still demurely shrouded, and from a window above, Maddalena was watching. "*Amore!* Did you see—?"

"I miss nothing," she said, and shot him with an imaginary crossbow. Geta mimed pulling the quarrel from his chest. "I know it," he said, returning fire with blown kisses.

They wore long black cloaks and spread out in prearranged formation after they crossed the bridge. The southside bandieratori had been given the choice to join the condottieri; to the south's eternal shame, only a few chose death. The traitors were charged with creating a topside perimeter around the bandieratori towers. Geta had fuel catchments—dry straw, wool, oil and black powder—already prepared and stashed northside and now his condottieri used the venerable *cap-a-pie* technique: as the tower base was set burning, brands were simultaneously thrown through upper windows and onto the rooftops.

The preponderance of black cloaks climbed the "healthy hills." Geta expected most resistance in the old Bardini highlands, and Workshop Scaligeri was besieged as it burned. The students who rolled out, coughing and gasping for breath, were quickly dispatched, regardless of age. Bandieratori skill meant nothing in the inferno within: the flames consumed flags and flesh indiscriminately.

Uggeri and the fastest of his old decina escaped by the adjoining corridor to Tower Scaligeri before it collapsed. The lower stories were already burning, so they climbed, blinded and choked by smoke, knowing every misstep would be fatal. The survivors burst out onto the rooftop, gasping for air. Tower Scaligeri was the highest vantage point in Rasenna. Uggeri batted out the flames licking at the edge of his flag and looked around at Geta's revenge.

The burning towers overpowered the night. Across the river, the few towers that had refused to collaborate had already collapsed into smoldering heaps. Here on the northside, the air was thick with whirling ash. Bandieratori leapt hopelessly from towers, or were thrown, or fell to their deaths. There were few options besides burning; but Uggeri's men did not panic. They looked to their capo to decide their fate.

"Tartarus," Uggeri said simply. "Get to Tartarus. Pedro'll know what to do."

The nearest tower to Tower Scaligeri was Tower Cammertoni. Its roof was thronged with waiting condottieri.

"Get ready, men," Becket shouted as he saw the bandieratori preparing to jump.

"Go together," Uggeri ordered, "and some will break through." Not waiting for objections, he jumped, and whether it was loyalty or desperation, all followed. Uggeri landed fighting, his flagstick immediately pushing the nearest swordsman into others behind. Uggeri saw one of his decina land straight onto a waiting sword; the bandieratoro fell over the side, but he dragged his murderer with him. As the rest landed, Becket's men fell back.

"Go! I'll hold them." Uggeri pushed into the center while hiding his body behind his flag, drawing in swords, then crashing his stick down to disarm them.

His bandieratori leapt from Tower Cammertoni and spread out, each taking a separate path across the rooftops. Soon Becket's men were down to four, but Uggeri's flag had been sliced into rags. He kept them at bay with his stick, but he knew he wouldn't be able to hold so many swordsmen for long. He circled until their backs were to the burning Tower Scaligeri, listening to the small explosions as the fire consumed each floor.

"You'll never have Rasenna as long as one of us lives," he shouted.

"Look around. The bandieratori are finished," said Becket gaily.

Something seemed to break within Uggeri and he threw his tattered stick away. "All right, damn you! I'll come quietly." Then, "What's so funny?"

"We're not taking prisoners."

A rumbling shudder filled the air. "I guess I knew that," Uggeri said, and with a silent prayer, he stepped back into nothingness.

He dropped vertically down the side of the tower, and caught the Cammertoni flag. Up above, he heard Tower Scaligeri moving with a great grinding noise, slowly tilting toward Tower Cammertoni, gathering speed . . . until Becket and his men were crushed as the towers annihilated each other.

Hot stone rained down on Uggeri and he felt the shadow of death's wing fall on him. All at once fear was absent. He did something he'd never before attempted.

He let go.

And fell.

Forever. The stars above meshed with the sparks and the beams of fire that were once towers. Two burning flags sailed by him, entwined and writhing like dying dragons. *This* was what Sofia had tried to show him, the peace at the heart of the fight—the wonder of it. He only regretted discovering it too late.

He crashed into a roof, and the tiles gave way beneath him. A moment of darkness was followed by an unexpectedly soft landing, and surprise—

—he was alive! He'd landed in an abandoned weaver's attic and was practically entombed in yellow dust. The wool he rested on was damp, sticky and rotten, but it had saved his life. No time to thank the Madonna. Through the hole in the roof he could see Tower Scaligeri had caused a domino collapse, and to judge from the thunder, it was happening all over the northside.

Sparks and embers fell through the hole and the attic began to fill with a thick, noxious smoke. He attempted to sit up but the wool clung to him until it felt like drowning. He held his breath and fell to the ground as he pulled himself free. He crawled along the floorboards, searching, but there was nothing there, just roiling, creamy smoke that cut his lungs like broken glass. He collapsed coughing, and his flailing hand came to rest on the stick of an old combat flag. He closed his fist around it and opened his eyes. Through the tears and smoke he could see the banner was black. Imagine Doc Bardini allowing himself to die choking like a dog and unavenged—never! Uggeri picked himself up and searched until he found the trapdoor. With strength failing, he dragged it open and all but fell down the ladder.

He was dizzy and bruised and bleeding, but he was alive! A surge of ecstasy lifted him to his feet. He opened the workshop's front door a crack: Piazza Stella was full of condottieri. At the back of the workshop was another door. He kicked it open, flag ready.

The alleyway was empty.

The glowing orange sky proclaimed that the topside was a dead zone for bandieratori. Sparks drifted among the stars as darkness once more descended on the streets, this time as a cloud of smoke and dust. The screaming continued over a steady percussive rumbling, interrupted by periodic explosive impacts. The bellows of falling towers pushed a river of scalding air through the alleys. He ignored the hair-singeing heat and ran to Tartarus.

Chapter 79

THE LAND ACROSS THE WATER

Apotheosis

Just as plague erupts every seventh year, so every seventh century Tartarus, that sea of grass at the world's roof, expurgates its unruly children. In the middle of the last century, the hordes of Gog abandoned the steppe and invaded . . . everywhere. The thundercloud rolled swiftly over Russ-Land, surveyed Europa's poverty and turned south to the Holy Land. The horsemen did not distinguish between Ebionite and Marian; all life was their enemy. The Oltremarines and the Ebionites had to choose whether to fight together or die separately.

Their combined armies, led by the Old Man of the Mountain, turned back the storm at Ain Jalut.[43] Afterward the Old Man vanished as suddenly as he had appeared, and with him, the alliance. One question remained: who would strike first? King Tancred,

43. Ebionite for "the Spring of Goliath"—an appropriate venue for giant-slaying.

in whom the Guiscard bloodline had reached an apotheosis of sorts, did not hesitate. Following his recapture of Jerusalem,[44] he scattered the Radinate into the desert from whence it had sprung.[45] The tribes returned to scavenging,[46] and Akka[47] began to look covetously on the Middle Sea. Crusade is riddled with ironies, but the greatest[48] must be that it created a rival to Etrurian interests much worse than the Radinate.

44. Oltremarines still use clappers and cymbals in memory of this victory. The custom originates in the second Ebionite occupation of Jerusalem: Marians were allowed to pray on the Mount, but they were forbidden to ring bells.

45. When Oltremare conquered Byzant, the Ariminumese merchants in the city assumed the existing arrangement would continue. They were shocked to be expelled along with the Ebionites.

46. Those who chose the safety of Oltremarine cities paid the price in the degrading trades allowed to them: servants, tanners and blacksmiths, horse traders, executioners and accountants.

47. Meanwhile, far from Akka's influence, Byzant pursued its own destiny. Though Marian now, Byzant's traditional cycle of war and trade with her neighbors went on exactly as before. As time passed, and Byzant's spheres of influence drifted westward, Akka's seniority became but a legal fiction.

48. The other contender is how a scheme designed to bolster the Curia finally destroyed it. The legal innovation of selling Atonement, concocted to finance the Crusades, opened the floodgates for a wave of corruption. When the flood of opprobrium subsided, the cardinals had been replaced by engineers and the world upended.

Chapter 80

The queen stood on the south wall facing the empty immensity. "The patriarch says the Sands must consume Akka one day. I don't believe it. God would not allow it. We're meant to be here." Behind her, Sofia looked silently on that unlimited desolation, hearing again the threat: *Wherever you run, he'll find you.* There was no sanctuary then, even here.

Catrina assumed Sofia was brooding on other things and praised her mothering abilities. "I've never seen such a natural."

Sofia demurred, "I've never been very feminine."

"Feminine. Bah! A word describing the ideal slave. Obedient is what they mean. Weeping, fainting, mooning over idiotic men, laughing at idiotic jokes, marveling at idiotic deeds. We are *queens*, Contessa. We have frail bodies, but we must have manly hearts to win men's hearts, and to do what must be done."

Sofia cupped the back of the baby's head, feeling its downy warmth and the small chest moving against hers.

"There!" the queen cried triumphantly.

Sofia saw only a dust cloud on the horizon. "Could be a Jinni."

She shook her head. "It's getting larger, and staying in one place. That's riders coming toward us—two, I'd wager. Must have him bound. Oh, Papa's coming back home, isn't he?" She clapped her hands, then reached over to pinch the baby's cheek. In her enthusiasm, she made her howl.

Down in the courtyard, Fulk and his men helped Levi and Arik tie up their camels. As they began to climb the stairway, Catrina said, "Contessa, give me the child. I want to show my uncle how well I treat his child despite the way he treated me." She eagerly shouted down, "Well, where is he? You *did* find him?"

Arik exchanged a look with Levi. "His body."

The queen's face reddened with fury. "I told you I wanted him *alive!*"

The baby started crying and Sofia offered to take her again, but the queen ignored her, demanding explanation.

"He was dead when we found him, Majesty. He must have panicked. He'd entered Sicarii territory."

"Nonsense! Andronikos grew up in this land—he knew where he was going. The scoundrel made a deal with them."

Arik was skeptical. "To what end?"

"To my throne, of course. Lord knows what concessions he promised them—as long as those bandits exist, my throne is not safe. Your father was a real idiot, wasn't he, little one?"

"He was desperate. He thought he'd be executed," Sofia said.

"He wasn't wrong." Catrina laughed. "I just wish he'd lived to see *this.*"

She cast the baby over the wall before Sofia knew what was happening. The child screamed all the way down. Levi, stunned though he was, managed to restrain Sofia before she assaulted the queen. Fulk and his men surrounded Catrina and stood facing them.

"How—how *could* you?"

Catrina was implacable. "It was self-defense. Nothing threatens a queen more than a princess—Andronikos should have known better. He always did underestimate me."

"Monster!" Sofia cried.

"Silence! I don't owe you an explanation. Would it have been better if the Grand Master had done it? I'm no hypocrite."

Sofia looked at Fulk. "He wouldn't!"

"I know my men." Catrina's lip curled. "Better at least than a foreign whore."

Levi looked at the Lazars surrounding the queen. "Sofia, leave it."

But Sofia couldn't. "You never intended to help us, did you? You just used us to draw Andronikos into rebellion."

"Child, *this* is what it means to be queen. Your people abandoned us to our struggle and it made us strong. I return the favor."

Weeping, Sofia broke away from Levi. Fulk caught hold of her, but she flung him off too. "Don't touch me, *Leper!*"

"Sofia, come back!"

There was nowhere to flee but the palace.

On her way to her chamber, Sofia passed the patriarch, standing alone in the Ancestor Room. He was staring lovelorn at a particular mask and he started away guiltily at the sound of her feet. "Contessa! I was just—that is—"

"You know what your mistress did?"

"Ah. Done, is it?" he said quietly. "Unfortunate business."

"You too," Sofia said numbly.

"Contessa, be fair. Queen Catrina cannot allow rebellion to tear apart her kingdom. Andronikos was a viper."

"But the child—how could she?"

"How could she not? Anyone close to the throne is close enough to be tempted: guards, courtiers, family. That's what makes the Lazars perfect praetorians. They die young and cannot reproduce—even if one persuaded a woman to sell herself, the disease makes them sterile. Don't judge Catrina too harshly; you don't know the wars she has survived."

"So others should suffer?"

The patriarch looked at Sofia sadly. "She suffers too. The queen is God's anointed, and as He gave His only son, so Catrina gave Fulk to a leper wet nurse. With the milk, the child consumed death."

Sofia stared at the patriarch. "He's her *son*?"

"Etruria left us to die. To survive this merciless land we had to become merciless too."

Sofia looked around hopelessly at the imperturbable cruel masks. Beneath his scars, Fulk looked like them.

Later that evening, Sofia found Fulk and Arik talking on the wall. Fulk stood. "Perhaps I should go."

"Please, don't. I'm sorry for what I said. You didn't have a choice. She condemned you."

"We're all condemned, Contessa. A knight's life is not measured in years." In the darkness behind the mask, Fulk's soft eyes shone with the loyalty of a hound.

"Why do you still defend her?"

"There's no greater joy than to know one's duty in life." He bowed to her. "I understand you're upset, but I will not blacken my queen's name."

"She blackens her own name!" Sofia shouted as Fulk walked away.

"Nice apology," Arik said.

She turned on him. "Did *you* know what she planned?"

"No, but the crimes of the *Franj* have long ceased to surprise me. The queen's actions, repugnant as they were, were logical. Your title, Contessa—did many siblings aspire for it also?"

When Sofia admitted that she had none, Arik said, "That follows. Familial bonds are helpful when a family is striving to rise, but when it reaches the summit, the competition does not cease but intensifies. Your sister, your brother, formerly your closest allies, become your closest rivals." He paused. "I speak, as you know, from experience."

"You never told me how you escaped."

"When I was very young my father made me a hostage to the queen's grandfather. That's when Fulk and I became friends. My father wanted me to learn the ways of the *Franj* and I cursed him for it. Now I know he was giving me an escape route. When I saw Yūsuf sharpening his knife, where else could I go? One man in the desert is a dead man. I fled to Akka and offered Catrina my dagger." He smiled with embarrassment. "I know the land as well as any Ebionite, better than any of her men. I see how you look at me, Sofia. You are thinking, 'This scoundrel betrayed his people.' I will tell you the manner of men I betrayed. The Prophetess led a righteous rebellion against foreign oppressors. My brother's running dogs dishonor the name of Sicarii. Freedom fighters—*ha!* They prey on the baggage trains that cross the desert, murdering Oltremarines and extorting Ebionites. What courage. What *folly*. The last hope of overthrowing the *Franj* vanished with the Old Man of the Mountain. My brother knows that, as do the other Ebionite tribes. Individually you will find no men stronger, but they value their freedom too much to submit to a king and that's what keeps them weak."

"Do all Ebionites think their cause so hopeless?"

"The Sicarii believe there is hope, but what does their sincerity count for? They are misguided. My brother—a black year on him—is no patriot."

Sofia was sickened by this compromised, hedging world. "And you are a slave!"

Arik's hand went quickly to his dagger, but there he stopped. "Perhaps," he said at last. "And what are you, Contessa?"

She could no longer deny it. "A prisoner."

Chapter 81

Though the young Prince Jorge had managed to maintain order after word came north of Andronikos' death, the army was likely to stay in the vicinity of Byzant until things were more stable. This allowed Leto to withdraw some troops from the Dalmatian frontier to Concord, enough to restore absolute order in the Old City and to mop up the last of Geta's bravos, who had outlived their usefulness.

The next step was bringing Etruria to heel.

The Ariminumese delegation sat opposite Torbidda and Leto at the stone table. Leto had left Ariminum on bad terms and his attitude to the smiling procurator was not conciliatory.

"I was most gratified to receive your invitation, First Apprentice. Though we afforded General Spinther every opportunity to catch Contessa Scaligeri, he was—if I may say—rather rude when she escaped. How it was our fault, I can't imagine. Look, things were said in the heat of the moment . . . we are willing to forget. For our part the deal negotiated still stands."

"I would have promised anything to scupper the league," said Leto.

"Of course. Nevertheless an alliance between Concord and Ariminum is logical. Our ambitions do not overlap, but our common enemy, if we are to realize our ambitions unhindered, is Oltremare."

"So you want our siege-engines?" said Torbidda neutrally.

"And engineers to teach the arsenalotti to operate them. Give us the sea, First Apprentice, and Etruria is yours."

The procurator had brought Admiral Azizi along "for his expertise," though the Moor did little beside study Torbidda with unconcealed curiosity. The procurator's giddiness made up for the admiral's reserve; since Torbidda appeared willing to countenance the alliance, he was full of ideas for postinvasion arrangements.

Leto felt obliged to sound a note of military caution. "First Apprentice, it's one thing moving markers on a map, quite another in the field. Sappers can only do the job *if* they land. I'm sure Admiral Azizi will agree that establishing a beachhead in Akka would be difficult."

When the Moor said nothing, the procurator waved his hand dismissively. "The Queen's navy is old. Pirates like Azizi here are as much as they can deal with. Our armada will overwhelm them."

"You're being complacent," said Leto. "I saw no galley equal to the *Tancred* in all Ariminum."

"The *Tancred* is but one ship," said the procurator. "Our Arsenale can churn out a galley a day. And our munitions a—"

"May I interrupt?" the Moor boomed suddenly.

"Oh," the procurator said doubtfully, "by all means."

"With Concord's recent convulsions, First Apprentice, I understand construction of the sea-corridor has been postponed. Is this so?"

"Among other things."

"Why go to the trouble of building a harbor when I can give you one?"

Leto looked at the Moor as if seeing him for the first time. "I think the Ariminumese government might object."

"Not if they're hanging from the yardarms of my galleys."

"Praetorian." Torbidda pointed at the stunned procurator. "Arrest this man,"

Leto was startled. "Are you mad, Torbidda? What is this?"

"A gesture of good faith. Admiral Azizi works for Queen Catrina, Leto."

When the Moor bowed in acknowledgment, the procurator leapt up, spitting, "Slave, you bite the hand that feeds you!"

Slowly the Moor turned toward him. He held up his bejeweled hand and commanded, "Look *here*!" The procurator stared mesmerized as the Moor's hand closed around his neck. "Here's the hand that feeds me!"

The struggling procurator could not break free, and as the Moor turned back to the Concordians, the gasping stopped abruptly with a wet, crumbling sound.

"Let me get this straight," said Leto as the guard dragged the procurator's body away. "When you were receiving a stipend to attack the Oltremarines—"

"—I was in her Majesty's employ, yes. I like a diverse portfolio."

"And she sent you as a prisoner to Ariminum—"

"—knowing the Ariminumese would free me. Even she didn't think they'd be so rash as to promote me to admiral."

"And when we chased the *Tancred*, and that Rasenneisi bitch gave us the slip . . ." Leto stood up suddenly.

"Please, Spinther, be seated," the Moor said smoothly. "I was under orders."

"Queen Catrina must be terrified of the Ariminumese," said Torbidda lightly.

"With good reason. For once the procurator spoke the truth: she's not ready for an invasion. She's been dealing with the Ebionite tribes and—how to put it?—family disputes for the last few years. How can we help each other?"

"The Contessa of Rasenna's child. I want it. Failing that, I want it dead."

Catching on, Leto said, "Remember, Azizi: we could clap you in irons, then sail over and take her."

The Moor gave Leto a dismissive look. "You need to concentrate on Etruria before starting another war. You asked for the child returned or killed, First Apprentice, and made no mention of the mother. This isn't about Rasenna, is it?"

"Queen Catrina should fear this child as much as I do," said Torbidda. "He threatens all princes."

"What matter if she loses her kingdom to him or you?" The Moor smiled. "She has a foolish notion—the female mind defies all understanding, does it not?—that you don't want this child to grow up . . . Cross her, and she'll hide it away where you'll never find it."

"Or?"

"Or we can send the Contessa back on the next west-bound galley."

Torbidda didn't attempt to bluff. "Your terms?"

"Ariminum."

"Torbidda, don't let this dog manipulate us too," Leto said. "If we attack Ariminum, it'll chase them back into alliance with the rest of the south."

"You misunderstand, Spinther; I only ask that you stand aside. The arsenalotti are loyal to me and poised to take over every ward and bridge in Ariminum. All we want, First Apprentice, is that when the Consilium Sapientium petitions you for help—"

"—that I say no. Done. I *need* that child."

Leto followed Torbidda to the Guild Hall. "Tell me what you're thinking. Why's the Scaligeri girl so important? I really thought that was just a ploy to break up the league—and it worked. Does it really matter what happens to her?"

Torbidda bared his teeth in rage. "After all this time, you still understand *nothing*! I *need* that child, Leto!" Moving impossibly fast, Torbidda grabbed Leto by the collar. "There's *nothing* more important—not you, not this, not any of it!"

Leto pulled himself free, breathing hard. "You're going crazy, you know that? That damn preacher has addled your mind. I don't know why you keep visiting him. Stay away from him—or better yet, cut his throat and be done with it."

"I may need him yet," Torbidda said, calming.

When they reached the Drawing Hall, Torbidda unlocked the door—he had the only key—and turned to Leto, tears streaming down his face. "Don't you get it?" he cried. "I can't solve it. I *can't*!"

Leto was mildly shocked to see Torbidda so emotional. "You can solve anything," he said firmly, gripping him by the shoulders. "You're Cadet Sixty, for goodness' sake!"

"Remember the day they made us into numbers?" Torbidda said, gazing beyond Leto. "Agrippina told us to take nothing that would slow us down, and I did it, Leto! I discarded *everything*—conscience, morality, friendship. I think what's slowing me down now is my soul."

He locked the door before Leto could respond.

Chapter 82

"If this tower is *not* sheltering outlaws, how do you explain the rumors?"

After the night of black towers, every Rasenneisi finally understood the truth: that the bandieratori, for all the mayhem they caused, had kept citizens good neighbors. Before that night, it was understood that one who used his tongue to lie about his countrymen would have the offending organ cut out. Now there was no recourse when Geta's men came knocking. If it took just a whisper to knock down an enemy's tower, who would not whisper?

The Mercanzia met secretly. They were stunned and frightened by the massacre they had authorized, and belatedly realized that in letting Geta destroy Rasenna's fighting stock, they had surrendered the reins of power. Perhaps, they whispered, Geta didn't realize how vulnerable they were now—he certainly wasn't acting any different. Collectively, they agreed to maintain a strong front—but on hearing that Geta's new wife was pregnant, each prior rushed separately to be the first to congratulate the royal couple: like shepherds, they paid homage; like kings, they bore gifts.

And in the Palazzo del Popolo, they listened with new attentiveness to the podesta's counsel. Peace with Concord—why not? It was better than the alternative.

Deep below Rasenna's cautious streets, the tunnels were alive. Uggeri was exhausted by his explorations by the time he returned to the base Pedro had set up, and the generator's light hurt his eyes. "*Madonna!*" he said, "I've traveled *leagues*. How deep does it go?"

"I don't know—but we can get to either side of the river," Pedro said.

Uggeri swigged some water and said, "Okay. It's important we know our territory. I'm going back. Don't wait up."

"No," Pedro said firmly, "you haven't eaten all day and you're too important to let yourself get sick. Sit and eat."

Gruffly, Uggeri assented, concealing behind his grave demeanor the sheer joy he felt at having a foe worthy to test his mettle. Even with the stench of sulfur, the taste of burned dust and wool in his mouth, the boiling blood and sweat still raw, Uggeri rejoiced: in Geta he had found an adversary who would fight to the death.

Pedro told Uggeri the plan as he ate.

"Even if possible," Uggeri said incredulously, "what good would it do? When Concord's legions arrive they can throw up a pontoon in a day—"

"—that's even more vulnerable. Don't you remember how slow everything was before the bridge? If we separate north and south, we force Geta to pick which side he wants to protect. We can tie up resources, make travel difficult. We won't win this with one blow in a single day. We'll win it step by step, day by day."

"Or blow ourselves up."

"It's worth the risk. Geta isn't expecting it—"

"—so he'll overreact. I get it: the worse he acts, the more people will join us. But, Pedro, it's *Giovanni's* bridge."

"It's *ours*. It saved Rasenna once by bringing us together; we can save Rasenna now by destroying it. Don't be sentimental." Pedro spoke boldly because it was necessary, but really, he shared Uggeri's doubts. It felt like sacrilege.

"You're right," Uggeri said, "whatever's necessary now, we can't hesitate. But let's make sure we blow up more than a bridge."

Just before dawn the baptistery bell rang out over the river. The clock tower delicately chimed its answer. Where the river ended and land begun was lost in the mist that had invaded Piazza Luna. Only the red banner of the Palazzo del Popolo interrupted the pervasive whiteness. Two gray guards stood at the entrance of the fortezza.

"What's that?"

"*Tranquillo*, kid," said the older, a veteran. "I don't see anything."

"There, look!"

Sure enough, a figure was crossing from the mouth of the bridge, tottering first left and then right, as if drunk.

"Probably got up enough courage to give us a right old talking-to."

"This ought to be good." They waited, chuckling together in anticipation. The night-watch was dull, and one of its few diversions was slapping drunks sober. The drunk was closer now, and he suddenly straightened up and produced a flag-stick that had been concealed in the silhouette of his body. The banner unfurled and they had time only to register that it was black before he came running toward them. They fumbled for their weapons, but the gap closed too soon.

The condottiere on the last watch of the night stretched himself and yawned, still groggy from last night's drinking. Every night since the raid had been a celebration. He slid open the spy hole. "Mornin' lads—"

He slammed it shut and leaned against the door as he rebolted it, breathing fast, trying to master his panic. He rang the bell hanging beside the door. Condottieri were used to quick mobilization, but the first to answer the call to arms was Geta. Others soon appeared, tucking their nightshirts into their pants.

"Mount up!" Geta shouted, pushing the guard aside and unbolting the door. The sun was coming up, but he did not need it to see the Palazzo del Popolo across the piazza. Flames licked out of its windows and the clock tower glowed from the spiraling inferno within. Geta walked forward a few steps, then spun around. The night watchmen still stood on either side of the door. "Why are you two just standing—?" he began, but stopped abruptly as he saw they wept blood. Then he noticed that their bodies dangled an inch above the ground, from ropes tied to the cressets above the door.

Geta dashed back inside, found his charger and mounted up. *"Avanti!"* he cried as he led a dozen men through the gate into the piazza. They rode three abreast, and the clatter of hoofs on cobblestones echoed over the roar of the fire. Up ahead, a black figure holding a bottle stuffed with a burning rag backed away from the palazzo. In a fluid practiced motion, Geta released his reins, slowed his horse with his legs, reached for his harquebus and whipped out the weapon. He took aim, snapped the flint and fired. The figure in the distance spun where he stood, but did not fall; instead, he ran limping for the bridge, and when he reached the lions, threw down his bottle. It exploded, leaving a rather feeble line of fire at the bridge entrance.

The recoil had knocked Geta out of the saddle, but he sat up laughing. "There—clipped the bastard!" he shouted. "On, lads! Ride him down!" Other riders leapt over Geta, swords drawn, prey in sight and the scent of blood in their nostrils. Their trained destriers effortlessly leapt the fire and thundered onto the bridge.

As Geta remounted, he glanced at what remained of the Palazzo del Popolo. The clock tower struck its final hour, then tumbled with a great groan of cracking metal and the muffled dusty pops of bricks exploding from the heat and pressure. Geta considered himself something of an expert when it came to arson; he realized that it needed more than a few oil bottles to set that blaze. This had taken time. He thought of the night watch's eyes so carefully removed and without thought, slowed his horse to a standstill. A second wave of cavalry rode by, hastening to the bridge, and Geta looked at the other side of the bridge. The fleeing figure was escaping into Piazza Stella, his limp miraculously cured.

"Get off the bridge!" Geta roared. "It's a trap!"

Some already halfway across heard the warning and turned around, and Geta realized his mistake. "No!" he screamed, "keep going!"

They turned again in confusion, more running into them even as others turned back, causing total mayhem.

Cursing all fools, Geta pulled his horse around and jammed his spurs in its haunches mercilessly—

First there was a patterning drumroll, barely perceptible, except for the soles of the feet, the fingertips.

Pah-Pah-Pah-Pah-Pah-Pah

Then came a world-rolling pounding, like a wave breaking overhead.

OOOooooommmmm

The bridge suddenly turned black, its graceful arch silhouetted by the synchronized explosions around the supporting pillars, glowing yellow as the flames licked greedily around it. Bits of horse and men and lumps that could have been either slowly floated upward before raining down in sizzling blobs that congealed in greasy pools on the river surface. White glowing stones that had been balustrades, pillars and archways hurtled up into the sky and tumbled beside the stars.

The explosives had been tightly packed at either end of the bridge and now the arch appeared to expand for a moment, even as its components came apart, before losing cohesion, sending great boulders crashing into the piazzas on either side, smashing cobblestones into pebbles. There was a rapid *pat pat pat* as the three lions that had survived the Wave and years under the Irenicon vanished and the stones, all that was left of the huge beasts, rained down into the river with serpentine hisses, their individual splashes lost in the majestically billowing steam clouds.

Then . . . *it was gone.*

Rasenna was bisected once more. The last few years were exposed as an impossible, aberrant dream, now dissipating just like the ringing echo of the explosion, fading away and leaving the roar of the Irenicon unchallenged. The few disorientated riders who made it across to Piazza Stella were felled by arrows and rocks and banners, then finished off by a giant death-dealing figure with hammers in place of hands.

Geta had been thrown off his horse again, this time by the explosion. He landed badly and was knocked unconscious, but he was lucky: he was far enough away to avoid the heaviest of the falling debris.

When he awoke, he was covered in gray dust that streaked black where the water streamed from his eyes. He limped back, but headed not to the fortezza but to the adjoining stable. The doors swung open. He stepped inside and found all the cells were open and empty, as was the trapdoor to the cellar, where the Hawk's Company's powder reserves had been stored.

Those condottieri who saw Geta emerge couldn't understand why he looked so merry. How could he explain to men to whom war was only a profession? This was why he'd come back to Rasenna. Mayhem was home here.

Chapter 83

"Torbidda?" The Drawing Hall's door was ajar and though Leto walked in feeling like an interloper, he found himself remembering many happy hours spent in that room. He stopped in front of the warped mirror to examine his uniform, and to compare his current self with the boy he'd been. The comparison was not pleasant. Through old, experienced eyes he saw the endless deceit that marked his still youthful boy's face like acid-etched metal. How did Torbidda *live* with it?

Outside, a cloud moved away from the sun and a sudden shaft of light struck the desk behind him. He saw the reflection of the drawing first, and he turned and approached it with a feeling of transgression, the sense of spying some forbidden thing. The scale was impossible, insane, and mildly nauseating, though it was just a drawing. All around the desk were crumpled pieces of paper, all scarred with the same dense scribbling, rows of digits overlapping each other, sometimes scratched out, with lines drawn between the rows at various angles. Scattered around the floor were old Ebionite and Etruscan texts, with passages underlined, and etchings of Solomon's Temple and the Molè had been torn apart and taped together in mad combinations that were almost unbearable to look at.

Fra Norcino watched through the bars with a patronizing smile as the coffin descended and slowed. His cell was near the bottom of the pit now. "Seems I shall meet the Master before you. What shall I tell him?"

"Tell him I've achieved everything he did—I control Concord. Rasenna and Ariminum are broken. Tell him my cathedral will be as beautiful as his Molè was terrible. Tell him the Handmaid's child will soon be brought to me."

"And you have not the wit to make use of its blood. Shall I tell him that you're still afraid?"

"I am master here!" Torbidda shouted.

"You can't even master yourself. I can smell your fear, even here where the air is saturated with the stuff. You're still a little boy, weeping for his mother. If you weren't, you'd confront him."

"Confront *him*?"

"Come, we both know why you keep returning. It's not to keep me company. You want his wit as much as he wants your flesh. *Why not fight for it?* Your will against his. If you were truly a wolf, you'd fight."

Torbidda said nothing and Norcino showed his black teeth as he laughed. "Fearful child, take off that red. You won it on false pretenses. You're no Apprentice. You will always be afraid until you confront him . . . Agrippina would not have hesitated."

"She should have won," Torbidda said, watching himself backing into the pod. "What if I'm not strong enough? What if I *am* just a lamb?"

"Courage, lad. I know a king when I see one."

When the door hissed closed and there was no one to hear, Torbidda whispered, "*Madonna* preserve me. I'm afraid."

As the pod started to descend and the blue light danced between the grinding torque of the rows, Norcino started cackling. "Alas for thee, child, blind men make poor guides."

A storm cloud churned around the summit of Mont Nero, and purple lightning stabbed the summit, again and again. Those watching from the streets and canals of New City swore next morning that they saw the Molè's ghost appear every time the lightning struck. Finally, one swollen sea-blue bolt exploded in the air at a point where once Argenti had looked at the stars and wept, where once the lantern's flame had been lit to call back a boy running for his life. The writhing electric charge dropped, straight as water falling, and impaled itself on the upraised sword of the angel, the only part of the Molè still standing.

It emerged a second later, searing the darkness of the pit like a razor, shooting past Norcino's cell to the lake into which the coffin had just sunk.

The buio leapt and clawed and climbed over one another, each particle of the filthy water striving to separate itself from the rest to escape the writhing agony that churned the depths until the ascending coffin parted the surface, wreathed in fronds of black-green scum, and rose.

The exhausted water went still.

The *thing* inside it was no longer crying. A talented, terrified boy had descended moments before; what stepped out was something else; Fra Norcino's blind eyes could see that plainly.

"Welcome back, my king."

"Come, astrologer. The hour is late and we have work."

The story concludes in

SPIRA MIRABILIS

BOOK III OF THE WAVE TRILOGY

Acknowledgments

They say that Labor Vincit Omnia, but it's nice to have help:

Seth Grodofsky assisted my research by showing me Israel, not quite from Dan to Beersheba but near enough, while Merav and the girls showed me great hospitality. Michael Harte lent me a critical pair of eyes on the first draft (he can have them back now—they've gone dry). Jo Fletcher deftly nipped and tucked a somewhat baggy version of *The Warring States* into something presentable. Throughout this my agent Ian Drury has been a constant support.

My thanks to all.

Thanks too to Nicola Budd, Lucy Ramsey, Georgina Difford, and everyone at Jo Fletcher Books and Quercus who are working hard to spread the word.

Lastly, most especially, my wife Bronagh deserves a bathtub of diamonds. Since I can't afford one yet, I give her my love.

AH

About the Type

Typeset in Minion Pro 11.5/15pt

Minion Pro was designed by Robert Slimbach and released in 1990. Its letterforms are rooted in classical typefaces and designed to be highly functional, graceful, and multi-functional.

Typeset by Scribe Inc., Philadelphia, PA